Fairytales do come true...

Katarina Bennett stopped believing in fairytales a long time ago. Prince Charming doesn't exist. Careful planning is what makes dreams come true and that's what she's spent her adult life doing. Now those plans have fallen apart. She's lost everything; her fiancé, her job and her home.

Determined to make a new start, Kat takes a job as a governess and teacher for five orphaned children and finds herself in an old Gothic mansion in the middle of nowhere with people who aren't what they seem.

Charles Goodman is the Alpha of his wolver pack, the modern descendants of an ancient line of man/beasts who've hidden among the human race for centuries. Charles has his hands full with taking his pack in a new direction and dealing with dissention in the ranks and doubts about his own abilities to lead, but when he meets his feisty new employee, he begins to believe in a future he didn't think feasible.

Together, Charles and Kat, Alpha and Mate, set out to prove all things are possible and fairytales do come true.

Other Titles by Jacqueline Rhoades

Paranormal Romances

The Guardians Of The Race Series
Guardian's Grace
Guardian's Hope #2
Guardian's Joy #3

Alpha's Mate Series
The Alpha's Mate

Contemporary Romances

Hidden Mountain Series
Preston's Mill

THE ALPHA'S CHOICE

By
Jacqueline Rhoades

Copyrighted 2013 by Jacqueline Rhoades
Cover Art: Georgianna Simpson

My Thanks
To my daughter, Heather,
who took the bull by the horns
and forced me to publish my first book.

I'm so proud of you.

Chapter 1

Someone had stolen the idea for this house from one of those gothic mysteries she used to read as a girl, the ones where she'd shout at the not very bright heroine, "Don't go down those dark, drafty cellar stairs in the middle of the night with only a candle to light your way, you idiot!"

The brainless twits never listened to Kat. They had to follow the clues to the damp and musty cellar of the old and creepy house where something awful was guaranteed to happen. How else was the heretofore unattainable hero supposed to rescue said twit from the clutches of her villainous uncle/brother/pseudo suitor/someone-she-trusted? How else could the handsome, brooding fellow fall in love with the plucky fearlessness of the heroine unless she went off investigating on her own and almost got herself killed?

The pragmatic Kat never understood why she bothered yelling at those books. She knew she was wasting her breath. The totally-unaware-of-her-remarkable-beauty ward/governess/poor relation's fate was sealed the moment she entered that house.

The romantic Kat always shouted her warning anyway. Worse, she followed the daring darling right down those cellar steps to whatever fate awaited, praying the hero would arrive in time to save his one true love so they could live happily ever after.

Kat was a big girl now and knew there was no such thing as

fairytales or happily ever after and if she was ever in need of rescuing, she damn well better do it herself. No handsome hero was going to do it for her. She'd learned her lesson on that score.

She double checked the directions in the manila folder she'd received from the agent. Yep, this was the place.

Mr. Begley, the man who'd hired her, called it a former hunting lodge and Kat envisioned a rustic country retreat, a one story log structure perhaps, with a broad front porch and a stone fireplace. It would be a cozy, masculine place with worn leather furniture and scattered throws and a moose head over the fireplace built from stone hand carried from the nearby creek. She wasn't enthusiastic about the moose head, but she'd lived with worse and it was a former hunting lodge after all. She'd add a few softer touches of her own once she saw what was needed.

The place in front of her had nothing in common with her bucolic image, unless you counted the stone; lots and lots and lots of stone. Three stories worth of stone, all of it square cut and gray. Dark gray. Even the window frames were painted dark gray. This was not what she would picture as a cheerful home for orphaned children.

Keeping with her gothic theme, a sinister looking gardener viciously snapping at the shrubbery with a wicked pair of shears would not have looked out of place. But if this place had ever had a gardener, sinister or otherwise, he was now standing in line down at Unemployment.

Hell Hall, as Kat already dubbed it in her mind, might not look quite so dreary with a little bit of landscaping, but the patchy spots of green she suspected were weeds and not grass, ran from the curved edge of the gravel drive right up to the stone foundation. There wasn't a shrub to be seen.

Two walls of the same ugly stone jutted out from either side of the huge square structure, cutting off the view of the rear of the house. Arches were built into each wall about halfway down their length, their keystones rising another two feet above the row of short, iron spikes capped by fleur-de-lis finials that lined the tops of the walls.

This place looked more like a prison than a home. Torn between investigating what lay behind the garden walls or facing the horrors she was now convinced lay inside, Kat chose the interior. If there was a stern looking housekeeper dressed head to foot in gray bombazine waiting to greet her, she'd best get it over with.

Exiting her little compact car, Kat felt tiny fingers of warning crawl up the center of her back and she looked both right and left and up to the windows towering above her. No eyes peeked around the corner. No telltale curtain moved. Mr. Begley assured her the house was vacant, but she had the strangest feeling she was being watched. She shook the feeling off and laughed at herself.

"There you go letting your imagination run away with you again," her practical side scolded. "It's the silence that's getting to you. No traffic, no car horns, no flashing lights or sirens, no clatter of feet on the sidewalk. All this quiet is downright creepy."

Boldly, she walked to the wide front door and took the key that Mr. Begley had given her from her pocket and fitted it into the lock. It was an unnecessary action. The door swung inward at her touch, squeaking eerily.

The little girl Kat used to be was shouting, "Don't go in that dark and creepy house all alone!"

But the grown-up Kat knew her fate was sealed the moment she signed the contract and she was done with scaring herself over nothing.

"You've lived in creepier places than this," she told herself and pushed through the door calling, "Hello! Is anybody home?"

And then laughed at herself again. If anyone had answered

her call, she would have been back in her car with the doors locked before she finished saying, "Whoa, shit!" The entrance hall was huge… and dark… and creepy. A ghost wouldn't feel out of place at all.

Kat's eyes skimmed across the dark paneled walls searching for a light switch and finally located a row of four, none of which turned anything on that she could see. The electricity was either turned off or, heaven forbid, there wasn't any to turn on. She waited, still as the stone walls, until her eyes adjusted to the dimness.

Ahead and to the right, a wide staircase climbed up one wall to the second floor and looking up through the towering height of the ceiling and a balcony rail, she could see where it continued from the hallway above up, up, up to the third floor.

Pocket doors, their glass panes neatly covered in brown paper and blue painter's tape opened to either side of the foyer leading to two very large rooms. Both appeared to be sitting rooms judging by the shapes of the sheeting covering the furniture. Each of these rooms had four large windows swathed in dark and deeply fringed draperies that kept out the light. Both were dusty and dirty with cobwebs hanging in the corners and from old fashioned chandeliers.

This was not the place she'd envisioned when she planned to spend a few days relaxing on her own. A highway rest area would be cleaner and more inviting.

She passed more doors on her way to the back of the house, but assumed the rooms would be in the same condition as those at the front.

On the right at the end of the hallway, she found the kitchen and it made her rethink what she'd seen of the rest of the house.

"Holy…" She snapped her mouth shut and wandered into something out of a magazine. Someone had taken great pains to combine the essence of the house's origins with every modern kitchen convenience.

A massive bank of windows ran along the back wall above a row of freshly painted white cabinets. These were topped by a black granite countertop that ran the length of the kitchen to either side of a soapstone sink that looked big enough to bathe in.

Three of the four walls of the long room were broken up by doors behind which were two large pantries lined with overflowing shelves; one with food, the other dishware. A large, minimally furnished bedroom with attached bath was behind another and then two sets of stairs, one leading up which Kat assumed was for the long ago servant's use and one leading down to the proverbial dark and drafty cellar.

A quick inspection of the cabinetry separated by the doors revealed not cupboards, but appliances; two refrigerators, a freezer, a fully stocked wine cooler and a series of drawers holding enough soft drinks to supply the small army being fed with the food that stocked the freezer and fridge.

A monstrous looking eight burner stove was centered on one wall capped by an elaborate exhaust hood and backed by beautiful mosaic tile work. The multicolored tile depicted a bright and sunny woodland scene of a girl or young woman carrying a basket as she walked along a path that ran through the forest. The girl wore an old fashioned red cloak and hood.

She leaned across the stove to get a better look. This was detailed, intricate work and not your usual pre-painted tile.

Someone had spent a small fortune on the renovation of this kitchen. Kat flipped a switch and cheered aloud as the kitchen was flooded with light from strategically placed fixtures throughout the room. Maybe this wasn't going to be so bad after all.

She ran back along the hall, opening the doors she'd neglected before. Directly across from the kitchen was another room with a full wall of windows that appeared to be a small dining room or breakfast room, she corrected when she opened the door at the end of the dish pantry to what was obviously the 'real' dining room with a table that could easily seat twenty. There was another small room with a desk and computer and two more moderately sized that were empty. Every room was clean and freshly painted.

"See?" Kat laughed with relief, "Nothing to worry about."

Mr. Begley wasn't exaggerating when he said it was a large Victorian home. There must be at least twenty rooms in this house, but the light housekeeping part of her contract? This place was going to take a lot more than light housekeeping to keep it tidy. Then again, they were paying her a helluva lot more than she'd ever been paid for anything else. She'd see they got their money's worth.

She hadn't realized how worried she was over her first impression of the house until the weight of it was lifted from her shoulders. Kat was a planner, an organizer. She hadn't done a spontaneous thing in her entire life and yet she'd fallen for everything the agent, Mr. Begley, told her about the job and the place where she would live. She'd been hurt, angry, and not quite in her right mind when she'd spoken to the man and feared she only heard what she wanted to hear. Not that there was anything she could do about it if that was the case.

After the mess she'd left behind, she doubted her ex-landlord would let her back in even if her old apartment was still available and if he did, she had nothing with which to pay first and last month's rent. Every dime she'd made in the last eight years had gone to The Bastard in one form or another. Now he had everything and she had nothing; no job, no home, no family and no future prospects.

Mr. Begley insisted the house would be vacant and no one would be inconvenienced by her early arrival. He promised to make the arrangements, but surely all that food in the kitchen was not for her alone. Once more she was beginning to doubt her decision.

The bedroom at the top of the stairs chased away those doubts and the view from the kitchen window sealed the deal.

Her bedroom and she knew this because of the notes Mr. Begley had given her along with directions, was larger than her first apartment. A huge four poster bed took center stage with a mattress raised so high off the floor the little set of steps alongside weren't just for show. On one side of the room, two wing chairs angled toward a fireplace with a hand carved surround and mantle. A desk filled the corner on the other side of the bed leaving plenty of room for a dresser between two doors; one of which led to a luxurious bath with a huge claw foot tub beneath the window and a glassed in shower stall along the back wall. The other door led to a closet the size of Rhode Island.

It took ten minutes to run down to her car, grab her bags and unpack every piece of clothing she owned. They filled a corner of the closet.

In spite of the open wall of windows, Kat hadn't bothered to take a good look outside the first time she was in the kitchen, but when she finally did, the patio beyond the kitchen made leaving the house impossible. She instantly took back every bad thing she thought about the landscaping. Who cared about the hellish front of the house when the back was heaven?

Within fifteen minutes, she had a piece of salmon on the grill and a patio table set for one with real dishes and flatware, a cloth napkin and a glass of white wine. The wood for a fire was laid ready in the pit with a lounge chair beside it where, after her delicious dinner, she would relax and enjoy another glass of wine. Or two.

If The Bastard could enjoy a vacation, why shouldn't she? Kat filled her plate and sat down to enjoy her surroundings.

In addition to the fire pit and outdoor kitchen, the backyard paradise included a heated pool, a hot tub, two dining/seating areas and a putting green. Her former students vacationed at fancy hotels that didn't equal this and beyond the grassy area on the far side of the pool it was evident more was planned.

Beyond that, the land went wild, beginning with open field and ending in forest which rose up and up into one of the many small mountains that dotted this part of the Appalachian range. She wondered how much of this small valley her employer owned. There didn't seem to be another house for miles.

For the first time in years Katarina Bennett felt completely relaxed and at ease. With a bath towel wrapped around her shoulders and a small fire to ward off the evening chill, she closed her eyes and exhaled noisily as she allowed her body to collapse in her patio lounge.

She was barely thirty years old and yet she felt old and worn out and for what? What did she have to show for all those hours and years of hard work? Except for her degrees? Not one damn thing, that's what.

She had no savings or investments and even her 401K was minimal. Her checking account had a whopping seven hundred and thirty five dollars in it.

She owned a twelve year old car and enough clothes to fill two beat up suitcases. She'd disposed of her half of the furniture which was purchased second hand to begin with and was worth nothing now. The Bastard's portion was still in the apartment. All her worldly possessions were stuffed in her compact car. Nothing of hers was left behind unless she counted her half of the flat screen TV. That was something she found too difficult to divide so she'd left it with a table leg sticking out of one side of it, a table leg from his half of the ancient kitchen table. The rest of the table lay on the kitchen floor surrounded by his half of the chairs she'd neatly sawed in two.

It took her eight years, but she'd learned her lesson. From here on in, Kat came first. She was tired of playing it safe; tired of living her life by a set of rules that seemed to benefit everyone but her. She was still young enough to make a new start and the year she would spend at this job would give her that. The pay was excellent and she would have none of the expenses she'd had before.

She laughed bitterly and poured herself more wine. Her major previous expense was somewhere in the Bahamas with his pregnant new wife.

Chapter 2

The sun had set, the fire had burned low and the wine bottle was half empty when she saw them. She was also half asleep, her chin bumping on her chest in a heavy-headed nod that brought her head snapping upright and her eyes popping open. She almost looked around to see if anyone had witnessed the embarrassing display before she remembered she was alone. Movement along the tree line caught her attention.

The warm earth and cool night air had merged to form a mist that settled low across the field stretching beyond the back of the house to the edge of the woods. The waning moon was almost full and brighter than Kat's urban eyes had ever seen. It rose above the trees, a bright, slightly misshapen opalescent ball that illuminated the swirling vapor and gave ghostly form to the shadows that played within.

She watched those shadows in the same way she used to watch white fluffy clouds flit across a bright blue sky. Her mind would form them into images only she could see and when they disappeared with the motion of the wind, she had only to reform them into something else from her imagination.

These shadows did the same, but without her mental manipulation. They formed and reformed, vague dark images engulfed and released by the mists to finally coalesce into darkened and undefined animal shapes travelling through the brown and gold of the tall, dry grass.

Kat blinked her incredulity and squinted into the haze, only half believing the reality of a line of animals trotting along in single file. They were too small to be horses and yet too large to be dogs. She dropped her feet to either side of the lounge and leaned forward to get a better look. The lead animal stopped and turned toward her as if it heard the faint thump of her feet touching ground. The others passed behind it in a steady line into the woods while their leader stood guard.

Like a curtain being parted for a stage performance, the mist gave way, giving her a clear vision of a great beast watching her as intently as she watched him. Moonlight glinted off his head and massive chest as he raised his snout to the heavens and Kat held her breath waiting for the long, mournful howl that never came. It didn't matter. Just the sight of the animal sent a fingernail running along the blackboard of her spine.

When he lowered his head, he looked across the field again and Kat knew he was staring at her. She nodded slowly in acknowledgement of the warning, blinked and the animal was gone.

They were wolves, she was sure of it, though what wolves were doing here, she couldn't fathom. She'd read about the reintroduction of elk in the higher elevations to the east, but nothing of the predators that might endanger the new herds. On the other hand, it wasn't the kind of thing she kept up to date on though she had read articles about deer populations growing out of control. This place was close to Federal lands. Maybe they were introducing the predators through some program there.

Not that it mattered. Except for the leader, the animals showed no interest in her and stayed at the far edge of the field and watching them, she felt no fear. Once there was more activity around the place, she expected the wolves to give the place even wider berth.

A look at her watch told her it was late and she rubbed her

arms against the night air. Spring was already giving way to summer, but the nights were still cool. Too lazy to retire upstairs, she replenished the fire from the stack of wood beside it and shifted her body this way and that until she was comfortable again and closed her eyes.

She'd just released that final sigh of breath that passes into sleep when a scream echoed through the night. Kat bolted upright, the hair at the back of her neck rising with the chill that ran the length of her spine. Another shadow rose out of the mist, rising into the night sky, great wings flapping silently as it rose.

As the huge owl flew across the field with its rabbit dinner dangling from its talons, Kat tried and failed to laugh away her city girl squeamishness. She pulled her terry cloth cover more tightly about her shoulders and scrunched down into her chair. As soon as she closed her eyes, visions of cute little bunnies danced through her mind.

"Poor baby bunnies," she pouted.

Something snorted behind her and her breath froze. Whatever it was, it was at the back of her right shoulder and it was larger than a bunny. Much, much larger. The sound was coming from behind her ear.

She glanced down at the fire wondering if the creature behind her could sense the movement of her eyes. A piece of branch, a couple of inches in diameter, stuck out from the fire and ended about two feet from the lounge. The tip was glowing brightly with flame. Kat was calculating how quickly she could grab the branch and turn, when the creature behind her snarled. It was a low, barely heard growl, but it was enough to cause Kat to change her mind.

"Sorry," she squeaked. Her heart was pumping so hard her sweatshirt moved to the pounding rhythm. Or maybe that was just her body shaking uncontrollably. The animal snorted again, a chuffing sound that almost sounded like a laugh.

"I think I should warn you," she whispered in the same squeaky voice. "I'm human. I read somewhere that we don't taste very good and you don't strike me as a Red Riding Hood kind of guy."

She heard the animal chuff again and this time she got the distinct impression of laughter. Did animals laugh? She had a hamster named Bernie once when she was seven, but he wasn't very personable. He bit her every chance he got. That was the only up close experience Kat had with animals and it only lasted about a month before Bernie ran away to live and die in the living room sofa.

She pointed to the field, lifting only her finger from the arm of the lounge. "There are bunnies out there. Big, fat juicy bunnies. I saw one earlier. I'm sure they taste much better than me and they'd be a lot more fun to catch."

The animal laughter sounded again.

Slowly, ever so slowly, Kat turned her head until she was looking directly at the beast behind her. As she suspected, it was a wolf, a different wolf from the one that watched her earlier and under any other circumstances she might have admired this one's strength and magnificence.

He was a beautiful animal. At first, with only the moonlight to cast away the darkness, his coat appeared as a solid gold mane, but when she shifted her shoulder and the firelight flickered over his velvety fur, she could see a variety of reds and golds and browns with a soft, silky sheen that made her want to reach out and touch it. He was a golden god of the wild.

She didn't realize she'd swung her legs over the side with her hand stretched toward the tawny head until the animal curled his lip at her approach.

"Why Grandma, what big teeth you have," she whispered while she withdrew her outstretched hand.

As if the animal understood, he showed her more of them, a

wolfish grin that almost made her laugh.

"Uh, I hope that's not an all-the-better-to-eat-you smile," she said nervously.

The wolf cocked his head, first to one side and then the other as if considering the idea. He licked his jowls before giving her another wolfish grin. With a sharp shake of his head and another chuff of canine mirth, the wolf sat, completely relaxed and comfortable.

"You're making fun of me."

The great beast closed his eyes and bowed his head.

Kat took the opportunity to make a move toward the safety of the house. The wolf was immediately on his feet, taking a step to block her retreat. Kat stamped her foot.

"Fine," she snapped, "Have it your way." She crossed her arms over her chest and gave the wolf her coldest stare, one that usually stopped teenagers in their tracks.

It hit her then that she was no longer afraid. Her initial terror had receded into simple cautiousness and it was only a residual distrust that kept her from walking into the house. This animal wasn't going to hurt her. She was sure of it. Well... pretty sure.

"I'm not sitting here all night. The fire is dying and I'm cold. Some of us," she sniffed, "Don't have fur coats." As if to emphasize her point, the towel slipped. She snapped it back in place.

The wolf snorted and Kat huffed right back while recognizing how bizarre this situation was. Anyone with half a brain would not be standing here talking to a dog, okay a wolf, she corrected when the animal's head snapped up as if he'd heard her thoughts. Anyone with an ounce of brains would be peeing their pants.

The wolf slowly closed his eyes and sighed. When he opened them again, he turned toward the house. His haunches collapsed and he laid down with his legs folded in such a way that he could easily leap into motion should the need arise. The eyes slid from the house to Kat.

OMG, she thought in the texting shorthand she'd picked up from the kids. The wolf's eyes were green!

Dark, thick lashes surrounded eyes like glowing emeralds. She'd never seen a dog, a canine, she corrected, with green eyes. How strange. Weren't wolf eyes yellow? If you crossed a yellow-eyed wolf with a blue-eyed husky, would you get a green-eyed wolf-dog? Kat found herself melting into those mesmerizing eyes. Suddenly she reared back and snapped her eyes shut. Holy shit!

She forced herself to look away from the beautiful beast. She'd never heard of wolves mesmerizing their prey, but then again, she didn't know they had green eyes, either. Was this a mutation? Or was this handsome fellow a throwback to his mystical forbearers? Was that a bit of fairytale magic in the wind? Of course not, but bright stars and firelight had probably given birth to such myths.

Wolves chased down their prey, ran it to ground. Running was what triggered the instinct to chase. Was that why this wolf showed no aggression toward her? Or was it simply because he had already hunted and his belly was full.

Eyes shuttered with half closed lids, the wolf cocked his head to the side again, this time not contemplating, but listening. He gave a slight downward shake of his head as if a decision was made and opened his eyes. Lip curled in a snarl, his head snapped up as he rose and took a step toward Kat, swinging his head and clearly herding her toward the back door of the house. His chest seemed to broaden as he brought himself up to his full and majestic height.

The wolf might not be King of the Jungle, but this one was definitely Lord of His Domain. The change in the wolf's demeanor was striking and a little frightening. Kat had forgotten for a moment just how powerful this animal was.

Not needing a second invitation, Kat threw herself off the lounge and headed for the door, pulling it closed behind her and bracing her back against it. In her mad dash to safety, she'd lost her towel.

As if to emphasize how ludicrous her precautions were, the wolf butted his head against the door, knocking her back. His nose jiggled the handle.

Whatever the wolf's mission, it was aborted when his head rose again, scenting the night. His howl broke the stillness, the final note of it echoing eerily through the darkness. When the last faint echo died away, the wolf outside her door snarled and then there was silence.

Kat pushed the door closed once more, this time listening for the solid click of the latch and driving the locking bolt into its seat. Standing motionless with her ear to the door, she listened closely, but all she heard in the quiet of the night were the small chirps of tiny creatures and clicks of insects who found safety in the dark. There were no more screams from nature's small victims, no more howls and nothing to indicate the great golden beast was still outside her door.

Shivering with the full import of what could have happened to her, she ran for the stairs, threw herself into the bed and had all she could do not to pull the downy comforter over her head. What was she thinking, trying to converse with a wolf?

She had no intention to sleep, didn't think she could, but the long day, the warmth of the covers and the stillness of the night conspired against her. Twice she awoke, startled by dreams of the green eyes staring at her through the darkness. In the dreams, those green eyes belonged to a man and not a wolf. They were only dreams, but they left her shaken and a little breathless and they frightened her more than the wolf.

Chapter 3

In the morning, there was no sign of the wolf, if it was, in fact, a wolf. She wouldn't pretend that the creature was a figment of her dreams. It wasn't, but in the bright morning light it was easy for Kat to believe the animal could not have been what she thought. It was dark and hearing it breathing behind her had been disconcerting. Oh hell, who was she kidding? Seeing that great beast behind her had scared her shitless!

First, it was much too large. She knew grey wolves were big, but that animal had to weigh close to two hundred pounds. Secondly, it was much too tame. Unless it was raised in captivity, no wolf would be that comfortable around a human. And those eyes! It had to be a cross breed of some kind, a wolf mix perhaps. Either it lived nearby or some cruel and thoughtless person had abandoned their pet, probably when it grew from an adorable puppy sized ball of fluff into something that would cost a small fortune to feed.

And the pack she saw along the edge of the trees? Swirling mists and moonlight could easily distort one's perception of size and it wasn't unheard of for stray dogs to revert to their primal ancestry and form a pack. That was certainly a more likely explanation than wolves.

Still, Kat was cautious as she peeked out the back door. She was determined to have her early morning swim, but not at the risk of another canine confrontation.

Her towel was on the lounge where it had fallen the night

before. The fire had burned away to ash. There was no sign of her furry friend, not even a paw print in the newly seeded soil around the perimeter of the patio.

Kat hummed the theme from the *Twilight Zone* on her way back to the pool. What happened last night was a tale to tell, nothing more and she wasn't about to spend precious vacation time worrying about it.

The air was chilly, but the water was warm and Kat wasted no time stripping off her short, thigh length silky robe and tiptoeing down the steps. She ducked her shoulders beneath the surface and made her way out to the middle of the pool where the water reached just below her breasts.

The mists that hovered over the fields the night before now gathered above the water's surface obscuring the reality of the world beyond the pool. It was easy to imagine herself alone in a fairy world of clouds and shimmering water, her nakedness a water nymph's natural attire. She raised her arms, threw back her head and closed her eyes in bliss.

"Thank you, Mr. Begley, for finding me this job and thank you, Mr. Goodman, for providing me with this beautiful heated pool. I don't know who you are, but I think I love you."

This was the perfect way to start the day and she made up her mind to make it a regular part of her routine, after she bought a bathing suit, of course. It wouldn't do to skinny dip in front of the children. And then she laughed, the sound of it echoing in the soft stillness of the dawn.

She turned onto her back and waved her arms and legs and came sputtering back to real life when she sank, butt first, beneath the surface. A poor kid from the wrong end of town didn't have much chance of learning how to swim, at least not well.

Kat shook the water from her short, tight curls and made her way over to the side of the pool where she could hang on to the side while she kicked her feet and made plans for the arrival of her small charges.

On her way to the pool, she'd taken a quick detour into one of the rooms off the foyer, the one that would receive the morning sun once those godawful drapes were gone and decided it would make the perfect schoolroom. Peeking under the drop cloths she uncovered a very comfortable looking overstuffed chair covered in bright red cotton duck; a good, sturdy, child friendly fabric if there ever was one.

A sofa, another chair and a wonderful wood rocker started the wheels turning in her head and once she passed the exercise portion of her morning swim, she rolled onto her back, this time hanging onto the edge with one hand, and began to knit the bits and pieces of ideas into a plan for a classroom that would make Mary Poppins proud.

With a more relaxed reading and study area at one end of the long room and a table for lessons at the other, all bathed in glorious morning light from the tall windows, the room would be perfect. She could almost see her young charges reading before a cozy fire on a chilly winter morning. She could picture them perusing the books of their new library in the bookcases to either side of that glowing fireplace.

"How's this one, Miss?" a sweet little girl in pigtails and a pretty pink dress would ask.

"Oh, that's a lovely choice," Kat would answer sweetly, patting the seat beside her for the little girl to sit and share her newfound treasure.

A chilling breeze interrupted the fantasy. Kat shook her head and sighed in disgust. She was doing it again; daydreaming about the way she wanted things to be instead of the way they were. Her little girl could be a tomboy in overalls and sneakers.

She rubbed her forehead and frowned. Was there a girl in the group? She didn't know. She didn't know their ages either. If someone had asked her right after her interview with Mr. Begley, she was sure she could have answered those questions. She was excited about this job. Mr. Begley had made it all sound so perfect. But now? She couldn't remember how many were coming. How many were boys? How many were girls?

Frustrated, Kat thumped the side of her head with the heel of her hand. The information wasn't there. It worried her. She'd never been a forgetful person, certainly not about something as important as this.

Of course, the interview followed the most disastrous week of her life. That was what she remembered and wished she could forget; The Bastard tearing her life apart and then expecting her to wish him well.

Damn! Vision blurred as tears welled in her eyes and the anger twisted her insides into knots. This was what came from too much time to hang around and think.

She swiped at her eyes with the back of her wrist, exchanging the salt water of tears for the chlorinated stuff in the pool. Her morning swim was ruined. It was time to get on with her day. Her stomach growled in agreement. Breakfast would be the first item on her agenda.

Hunkering down in the water's warmth, she made her way to the end of the pool. Goosebumps rose along her arms and torso as she emerged and she shivered in the cold morning air. She reached for the hand rail, looked up, shrieked and went windmilling back into the pool.

Once again she came up sputtering only this time to face the wolf. And there was no denying it. He was definitely a wolf and seemingly a playful wolf at that.

The golden god of the forest stretched out his front legs, and raised his rear end and wagging tail. He pounced toward her, not threateningly but in fun and woofed much like she'd seen his domesticated cousins playing with their masters in the park.

"Shoo!" Kat splashed water with her fingers.

The wolf dodged the water and woofed again, daring her.

She took the dare and drove her flattened hands along the top of the water creating a wide wave the edge of which caught him in the snout as he dodged away. He shook his head and sneezed.

"Serves you right," she laughed, both thrilled and astounded that she was playing games with this wild creature. Nature chose that moment to send a cold breeze skimming across the open field and yard to remind her it was only spring. She shimmied with the chill. "Game's over," she told her wild friend.

Starting with his head and wiggling down the length of his body to the tip of his tail, the wolf mimicked her shimmy and playfully bobbed his head.

"Game's over," she said and pointed to her tightly pointed nipples. "You see these? If I don't get some clothes on, they're going to freeze right off." She started up the steps. "Besides, it must be getting close to seven. What if someone shows up and finds me naked in the pool playing with a wolf. Fine first impression that would make."

The animal bowed. Kat was sure of it. He bowed to her, her gentleman wolf, and then he turned and trotted off toward the woods and never looked back. She was amazed, astounded and thoroughly charmed.

Tying the belt of her silky robe, she entered the kitchen in search of breakfast, her mood lightened by her encounter with the wolf. After a lifetime of trying to prove she was just like everyone else and an adulthood of reaching for the life she thought every woman was supposed to want, her exchange with the wild and beautiful creature made her rethink her whole future.

Maybe, The Bastard leaving her wasn't such a tragedy. Maybe resigning from her teaching position wasn't a catastrophe. Maybe, just maybe, Grams was right and she wasn't meant to be like everyone else. Maybe she wasn't meant to be ordinary. Maybe she was meant to be different. Maybe she was meant to talk to the wolves.

Her pragmatic side snorted and Kat laughed. And maybe that was the biggest load of fanciful bullshit she'd ever concocted. It didn't matter. For the first time in a long time, she felt happy.

She started the coffee, tossed a package of bacon on the counter and turned back to the refrigerator to grab a couple of eggs singing aloud the song her father used to sing to her Mom before the bad times came.

"Hey there Little Red Riding Hood, you sure are looking good..."

"You're everything that a big bad wolf could want," a deep bass intoned behind her.

"Aaack!" The eggs went flying as Kat whirled to face the owner of the voice.

Two hands shot out and caught the eggs. Those hands were attached to the best looking piece of manhood Kat had ever seen outside of a movie screen

Chapter 4

"Good God Almighty!" whooshed out of her mouth and Kat wasn't sure if it was fear or astonishment.

"No, I'm not Him," the man said slowly with a bit of a drawl she couldn't quite place, "But you're not the first to make the mistake." His smile was disarming, like a small boy who was up to mischief. Except he wasn't small. Anywhere. "But now that you mention it, there have been a few women who referred to a second coming...or third...or fourth."

She changed her mind. His smile reflected a dirty little boy's dirty little mind. What she found disarming was that he didn't try to hide it. He was watching her and waiting to see if she got the joke.

With her hand still plastered to her chest where it flew to keep her heart from leaping out, she sputtered, "And probably a few more who questioned their sanity the next morning. Do you always use such outrageous lines?"

He raised his hand in the Boy Scout sign, three fingers up, thumb and pinkie folded across his palm. "Never, but I've been waiting years for the opportunity to use that one."

"You should have waited longer. Who are you?" and then her eyes managed to get past his face and physique to his clothes, "Oh, sorry," because the answer was obvious. "Duh."

He was wearing a pair of paint spattered white canvas pants, work boots and a faded blue oxford shirt that had been washed to threadbare softness. The sleeves were rolled up to his elbows and showed off a pair of long, muscular forearms dusted with golden hair that attested to the fact that the golden blonde locks brushed back from his forehead and held in place by a pair of sunglasses were natural. Kat marveled at the great cosmic blunder that had turned this guy into a house painter when he should have been adorning the covers of magazines or romance novels.

"Move over, Wolfy. You've just been replaced by a human golden god," she thought and then blushed deep red when she remembered her earlier comment to the wolf. What if this gorgeous painter had shown up while she was naked in the pool?

"No need to apologize." He smiled with gleaming white, even teeth. "I'm the one who came in unannounced. I didn't mean to frighten you."

Maybe not, but he was enjoying her discomfiture once he did. She'd met his kind before when she tended bar during her last two years of college. Men like this one liked to keep their intended conquest off balance, were masters of the double entendre and sly remarks and if a girl wasn't careful, the really talented ones could charm her panties right off her rear end while her jeans were still in place. Most of the time, their banter was harmless and they took no offense when their advances were turned away.

The handsome house painter stepped past her, placed the rescued eggs next to the stove, and gave her a friendly wink. His next stop was the coffee maker where he poured himself a mug and settled his backside against the granite countertop, crossing his legs at the ankle.

The painter's pants were loose along the leg and left much to the imagination, but there was no disguising their length and leanness. A tailor couldn't have fit them better across the hips and Kat was looking forward to the rear view of him walking away. She glanced up to find him watching her watching him and reddened again when he grinned.

"Like what you see?"

What was the matter with her? She wasn't fourteen! She knew better than to blatantly stare at a man as if he was a box of Belgian chocolates, even if he was drool worthy. She turned her back on him and grabbed a frying pan from the rack.

"I was just about to make breakfast. I imagine you've already had yours," she hinted, hoping he'd go back to work at the front of the house and leave her alone. Out of sight, out of mind and all that. "My name's Kat, by the way."

"Cat?" he chuckled, "Meow. That's a bit unusual or did someone have a sense of humor."

Kat frowned. Her name wasn't common, but unusual? Funny? "K, not C. It's short for Katarina, after my grandmother."

He must have heard the snap in her voice because he seemed eager to make amends. "Ahhh, Katarina. Now I like that. It's a lovely name for a lovely lady."

Kat gave him a look that said she was on to him and unimpressed. She began pulling off strips of bacon and laying them in the pan.

"Don't look at me like that. I was talking about Grandma. She was a lovely lady, right? They wouldn't have named you after her if she wasn't, right?" he asked, thus making her look like the bad guy for misconstruing what he said.

Kat shook her head in admiration. She had to admit the guy was good.

"I'm Charles and I would be delighted to share breakfast with you, Katarina. How about you frying up that package of bacon and I'll whip up the eggs?" He opened the refrigerator and pulled out the carton with the remaining ten eggs.

"The whole package?" The package was a full pound.

"Not enough?" Charles turned back to the refrigerator.

"No, no! I just meant..." Kat blew out her breath and laughed.

"There's only the two of us."

"That's what I thought," he agreed, "So one should be enough." He began cracking eggs into a deep bowl.

"Whoa, wait!" Kat held out her hand, palm forward. "How many eggs do you eat?"

"I don't know. Six, eight? Whatever's on the plate. Why?" He looked at her curiously.

"Because I can only handle two and a strip or two of bacon," she said aloud and muttered to herself, "And because I want to live past thirty-five," as she eased around him and into the pantry.

Had this guy ever heard of cholesterol? She risked another glance at the man now working at the stove. That high, tight rear end was every bit as enticing as she thought it would be and that long, lithe body of his sure didn't look like a heart attack waiting to happen. She grabbed the loaf of bread and removed three slices for the toaster.

"There's steak here if you'd rather," Charles offered. "I'm partial to pork chops myself."

Kat shook her head. "We'd better wait on that." He was awfully free with his employer's supplies, but then again, he'd worked here longer than she had and probably knew what was okay and what wasn't. "Inside or outside?" she asked as she took the dishes down from the second shelf.

From the corner of her eye she saw him lean back from the stove to answer her and do a little checking of his own. When his eyebrows rose slightly in speculation and his back arched a little more, Kat flushed, remembering what she wore beneath the tiny cover-up, which was absolutely nothing at all.

"Well?" She resisted the urge to tug at the hem of her robe.

"Hmmm?" Charles looked up at her and grinned and it wasn't a guilty grin. He wasn't trying to disguise his interest.

"Do you want to eat inside or out?" she asked again in a

reasonable attempt to sound casual. She grabbed the dishes up and hoped they didn't crack in her tight fisted grip. The robe was called a cover-up because that's what it did, right? He couldn't see anything. Then why did the look in his eye make her feel as if he could see everything?

"Do you want to eat inside or out?"

Charles licked his lips, eyes half closed, and then shook himself out of whatever reverie he was falling into. "Oh, outside, definitely. Let's enjoy it while we can. Rain's coming and I doubt we'll be doing any running tonight. Moon's waning anyway."

She piled the plates on the tray, reached up for a platter and looked back over her shoulder. "Ah, you're a runner."

"Yeah, sure. Aren't you?" He checked the sizzling bacon, removed some and added more before he looked her way. "With those legs, you'd have to be," he said appreciatively.

His eyes said he approved of more than her legs, so she held the Betty Grable pin-up pose a moment longer than she had to, watching him watching her. This was something she'd never done before. She was flirting outrageously and apparently doing a decent job of it. It was fun. That Charles obviously found her attractive made it more fun. Maybe Grams was right and she was a late bloomer, a really late bloomer. Kat did a mental shrug. Better late than never, right?

She'd always felt like she'd missed some rungs on the boy/girl attraction ladder. She'd climbed it just fine until she was twelve or thirteen. At that age, she could sigh and swoon with the best of them over boy bands or current TV heart throbs. Her sexual fantasies were normal for girls that age, at least according to the psych classes she'd taken in college.

But as her body reached its physical adulthood, something went wrong. She was sure her preferences lay with the opposite sex. She could definitely appreciate the male form in the abstract and fantasize about the usual what-ifs, but she never got that toe curling tingle of desire for any of the boys or men she'd dated and it wasn't for lack of opportunity. She was neither a wallflower nor a celibate when she met The Bastard.

Her relationship with The Bastard, she refused to call him by his name, had been based on common interests, compatibility, and future goals rather than sexual attraction and she had been content. They were both busy and their night time conjugal forays were about physical release more than passion. It wasn't great. It wasn't awful. It was supposed to produce two children when the time was right and then, she assumed, fade into the background. After the two children, if he'd wished to continue that side of their relationship, she wouldn't have refused, but she wouldn't have questioned his withdrawal from it either.

In their eight years together, she'd never once felt the tingle of anticipation she was feeling now.

"You want butter or jam with your toast?"

Thank heavens she'd already laid the plates on the glass topped table or they would have gone the way of the knives and forks, up in the air and clattering to the flagstone of the patio. She hadn't seen, heard, or felt him move up behind her.

"Oops, sorry," he said sounding not the least bit repentant. He set the platter of bacon and eggs on the table and quickly stooped to retrieve the knife that landed by her foot where he lingered a moment more than necessary.

"That's a good way to get you nose whacked," she told him, stepping away and folding her arms across her chest.

He handed her the knife with the same smirky grin used by the fourteen year old boys who used a dropped pencil as an excuse to look up her skirt. Kat didn't let them get away with it. She wasn't going to let the housepainter get away with it either. Unlike the boys at school, however, Charles didn't look the least bit guilty or offer up any lame excuses.

"Can't blame a guy for trying," he shrugged.

"I can if he's old enough to know better," she told him while trying in vain to keep her shame-on-you face from breaking into a smile.

"Ah," Charles said, rising and raising his finger. "But then he'd also be old enough to calculate the risk/reward ratio." He took a step toward her and she took a step back. He placed the dropped knife on the table. "In this case, the risk would be minimal. I knew you wouldn't hit me."

"You didn't get a reward either," Kat laughed. She knew she shouldn't. The man didn't need any encouragement and while she was having fun, she didn't want him to think there was anything more to it than that.

"Not yet, but I'm patient," he stated confidently.

"Good," she said, "Then you won't mind waiting while I run upstairs and put some clo... something else on."

"Your breakfast will go cold," he called after her as she ducked through the door.

"That's why they invented microwaves!" she called back.

Kat tossed the jean shorts she was going to wear back in the closet and reached for a newer pair, the ones that showed off her rear end to best advantage. She had both feet in and was wriggling them up over her hips when she stopped, frowned, and wriggled them back down. She retrieved the old baggy pair with the torn pocket and put those on instead.

She'd had her moment of fun. It was time to get back to the real world.

Charles nodded his approval of her Race For the Cure® t-shirt or that was what she told herself since his eyes dwelt on her chest for an extended moment before the microwave dinged. He removed her small plate and slid his much larger and full to overflowing one in. As he passed Kat the plate, he gave her a look of resignation.

"I was hoping you'd come back in one of those little black

and white jobs," he told her, "You know, with little bits of white lace up here." He ran his finger along his chest outlining the twin arches of a bra. "And all around the edges of the poufy little black skirt. You'd be wearing fishnet stockings and six inch heels. Oh yeah, and the apron." He rolled his eyes heavenward. "I love the tiny apron."

Kat shook her head in disbelief. "Here I was, beginning to think you were original and all you can come up with is a Halloween costume. A French maid's costume? Really?" She took her plate from him and headed back to the patio. "In your dreams, buddy," she said, laughing. She tried to muster some outrage at his blatant harassing behavior, but she couldn't.

"Exactly!" he called after her, undaunted. The microwave dinged again and he followed her to the table. "A dream come true! A fantasy! But it doesn't have to be Halloween," he laughed as he took a seat, "I mean, who says you can't play a little dress-up outside the holidays. You pick the day and I'm there."

It was one of those times when she wished her hair was long enough to hide behind, but even with her head bent and her eyes on her plate, she knew he could see her trying to control her smile. "Does this routine usually get you where you're trying to go?"

Charles frowned in disappointment and sat back in his chair.

"It's the outfit, isn't it? You don't like the idea of playing a lowly maid."

"I've worked as a maid, actually," Kat said, hoping to steer the conversation in another direction. "A hotel maid and I don't consider it lowly, just very hard work."

She forked another bit of egg into her mouth and watched Charles steadily plow through his breakfast. He didn't shovel his food, but he never laid his fork to rest, either. He started at one side and worked his way across the plate barely leaving a crumb in his wake. Where did he put it?

Swallowing the latest bite of bacon, he asked, "What hotel was that?"

"A very respectable one." Kat watched him over the rim of her mug as she took a last sip of coffee.

Charles left off eating long enough to wave his fork back and forth. "Ah, ah, ah," he admonished, "I smell a teensy little pile of bullshit in there." He sounded very serious, but his eyes danced.

"Okay," Kat confessed with a regrettable laugh, "It was a seedy motel that did most of its business in hourly rates, but the owner was willing to hire underage help and the money was good, especially when you added in how much change you could find on the floor or under the bed where it rolled from the men's pockets. Some of the working girls tipped pretty well, too, to keep the sheets in their favorite rooms clean."

She was barely fifteen and desperate as only a teenaged girl can be to have the clothes and things other girls had and there was nothing left of Gram's Social Security once all the bills were paid. They didn't dare call Children's Services for fear Kat would be taken away.

"The uniform came from the thrift store. It was dull gray polyester with a white collar and huge buttons up the front. It was two sizes too big and hung like a sack on my skinny teenaged frame, which was exactly how I liked it because it said very clearly 'I am the maid'. I bought it after two guys mistook me for, well, not the maid."

"Did they hurt you?" He wasn't laughing now.

"No." Kat's laugh was a little shaky because of the look on his face. "Scared me a little. No big deal."

In fact, it had terrified her, but she had a plan and she needed the money to see it through and so she bought the uniform and forced herself to go back... and kept a container of pepper spray in the pocket. Luckily, she never had to use it.

"What happened to them?" he asked with a little more than

curiosity in his tone.

"The two guys? I don't know. They went home to their unsuspecting wives, I guess." She rose and started collecting dishes and flatware.

Charles rose, too. "Who stood for you? Who stood against them? Why were you allowed to work in a place like that to begin with?"

He reached for her hand, but she pulled it away, uncomfortable with his concern. He sounded fierce, affronted on her behalf.

"You mean like who stood up for me? Who rescued me?" This last was mocking and sarcastic. "No one," she answered her own question. "There was no one *to* stand up for me."

Her mother was long gone by then and her father was reduced to a shadow that flitted in and out of her life according to how much he drank that week and how guilty he felt about it. Grams was already confined in their fourth floor walk-up by the wheeled chair she spent her life in, as effective as any prison guard.

"There should have been," Charles said and Kat was surprised at the anger in his voice. "You'll find it very different here. I stand for those who stand for me. We stand for those who stand with us. That's what makes us who and what we are. My father taught me that. It's one of the few things we agreed on."

Charles looked around as if suddenly remembering where he was. He grinned sheepishly. "I sound like a pompous ass instead of a... Oh, never mind," he laughed and the anger melted away as quickly as it had come. "I'd better get my pompous ass in gear. My crew will be back here tomorrow night and I've got money riding on having the place ready for them."

Chapter 5

Charles was right about the weather. By late morning, the sky had turned into a solid sheet of dull and leaden gray that leached all remaining color from the gold and pale green tones of the earth and left it gray and dingy looking, too.

Paint roller held like Liberty's torch, Kat stared out through the uncurtained windows of what would be her future schoolroom. They'd torn the window coverings down and tossed them out the front door when Charles declared them good for nothing but burning.

She'd spent the morning scrubbing the grime from those windows while Charles washed walls and prepared them for their first coat of paint. Then, while he trimmed out the walls along the ceiling and woodwork with precise even lines, she rolled on the light, buttery yellow that had been chosen for the walls. At first, Charles objected to her offer of help.

"I thought you came down here early for a few days' vacation?" Once he pulled out his paint buckets and brushes, all flirtatious bantering stopped. Charles was all business as he skillfully unrolled a line of blue tape along the edge of the dark stained paneling that ran around the bottom half of the room. "Your job doesn't begin until next week. Relax and enjoy."

"Truth? I'm not sure I know how. I've never had a vacation before. I always wondered what it would be like. It seemed so wonderful to be able to kick back and do whatever you want even if that's do nothing at all. That's what I did yesterday. I built myself a fire out on the patio, relaxed in the chaise lounge, had a glass or three of wine..."

"Swam in the pool," Charles filled in her list. He snapped off the last bit of tape with his thumbnail and folded the edge over in a self-sealing flap, ready to be pulled from the roll when he needed it next.

Kat blinked. "Yeah, how did you know?" She'd been admiring his taping efficiency and the way his shirt molded to the muscles of his back when his arms reached forward.

"Lucky guess?" His eyes crinkled at the corners and he looked like he was waiting for her to say something more and then looked at her strangely when she did.

"Do you know anything about wolves?"

"Real wolves?"

Now she looked strangely at him. "Well they weren't stuffed." She turned to the window and pointed with the roller. "I saw them last night, five or six maybe more, out there along the trees."

"No you didn't." He sounded so sure of himself Kat was taken aback.

"Yes I did," she said with more conviction than she felt. The nerve of the man. She might have been mistaken about those animals along the trees, but there was no mistaking the big fella at the pool.

"No. You didn't," he insisted.

"Yes. I did," she snapped, "If they weren't wolves, then they were the biggest damned dogs I've ever seen." She turned from the window, shaking her paint roller for emphasis...

...And laid a swath of yellow paint like a blindfold across his eyes. The stripe, running between the upper edges of his slightly arched eyebrows and the tip of his aquiline nose, was perfectly straight and even like the brushwork he'd used throughout the room.

Kat was so shocked by what she'd done, she couldn't speak, could only stare at the yellow striped face in front of her which showed no response to the assault other than to tilt its chin a little higher. The reaction was all in his hands which were held closely to his sides and clenched into white knuckled fists. He made no move to wipe the mask away.

His jaw tightened. His Adam's apple bobbed in his throat as he swallowed. The yellow lids and lashes lifted slowly, exposing the flashing eyes beneath. Kat found her voice.

"Holy shit," she said, steeping back from the blazing eyes shining from the yellow bandit's mask. "Why didn't I notice that before?"

Of course, she knew why. She'd been too busy checking out the imagined beefcake body beneath the loose fitting clothes. Damn, how many times had she complained about guys undressing women with their eyes and here she'd been doing the same thing to the painter. Shame on her.

Charles' jaw tightened some more and his eyes rolled heavenward in an exaggerated petition for patience. "What, pray tell, did you not notice before? What could possibly be more obvious than my face full of paint?"

A tick started in Kat's cheek and then the corners of her mouth started pulling upward in a smile. She sucked her cheeks inward to stop both tick and smile, but it was no use. The laugh snickered out between her compressed lips in a crude and unladylike spurt.

"I'm sorry, so sorry," she sputtered. She grabbed the rag that hung from her torn back pocket like a tail and began to dab at the paint with one hand while resting the other on his chest for leverage, forgetting the roller still clutched in her fist.

"Oh! Shit! Sorry!" The bandit now had a yellow paint beard.

"Give me the damn rag and go stand over there," he growled, snatching the rag and running it over his face which only served to smear the paint further.

Kat dropped the roller into its tray and reached again for the rag. "No, no, you're making it worse. Here, let me, before you get it in your eyes."

Her hand, now free of the roller, went to the last clean spot on his face and held his cheek. His hand gripped her wrist as she gripped the rag. Both painter and painted froze in place.

A surge of sexual desire such as Kat had never felt before coursed through her. Like a wave of electric shock, it began where Charles grasped her wrist and zinged up her arm and through her chest, a heart attack in reverse. It tightened her breasts and curled downward into the lower, most private regions of her body. It made her gasp.

Kat stared into the vivid green eyes that had startled her into this fiasco, unable to look away. Charles' eyes held hers for a startled moment, and then dropped to her open and quivering lips. His tongue darted out, moistening his own lips before his mouth descended on hers.

Practical and pragmatic Kat knew this wasn't right. She'd only met the man that morning and as attractive and charming as he was, she wasn't foolish enough to fall for a pretty face and form. She knew nothing about him except that with his charming ways and handsome face, he was probably a great one with the ladies and she had no wish to be another notch in his belt or on his bedpost. The only sensible thing to do would be to turn her head away and her rational mind called to her to do just that.

But fanciful and romantic Kat, the Kat she kept caged and silent because no good ever came from daydreams and fantasies, chose that moment to make a break for freedom and regardless of what good sense dictated; her body sided with the rebellion. She'd never felt like this before, never felt this swell of want and need, this rush of heady emotion she'd only read about in her silly books.

In spite of her desire, she met his mouth hesitantly, almost timidly, unsure of what to do with this new craving. She needn't have worried.

Charles' lips met hers with a demanding force that overwhelmed and put to rest any hesitation she might harbor. He claimed her with that kiss. No sweet and diffident touching of lips in a tentative first kiss, this was deep and devouring. Consuming. And she wanted to be consumed. By it. By him.

His fingers slid through the loose curls at the back of her head, holding it in place as he slanted his mouth over hers. The hand holding her wrist released its grip to wrap around her waist and mold her body to his. Her back bent with the pressure and she dug her fingers into his broad and muscled shoulders to keep from falling backward to the floor. She could feel the heat from his body searing through the layers of cloth that separated them and she wanted that clothing gone.

His lips left hers to work their way along her chin and neck and her head fell back to give him access to the sensitive place in the hollow of her throat and she released a small whimper of pleasure when he found the perfect spot to attack with fluttering kisses.

Her hands had teased their way around to his back and after a frenzied bout of pulling and tugging his shirt from the waist of his pants, she found what she was searching for, the smooth, warm, rippling muscles of his back. She felt his body sigh beneath her kneading fingers and another sensation swept over her.

It, too, was one she'd never recognized before. Charles' desire was as great as her own. That such a man wanted her and so desperately, gave her a heady mix of potency and pleasure. There was power here and it was hers.

Charles moved forward toward the canvas draped sofa, leading her in a dance of passion toward the next series of steps and she was ready, oh lord, how ready she was to follow his lead.

Just before he reached their destination, Charles stopped so suddenly, Kat stumbled and had it not been for his strong arms circling her waist, she would have fallen.

His head snapped up and cocked slightly to the left, listening. He blinked, twice, and looked at Kat as if he was surprised he held her in his arms.

"Fuck!" he hissed and pushed away from her. This time, it was her grip on his shoulders that kept her from falling.

Charles stared at her in horror, as if she'd grown another head. A glance at her reflection in the glass of the window showed he wasn't far from wrong. Her face was smeared with the same yellow paint as his and her chocolate brown curls were now streaked as well.

As soon as he released her, the overwhelming passion she'd felt began to recede and sanity prevailed. And why shouldn't it? Between his curse and shove and horror stricken face, she felt about as sexy as a snail, yet not so lucky as the slimy little mollusk. She had no shell to crawl into and hide.

"Who put you up to this? You're not one of us," he accused.

"That's a relief. I wouldn't want to be whoever the hell you think you are," Kat snapped. She was humiliated and furious with him and with herself for whatever it was that came over her and made her act like a common…

Something in the other room caught Charles' attention. "Quick. Wipe your face," he ordered. He scooped the paint spattered rag from the floor, tossed it to her and began tucking his shirt back into his pants.

Kat scrubbed the rag, now stiff with dried paint, viciously over her nose and lips. It was too late to remove the paint which had dried to a thin crust, but that wasn't why she scoured her skin and it sure as hell wasn't because he told her to.

She could still smell him and the lingering scent of woods

and meadows irritated her nose. She could still taste him, coffee and bacon and that unique flavor that was all his own and she was sure she'd never look at breakfast the same way again. Damnit! She still wanted him and that angered her more than her initial lapse in judgment.

Her cleaning efforts only added the faint odor of paint to the mix. Kat scrubbed harder. Foul words were on the tip of her tongue when she heard the heavy front door in the foyer open.

"You just set those right there, Buddy, and go on out and get another load while I see what's what." The voice was a woman's, high pitched and sing-song with a no nonsense tone about it. "I can see right off this front hall won't do. Yes sir, Buddy, we've got our work cut out plain as day. Go on, now, move that truck and get those things under roof before it rains."

Chapter 6

Kat stood straight and hid the paint covered rag behind her back as the woman came through the door to the room where they stood and greeted them with a judgmental "humph".

Taking them in with hawklike eyes, her head snapped from side to side like the predatory bird she resembled. She folded her skinny arms over her nonexistent bosom and tapped a foot that looked too large for her long, skinny legs.

Holy smokes! It was one of those dour housekeepers from those awful gothic novels. If she'd been wearing gray bombazine, Kat would have wet her pants.

This woman wore a cotton print dress buttoned up the front to just below her neck and cinched at the waist with a matching belt. Her shoes were black, heavy heeled and sturdy, the kind Kat remembered the nuns wearing in the school she attended until she was nine.

"Humph," the woman said again and there was no doubt about the opinion expressed in that one sound. "Looks like I wasn't a minute too soon." She looked them over again, pursing her lips into a disapproving frown, and pointed a bony finger at Charles who stood there with a belligerent look on his yellow face.

"You, young man, had best be about your business. Save your foolishness for the Road House and your hanky-panky for a motel room. And you!" she turned to Kat. "You look to be an intelligent young woman, once you get that paint off. Not the kind to be charmed by a handsome face and lustful body. You want to keep your reputation here abouts, you'll use that sofa for settin' and nothin' more." She ignored Kat's flaming face and looked around the room. "There'll be no more carryings on in the parlor."

"Schoolroom," Kat corrected without thinking and then blatantly lied, "That wasn't what we were doing."

"You're the housekeeper." Charles was clearly bewildered.

"What you were doing is as plain as that paint on your face… and elsewhere." The woman stared pointedly at Kat's chest. Swiveling her head to Charles, she said, "Of course I'm the housekeeper. Who else would I be?"

Yeah, who else? Kat looked down at her chest. A perfect yellow handprint like the kind children make with finger paints was emblazoned on her chest completely covering her left breast and the hand that made it was clearly not a child's. Well, damn. The evidence was pretty incriminating.

"You aren't the housekeeper," Charles was saying and it took Kat a minute to realize he was talking to her, "Who the hell are you?"

"I think you'd best be on your way, young woman, to do whatever it is you're supposed to be doing. And you, young man, better get back to work. This place will be full up tomorrow and the Alpha expects it done."

"I never said I was," Kat answered. "I'm the teacher," she explained, though at that point she wasn't sure anybody was listening or cared. "I'm supposed to be here."

"I *am* the Alpha!" Charles snarled at the woman. "No, you're not!" he turned on Kat.

"Yes, I am." Who the hell did this guy think he was?

"Good God Almighty," the woman breathed.

Having said pretty much the same thing when she met him, Kat almost rolled her eyes, particularly since the woman's hand went to her chest in the same heart protecting way. She would have laughed if she hadn't been so angry at the man who caused such a reaction.

The woman winced as she peered more closely into Charles' yellow face. "It is you." She took a step back and looked him over once again and shook her head. "Well ain't that a fine howdy-do."

Charles looked more closely at the woman. "Mrs. Gregory?" he asked, looking a little shaken himself.

"What was. It's Martin now. After Bill died, I married Stuart Martin and went north to live with his folk. Now he's gone, too," the woman said with a hint of defiance as if daring Charles to ask another question.

Charles didn't ask it. "I remember now," he said instead and then he smiled his most charming smile and Kat was amazed to see the older woman thaw under his warming gaze.

What was it about this guy that he could melt the drawers off every woman he met?

"I didn't recognize you either," he continued, "Good God, how many years has it been? It must be twenty-five at least."

Mrs. Martin suddenly closed her eyes and swayed dangerously. The woman's mouth opened and closed and opened again. Her eyes popped open and her face paled. She swayed dangerously. The predator had become prey; a gasping fish out of water.

Kat ran to catch the woman before she fell. "Don't just stand there. Help me get her to the chair," she snapped at Charles.

Charles did more than help. He scooped the woman up and carried her to the chair where he set her down gently and knelt on the floor in front of her.

Mrs. Martin took a deep breath, shook her head to clear it, and opened her eyes to the kneeling Charles. This seemed to upset the woman even more. Fanning her hand to shoo him away, she tried to rise.

"Don't need to sit. I got work to do. I'm fine," she insisted. She tried to rise and quickly sat back down. "Just give me a minute."

Charles lifted her chin with the knuckle of his index finger. In an odd gesture, he leaned forward almost as if he was zooming in for a kiss and sniffed sharply, twice. "When was the last time you ate?"

"I'm fine. You go clean up and leave me to my business. It's almost lunch and I got work to do. Leave me be," she said bossily.

"When was the last time you ate?" Charles asked again, his tone demanding an answer.

Maybe it was the tone of his voice which now sounded deeper and more commanding or maybe it was the way he stood up and over her that made his shoulders look broader, his legs look longer, his whole body look more powerful. Whatever it was, Mrs. Martin shifted back in her chair and averted her eyes.

"Day before yesterday," she confessed.

"Why?" It was another demand.

Mrs. Martin hung her head, clearly ashamed. "I spent the last of our money on the gas to get us here."

"Why didn't you tell Begley you needed money? He would have billed it to me." Charles' eyes never left the older woman's bowed head.

"I didn't want you to think we came a-begging," she whispered. She started to rise again.

"You sit until I tell you to do otherwise," he snapped and Mrs. Martin sat.

Kat wanted to be anywhere but in that room witnessing this proud woman confess her penury and she was shocked by Charles brow beating her. Her fist was clenched, ready to do battle on the older woman's behalf. She started forward.

Charles hand snapped up, one finger raised. Stop. Kat was brought up short. Charles didn't look to see if his gesture was obeyed. His eyes never left Mrs. Martin.

"Becoming a member of this... family," he went on in a stern voice, "was a condition of your coming here; that and a release from your previous... employer. Do you honor that agreement? Do you stand for me?"

At his repetition of the same words he'd used when speaking to her, Kat's fist unclenched, her curiosity aroused. It was like being eight years old again, sitting at the kitchen table doing homework, listening to her parents talk about one thing while meaning something else. She'd known they were talking in code, but didn't have the key to break it.

"Of course I do and Buddy, too," Mrs. Martin said, offended. "Where I go, he goes and you know he'll be loyal to you." A little of the snap was back in her voice.

"Then why would you shame me."

"I didn't..."

"You did! It's my duty to see my p... people are cared for, fed, housed. What would it look like if I let someone I stood for go hungry, a widow no less?" His finger poked the soft arm of the chair for emphasis and Mrs. Martin jumped. "We're small. We're new. I'll be observed and tested and I will not be found wanting. I stand for those who stand for me, Tilda Martin. Don't you forget it."

"I won't, sir," Mrs. Martin said, nodding her head sharply. She smiled at Charles like a mother proud of her son. "It won't happen again."

"See that it doesn't."

He held out his hand and the housekeeper placed her hand in his, he patted it and smiled affectionately. His whole bearing changed as he returned to role of affable painter.

"You sit right there. I'll get you some water. Katarina will keep you company."

"It's Kat and I want to know what the..."

"So do I. We'll talk about that later," Charles said in that voice that oozed authority and expected obedience. He turned to Mrs. Martin lowering his chin and raising his eyebrows in a significant look. "You're right, she doesn't belong here. You keep that in mind."

Mrs. Martin's nod contradicted her words as a body hurtled across the room.

"No!" she shouted as the huge man wrapped his arms around Charles and lifted him from the ground in a bear hug that had the power to break the smaller man's ribs. "Buddy, no!"

"Charlie!" Buddy danced around the room with Charles dangling from his arms like a big rag doll. "I'm back, Charlie. I'm back. I come home."

"Buddy Gregory, you put him down!"

"That's great, Buddy," Charles choked out in a strangled voice, "Could you put me down now."

"Sure, Charlie, sure."

Charles bent in half and rested his hands on his knees while he gulped in enough air to replace what had been squeezed from his lungs.

"Well," he rasped out a laugh, "Buddy hasn't changed much." He straightened and then bent backward with a groan to realign his spine. "Good to see you, man, but I sure hope you don't hug the girls like that."

Buddy was tall, six-six or seven to Charles' six feet and where Charles' well-muscled shoulders and chest narrowed to slim hips and long legs, Buddy was simply huge. He dwarfed Charles with his massive neck, hulking shoulders and thick arms. His broad chest crowned a thick torso and wide hips that were supported by thighs the size of telephone poles. Even though his back was to her, Kat could see the blush creep up the pale skin of the ears that stuck out on either side of his red ball cap.

"I wouldn't hug a girl like that, Charlie," the man said

seriously and as if Charles should know better than to say such a thing. "You got to be careful with girls. They're like Mama's china tea cups and break real easy. And no huggin' lessin' she's your girlfriend," he continued as if reciting a rule. "I don't got no girlfriend. But you do," he said slyly and turned and winked at Kat.

Three voices sounded at once.

"Buddy!"

"No, she isn't."

"N-no. I'm not." Kat was as quick to answer as Charles and she hoped the others thought her stutter was caused by the comment and not by her first good look at Buddy's face.

Buddy Gregory was an albino with snow white hair, colorless brows and lashes and pale, almost transparent blue eyes. His lips, too, showed only a hint of color against the gleaming white of his teeth bared in a childlike grin. It was hard to put an age to his innocent and unlined face, but if she was forced to guess, she'd say his late twenties.

The white haired giant blushed fiercely. "But Mama said if Charlie was gonna be..."

"Maybe you better pay less attention to your Mama's mutterings and more attention to your manners," Mrs. Martin interrupted before Buddy embarrassed them both. "Instead of tossing Mr. Goodman around, maybe you should have been holding out your hand and introducing yourself to the lady."

Poor Buddy looked like he wasn't sure what to do. He looked at his mother, looked at his hand, and looked at Kat.

Kat took pity on the confused man and held out her hand. "Hi, I'm Kat. It's nice to meet you, Buddy."

"Kat?" he grinned as he shook her hand, very gently, she noted. Still shaking and grinning, he looked to his mother. "You were right Mama. We got us another Kitty Kat." Buddy laughed at his joke. "Our other one died," he explained to Kat, "But I didn't eat it. We don't eat cats." He emphasized each word with a shake of his finger as if it was another rule.

"I'm glad to hear it" she laughed.

Chapter 7

"What do you mean he's not there?"

Charles was shouting so loudly into his phone, they could hear every word from the kitchen. He was pacing like a wild animal held in a cage, back and forth, back and forth, in front of the windows looking out over the patio. He'd been making phone calls for the last half hour, becoming louder and more frustrated each time the people he tried to contact were unavailable.

By the sound of it, he'd gone back to the top of his list.

"Don't give me that out-of-town shit, Henry. We both know he's not on vacation. Saint Marshall wouldn't leave his precious Rabbit Creek unattended." His jaw clenched as he listened to what Henry had to say.

"Bullshit! Elizabeth'll be ready to whelp any day now. Hell, half your female population must be ready to drop their cubs, so you know as well as I do, nobody's going anywhere any time soon."

Whatever was said on the other side of the line made him grin, but no one would know it from the sound of his voice.

"You're welcome," he snarled, "If you weren't my cousin, I'd come down there and rip your throat out. What kind of a Second are you? You don't know where your Alpha is. You don't know where the goddamned kids are and you don't have a contact number for Eugene Fucking Begley." He held the phone out and looked at it as if he couldn't believe what he was hearing.

"I didn't call him," he yelled at the phone in his outstretched hand, "Elizabeth did. She said she'd take care of finding me a housekeeper for this place and a teacher for the kids." A pause. "Yes, dammit, but she knew damn well they weren't both supposed to come here. Shit, the teacher isn't even one of us!"

"You know damn well what she is! Keep laughing and I really will come down there and rip your throat out. You tell Marshall the same goes for him and don't think that pretty little mate of his is going to save either one of you."

He looked at the phone in his hand again and for a moment, Kat thought he was going to hurl it into the pool, but then he punched it with his thumb without saying goodbye and jammed it into his pocket.

Mrs. Martin's whole head followed each time Charles changed direction, like this was a tennis match and his head was the ball. She pursed her lips and sighed.

"Looks to me like Buddy isn't the only one who hasn't changed. Listen to that language. I told his mother long ago she should wash that filthy mouth out with soap, but poor Emily, God rest her soul, thought he'd grow out of it. Don't see why. His Daddy never did. He had the same foul temper peppered with the same foul words."

"Like father, like son," Kat commented.

"Lord, I hope not."

They'd eaten lunch in the small eating area off the kitchen, the Breakfast Room, and over sandwiches piled impossibly high with slabs of ham and thick slices of cheese, Kat learned that Mrs. Martin had worked for Charles' mother when he and his brothers were boys. She'd been Mrs. Gregory then and her son, older than the Goodman boys, had worshipped Charles, the eldest son, and followed him about so closely, Charles couldn't stop short without the bigger boy bowling him over.

Kat did the mental math and came to the conclusion that Buddy, the man she'd judged to be in his twenties, was a good twenty years older than that!

As for the grownup Charles, he all but ignored Kat during the meal and spent his time trying to chat with Buddy about how the other man had spent his time during the years they'd been apart. It wasn't easy. Buddy only wanted to talk about Kat.

"She sure is pretty," he told Charles as if Kat wasn't in the room.

"She is that," Charles agreed, "So you say you couldn't find much work, huh?"

"No. I think she'd make a fine Mate. She's a teacher, you know."

"So I gathered. You think you'd like to work for me?"

"Mama says I got no choice if I expect to eat. You think she'd like having babies? I could help take care of 'em. I do good with babies, 'specially if they was your babies, Charlie. Mama says it's important for a Mate to like babies and if she's a teacher, she must like 'em, right?"

Charles was beginning to look uncomfortable and Kat didn't feel much better. "Maybe we can go for a run later, Buddy. Would you like that?"

"Sure would!" Buddy nodded enthusiastically. "If Kat was the Mate, she could run with us. I bet she'd look fine a-runnin' wild. You like to run Miss Kitty Kat?"

"I used to," Kat told him, "But mostly when I had to catch a bus"

It was true. When she was young, she ran for the sheer joy of it, but like so many things she enjoyed, running was set aside because it got her no closer to her goals and running on city sidewalks held little appeal.

"See, Charlie? Miss Kitty Kat is just about perfect." Buddy folded his arms and sat back in his chair and nodded, argument won, conversation over.

"You need to talk to him, Mrs. Martin."

"Indeed I do, Mr. Goodman, but you have to understand. Buddy's not a child anymore and he has his own opinions."

Charles spent the rest of the meal in silence before he went outside and started making phone calls.

"Wes Goodman, Charles' daddy, was a hard man, but a just leader and fair in his dealings with his people," Mrs. Martin went on. "He did right by them, took good care of them and he was soft and sweet as marshmallow when it came to Emily. It was them boys he was tough on. Toughest on Charles because he was the oldest and supposed to take his father's place." She glanced over her shoulder at Kat. "You need to remember that."

"I don't see why. According to Mr. Goodman, I don't belong here." It was like she'd suddenly grown warts on her nose, turned wall-eyed, lost half her teeth and contracted plague. The man wouldn't even look at her. "I'll be leaving come morning."

"I wouldn't count on that if I were you." One side of the woman's mouth curved up into her cheek in a lopsided smirk that Kat already recognized as Mrs. Martin's version of a smile. "If Eugene Begley sent you here, he must mean you to be here."

"You heard Mr. Goodman. It was a mistake."

"Eugene Begley don't make that kind of mistake."

"Charles' plans for this place didn't include me or kids. I thought he made that pretty clear."

Looking only at Mrs. Martin across the table from him at lunch or at Buddy to his left, Charles explained in code again (and that was really ticking Kat off) that he'd purchased this place in the middle of nowhere as a 'retreat' for his people, to be used mostly on weekends for adult relaxation and pursuits, emphasis on 'adult', and not for a schoolhouse.

You didn't have to be an expert at code breaking to understand the meaning of that! With the pool and hot tub, food and liquor enough to stock a neighborhood bar and six bedrooms and baths above, he was looking for party time, not foster parent time and he had thought to begin this week's party early with Kat. The flaw in that theory was Mrs. Martin herself who didn't find their circumstances amusing when she walked in on them this morning, but later nodded her head in understanding at Charles' plan. Of course, at the time, Mrs. Martin thought Charles was the painter and not the boss. The guy who signed your paychecks always had great ideas.

Kat brushed the last of the crumbs from the counter into her palm, tossed them into the container under the sink and came to stand next to Mrs. Martin. Together they watched Charles look up at the gray and water swollen sky and frown.

He held his hand out, palm up, catching the first fat drops of rain and then his hand went to his mouth and with two fingers between his lips he issued a piercing whistle before waving his arms to call Buddy in.

"You're supposed to be sitting down."

Kat touched the other woman's arm and indicated the wooden rocker in the corner, mostly because she didn't want to watch Charles' high and tight rear end move beneath the canvas work pants. She didn't want to imagine how the muscles of his tapered back rippled under the faded oxford shirt.

Damnit! What was the matter with her? She didn't even know this guy and if they hadn't been interrupted, she would have been stripped and spread after only a grunt and a nod from him. She'd never done a one night stand in her life and she sure as hell never felt like that about anyone, never mind a guy she just met. After the way he'd treated her, what he'd said to her, the way he ignored her at lunch, how could she still feel this disgustingly insatiable interest?

"You don't belong here," Kat said aloud, "That's what he said and he was right." He might as well have slapped her.

She'd heard and felt those words so many times, they

shouldn't hurt any more. Repetition had taken the sting out of those words long ago or so she thought. Kat had spent a lifetime trying to belong, trying to have what other people had, trying to live the way other people lived. Trying and failing.

She never belonged; not in her old neighborhood, not in high school or college, not with her colleagues at Greenwood Preparatory Academy and apparently not with those of the Bastard, either.

"Seems to me, men say a lot of things they don't mean." Mrs. Martin rocked that chair the way Kat suspected the woman did everything, in double time.

"Trust me, Mrs. Martin, this one means it. He wants me gone," Kat said bitterly and wondered again why it should bother her so much.

"Don't know you well enough to trust you and call me Tilda. I expect we'll be spending a lot of time together. No sense being formal."

Before Kat could reply, Charles stuck his head in the door.

"I'm going for a run," he said, "See if I can catch up with Buddy."

At the sound of her son's name, Tilda's head snapped up. "You let him run?"

"I did," he nodded. "He said it had been a while and he missed it, so I let him go."

Tilda looked ready to run out the door after her wayward son and Kat could understand why. In the few hours she'd known them, she'd already seen that the man had the mind of a child and was actually older than Charles though he didn't look it.

"He can't run, not alone. He gets distracted, confused... lost."

"He'll be fine. He can't have gone far. I'll call and he'll come," Charles said confidently.

"He won't," Tilda told him worriedly with a sharp glance at

Kat. "When he runs, he turns deaf. All he hears is the wild. They'd get so mad at him, but he can't help it. The pull is too strong, he doesn't hear."

"He'll hear me." Charles stripped his belt from the loops of his spattered painter's pants. He crossed his arms and gripped the hem of his shirt in that way men have of stripping off their shirt and leaving it inside out. Arms stretched above his head, he offered a perfect display of pectorals and abs.

His chest was every bit as beautiful as Kat imagined. Unprepared for her reaction, she sucked in her breath on a wave of longing and had her arm outstretched to touch him before she realized she'd moved. Disgusted with herself, she turned the gesture into a comforting one and laid her hand on Tilda's shoulder.

"I can look for him, too."

"No, you can't. I want you here, with Mrs. Martin," Charles ordered.

"Yes, I can. I'm perfectly capable..."

The closing door told her what he thought of that.

Being a mature adult, Kat wrinkled her nose and stuck out her tongue at the back of the man striding away from the door. "Asshole. I wonder if he orders everyone around like that or just me."

"I imagine he's used to being obeyed," Tilda observed vaguely.

She was watching through the window, eyes squinting to see through the sheets of rain that beat against the windows as the sky released its burden. Her thumb rubbed against the tips of her fingers in a nervous gesture and her jaw was tight. Even on such short acquaintance, Kat knew this woman wasn't one to worry over trivial things. If she was concerned for Buddy's safety, she had reason to be. A tear formed in the corner of the woman's eye, just one tear, but it was enough for Kat to make up her mind.

"I'm going out to look."

Poor Mrs. Martin looked truly alarmed. "You can't. He said to stay here."

Kat grinned. "Ever hear the words you're not the boss of me?"

"Don't claim to be, but the Al... Mr. Goodman, he..."

"Isn't the boss of me either."

Technically he was, but at the moment Kat didn't care. He was probably going to fire her anyway.

"You don't know these woods. You'll end up lost, too."

Kat grabbed her keys off the rack by the back door where Charles had hooked them along with several others when he returned from pulling her car into the barn along with his truck. She dangled the keys from her finger for Tilda to see.

"I won't be running around the woods. I'll stick to the roads. If Buddy comes across one, he'll probably stick to it, too, and try to follow it back here."

"Wait!" Tilda raised her finger and hurried to the bedroom off the kitchen, returning with an old purple umbrella, the kind you didn't see any more with the deadly silver point at its tip. "Just in case you have to get out of the car," she said, holding it out to Kat.

Kat took it as an offering of approval and thanks for what she was doing, though the woman couldn't say it out loud.

Without it, she would have been soaked by the time she entered the barn, soaked and already shivering with cold. She couldn't imagine what poor Buddy must be feeling. Hauling back the doors on their screeching metal rollers, the first thing she saw was a very sleek and very expensive Mercedes roadster and just beyond it a metallic blue Tahoe. Kat couldn't imagine owning either one and wondered which one Charles drove here and which one he kept as a spare for weekend pleasure.

Beyond them was an older pickup truck with huge tires. It

was obviously a work vehicle if one took into account the ladders, buckets and tarps in the back and next to that, the old beat up rust bucket Tilda and Buddy had arrived in. Next to that was her own little rust bucket that had served her faithfully since she bought it used ten years ago.

Kat tossed everything that filled her front seat out onto the floor. She would pick it up later when she had time. For now, finding Buddy was priority number one.

Chapter 8

Kat searched for hours along the half mile lane that led to the house and five miles in either direction once she got out on the county road. She followed every side road and lane. Steven's Bridge, Duck Creek, Twenty Mile, Old Mill; the names became familiar as she traveled them over and over.

Twice, heart thumping in fear of what she might find, she stopped her slow crawl and got out of the car to investigate the ditches that ran alongside the road when her eyes detected something not quite right. The first was a dead deer, decaying and bloated, and the second, a bag of garbage tossed by a passerby and torn open by some wild creature in search of a meal.

Twice she stopped for odd flashes of bright light from the edge of the trees and once, left the car at the side of the road to run across a stubbled field to find nothing when she could have sworn she saw a man.

Every hour or so she stopped by the house to check in with Tilda and the news was always the same; no word from Charles, no sign of Buddy. Each time, Tilda begged her to stay. Each time, Kat refused and Tilda exchanged Kat's empty travel mug for one filled with coffee.

Kat was wet, muddy and tired, but she wouldn't give up. The rain had stopped, but the sky was still overcast and full darkness was falling fast. Her gas gauge showed almost empty as she swung onto Fulton's Bend, a narrow gravel road she'd learned would bring her out to the county road about a mile beyond the turnoff for Hell Hall, the facetious name having taken on a more sinister connotation when she thought of the possible outcomes of Buddy's disappearance. This would be her last pass before she ran out of gas.

Charles must be exhausted. While she was riding in semi-comfort, he was tramping through the woods and fields on foot. He too, was MIA and Kat thought it odd he hadn't checked once with Tilda to see if Buddy had returned on his own. As much as she wanted not to, Kat was worried for his safety, too.

He was arrogant and rude and since Tilda and Buddy's arrival had gone out of his way to ignore her existence and yet she couldn't get him out of her mind. It was as if after that one wild and passionate encounter, he was inside her, had become an intrinsic part of her and she didn't like the feeling at all.

She felt used and humiliated, a been-there-done-that sensation she had no wish to repeat. The first time was in high school when the football team's star running back asked her out and dated her regularly, only to leave her with her first formal dress hanging in her closet with the new shoes and bag to match two days before Homecoming. His grades were solid and the two papers she'd helped him with would carry his eligibility through the season. He didn't need her any more.

He didn't feel the need to tell her that, but the blond chick with big boobs and bigger hair that ended up on his arm for Homecoming couldn't wait to give her the news.

It happened again when she was a college freshman and let's not forget The Bastard who waited until the final med school bill was paid before he told her he'd fallen madly in love with a twenty one year old nurse.

No, being used wasn't a new experience, but it had never felt quite like this.

Charles had treated her like some two bit tramp, a quick

fuck, a dirty little secret not to be exposed in respectable company. Okay, they didn't quite get to the fuck part, but they would have if Tilda hadn't shown up when she did.

During those other times, Kat hadn't known she was being used, not until the end when it was too late and therein lay the difference between this and those other times. What did she expect throwing herself at a man she barely knew? Sure, she'd slept with men she didn't love. She wasn't sure she was capable of such a strong emotion, but she'd known them and cared for them and certainly hadn't thrown herself into their beds after knowing them for only a few hours.

Charles wasn't the cause of her humiliation. She was. She'd never acted that way in her life. People farther up the social ladder made assumptions about girls raised in her part of town and she'd always gone out of her way to prove those assumptions false. She wasn't a skank. She wasn't loose with her favors. She wasn't a tramp.

Until today when she sure as hell acted like one. Worse, those incredible feelings were still there even after Charles had metaphorically slapped her down and put her in her place. She still felt a sexual tingle when he came within a few feet of her. Thinking of him now made her insides quiver.

Damnit! What was the matter with her? She would have to be very careful when she was around him. If he didn't fire her. If he didn't send her away to where he thought the children should live. If he let her stay.

The little red finger of her gas gauge was bouncing above the E. With luck she'd be coasting back to the barn on fumes. She was close enough now she could walk it with ease if she ran out of gas.

With the coming darkness, she'd slowed to a crawl, squinting into the dusk to see beyond the almost useless beam of her headlights. She was so used to staring out and seeing nothing of interest that she almost missed the shadowy shapes of people in the middle of the field to her left. She stopped and stared and then backed up and angled her car so the headlights shone on the men.

They were concentrating so hard on what they were doing they didn't notice they were being observed or else had no fear of being watched. Her stomach clenched when she realized whatever they were kicking and poking was alive, an animal of some sort. It rose up and tried to crawl away, but a brutal kick from one of the men sent it sprawling back down with a howl of pain. She heard one of the men laugh. The cruel sound of it set her in motion.

Kat scrambled for the glove box and the small black canister within and looped the cord over her wrist. She grabbed the tightly furled umbrella for good measure. Leaving the headlights on, she ran from the car and across the field.

"Stop! Stop it! Leave it alone!"

She was almost on top of them before they turned. The older one took a step toward her while the younger turned back and kicked the animal again. It whimpered with the blow.

It was a dog, a big dog, so covered in mud she could barely see the white fur beneath, but what stood out more than its bedraggled coat was the blood matting its leg and the iron jaws clamped around it. The poor thing had been caught in a leg hold trap.

Kat's vision blurred to red.

"You bastard!" she screamed and swung the umbrella with all her might.

It clipped the kicker behind the ear and sent him to his knees over the struggling animal. The older man continued his advance, arm raised to hit her with a back handed fist. Kat swung the umbrella again and it was enough to interfere with the blow, but not enough to prevent its connection. Her head exploded with pain. She staggered back and fell, but she kept her grip on the umbrella and stabbed out at the man looming over her with his fist raised again.

The point caught him in the side just below his ribs and above the waist of his jeans. He bellowed in rage and pain, grabbed the umbrella and wrenched it from her grip, hurling it behind her. Kat flipped onto her stomach and clawed at the muddy ground in a futile attempt to scramble away.

He grabbed her ankle and twisted her easily onto her back. In spite of her flailing kicks, he held her easily with one hand while the other went to the buckle on his jeans.

"You should have minded your own business, bitch." He turned to his partner who was crawling away from the dog that now lay still as death. "Go get the fucking truck."

"It bit me," the partner complained. "The fucking thing bit me." He held his hand to his neck. "It could have torn my throat out."

"I wish it had," Kat hissed. She stopped fighting and stared at the two men, squinting in the fading light. She needed to memorize their faces. If she got out of this alive, she wanted to be able to identify them, to make them pay.

Her arm was pinned beneath her and she could feel the canister of spray digging into her back. It was her only chance and only good if she used it while the partner was away at the truck.

Her captor ignored her comment. "Good," he said, "Give it a taste of blood it might fight harder in the ring. Shame to use a dog that size for bait."

"That's no dog. It's a wolf, I tell ya, a fucking wolf. I told you there were wolves up here."

Kat risked another look at the dog, relieved to see its sides heave with labored breath. It was certainly big, bigger than her friend from the pool. Could it be another wolf?

Beyond the dog, a good distance away across the field, she saw the figure of another man, little more than a darker shadow in the night, running toward them. Her heart knotted in her chest and she shrank with the knowledge that her luck had just run out. Her chance for escape was now reduced to nothing.

All those nights in the city walking home alone in the dark, she'd often worried that she'd end up raped or dead in some dark alley. How ironic to meet her fate in the peace and quiet of a country meadow.

Kat's eyes widened and she gasped again as the running man burst into a flash of light moving faster than any man could. The light seemed to leap through the air momentarily blinding her and then the light was gone, leaving in its place not a man, but a beast. The beast soared over the injured animal on the ground, a vicious snarl contorting its face. She knew him in an instant. She knew his golden coat and blazing green eyes. It was her Wolf Lord from the pool.

Before her captor had a chance to turn, the wolf was on him, knocking him away from Kat and driving him to the ground. Kat rolled in the opposite direction and shoved herself up onto her knees. One foot planted firmly on the ground, she started to rise, saw her attacker's companion fumble with his hand in his pocket. His eyes were wide with panic and his hands were shaking badly as he withdrew the gun.

In a half leap, half stagger, Kat lunged forward and reached for the arm rising with the gun while she drove her shoulder into the stomach of the frightened man. The gun went off with a deafening roar in the stillness of the night as Kat and the gunman tumbled to the muddy ground inches from the trapped and beaten animal's head.

The white wolf, and this close she was sure that's what it was, made one last effort to slice its tormentor with its wicked looking jaws, but it hadn't enough strength to finish the job. It collapsed back onto the ground.

The sight of those jaws snapping so close to his face was enough, however, to send the gunman into a screaming panic. Screeching obscenities, he threw the gun aside and kicked and punched his way out from under Kat who was clawing her way up his body to do her own damage to his face. He ran, stumbled, fell, clambered to his feet and took off at a dead run.

Kat, screaming obscenities of her own, scuttled after him on all fours, until she too, collapsed face first in the mud. Her nose landed on Tilda's muddy umbrella. Grunting, she pulled herself to her feet and shook her purple weapon at the retreating man.

"Fucking bastard! Come back here so I can kill you," she shouted irrationally.

Bright light burst behind her and she spun around to find Charles Goodman brushing flecks of dirt from his bare chest. "I doubt he'll take you up on that offer," he said.

Kat poked her finger in the air and opened her mouth to speak, closed it, opened it again and closed it once more. Her knees gave out and she sat, splat, in the mud, staring speechlessly up at a man who a moment before was a wolf. Her wolf.

"I know. Pretty amazing, isn't it. I often leave women speechless."

Kat began to shake, not quiver and tremble, but earth quaking shake. She dropped the umbrella as her hands flapped uselessly in front of her face. The unused canister of pepper spray flopped dangerously close to her nose. Her teeth chattered so forcefully she couldn't hear herself think.

The man who was her new boss, the man that owned that house and those cars, the gorgeous man who made her insides turn to jelly, the man she almost dropped her drawers was..."A W-w-w-werewolf?" she sputtered.

"No. A Wolver. There's a big difference and we don't have

time to go into it now. We've got to get Buddy home or he'll die."

Charles knelt beside the white wolf and began to feel along the leg held by the trap.

"Buddy?"

Kat stared at the mud covered animal, its pale mouth and pink rimmed eyes evidence of its condition. Of course. Albino man, albino wolf. What was she thinking? If Kat could have found her voice, she would have given in to the hysteria rising up through her throat and attempting to form a scream. Fortunately, when she opened her mouth, nothing came out, because she had the feeling once she started, she wouldn't stop.

"Katarina." Charles' voice was stern and commanding. "You were willing to save the wolf. Come help me save the man. Now!"

That gave her something other than the bizarreness to focus on. Wolf or man, Buddy was a sweetheart and he was going to die without help. She knelt beside Charles.

"What do you need me to do?"

"Hold his leg here and here." Charles showed her where he needed her to steady the leg so he wouldn't do more damage while he forced the iron jaws open. He looked around and shook his head. "The ground was softened by the rain. He must have pulled the spike loose and dragged it with him. Those two must have found him here, struggling."

At the mention of the two tormentors, Kat became alert and looked around for the one that didn't run off. His body was sprawled a few feet away. "Did you...?"

"That was the plan, but I didn't have the pleasure. His partner got him first. Shot through the heart."

He forced the trap open and Buddy screamed and thrashed with the pain of blood rushing back through the mangled limb. Without thinking, Kat threw her body over the wolf's to keep him still. Buddy's head snapped around to lash out at her with bared fangs, one of which scraped the back of her hand.

Before she could move, Charles' hand wrapped around the wolf's throat and pinned its head to the ground. "No," he said and it was almost a growl. "She's mine."

Buddy the wolf whimpered and lay back.

"Yours?" Kat squeaked.

"Best to keep it simple," Charles said, "Easier for Buddy to understand."

Chapter 9

Charles hoisted the giant wolf into his arms and slowly straightened his legs. He started forward, staggered a few steps and then readjusted the weight.

"Leave that," he ordered when Kat bent to pick up the muddy umbrella. "We can't get any wetter than we already are."

The rain had started again, a slow drizzle that clung to their faces like cobwebs of mist, but Kat wasn't thinking of protection from the rain.

"It's Mrs. Martin's umbrella. She's had it for a long time and she'll want it back." It was a handy weapon.

Kat tried to picture Mrs. Martin using her purple umbrella to protect her little wolves from whatever it was that frightened little wolves and saw nothing peculiar about the vision. By taking the umbrella with her, Kat was protecting them, too.

She shook off what mud she could and tucked the furled umbrella under her arm. She turned to follow Charles and her toe caught the edge of the steel trap, closed and harmless now that its damage was done. With her free hand, she followed the short length of attached chain to the stake that was supposed to anchor the trap, grasped it and began to drag it along behind her.

"I said leave that stuff," Charles called back over his shoulder in that you-will-obey-me voice.

Kat ignored him. Her mind was running on a kind of autopilot where she knew what she had to do, but couldn't articulate why. The umbrella had to go. The trap had to go. The gun had to stay. The body? Every time the word entered her thoughts, her mind shut down a little more. Body? What body?

Charles already had the unconscious Buddy settled in the back seat by the time Kat caught up with him. He stood aside and held the passenger door for her, the perfect gentleman. She nodded her thanks, slid into the seat and arranged the umbrella along her leg and the leghold trap on her lap as if it was her purse, the perfect lady.

"Seat belt," Charles ordered as he climbed in the driver's side. He frowned as he jerked the seat back as far as it would go which apparently wasn't far enough because he muttered something about a piece of shit car.

"But it's my piece of shit, so watch your mouth," she snapped without thinking. "You don't like it, you can walk."

She turned in her seat to check on Buddy and heard Charles sputter. She couldn't tell if it was indignation or a laugh and didn't care. She was still trying to make sense of what was before her eyes.

Charles threw the car in gear and said, "As soon as we get there, I'll carry him upstairs. The wounds need to be cleaned..."

"You'll carry him to the kitchen," she said, staring out the window, "You'll lay him on the table. He'll be easier to work on and it won't be so back breaking. Is there a doctor or a vet you can call or is this all on us? Because I can stitch, but I can't set bones," she said earnestly.

Her autopilot mind didn't even register the absurdity of the questions. When Charles didn't answer, she looked over at him. "Well?"

He was staring at her with a dumbfounded look on his face. "You're taking this all pretty well," he said.

Kat thought about that and nodded. "I suppose I am," she told him truthfully, "Though I'm not sure how else I could take it. Like you said, Buddy needs our help. There'll be time enough later for me to fall apart." She pointed at the windshield. "Keep your eyes on the road. It won't help if you run us into the ditch."

"You must have questions..." he began.

"I guess I do." She had a hundred questions and by the time her befuddled mind was working smoothly again, she'd have a hundred more. Right now, she needed to sort out the most important ones, the ones that would help Buddy. "First off..." she began.

"No," Charles cut her off.

"What do you mean 'no'? I haven't asked anything yet."

"The answer to your first question is no, you won't turn because he bit you. It doesn't work that way."

Kat looked at the back of her hand where a thin line of blood defined where Buddy's razor sharp tooth had broken the skin. She hadn't thought of infection until Charles brought it up.

"Nice to know you're not a mind reader," she said wryly. "I wasn't thinking of biting. I was thinking of changing. What's the chance of him changing while I'm stitching?"

"He won't change. He can't. And you won't be stitching."

"Really? Why not?" she asked curiously, "Is he stuck this way? How does he, uh, do you, uh, change, anyway? Is that the right word? Change? Does it hurt? Do you think like a man or an animal when you're, uh...?" So much for holding her questions.

"Over the moon."

"Is that what you call it? Over the moon? Over the moon." Kat tested the words out several times before nodding her head. "I like it," she said and then she frowned, "I can stitch, you know. My grandmother taught me. Brandon thought it was horrible when I told him about it. She'd use white cotton thread and a sewing needle."

"Brandon?" Charles said the name as if he didn't like the taste of it.

"My ex fiancé, the doctor." It was the first time since he left that she referred to him by name instead of The Bastard and she was pleased and not a little surprised that mentioning him didn't hurt that much anymore.

"Ex," Charles said and nodded, "Good. Good that you can stitch, I mean. Just in case."

He pulled the car up as close as possible to the front door where Tilda met them with a cry of anguish.

"He's alive," Charles assured her as he rounded the car and opened the back door. "Get hot water, towels, any antiseptic you can find. We've got to clean him up before I close him up."

Tilda froze mid turn. "You? Are you sure?" She stepped back as Charles pushed past with the limp wolf in his arms.

Kat watched Charles' shoulders sag as he continued on to the back of the house, evidence that Tilda's words only added to his burden.

"I'm not that boy any more, Mrs. Martin," he said. "I can take care of the worst of it and if I can't finish, Kat can take care of the rest."

Tilda's eyes slid to Kat. The worry in them didn't lessen, so Kat smiled to reassure her.

"I can sew a fine seam as my Grams used to say. Come on now, worry won't fix it." It was another thing Grams used to say. "You go gather up the things we'll need and I'll go help Charles get Buddy settled and put some water on to boil."

Kat squeezed past Charles to pull the chairs away from the table and helped him arrange the wolf with the best access to the damaged leg. Buddy's mouth sagged open and his tongue lolled. His breathing was reduced to a shallow pant and the pink around his mouth and nose and tongue had turned a sickly gray. It was obvious he was in shock and dying.

They worked together to quickly clean away the mud and the grit from the fur of the wolf and stroked it back from the open wounds. There was massive bruising along his sides and along his soft belly and Kat was concerned he was bleeding inside.

"Stitching won't fix this," she said bleakly as she stroked the matted fur of his face and ruff. She'd only known the man for a few hours, the wolf not at all and yet her heart was breaking at his loss.

"No, it won't and in spite of what I said to Mrs. Martin, I don't know if I can. There might be too much damage. I might be too late. I don't know if I should even try."

Here in the light of the overhead light, Kat saw clearly what the night's darkness hid. The man was tired, worn to the point of exhaustion and she was reminded once again that Charles had been on foot while she had driven.

"You'll try and you'll succeed," she said with a confidence she didn't feel. She straightened her back and squared her shoulders. "What do you need? Tell me what I can do." She heard Tilda's indrawn breath and left Charles and headed across the hall for the kitchen sink. She turned on the tap to let the water warm. Ignoring the frozen woman with the pile of towels and bottles in her arms, she asked, "Is this okay to scrub with?" She held up the container of liquid soap. "It says anti-bacterial."

She turned back to the breakfast room for the answer that never came. Mrs. Martin had disappeared and there was a light shimmering inside the room, brighter than that cast by the small chandelier and similar to what she'd seen in the field tonight, though not nearly as brilliant or blinding.

Was he…? Changing? Shifting? What the hell did he call it? Going over the moon? No, that was the word for changing to the wolf. Oh God, would Buddy change back if the worst happened and he…? Suddenly worried, she inched a little closer, craning her neck out to the side to get a better look and yet frightened by what she might see.

What she saw was Charles holding a glowing ball of light in

his hand. Holding it in his palm, he ran it over Buddy's wolf chest, paused, closed his eyes and frowned in concentration. She inched closer and jumped when she heard a gasp behind her.

Tilda looked over Kat's shoulder at what Charles was doing to her son. The housekeeper's eyes were huge and frightened.

Kat gripped the hand that gripped her shoulder. She wasn't sure what was happening, but she understood from Tilda's shaking body that it was important, maybe dangerous, though for whom she couldn't tell.

Charles ignored them and continued to slowly pass the glowing light back and forth across Buddy's body, spending a great deal of time over the wolf's chest. He stopped his movement now and then to concentrate the light on a single area.

Kat watched in growing amazement as a dark and swollen area shrank back to healthy tissue. The wolf on the table began to breathe easier and so did his mother. Tilda's hand gently pulled Kat back into the kitchen. Her relief was evident when she began briskly pulling food from the refrigerator.

"They're going to need food," she whispered, "and Charles is going to need someone to watch out for him. I'll take care of the food. You take care of Charles."

Take care of Charles? Kat nodded her understanding, but she didn't understand at all until she returned to the smaller room to find him pale and shaking with fatigue. The power he was using was nothing short of miraculous, but it was taking its toll. With each pass of his hand, with each flare of the iridescent light, Charles became weaker as if it was his personal strength infusing Buddy.

He was guiding the light over the animal's mangled leg and she watched in fascination as the deep and bloody wounds closed to faint pink scars. Charles faltered and he gripped the table's edge with his free hand to steady himself.

"That's it, you're done. Sit down before you fall down," Kat said when he started to sway and she shoved a chair behind his knees.

Charles tried to wave her out of the way. "I have to bring him home." His words were slurred. He sounded drunk and with the silly grin he wore, he looked it, too.

"Home?" This was code again, but she was starting to get the hang of it. "You mean make him human? Can it wait? You look like you're about to pass out and if you go down, you're staying down. I'm not strong enough to get you up." She tugged his arm to force him into the chair where he sat, heavily, and gave her another weak grin.

"You don't have to be strong to get me up, just willing." He tried to wink, but it came across as more of a squint.

"Your come-ons stink, Rover." She pursed her lips in an effort not to smile. This guy was a master of bad pickup lines.

"Oh come on, you know you were impressed."

This time, Kat laughed aloud. She stroked the air with wiggling fingers. "I was definitely impressed with the hoo-doo. It was amazing, miraculous, like magic," she said and then she sobered. "That's not the same as being impressed with the guy doing it. Don't let what happened earlier fool you. I'm not that easy to impress."

"I acted like an ass," he admitted.

He looked repentant, but Kat wasn't letting him off the hook that easily. "I was thinking dirty dog, myself, but ass will do."

Charles groaned. "That was low."

"So was how you treated me this afternoon."

He let his head fall back and he blew out an exhausted breath. "Yeah, about that. I thought you were one of us."

"I get that. What I don't get is why you reacted the way you did when you found out I wasn't."

The albino wolf whined and lifted his head. He looked

blearily at Kat and the corners of his mouth pulled back to show a fringe of teeth below the thin pink again lips. He sighed, lowered his head to the table and closed his eyes on a contented sigh.

"Did he just smile at me?" she asked in a whisper.

"He surely did. Ole Buddy recognized you right off. He's got a talent for it and good taste." Charles wiped his hand down his face, never taking his eyes from the sleeping wolf. "Look, I need food and Buddy needs to get back to being a man. Can we take this discussion up later?" Charles moved past Kat to the door where he hung on to the jamb to steady himself.

"What if I said no?" She placed her hand on his chest and looked up into his face.

"Then we wouldn't have the discussion at all." Charles looked pointedly at the hand splayed against his chest and then into her eyes. "Now, I suggest you take your hand, lovely as it is, off my chest and let me pass or we may both end up in a place neither of us wishes to be."

Kat wasn't sure where that was, because at that moment, she didn't want to be anywhere else. The same tingle of sexual excitement she'd felt that morning now coursed through the fingers spread over the warm skin of his chest and sent a happy shiver to her core. She snatched her hand back as if burned and stared at her palm.

"How the hell do you do that?"

Charles sucked in his cheeks and raised his eyebrows and for a moment Kat had a glimpse of the boy Mrs. Martin must have known; full of the devil and ready to raise hell. Then the glint in his eye faded and he sighed.

"I'm exhausted. You have no idea how exhausted." He looked back at Buddy sprawled peacefully across the table. "I barely have enough magic left to take care of him. I can't tamp down the call for you, too."

"Magic? The call?" she asked, though if she thought about it, magic was as good an explanation as any. How else could he conjure up a fiery ball of healing power? How else could he conjure such feelings of arousal in her? Magic.

Kat stepped aside and Charles moved past her, not into the kitchen, but into the hall where he called back over his shoulder.

"I'm going to shower and change into something warm. Tell Mrs. Martin to give me twenty minutes and I'll be ready to eat. Then I'll take care of Buddy." He shook his finger over his shoulder. "Then and only then will I take care of you."

"Oh how I wish you would," Kat whispered as she watched him walk away. Charles Goodman was the stuff of fairy tales; a sexy man/beast/prince who took her breath away and just once she'd like to play Beauty to his Beast. It never dawned on her how out of character those thoughts were from a woman who just found out the sexiest man she ever met was a wolf or from a woman who took such pride in her self-control.

Chapter 10

"I get the magic part or at least I think I do," Kat told Tilda while they waited for Charles to return. What she wanted to know was what he meant by 'the call', but Tilda kept evading the answer.

"I doubt you do." Tilda stirred the huge pot of chili simmering on the stove, releasing the aroma of peppers, onions and tomatoes into the air. "The magic isn't just the healing, though any pack would be fortunate and proud to have a healer for their Alpha. His father had the gift and so did his brothers, but Charles?" She shrugged. "It wasn't the same."

"You didn't believe he could help Buddy." Kat winced as soon as the words were said. She hadn't meant to sound so accusing and she tried to soften her tone. "You were so worried. I can understand you're having doubts."

Not easily fooled, Tilda gave her a wry look. "You make a poor liar, but I'm mindful of the attempt and shamed to admit you're right. I didn't have faith in my Alpha when I should have."

"Why? Why didn't you believe?"

"I forgot for a moment that the boy became a man, maybe because my Buddy never did. That's twice I've doubted him and twice he's shown himself to be a Wolver of his word. I won't doubt him again. He's our Alpha and he's taken us in when we had nowhere to go. The other pack wasn't so kind after my mate passed away."

Tilda loaded a tray with generous slabs of cheese and turkey and thick slices of bread and a few token carrot and celery sticks Kat suspected were for her. Charles' penchant for protein was a little more understandable now that she knew what he was. Now that she knew what he was?

"Tilda, shouldn't I be more upset about this than I am?" she asked, a little bit panicked. She was surprised when Tilda didn't laugh.

"I've only met one other like you," Tilda said in all seriousness, "That was Charles' mother and she spent three days locked in the bathroom. So I'd say you're takin' it pretty well."

"What about you? How did you find out?" Maybe Tilda was so young she didn't remember.

"Oh, I was born this way. I've always known." The older woman waited for Kat's reaction with a sparkle in her eye.

"Y-you, you're not...?" She wanted to say a human, but Tilda was as human as a woman could get. "You're a Wolver? You can do that?" Kat pointed to the room where Buddy lay. "You can go over the moon?"

"Only once a year unless the Alpha is feeling generous. The men can go over any time the moon is full, but they need the Alpha to do it any other time." Tilda stood with her hands folded in front of her, patiently waiting for Kat to take it all in.

"So Charles mother wasn't a Wolver," Kat said hesitantly. "She was like me."

The housekeeper smiled and it changed the whole appearance of her face. She no longer looked dour at all and Kat could see a glimpse of the pretty girl she once was.

"No, not a wolver, but not full human neither. She was a pretty thing got thrown from her horse when it was spooked by the Alpha running as a beast. Of course, she didn't know that then. The Alpha, he came home in an instant and came a-runnin' as a man and a fine looking man he was, too. Emily always said it was love at first sight. With the man that is, not the beast. Took her a mite longer to get used to the beast." Her eyes on the distant past, Mrs. Martin laughed.

"Three days in the bathroom?" Kat asked

The housekeeper nodded. "Yes ma'am. She did a bit of wailing and cried some and wouldn't listen to anyone who tried to offer comfort. She just sat in that bathroom and wouldn't come out."

"And?" Kat rolled her hand urging Mrs. Martin to continue. "Then what?" She'd half forgotten how this conversation started.

"Well," Mrs. Martin lowered her voice to a confidential whisper, "Nobody's rightly sure, but we have our speculations. You see, the Alpha wasn't what you'd call a patient man and he finally got tired of trying to sweet talk her through the door and kicked it open. He slammed it shut behind him, but we never heard no hollerin' and when they finally come out, Emily was smiling sweet as could be and happy to be with the Alpha. We figured the Alpha used that charm they're all blessed with and it appeared to work. They had their disagreements as all folks do, but they were as happy together the day me and Buddy left as the day he handed her from that bathroom."

"Just what kind of charm are we talking here?" Kat asked suspiciously.

"I couldn't rightly say. No Alpha ever courted me." Tilda turned away to hide her smile.

"You're not a very good liar either," Kat told her.

Tilda tilted her head as if listening. Charles sometimes angled his head in just the same way and Kat wondered if these Wolver's hearing was as good as their canine cousins.

"The Alpha said twenty minutes and it's been a good deal longer than that." Tilda pointed to the door that led to the back stairs. "Why don't you go up there and fetch him down. Your legs are younger than mine and I'd like my boy back sometime before bedtime."

Kat was sure there was an ulterior motive in the request, but she couldn't very well tell the woman no. She climbed the back stairs and found herself at the far end of the hall from her bedroom. She knocked and called quietly at each door along the hall before opening each one to check within. She wasn't sure which room he had chosen for a bedroom, but she should have known it would be the largest and the best, the one she'd chosen for herself.

He was sprawled across the bed on his back, barefooted, jeans zipped but unbuttoned, and shirtless as if he'd laid back to rest for a moment before he finished dressing. His skin was still damp as was his hair and his lashes were long and dark against the paleness of his skin.

Damn, the man was beautiful and Kat had to dig her fingers into the door frame to keep from going to him and smoothing the naughty boy curl back from his forehead. She wanted to do much more than that and the thoughts that were running through her head shocked her. Were these her thoughts? Or were they the result of that Alpha's charm Tilda spoke of? And Kat wondered if that charm might have a bit of magic in it, too.

"Charles," she called softly from the doorway and when he didn't answer or open his eyes she giggled a little. "Char-lie, oh Char-lie," she called in the singsong voice. "Wake up, beastie boy"

Charles still didn't open his eyes, seemed to be sound asleep and then he smiled and she knew it was the sound of her voice that put that blissful look on his face. He looked relaxed and happy and she wondered how often he looked that way. She didn't think he was a happy man and the thought touched her heart in a place that hadn't been touched since she was little girl.

Again she had to fight the urge to go to him, to comfort him, though why a man who could afford a house like this and those cars in the barn would need comfort she had no idea. She only knew that when the smile left his face, her smile disappeared as well.

She tiptoed across the carpeted floor to the bedside and touched his denim clad knee, thinking she was safe enough if she didn't touch him skin to skin. She was wrong. As soon as she laid her hand on his knee, the hum of sexual awareness began. She closed her eyes and savored it for a moment before she shook his knee and called his name again.

"Charles," she called softly, "Mrs. Martin has your supper ready. You need to bring Buddy home."

He smiled again and reached out his hand to her and slowly opened his eyes...

"I was dreaming about you," he said sleepily and grasped her hand and pulled her to him.

For a man half asleep, his grip was remarkably strong. Already off balance, Kat fell across that long lean body and couldn't bring herself to resist when his other arm wrapped around her back and pinned her to his chest. His hand slid up her back and into her curls and held her face close to his.

She moistened her lips and closed her eyes in anticipation of his kiss, but they snapped open again in surprise when he kissed her nose instead. She laughed at the affectionate gesture.

"What are you doing here?" he asked.

The buzz of attraction was still there, but subdued when compared to what it had been before. At least now she could think clearly.

"Mrs. Martin has your supper ready. You said you'd be down in twenty minutes. It's been more like forty-five." She pushed herself up from his chest. "You need to let me up or you'll need another shower. I'm filthy."

Charles laughed and it was deep and rumbly and sexy. "Mmmm, I like my women filthy... and dirty... and a little bit kinky, too. How about you?"

Kat laughed and it was rich and throaty and relaxed. "Not into women, sorry." She tried, not too hard, to wiggle back onto her feet, but Charles wouldn't let her. "And your sexy lines aren't the least bit tempting. You'll have to work harder if you want to attract a really good woman."

"But that's my point, sweetheart. I prefer the bad ones."

"And that's my point, beastie boy. I'm not interested." This time she forced herself to wiggle free and stand between his knees at the edge of the bed. "You better get your rear in gear or you'll have to face the wrath of Mrs. Martin. She strikes me as a woman who doesn't like to be crossed."

"Maybe for you, but she adores me."

Kat headed for the closet where she'd stored her meager supply of clothes and pulled a pair of navy slacks and a light blue tailored blouse from their hangers. Jeans and a T-shirt would've been fine, but she's had the sudden urge to look a little nicer and put together.

"She'll be sweeping up her adoration along with the rest of the trash if you don't get down there and fix her son. He's beginning to get restless and we don't want his muddy pawprints all over the floor."

She headed for the bathroom keeping her eyes averted from the man on the bed. His presence pulled at her and she wanted to return to the position she had just left. She was at the bathroom door before he spoke again.

"You are you know." She heard the bed creak as he arose from it.

"I am what?" She stopped in the bathroom doorway, but didn't turn around.

"Interested. You can't help yourself."

She had a funny feeling he was right, but she wasn't about to let him think so. "If you're thinking about your Alpha charm, you'd better think again. It's not working and even if it was, you'd be surprised what a girl can resist when she puts her mind to it."

He didn't reply and when she glanced over her shoulder she saw that he was already gone.

Her shower was a quick one, enough to sluice off the accumulated dirt and wash her hair for the second time that day. She thought about shaving her legs, realized she'd already done that earlier and decided the little bit of stubble would be another incentive to remain on the straight and narrow where Charles was concerned. She was dressed and ready for supper in fifteen minutes.

She found them in the dining room. Mrs. Martin had spread a small cloth over one end of the long table and set it for four, two to each side, with a full complement of glasses, silverware, and folded cloth napkins. She'd gone to a lot of trouble for a chili supper.

"Hey Kitty Kat, don't you look pretty. Doesn't she look pretty Charlie? That necklace is real pretty too, almost as pretty as you. I know what that is. That's a sapphire. That's for September. It's Mama's birthstone. Right Mama?"

Kat reddened at the complement and fingered the stone of the necklace she'd worn to match her slacks and blouse. It wasn't a real sapphire, but it was her birthstone, too. Her father had given it to her for her ninth birthday, the birthday before the world fell apart. She treasured it as a reminder of the happy life she lived back then.

"Thank you, Buddy. You're looking pretty good yourself."

He was, too. His face was shining and his hair was combed back neatly from his forehead. Because of his natural coloring, or lack of it, it was hard to tell if he was still pale, but his cheeks showed a faint pink as did his lips and tongue. He was dressed in a clean T-shirt and jeans. She was sorry she missed his 'coming home'.

She would have liked seeing his transformation, but thought it might be a private matter and didn't want to embarrass him if he came back naked. Maybe she should ask Tilda about that next time they were alone.

She took the empty seat beside Charles, who looked much too pale, and resolved to trade her place for Buddy's the next time they sat down to eat. If there was a next time. Even without touching him she was acutely aware of Charles' body just a few inches from hers.

"I'm sorry if I held things up," she said self-consciously, "I didn't think we would be sitting down to supper. I thought we would just grab a bowl in the kitchen. My apologies."

"Nonsense." Mrs. Martin looked a little offended. "There'll be no grabbing a bowl of anything for a meal as long as I'm in charge of the kitchen." She began to ladle chili from the tureen set in front of her.

"I'll remember that," Kat said and lowered her eyes and accepting the rebuke.

Charles hand trembled a little as he passed his bowl to Mrs. Martin. Kat followed Mrs. Martin's lead and ignored it, though her instinct was to force him back into bed and feed him herself.

He waited patiently for everyone to be served before attacking his bowl as if he hadn't eaten for a week. When compared to Buddy, Charles looked the worse for wear and Kat wondered again about how much energy he expended in saving Buddy's life.

Buddy matched him spoon for spoon. When his bowl was empty, he laid aside his spoon and would have picked up the bowl in his hands had his mother not sternly cleared her throat and held out her hand for the bowl to refill. She did the same for Charles.

"It's to bed early for you tonight, my young wolf."

"Aw, Mama. I don't want to sleep up there alone." Buddy

looked bleakly up at the ceiling.

Charles gave Mrs. Martin a questioning look as he passed his bowl for another refill.

"I've put Buddy up on the third floor," she explained as she filled the bowl. "I thought I would make the room off the kitchen into the sitting room for myself and Buddy. We can take our meals in there when the others are here. There's plenty of room for a small table and a comfortable chair or two and a television for Buddy. He enjoys his TV in the evening."

"Ghost Detectives. That's my favorite." Buddy bobbed his head in agreement. Every night at eight o'clock p.m. on channel forty-six."

"Which is why you have trouble falling asleep," his mother told him. She paused from her ladling duty to give his hand an affectionate pat and then turned back to Charles. "I'll take the room upstairs next to his."

"I don't like the idea of you running up and down those stairs." Charles accepted his bowl but left it sitting in front of him. "The house is big enough as it is without you taking extra steps and I see no reason why you can't continue to take your meals with us."

Mrs. Martin smiled and nodded her thanks. "This is fine for every day, but not when you're holding court. When folks come to visit, we'll take our meals separate, as we should. I won't have folks here about looking down on you. You have a reputation to uphold. Fine man like you can't be eating with the hired help. As for moving upstairs, Buddy doesn't like to sleep alone. He sleeps better if I'm nearby. We'll be fine. You take care of your business and we'll take care of ourn."

"You are my business. If you want to move upstairs, that's fine, but you'll move to the second floor."

"And what will your company think when they're tucked up under the eaves in the servant's quarters?" Mrs. Martin was clearly displeased, having her own ideas of what was proper and what was not.

"They'll think my housekeeper and groundsman must be worth their weight in gold. They'll probably try to lure you away with promises of better pay," Charles laughed.

Mrs. Martin suddenly looked like she was going to cry. She fanned her face with her hand and jumped up from the table. "I forgot the dessert," she said and fled to the kitchen.

"What did I say?" Charles asked.

"Maybe I should go check on her." Kat was about to rise, but there was no need.

Mrs. Martin came through the door and plopped a bowl of strawberries and cream in front of Charles. She straightened her back and took a deep breath.

"I've been keeping other people's houses for as far back as I can remember," she said in a rush, "And nobody's treated me and Buddy with such care and kindness as you have since we left your mama's house. There's no money in the world that can buy that." Her eyes filled again and she flapped her hands. "Dammit, I forgot the spoon," she said and fled to the kitchen again.

Charles sat back and just shook his head in bafflement.

"I think that was a thank you," Kat whispered.

"What's a groundsman, Charlie?" Buddy asked looking up from his bowl. "Where's he going to sleep?"

"You're the groundsman, Buddy." Charles nodded to Mrs. Martin as she took her seat and began to spoon out the strawberries as if nothing had happened. "It's your job to keep the outside of the house neat and tidy and to keep an eye on things when I'm not around. It's an important job and I need someone I can trust."

Buddy beamed at the complement and leaned across the table to pat Kat's hand. "Don't you worry, Miss Kitty Kat, I won't let you down." He turned to Charles "I got to keep an eye on her,

Charlie. She's from the city and she says she needs someone to teach her country ways. She's just a bitty thing and real smart and won't take much watchin', so I think I can be your groundsman, too. But you gots to know, Charlie, Miss Kitty Kat comes first. She tried to fight off those men to save me. Mama says we was lucky she didn't get herself kilt. We're beholding to her, so she comes first."

"Absolutely, Buddy," Charles told him solemnly. "Miss Kitty Kat should always come first."

Buddy grinned. "Besides, she's prettier than you." He laughed uproariously at his own joke while his mother dabbed at her eyes with her napkin.

Chapter 11

Kat couldn't sleep. She was too acutely aware of sleeping in Charles' bed while he was sleeping only one wall away. He'd played the gentleman and insisted she keep the room while he moved to the one next door while she graciously demurred and just as graciously changed her mind when she thought he might change his. This bedroom was as close to a five-star hotel as she was ever going to get and she wasn't going to miss the chance to enjoy it while she could.

She was paying for her subterfuge now. She tossed and turned and swore she could feel the heat of his body from where he had lain across the bed earlier. She kept playing the scene over and over in her mind and wondered if she had made a mistake in her refusal to play his game.

She wanted him. There was no mistaking that, but she couldn't figure out where his intentions lay. One minute he seemed to want her as much a she wanted him, but the next he seemed indifferent. All evening he'd been polite but distant. Was that playing the gentleman, too? Was he waiting for a signal that she had changed her mind?

If that was the case, he would have a long wait. Yes, she wanted him, but she wouldn't allow herself to be overwhelmed by that need. She refused to sell herself so cheaply to a man who was so obviously used to having his way in everything, including women.

The 'charm' that Tilda spoke of was real. It called to her like the moon to the tides. Was it another form of his magic perhaps? She would have to ask Tilda tomorrow. In the meantime, sleep was impossible and she'd learned long ago that hard work was the cure for her occasional bouts of insomnia. There was a classroom waiting to be finished.

She slipped into the clothing she'd worn before and tiptoed down the stairs, surprised to find the entrance hall lighted by a utility light hanging from the old coat tree to the right of the front door. The dark paneling of the foyer had been transformed with a coat of primer in readiness for a new coat of paint. Apparently, she wasn't the only one who couldn't sleep.

Charles was in her schoolroom, his back to her, rolling on the final coat of yellow paint.

"I could use some help," he said without looking back.

Kat nodded, even though he couldn't see her and picked up the roller she'd used that morning. It was wrapped tightly in plastic and her tray was clean and ready for a refill.

"How long have you been down here?" she asked. As far as she knew he'd gone to bed when she did, right after Mrs. Martin and Buddy said good night.

"Since five minutes after you went to bed. Did you miss me?" He still didn't look at her, but she could tell he was smiling.

"Don't flatter yourself. I always have trouble sleeping in a new place." She busied herself applying the paint to the opposite side of the room.

"You didn't seem to have any trouble sleeping last night," he laughed.

That was when it hit her. Charles didn't arrive this morning as she had thought. He'd been here all along. It was the eyes, those beautiful, thick lashed green eyes that tilted upward ever so slightly at the outer corners.

He was the Lord of his Domain. He was her Wolf King. He was the wolf at the pool and he had seen her naked as the day she was born. She advanced on him with roller raised.

"You bastard! You pervert! It was you by the pool scaring me half to death."

"You didn't seem too frightened to me." He raised his eyebrows and smiled with a definite wolfish leer. "In the pool, you seemed friendly and playful and... How should I say this?" He put his finger to his chin as if thinking and his eyes slid to her breasts. "Perky?"

Furious, Kat shook the roller at him. "You had no right."

"No right? In case you hadn't noticed, this is my house and it was supposed to be empty. I don't recall inviting you here." He eyed the roller in her hand and set his down in the tray. "And how was I to know you'd be swimming naked in my pool."

"You didn't have to stay in wolf form," she argued. "You could have... have... come home and showed up as a man."

"Because a naked man walking across the patio would be so much more acceptable." Those green eyes danced with devilish mischief.

The image of Charles, crossing the patio in all his naked glory sent a wave of heat down through her body beginning with her cheeks and ending at the juncture of her legs where her body gushed with pleasure, ready to meet and greet. Just when she was beginning to rethink the possibilities, he had to go and ruin it.

"I thought you were the housekeeper," he said.

"You're just digging this hole deeper and deeper. Another six inches and it will be deep enough to bury you." She threatened him with the roller again. "You think it's all right to coerce sex from an employee? Is that what it means to be an Alpha?"

"That was the point," he said and took a step toward her. "You would have known I was the Alpha and it wasn't coercion. If you were one of us you would've known that, too. I asked. When you didn't run, I backed off. No one forced anyone to do anything." Charles took another step.

Kat took a step back, but she still held her paint roller weapon ready. "You didn't ask anything and if you did I don't understand wolfish. One woof sounds the same as another. And what do you mean, I didn't run?"

There was something she was missing here. He should at least give him the opportunity to explain, right? Her nether regions eagerly agreed.

Charles smiled as if he'd scored a point and advanced another step. "We don't see sex the same way you do. A courting couple usually stays faithful, same as a mated pair, but most unattached adults see sex as a recreational activity."

"You just dug your last six inches. That hole is six feet deep and ready for the headstone." The paint roller kept Kat from putting her fists on her hips.

"You still don't get it," he laughed. "I played with you. You played with me. I indicated I wanted to chase. You refused to run. That's a Wolver's way of saying I don't want to play. Haven't you ever had a guy hit on you in a bar? He makes a pass. You say no. He smiles and goes away. No harm, no foul, Wolver style."

"Does, uh, getting together always involve a chase?" she asked and hated that her curiosity got the best of her. Again.

Charles raised his eyebrows. "No, but it sure adds to the fun."

"So if I'd run..."

"I would have flashed and come home and chased you up the stairs. Maybe we would have made it to the bedroom and maybe we wouldn't."

The stairs? Her eyes strayed to the door that led to them. She caught herself and forced them back to Charles where she avoided his eyes and mouth and focused on the spot just below his chin. It was a very nice chin with just a hint of a dimpled crease in the center. Kat shook her head and cleared her throat.

"We wouldn't," she said, purposefully misconstruing his reference, "And just so we're clear, I will never run from you." Though if he hadn't told her, she'd be running hard and fast right now. Damn, the man oozed sex appeal.

"Never say never."

The whole time they were talking, Charles was moving closer. Before Kat realized his plan, one hand slid about her waist pulling her close while the other hand grabbed the handle of the roller and raised her hand along with it over her head.

"You, me, and a paint roller isn't a good idea," he said as he lifted it from her fingers and tossed it onto the plastic covering the floor. "But if you're into body painting, I'm sure we can find something sweet and edible."

They were nose to nose, those piercing green eyes drilling into hers. Kat sucked in air and then found she couldn't release it. She swallowed hard and moistened her lips. It was all the invitation he needed.

"It seems we're right where we left off," he whispered before he kissed her.

Oh God, why did he have to be such a good kisser? Why couldn't he be one of those guys whose lips were so wet and sloppy you felt like you were drowning or so dry you may as well have been kissing your ancient Aunt Mildred? His kisses were perfect. His lips were warm and demanding and they perfectly covered hers. His tongue almost delicately probed its way between her lips to tango with her tongue. Why couldn't he be the kind of guy who acted like he was on a search and destroy mission for her tonsils instead of treating her to this sexy and playful dance?

Her hand was on his chest and she should have pushed him away, but her fingers curled into his shirt and clung to him. She closed her eyes and followed his lead, not caring for the moment where this dance would take them.

Some semblance of good sense remained for when he withdrew for a moment she opened her eyes and whispered, "I can't do this."

Charles' head drew back another few inches, looking genuinely concerned. "Why? Are you a virgin?"

"God, no," she answered, startled by the question.

He chuckled deep in his throat. "Good, then there's no problem. I've never been fond of cherries and you already know how it's done." He bent her backward to reach behind her and pull the dust cover from the sofa.

"That's not what I meant," she said not sure exactly what she did mean.

"Tell me about it later," he said as he eased her down onto the cushions. "I can only concentrate on one thing at a time."

There was something important she was about to say, but she forgot what it was because he was kissing her again and all thoughts of opposition fled. He slid his hands beneath her shirt, splaying his fingers over her stomach and ran them lightly up her sides, leaving a trail of fiery warmth until they reached her breasts and there they stopped. His thumbs rested along her ribs beneath the full mounds, while his fingers tested their weightiness at the sides.

Oh God, that wasn't where those hands were supposed to be. It wasn't enough. Kat wanted more and when she arched her back and moaned a little, Charles laughed.

"Let's see how much it takes to make this kitten purr." His hands slid back down her sides and his thumbs hooked the hem of her shirt to lift it over her head and remove it.

The chill of the air settling over her bared breasts soon turned to warmth as his hand covered one and his mouth covered the other. This was where he was supposed to be! She moaned, lost to the sensations coursing through her body. Her sensible half made one last attempt at protest, but it was drowned out by a mewl of pleasure when he nipped at the pebbled nipple with his teeth and then laved the tiny sting away with his tongue.

"I like that sound," he chuckled against her breast, "I want to hear it again."

She obliged when he addressed his ministrations to the other breast. From there he moved downward showering hot kisses along the center of her body.

"Oh. O-o-oh. Oh, my god," she breathed out followed by a sharp intake of breath.

"Not yet, but I will be," he whispered to the sensitive skin below her navel but above the metal button of her cut-off shorts.

He looked up at her as he undid the button and zipper below it and she saw in his eyes the same blazing need and want that she felt for him. Drawn by those eyes, she tried to rise to meet him. She wanted to feel his lips against her own, but he placed one hand between her breasts and gently pushed her back.

"No," he said in a hoarse whisper. "Stay where you are. This is for me. You'll have your chance when I'm finished."

Kat laid back and closed her eyes on a sigh. Charles' imperious voice commanded and she felt compelled to obey. He'd done nothing to her that hadn't been done before and yet his lips ignited a fire in her she had never felt before. His hands made her body sing; every nerve and muscle in her attuned to the melody his fingers played. She wanted nothing more than to please him, to give him all he asked of her.

"Lift your hips for me, kitten," he directed as he slid her shorts and panties from her hips. "You are the most beautiful thing I have ever seen," he told her as he took in her full length and because of the look in those beautiful, blazing eyes, she believed him.

He ran his hands up her calves to her knees and spread them wide and smiled knowingly at what he had exposed. That smile alone sent a shiver of anticipation through her. Her breasts tightened further and tiny goosebumps appeared on her legs and arms.

Charles pressed her knees together and with a short nod, as if he'd come to some decision, he took her hands and pulled her to her feet.

"This isn't right," he said as much to himself as to her and laughed at her whimpered protest. "We'll have plenty of time for odd places and adventure. Our first time should be done properly in a wide, soft bed. Wrap your arms around my neck."

Somewhere along the way Charles had lost his shirt and it was heaven to press her breasts against his bare chest, to feel the beat of his heart next to hers.

Charles must have like it, too, because for a moment he just held her there pressed closely to him and then his hands slid along her back to her buttocks and he hoisted her to his waist. Kat didn't need to be told where to wrap her legs.

He groaned and rolled his eyes at the sight of her breasts now bobbing conveniently in front of his mouth and Kat laughed. The sound of it was strange to her. It was deep and throaty and sexually charged and nothing like her laugh at all.

Deftly avoiding all obstacles and pausing only briefly on the stairs to nuzzle her breasts, Charles carried her to the bed she had so recently left. He laughed when he saw the tumble of covers.

"Restless sleeper or were you missing something?"

"I couldn't sleep," she told him honestly, "I couldn't stop thinking of you."

"Yeah, I'm that kind of guy."

He bent until her back was on the mattress, but Kat didn't let him go. He laughed and kissed her and unwrapped her fingers from around his neck.

"As much as I love to feel you close to me, this isn't close enough." He stood, kicked his shoes from his sockless feet, undid his pants and kicked those away, too.

With his broad shoulders, narrow hips and well-defined muscles, he was everything she dreamed of in a man. His legs were long and lean, but there was nothing skinny about them. There was a tensile strength to their leanness. In her eyes he was a perfect specimen and he knew it. There was no embarrassment as he stood before her and let her admiring gaze wash over him.

When she had looked her fill, Kat reached for him and he obliged, covering her body with his. She expected him to fill her, wanted him to fill her and she spread her legs in invitation, but Charles had other plans.

When she had been thoroughly kissed, he began to explore the rest of her body with kisses, teeth, and tongue. The bend of her elbows, the backs of her knees, the soft spot where her neck met her shoulder; he searched for and discovered every spot along her body that gave her the most sensual pleasure and Kat did the same for him.

They rolled about the bed, tangling further the sheets and blankets, kissing, licking, nipping, tasting, yet both avoiding the places most wanting of the other's caress. By the time they finished their exploration, they were each covered with a fine sheen of sweat and Kat was panting with her need for completion.

Entwining his fingers with hers, Charles brought her hands to her side and raised himself above her.

"What is it you want?" He asked huskily.

"You," she breathed and it was true. She felt as if he was the one she had been waiting for, had been wanting her whole life.

He freed one hand from hers to snake it down between them, lower and lower until he found her throbbing clit.

She was so wet and swollen with need that she thought she might explode with that first touch and Charles gave a satisfied chuckle when she gasped as he ran his finger over it. Kat moaned softly and arched her pelvis up to meet his dancing fingers.

"That's it. Purr for me, kitten. Come for me, my beautiful Katarina."

She wanted to save it until he was inside her. She wanted to share and savor that shining moment with him, but Charles had taken the lead, made his demand, and his dancing fingers insisted she obey. She exploded and cried out with the sensation.

Charles plunged his fingers within and she rode the crest of the wave on his hand, but it was not enough for him. Before she had fully recovered he took her to the heights again and this time she closed her eyes and begged.

"Please, please," she whimpered.

She gasped out her pleasure when he entered her, stretching her and filling her with his heat. Over and over he plunged into her, deeper and deeper until she felt consumed by him. Legs wrapped tightly around his hips, she met him thrust for thrust, rising higher and higher until another orgasm shattered conscious thought. She felt his body stiffen and heard his groan of release. She could feel his warmth mix with hers and she had never felt so complete.

Chapter 12

Kat awoke feeling cold and alone; abandoned. Bereft of his presence, her eyes snapped open. "Charles?"

"Miss me already?" Charles poked his head out the door of the walk-in closet, winked and walked back to the bed. He tugged the zipper of his jeans into place but left the button undone.

With the bright light of morning, Kat's doubts returned and she became self-conscious of her nakedness particularly in the presence of the man who stood before her. There was no denying the animal grace that was an intrinsic part of his being. Even the simple act of getting dressed was so smooth and sensual it took her breath away. He was the Alpha.

She looked around at the room at her luxurious surroundings, her employer's room. This was wrong on so many levels. She didn't belong here in this fairytale. Charles didn't know her and heaven only knew she didn't know him. Who was this man/beast who drove all rational thought from her head and made her feel things she never thought possible? The Alpha.

Kat turned away to shield herself from his view and reached for the tangled sheet to cover herself.

Charles went down on one knee beside the bed. She thought he would reach for the sheet to take it from her and she clutched it to her chest, but he didn't reach for her covers. Instead, his hand cupped her cheek and insisted she turn to face him.

"Tell me," he said and as before, the compulsion was there to follow his command.

"I don't know what I'm doing here. I don't know what you want from me," she whispered. "I don't know if what you make me feel is real. I don't even know if you are real. Wolvers? Alphas? You? It's all beyond belief and for all I know, the last two days are some kind of bizarre hallucination."

"Is this the 'later' where you fall apart?" he asked gently.

Kat pressed her lips together and nodded her head. She'd spoken all she could without an overflow of tears. Why was this happening now? Yesterday... Was it only yesterday? ...had been filled with rejection and brutality; wolves, leghold traps, cruel men and death. She'd held up through it all as Grams had taught her to do, facing down her fears and doing what must be done. So why now, after experiencing the most beautiful thing she had ever felt, did she feel like the world might be coming apart?

Charles slid his palms beneath her knees and shoulders and lifted her into his arms. He held her close to his chest and whispered into her hair as he rose to his full height.

"I'm real and so are you and the connection between us is real. I wasn't looking for this. When I first realized who you were and how fast this can happen, it scared the hell out of me. I don't know if I'm ready for this. I don't know that I'm even worthy of this." He turned and carried her across the room to the bath.

Charles continued, his voice a deep rumble in his chest. "My brother told me that when I found the one, I'd know it in my soul. I laughed when he said it, but I'm not laughing now. When I saw you stand for Buddy against those two men, I knew it. You were so strong and fierce and beautiful. You could be the one and if I don't pursue this, I may regret it for the rest of my life. What I want from you Katarina Bennett is to give this a chance and see where it takes us."

Kat wrapped her arms around his neck and buried her face in the hollow of his throat. Here in his arms, she was reassured that anything was possible. His magic made it real and if his magic was her insanity, she would gladly spend the rest of her life in such a delusion.

The tub was full and steaming. Charles was careful as he set her into it, waiting for her assurance that it was not too hot. He knelt beside the tub and began soaping a cloth.

"You don't have to do this," she protested as she settled into a more comfortable position. "I'm perfectly capable of taking care of myself."

"I'm sure you are," he said as he rubbed the soft cloth over her back, "But I gave you a rough time of it last night and I reckon I owe you."

"It wasn't rough. It was wonderful."

They'd made love several times throughout the night and yes, in his ardor he had at times used her rather roughly, but she reveled in the power of it and gloried in her ability to make him feel such passion. She'd expected to be sore this morning, but felt only the burn of unused muscles.

"No regrets?" He ran the cloth across her shoulders and down over her breasts.

"For what we did? No, never for that. But why? What is it that draws us together? I want to understand it."

Charles rinsed and added soap to the cloth again, washed her arms with it and ran it down her belly. "Spread your knees, Kitten, and let me clean you up." He ran a cloth between her legs and gently sponged her private parts. It was all done efficiently and impersonally and yet it made her feel cared for and pampered.

"What's to understand? You're special. And me? Well..." He shrugged and gave her a look that said, "What's not to like?" and moved on to her legs.

Kat laughed. "Were you born conceited or did it develop over time?"

Charles laughed with her. "Hey, if I don't blow my own horn, no one else will."

A sharp knock had them turning toward the bedroom door and Kat felt a moment's panic. Would he reject her again, pretend last night didn't happen in the face of Mrs. Martin's scrutiny? One panic was replaced with another when, with the door wide open and the tub in full view, Charles called out.

"Come in, Mrs. Martin. It's not locked."

Eyes averted but clearly unembarrassed, Mrs. Martin entered with a breakfast tray with the dishes covered by metal lids and on top of that Kat's neatly folded clothing from the night before, pink panties on top.

"Well, shit," Kat muttered as she sank down in the tub.

Charles wasn't bothered at all. "Thank you, Mrs. Martin, just leave it on the dresser. We'll be down shortly."

"You might want to hurry it up," Mrs. Martin said, clearly unimpressed with his more formal tone. "Your friends just turned in the Lane. Buddy's been keeping watch from the upper window. He's been up there all morning."

All morning? "What time is it?" Kat asked, peeking up over Charles' shoulder and forgetting for a moment she was supposed to be hiding.

"A little past ten. Neither of you said what time you wanted to be called and I figured you had a busy night..." she paused, "Paintin' that room 'n all."

It was said in Mrs. Martin's typical straight-faced manner, but Kat was sure she heard a little snicker in the housekeeper's voice.

"You're sure it's the pack and not the children," Charles and asked.

"Lessin them kids is driving fancy cars, I'd say it's pack."

Charles ruffled Kat's curls. "You'll have to wash your own hair, kitten. Duty calls. I have to go."

"Not until you've had something to eat," Kat and Mrs. Martin said at the same time. Mrs. Martin gave Kat sharp nod of approval.

*****

"I'll take my hundred in twenties if you have them. I knew you couldn't get it done."

Kat heard the voice from the school room as she came down the stairs and hesitated. By the time she'd finished her bath, Charles had finished his breakfast. He told her he would meet her downstairs when she was finished dressing. There was no hurry.

But of course there was. She was both frightened and eager to see how Charles would treat her in front of his friends. His pack? She had a whole new vocabulary to learn. And how would his pack react to her, a human? There were so many things she needed to learn.

"You'll get your money," Charles laughed in answer. "I'll get it back in labor anyway, when I make you guys help me finish the job."

"Aw, wait a minute, Boss, no one said anything about manual labor," complained a third voice. "I didn't become a lawyer to dirty my hands."

"No, that's what you did to dirty your soul," a woman's voice laughed.

A woman? That surprised Kat. For some reason she'd assumed Charles' pack would be all-male. She stepped through the doorway and into the room and glanced guiltily around. Mrs. Martin had obviously been busy. Not only had the housekeeper picked up Kat's clothes, she'd put away all the painting supplies and pulled the covers from the furniture.

Charles, whose back was to her, turned at her entrance and to her great relief, smiled and held out his hand to her.

"Ah, here's the someone I wanted you to meet. Katarina is

the teacher who was hired for our children." He drew Kat to him and continued to hold her hand.

"*Our* children? Good Lord, Charlie, those pups aren't mine. If they were, I'd seriously consider drowning them and then shooting myself for having the little beasts in the first place," the woman said and held out her hand to Kat, "Hi, I'm Joanne, Jo for short."

"Jojo if you want to piss her off."

Kat recognized the voice of the lawyer, a smooth, deep baritone that didn't fit the tall, skinny man giving her a two fingered salute. "Hyatt Thomas, Attorney for Wolf's Head Enterprises." He smoothed back his thinning hair with long, sticklike fingers.

"Stop preening, Hyatt. She's not impressed. You're a tax attorney, for heaven's sake. It's as exciting as watching your six hairs grow."

The woman wiggled her fingers at him and blew him a kiss. She was a stunning brunette, tall with a figure that would draw a man's eyes and those eyes wouldn't be disappointed when they reached her face. She wore a pair of jeans so tight they look painted on, a pair of ankle high boots with heels so long and sharp they could be declared lethal weapons and a tailored menswear shirt that only emphasized her femininity. Her shoulder length hair was held back with a plain silver clip that Kat was sure was the real thing.

Her makeup looked professionally done and her attitude reminded Kat of the pampered and polished women who picked their children up from the Greenwood Preparatory Academy where until recently, Kat taught the spoiled children of people with too much money and not enough sense. Kat disliked her on the spot.

"It's so much easier when you can sit them in the corner or send them to the principal, isn't it?" The man at the window, the one who'd won the bet, said of his bickering colleagues. "I've recommended firing them, but it's not my call. The boss is fond of them for some reason."

"It couldn't be the hassle and money you save him." Joanne said to the tall, balding man who laughed and replied,

"And it couldn't possibly be the millions you make over land deals."

"Oh, Hyatt, do you think he loves us?" Joanne asked with false excitement. "Do you love us, Charlie?"

Charles ignored their banter and introduced the man coming to join them from his place by the window. "Katarina, this is Alex, my Second and yes, it's a title."

"Like The Alpha?"

"No," Alex answered, extending his manicured hand. He was tall, fit, and too well groomed with every tiny spike of his salt and pepper hair perfectly gelled in place. "It doesn't carry near the power."

Kat got the impression that Alex would like more.

It was a power handshake, the kind where the right hand grasps your hand and the left hand grasps your elbow and draws you in. As they shook, Alex drew her toward him, past the comfort zone of personal space and shifted his eyes just a fraction to the right, glancing over her shoulder to question Charles with a bit of a frown before he smiled at her.

"Katarina. It's a beautiful name. Welcome to... do we have a name for this place yet?"

Kat tugged back from the unwelcome closeness. "Hell Hall," she said without thinking and then apologized to Charles with a laugh. "Sorry. That's what I called it the first time I saw it. The place was empty when I arrived and from the looks of the entry, I was sure I'd meet up with a ghost."

"And met a Wolver instead." Charles rescued her from Alex by pulling her to him and tucking her under his arm.

Kat heard her heart pound in the silence of the room and then a voice called from the front door.

"We loaded this shit and dragged it all the way down here. I'll be damned if we carry it in, too. Get your asses out here and give us some help."

*****

It was like the first day of class except Kat had no seating chart and would therefore never remember all these names. There were fifteen of them so far, ten men and five women, and more would be arriving later. They all worked for Wolf's Head Enterprises, an investment firm begun by Charles and Alex and they all lived two hours away in an upscale area of the city and by the time lunch was over, Kat's head was spinning with talk of interest rate risks and investment risks and rebalancing asset allocations and principles and principals which she'd only heard of in spelling lessons.

They laughed and argued and shouted and called each other names sounding very much like the guys at the bar she used to work at after a big game. The only difference was she understood football.

As soon as she could without seeming impolite, Kat escaped to the kitchen to help Mrs. Martin with the cleanup.

"I've got this under control," the housekeeper objected when she started to load the dishwasher. "You should be in there with the guests, not in here with the likes of me. You don't belong in here."

"I don't belong in there either. Frankly, I'm more comfortable in the kitchen serving lunch with the likes of you than eating it in there with the likes of them. They're all a couple of cuts above my pay grade and all that financial stuff is way beyond my education."

"Nonsense. You're smart and you'll catch on quick enough and don't let the clothes and talk fool you. Most of them came from humble beginnings that I reckon they're working hard to forget. They're thinking that fancy talk and a fancy education makes them better than their raisin'. It don't. It just makes who they are sound prettier. There's not a one of them out there that can hold a candle to you and don't you forget it."

"Thanks, Tilda, but I'm not so sure about that," Kat sighed, thinking about Joanne and the other two women who came in with the second wave. They were all dressed in expensive weekend casual. "Even in my best slacks and sweater I look cheap next to them."

Tilda hmphed. "Clothes don't make the man, nor the woman neither. You've got something none of the rest of them do."

"Yeah? What's that?"

"You can make the Alpha smile the way nobody else can and I'm thinking he ain't done much genuine smiling in a long, long time." Tilda closed the dishwasher with a swing of her bony hip. "Now you get back in there and show 'em what you're made of."

Chapter 13

Kat had to admit the Wolf's Head Pack knew how to work. Right after lunch Charles set them to it, moving furniture, painting walls, and scrubbing floors and windows until the whole house shone. Granted, there was a lot of grumbling and complaining, but for the most part it was good-natured.

Some of their initial hesitancy wore off as the afternoon continued and Kat worked with them side-by-side. She did lose points however, when she insisted the sunny parlor be used as her classroom.

"Those children as you so lovingly refer to them aren't children at all. They're animals," Jo laughed without humor, "and I don't mean like us. I mean animals. There's not one ounce of civilization in the lot of them."

"All the more reason to keep them here," Kat argued, "They're going to need examples of proper behavior and people around them to love them."

"There you go, Jo," Hyatt laughed snidely, "The perfect chance to exercise all those maternal instincts you've got hidden somewhere."

Another newcomer, a handsome young man with skin the color of rich, dark chocolate and golden flecked brown eyes that sparkled with amusement, sputtered a laugh. "The only maternal instinct Jo has is the one that would compel her to eat her young."

"All kidding aside, I think Jo might be right. Those pups

should be kept isolated until they're presentable." This was Alex, Charles' right-hand man and the one who'd been the least friendly to Kat after the initial shock of a human woman knowing about their race. Every time he spoke it sounded like a news bulletin. "It would be best to follow the original plan. I don't know why Charles decided to alter his decision."

"Alter what decision?" Charles entered the room carrying one end of a large flat box.

"The one that allows the cubs to come here. I think we need to rethink this."

The other end of Charles' box was supported by another man, older than the rest. His name was Ryker and his looks; square cut jaw, scarred face and military bearing made him perfect for the role of Security Chief. He frowned and grunted after Alex's comment, but Kat couldn't tell if the grunt was in reference to the comment or the huge flatscreen TV they were carrying.

Seeing what they were carrying, Alex changed the subject. "That doesn't go in here. I thought we decided that would go across the hall."

Charles glanced over at Kat and winked. "New plan. The lady doesn't want a television in her school room." He shrugged and laughed. "Damn, another decision altered." He pointed with is chin to the blank wall over the mantle. "The TV goes over the fireplace in here. The kids will be using the other room, and the lady should be happy."

"The lady is very happy." This, more than anything else he could have said or done made her feel like Charles saw her as more than a casual bed partner. He wanted her here in his home, though how often he would be here to share that home with her and the children was another question to be answered.

Alex looked like he sucked on something sour, Ryker grunted, and Jo eyed Kat speculatively. Charles assigned two of the younger men to help Kat find and arrange the furniture she wanted in her school room.

*****

Everything seemed to go smoothly until after their supper of steaks on the grill where Charles and Alex shared duties as chef. Kat was in the kitchen helping Tilda with the clearing up along with a friendly, freckled faced redhead named Becky and a short, round woman who said little, but whose eyes took in everything.

This far back in the house, Kat heard nothing, but the three other women in the kitchen did. Three heads turned as one to the door leading to the hallway. Their movement was followed a few moments later with someone hailing them from the front of the house.

"Halloo-oo," a sing song voice called. "Where is everyone? We have bags here."

Tilda, who was wiping her hands on a towel, started for the door, but was waved back by Jo who entered by the back door and must've heard the newcomer, too.

"I've got it, Mrs. Martin," she said. She walked over to the door leading to the hall, opened it, and shouted, "We're back here. Carry your own damn bags," and more quietly but still in a voice that carried, she said to Mrs. Martin and Kat, "Don't let her push you around."

Nothing happened for several minutes, but the women didn't take their eyes from the door. Charles came in, looked at the women, then at the door and laughed.

"I guess the others have arrived."

"The Queen and her entourage," Jo muttered to no one in particular.

"Jo," Charles warned.

"I know, I know. One for all and all for one and all the rest of that bullshit. You might mention it to her once in a while."

"I have."

"Then you might want to get her hearing checked because she's not getting the message."

Charles started toward the swinging door and had to step back to avoid being smacked by it as a woman strode through followed by three men for whom she didn't bother to hold it open.

"Charles, darling, all the guest rooms on the second floor are taken. Someone will have to move," was her greeting. She gave him a swift peck on the lips and patted his cheek with her long slender fingers. "There's a good boy. My bags are in the foyer." She pronounced it "foy-yay" and looked pointedly at Kat.

"There are twenty of us and only one Mrs. Martin. Like I said you can carry your own damn bags, just like the rest of us. Damn prima donna," Jo muttered as she turned back to the dishes she was stacking on the island that ran down the center of the kitchen.

"If you wanted one of those rooms, Stephanie, then maybe you should have arrived with everyone else as I asked," Charles told her pointedly, but gently.

"Ah, so this is some kind of punishment for my disobedience," the woman said, pouting, "The Alpha spoke and I didn't listen. Consider me properly chastised." She patted Charles' cheek again. Her voice became sensually inviting. "Put me on the second floor, darling, and you can punish me later."

"It's not a punishment, Stephanie. Simply a matter of first come first serve. I'm sure you'll make the best of it. You always do." He winked. "Let me get Buddy and we'll carry your bags up. What's still available?" Charles looked around.

"There are several rooms on the third floor," Jo answered sweetly.

"I will not sleep on the third floor," Stephanie declared.

"Buddy and I will move," Mrs. Martin said quietly, as if that would settle it.

"No, you won't," Kat said firmly. "Those are your rooms. The Alpha said so." It was none of her business, she knew, but Mrs. Martin had already moved once and it wasn't fair to ask her to move again. Besides, she didn't like this newcomer's rude behavior. She was, however, reassessing her opinion of Jo.

The woman looked Kat up and down as if she was something distasteful found on the bottom of a shoe. "And who, may I ask, are you?"

"I'm sorry, Stephanie. With all the fuss I forgot my manners." Charles held out his hand to Kat and she took it, mostly because she sensed it would tick the other woman off. "This is Katarina."

"And the shit hits the fan," someone mumbled behind them. Becky was coughing into her hand so it had to be the quiet one who hadn't spoken before.

Two of the men standing behind Stephanie had their lips pressed together as if they too, were suppressing smiles.

Kat could almost see the wheels turning in Stephanie's head as she assessed the situation and Kat's position in it. Smiling an attractive yet predatory smile, the woman held out her hand to Kat forcing Kat to let go of Charles in order to shake. Stephanie smile became a little wider when Kat complied.

They shook, but it wasn't a friendly greeting. It was a there, I've-done-my-duty-now-I can-ignore-her shake.

Unlike Alex, Stephanie didn't pull her in with the handshake, though she did inhale deeply as the men did. It was subtle and Kat might not have noticed it if she hadn't seen the others do it. Were they marking her scent or did she stink? Stephanie's slight curl of the lip led Kat to consider the latter.

"Everyone calls me Kat."

"Meow." Stephanie gave the crowd a feral smile.

"She's our new Kitty Kat," Buddy piped up and Kat half hoped he'd add a reminder about not eating them.

"Great! We're all here," Alex said, entering the kitchen, too.

"Come on, Stephanie, let's get you squared away so you can kick back and relax. We're all out on the patio, entertaining ourselves until it's dark and the fun can begin."

Stephanie's eyes lit. "Are you taking us over the moon?" she asked Charles. It was a simple question, but from Stephanie, it sounded seductive. She watched Kat for her reaction. "You promised."

"Sorry, Stephanie, only the men. Ryker thinks we need training. Plans have changed."

"I guess they have," Stephanie said to Charles, but she was looking at Kat.

*****

The wine and beer and hard liquor flowed, but no one got drunk. The night was clear and the patio was warm thanks to the propane heaters Charles had the men carry up from the barn. By the time the kitchen was set to rights, the group had gathered around their Alpha. Kat, Jo, and the other two women joined them to hear the tail end of Charles' story of Buddy and the trap and Kat's role in his rescue. He was laughing as he told it, but she could hear the pride in his voice.

"Here she comes, charging across the field like an avenging angel holding that umbrella like a flaming sword. Scared the hell out of me, she did. Scared hell out of them, too. The girl's got a mouth on her, let me tell you."

"It's a shame you weren't there in time."

Alex's comment turned off the light shining in Charles' eyes. He nodded in agreement.

"What do you mean he wasn't there in time? How can you say that?" Without thinking, Kat moved into position next to Charles. "You weren't there! You don't know!" Her voice shook and she didn't realize her whole body was shaking until Charles tucked her under his arm. "You don't know what they were going to do to Buddy, what that man was going to do to me. They wanted Buddy for dog fights. Dog fights! They were going to throw him in a pit! They were going to... to..."

"Hey, shhh, it's all right now. It's all right," Charles whispered.

It hadn't hit her until then how badly things could have turned out, how close Buddy had come to dying.

"It isn't all right," she sniffed angrily, looking up at him. "You were in time. You were," she said as if he'd denied it. "He tried to shoot you. He would have killed you, too."

"What's this?" Ryker asked.

Charles told the rest, again playing up her role in fending off the attacker while playing down his own, but Kat wouldn't let it rest.

"Buddy was dying and the Alpha used his magic to heal him and then he brought him home."

"It could have been handled differently. I've spent a great deal of valuable time negotiating with them," Alex explained.

"*We* spent a great deal of valuable time," Stephanie corrected. "And the one you were talking to wasn't the one in charge. He was a front."

"I'm afraid this will bring attention to us," the Second warned, ignoring the interruption. He glared at Kat as if she was the cause of it all.

"No it won't," Charles said. "The sheriff called this morning while we were still in bed. Mrs. Martin told him we were all indoors because of the rain. We heard nothing." He nodded to Stephanie in recognition. "I appreciate what you were trying to do, but there was no negotiating to be done out there. I made the call. I'll take the blame."

"What else did the sheriff say?" Alex drew the attention back to himself.

"He thanked Mrs. Martin for her time and warned her to keep an eye out for wild dogs. She's to give him a call if she sees or hears anything unusual."

"Like howling, snarling, growling?" someone quipped, "There's nothing unusual about that!"

Chapter 14

Kat pointed to the gathering of men in the field, pale shadows in the darkness. There was laughter and playful shoving as they shucked their clothing and tossed it to the ground. "Do they always...?"

"Yeah, pretty much. Too bad they're not closer. It's a sight to behold." Jo topped her glass off and offered the bottle to Kat.

Kat shook her head. These wolvers could consume a frightening amount of liquor without showing its effects. She, on the other hand, had already had one glass too many.

"I don't know about that." She giggled at the thought of a dozen men running around naked in what was, in effect, the backyard. "It's warm enough here, but out there it's cold enough to shrivel the goods. Charles wore jeans the other night," she added, remembering.

"Every pack is different. Back home, good old cotton longjohns were the norm. It gets cold in the Maine woods. As long as it's natural fibers, it works. Synthetics come home in shreds." She poked her chin in the men's direction. "These guys are always measuring the size of their dicks in one way or another. It gets old after a while. Not this, though. Watch. This never gets old."

Light shone from the center of the group, the same light Kat saw when Charles went over the moon in the field. How easily the term came to her now. The light grew brighter and another light flared and another and another until a soft glow covered the group of men. Only they weren't men anymore, but beasts; great wolves who yipped and nipped at one another the way their man-forms laughed and shoved.

Two of the women, red headed Becky and her quiet friend Nan, had already gone to bed. Stephanie and the two others shared gossip in the warmth of the hot tub, their short bursts of brittle laughter slicing through the stillness. Jo declined their offer to join them. Kat remained uninvited and felt a bit like High School all over again.

The wolves broke up into teams of three or four. Kat wasn't sure what game they played or if it was a game at all. It almost looked like keep-away although apparently there was a goal in mind as they moved farther out into the field. The snarling became more pronounced, the tackling more vicious. They circled, pounced, and tore into one another with a vehemence that was frightening.

Kat watched from the edge of her seat, eyes wide as one cried out in pain and then another. The waning moon rising above the treetops shed enough of its pale light to see one lone wolf hang back from the pack and limp off to the side.

"Poor Hyatt. He never was much good at games. My mother always said he lacked the killer instinct," Jo said fondly. "He's loyal, though, and one helluva a lawyer."

"Isn't he the one you were bickering with?" Kat asked.

They watched as the injured wolf lay down on the edge of field.

"He's my brother. Who else can I bicker with?" She spoke calmly enough, but her eyes never left Hyatt. "We've always been like that. Don't you have brothers, sisters?"

"Just me. My mother died when I was nine, but my grandmother said her trouble started soon after I was born. Grams is gone now, too." Kat changed her mind and poured a little more wine in her glass. After taking a sip, she spoke again.

"My father is still around somewhere. I think. I haven't seen him in years. He fell apart after my mother died, started drinking. The last good thing he did for me was leave me with Grams."

"You didn't see him? Didn't he visit?"

Kat took another sip of wine. It was another hurt that kept on hurting. "He would show up once in a while, sober up long enough for me to begin to get to know him and then start drinking again." As an adult, she knew he suffered from depression and self-medicated with alcohol, but knowing that didn't help the hurt she felt as a child each time he left. She often thought back then that it would be better if he didn't come at all, but when he stopped coming, it was worse.

"My dad and mom still live in Maine along with my sister, her mate and my two nephews. I miss them, but I couldn't live like them."

Kat raised her eyebrows in question and it was enough for Jo to continue.

"Most wolver packs live behind the times. Males are dominant, females subservient. The women are content to stay home and raise their families and take care of their mates. If they have jobs, they're secondary and devoting your life to a career is unheard of. That's okay for them, but it wasn't for me. I couldn't wait to leave the backwoods for the big city. When I met Charles and he offered me this job and a place in his pack, I thought it was a dream come true, though lately I've been wondering if I made the right choice." She waved her hand to indicate the surrounding area. "I miss this. The land, I mean. I miss the wild."

"I like teaching," Kat admitted, "and I never planned to set it aside, but all I ever really wanted was a husband, a house in the suburbs and two point three children. You know; a normal, average, regular life."

"Well, you sure ain't finding it here. We're not even normal by Wolver standards, though I think that might be about to change," Jo sat back in her chair and turned her eyes to Kat after the wounded wolver arose and limped after the pack that was now running toward the woods. "He doesn't have any money, you know."

"Who? Charles?" Kat thought of the cars in the barn, the house and the renovations, not to mention the pool and hot tub.

"Yes, Charles. Who else would I be talking about? Everything is held by Wolf's Head Enterprises except for this house and it's mortgaged to the hilt. Charles earns good money, but he likes the high life. If he lost his position as the Alpha, he'd lose everything."

"Not everything," Kat said with quiet confidence and then realizing she'd spoken aloud, she blushed. More to cover her slip of the tongue than curiosity, she said, "I guess I don't understand the whole concept. I thought he was born to be the Alpha."

Jo watched the trees where the wolves had run. "Every man out there is an alpha in his own right. Charles handpicked every one of them because they had those qualities. They're smart, aggressive, and strong. Hyatt is probably the weakest physically, but he makes up for it in intelligence. There are others, betas and below, who work for Wolf's Head. They also have strengths and talents, but not to the alpha degree. The Alpha, the leader with a capital A, normally has to earn that position through strength and cunning, but any alpha has the right to challenge for it at any time." She watched the women in the hot tub for a few moments and when she was sure they were busy with their own conversation she continued.

"Charles was raised to be the Alpha, but he didn't fight for his position. He created it. He wanted to break from the old isolationist ways to form a new kind of pack based on business principles, one that functions more as a corporation than a pack. The corporation would grow through recruitment rather than mating. He sought out others who were dissatisfied with the traditional packs, others like myself who wanted to live independent lives without going rogue. Applying our pack mentality to the business world has worked well for almost ten years, but now it's falling apart. No one says much about it, but we all feel it."

Kat shifted a bit to get a clearer view of Jo's face. "Why? What's happened to change things?"

"That's the problem. We don't know, but the theories are driving us apart." Jo checked on the women in the hot tub again. "Most of us were really young when the pack was formed. We thought the old ways were outdated. We thought we knew better than our elders. Now, some of us think they were right. About some things, anyway."

Kat thought of the many times she'd argued with Grams about how she went about planning her future and how things turned out. "That's nothing new. It's pretty common, isn't it? I've been guilty of it myself."

Jo shrugged and made a wry face. "That's just it. It's common for you, not for us. Tradition is strong in the packs and we believed that's all they were, traditions. Now, some of us are thinking it's more than that. The beast runs strong in all of us. We talk about our animal instincts that make us successful, but there are others instincts that we've tried to ignore; home, the family unit, mating, communal structure. Some of us believe those are instincts, too, and the beast within us is calling us to obey."

"You miss it." Kat whispered the commiseration. "We're not so different, you and I. You miss your home and family. I miss mine, too, and I want one more than anything."

"Some of us are beginning to feel that way, too."

"Some of you, but not all of you," Kat filled in.

Jo kept her voice low, barely above a whisper. "Some believe it's a matter of leadership."

"You don't mean someone might challenge...?"

"Yeah, I do."

"But..."

Jo's eyes flashed a warning. "Is there any wine left in that bottle?" she asked loudly, picking the bottle up and turning it upside down. "Guess not."

The women in the hot tub rose as one. There was squealing and laughter from two of them as the cool night air hit their water warmed bodies.

"I'm off to bed," said one as she wrapped herself in a heavy terrycloth robe. "When Tanner comes home, he always brings a bit of the beast with him. I want to be ready."

"Fine for you, sharing a comfy room on the second floor. Stephanie and I have to make do with those stuffy little rooms on the third." The speaker was short, plump and curvaceous. Kat thought her name was Sylvia. The woman briskly wiped down with a towel and then wrapped it about her shoulders.

Stephanie didn't bother with robe or towel, but struck a pose that showed off her perfect body to its best advantage. She stood so close to Jo's lounge, water dripped from her body onto Jo's bare legs. She didn't seem concerned with the chilly air and Kat thought, uncharitably, it was because of her cold heart.

Kat had met Stephanie before or at least women just like her. There was one in every bar she worked. They sauntered in, sat at the bar with their legs crossed and their skirt riding high and issued some nonverbal command that had six guys at their side within minutes. They'd flirt, pout, laugh, and lightly touch, but you could tell they didn't give a damn about the men. It was the power they got off on. If they came in with another woman, it was usually one who gratefully accepted the siren's leavings.

"Speak for yourself, Syl." Stephanie pulled away the plastic clip that held her hair above the water and shook her head. Her hair immediately took on that wind-blown look that other women took hours to achieve. "I have no intentions of sleeping on the third floor, like the hired help." She looked pointedly at Kat.

"Then I guess you'll have to knock on doors until someone lets you in. Just don't knock on mine. It's the one next to the Alpha's."

"Oh, give it up, Jo," Stephanie sneered. "We all know you're not Charles' type."

"So true, Stephanie dear, so true." It was clear Joanne was enjoying herself. "What you failed to notice is neither are you."

"We'll see about that, won't we?" Stephanie tossed her hair artfully over her shoulder and led her sisterly supporters into the house.

"And on that note," Jo laughed, "I think I'd better hit the sack, too. If I wait too long, I'm liable to find my things thrown out in the hallway."

"She wouldn't dare."

"Oh yes she would. Don't ever underestimate Stephanie. She's an alpha through and through."

This society was more complex than Kat had imagined. "I thought only men were alpha's."

Jo laughed and poked her chin at the woods the way she had before. "That's what they think, but in every pack there are strong woman that folks turn to for wisdom and guidance and support. In a strong pack, there may be more than one. They're the glue that holds a pack together. No one calls them alpha's, but that's what they are. Stephanie's just a new breed of the old girl. Strength and power aren't always found in tooth and claw. Remember that." She yawned and stretched. "And now that I've probably said more than I should, I'm off to bed. Rhonda's right, when the men come home, they'll bring the wild with them. I want to be rested if I'm going to get me some of that." She smacked her lips and rubbed her flat stomach. "With the male/female ratio, I'll have my pick of the litter."

"Anyone special?"

Jo pretended to be offended. "Do I look like a girl who kisses and tells?"

"Do you really want me to answer that?" Kat laughed. Plain spoken Jo was anything but reticent.

"Fine. It's Ryker." Jo huffed, "But there's nothing to tell until after the kissing, so the juicy details will have to wait for tomorrow." Jo wiggled her ass suggestively and headed for the door. "You coming?"

Kat laughed again and shook her head, wondering how she could have misjudged this open and forthright woman. "I think I'll sit here and ponder for a while. You've given me a lot to think about."

Jo turned back, all smiles and laughter gone. "Then let me give you something else to think about. You might be the one who has the power to make this pack what it should be."

Kat shook her head. "I'm no wolver and I'm sure as hell not an alpha."

"But you could be the Alpha's Mate." Jo winked and continued on into the house.

Kat turned off the propane heaters and added more wood to the fire before settling back into her lounge. She grabbed a towel to cover her legs, folded her arms over her chest and stared into the flames.

Charles' mate? Could that even be possible? She was human, after all. She wanted him; wanted to talk with him; wanted to watch him as he listened to her. She wanted to spend time with him and work beside him, even if that meant clearing spiders and their webs from the corners of the room they were about to paint. His body and his touch called to her. Just the thought of him in her bed made her body burn with the memory.

But a mate? And just what was that, anyway? A girlfriend? A

lover? Or was it something more permanent? Was it the wolver term for spouse? She hadn't known him long enough to be any of those things, really. And yet, there was something powerful between them. One night in his bed had shown her that. He felt it too. Hadn't he told her she might be the one? Could one person fall in love with another that fast? Did she even know what love was?

When Jo spoke of Charles establishing his new pack, Kat was filled with pride for his accomplishments. When Jo spoke of someone contesting his leadership, Kat was angered on his behalf. How dare they? And when Jo suggested she could be the Alpha's mate, Kat's insides fluttered excitedly at the possibility. Was that love?

Kat told herself she was waiting and watching for the men to return so that she could watch the change, watch them coming home. In truth, she was only waiting for one wolver to come home. She'd missed him in the short time he'd been gone.

Chapter 15

Half asleep, her legs tucked up under her chin so the heavy towel covered her whole body, Kat heard them coming. In the dark's silence, she heard the faint pounding of their feet accentuated by a sharp yip, a quiet snarl of reprimand and then a long drawn out howl that echoed through the night.

Opening her eyes, she saw them stop where they'd flung their clothes. They milled about and she could feel their excitement and then suddenly they stilled. Small flashes of light began with the outermost beasts, moving rapidly inward, lighting the whole area around them until the final blinding flash erupted from the center and the beasts became men.

For a moment, Kat couldn't breathe. She'd felt the power of that final flare at the very center of her core. It stunned her and thrilled her. Charles had brought his wolvers home.

The men laughed and pushed and shoved each other in playful camaraderie as they gathered their scattered belongings, tossing them about as each found their own. Only a few bothered redressing and those only in their jeans and shoes.

Embarrassed to be caught peeping, Kat pulled the towel over her face and pretended sleep as they drew nearer the house. Sheltered from the breeze, the lounge was tucked back in the darkest corner of the patio and her towel covering was a dark navy blue. With any luck, they'd never know she was there.

"That was ass crackin' fun!" Kat didn't recognize the voice.

"What the hell does that mean?" She thought that might be

Tanner; young, dark haired with a ready smile.

"Bend over and I'll show ya."

"Sorry, my ass is spoken for. Sweet Rhonda awaits." Hopefully Tanner.

"Don't know what the girl sees in you, Tanner."

"That's because I keep my drawers on whenever you're around. Wouldn't want to cause you any whatchamacallit, penis envy." Definitely Tanner.

"Anyone know what room Becky's in?" said another unknown voice.

"I do and if I find you anywhere near it, you'll be changing your name to Dick-less." That was Rawley of the silky smooth voice. That voice alone could bring a woman to the edge. Add it to that god-like body and... well... Becky was a lucky woman!

"I thought Dickless was his name."

"Nah. You're thinking of Dickhead."

"Asshole."

"That's his middle name."

All this was interspersed with good natured laughter and Kat locked her lips between her teeth to hold back the giggles. These alpha wolvers were nothing more than overgrown boys. She'd heard the same type of conversations in the hall by the boy's locker room after a game. Kat's internal merriment was cut short by her sharp intake of breath when another voice spoke.

"Time to put the beast to bed, boys, and there'll be no knocking on doors unless an invitation has already been issued. No invitation? You'll have to make do with a cold shower or your five fingered friend."

There were more comments and laughter, but Kat was no longer paying attention. Charles was standing at the foot of her lounge. She could feel the residual power emanating from him and goosebumps arose on her skin.

Moisture gathered between her legs and she tried to think of snakes and spiders and circus clowns, any creepy thing that would take her mind away from the thoughts that were buzzing through her head. She willed the group to pass her by unnoticed.

They did, all but Charles. He stood there at the foot of her lounge, his power curling up and around her like smoke from a candle, until the back door closed and the voices receded into the depths of the house.

"You were eavesdropping, Katarina, and eavesdropping is not nice. Eavesdropping makes you a very naughty little girl."

Kat could hear a sternness in his voice that she hadn't heard before. Was he angry? She didn't think so, but she left the cover over her face and squinched her eyes shut. If she didn't move and kept her breathing even, she could sometimes fool Grams into thinking she was really asleep instead of listening to the television though the paper thin walls.

Her ploy was ruined by her startled squeak when Charles whispered through the towel by her ear. She hadn't heard him move.

"And naughty little girls need to be punished."

He pulled the towel down enough to see her wide open eyes. "I knew you were awake. I could smell your arousal."

He could smell that? Oh, shit! Kat sat up straight and the towel fell to her lap. "Could they?"

Charles stood over her, dressed only in his jeans. His grin was evil. "Probably. Would you like me to call them back and ask?"

"No!"

He nodded. "Now, why were you out here eavesdropping in the middle of the night instead of upstairs in your bed where you should be?"

"I wasn't eavesdropping," she said indignantly and immediately recanted. "Well I was, but that wasn't why I was out here." It wasn't as if she'd overheard any wolver secrets. "I just wanted to see... the wolvers come home," she added quickly.

Charles shook his head sadly. "And now you've lied. That'll earn you another punishment I'm afraid." He peeled the towel from her body and stood looking down at her.

Kat pulled her knees up closer to her chest and wrapped her arms around her legs to keep them there. "That's not fair," she pouted, refusing to look up at the broad, muscled chest looming over her.

There was a thin patch of dark blond curls at the center of his chest that formed a winged vee over his pectoral muscles and if she looked at it, her eyes would be forced to follow the long tail of the vee down the center of his body to disappear into the waistband of his jeans. She licked her lips before she complained.

"You can't punish people for breaking the rules when you haven't told them what the rules are. You have to tell me what the rules are first."

"Where would be the fun in that?"

Kat's head snapped up to find Charles smiling with mischief. He held out his hand to her and waited patiently until she took it.

"Let the punishment begin," he said as he pulled her to her feet. He looked her up and down, taking in every inch of her, slowly.

Kat wasn't sure where this was going. Charles was still talking about punishment and yet the look he was giving her was anything but punishing. She watched and waited, goosebumps rising on her arms, this time not from the chill in the air, but from the heat of his gaze.

"You're going to run."

Run? She remembered what he said about her refusal to run and his refusal to chase. "So you're just playing the Big Bad, right?"

"The Big Bad?"

"Yeah. The Big Bad Wolf. This is a game, right? Not a real

punishment."

"We'll have to see, won't we?" He grinned evilly. "Your punishment is to run to the barn."

Kat looked out to where he pointed. She could barely see the darkened outline of the barn. It wasn't too far, about two hundred yards. She was in good shape. She could make that easily.

Charles wasn't finished. "You'll have four stops along the way; the woodpile from the dead tree, the pear tree, the big rock half exposed, and the bucket Buddy left out by the drive. Those will be your safe zones." He pointed in the direction of each as he spoke.

Two hundred yards just became five hundred. It wasn't a straight line to the barn, but a zigzag pattern. She could easily see the outline of the woodpile. It was huge. There were several trees clustered together with their buds just beginning to pop. How the hell was she supposed to figure out which one was the pear? Beyond that she could see nothing. His pointing only gave her a vague placement for the rock and the bucket.

"If I catch you before you reach your safe zone, you forfeit a piece of clothing."

"That's not fair!" She complained and she shivered, more at the thought of running naked than the cool night air. What if someone should see them? "You can run faster than me and I'm wearing sandals. I can't run in these."

He looked down at her feet. "You're right. I'm not wearing shoes. Take yours off. We want this to be fair." The grin Charles gave her told her he wanted this to be anything but fair.

Kat kicked her sandals off and giving it one last try, she ran her fingers over his chest. "Can't we just go inside and...?"

"Where would be the punishment in that?" He sighed. "Tell you what, I'll give you a head start. Ready, set, go!"

Startled, Kat stumbled as she took off, but she gained her

footing quickly and ran for all she was worth toward the jumbled pile of wood, the remains of a dying maple tree. The ground over which she ran had been turned and tilled and freshly seeded with grass. It was soft beneath her feet.

She could see the outline of each piece of wood and was only about ten feet away when she was grabbed about the waist and spun in a circle, her feet in the air. She squealed in the delightful fear she used to feel when she was a little girl and her father chased her around the house as a growling bear.

Charles set her on her feet and looked her up and down slowly. Kat stood still, arms to her side, awaiting his choice of forfeiture.

"Turn around and take off the shorts," he ordered, surprising her.

"I thought you were going to..."

"Ah, ah," he admonished her with a shaking index finger and then stirred the air with the same finger to indicate she was to turn. "No talking during punishment." He paused for a moment and when she didn't move he added, "I'm waiting."

Kat slowly undid the button and inched the zipper down. The shorts, cut down from an old pair of jeans, were tight she had to shimmy her hips to get them down. She bent to pull them off her feet and shivered a little as the cold night air hit her nylon clad bottom. Without looking back, she held the shorts out to him.

"We'll leave them right here on the wood pile," he told her and before she could straighten, his hand was on her back holding her in place. "Let me see that little wiggle again."

Kat giggled and wiggled and when she heard him hum in appreciation, she wiggled again.

"Ready, set, go!" he said in the middle of her wiggle.

Startled again, Kat ran for the cluster of trees, laughing now. Her legs were freer without the tight shorts, and she thought she might have a chance. The tilled earth turned to scratchy weed that prickled her feet, but she ignored it and sprinted on, reached the half dozen trees and grabbed the first branch she came to.

"That's a plum," Charles said behind her and she jumped. She hadn't heard him running.

She turned to him and huffed, "How was I supposed to know which one..."

The wagging finger was back. "That's twice. Don't make me warn you again. I think I'll take those panties now."

As before, she kept her back to him as she removed her panties, feeling more vulnerable and yet somehow aroused by being fully clothed on top and fully exposed at her bottom. She bent at the waist to untangle the panties from her feet, knowing she was exposing her cheeks to his view.

"This is very... weird," she was about to say, but gave a sharp shriek instead when Charles slapped her ass with his hand. It was hard enough to sting, but not to hurt. She brought her hand around to cover the spot.

"No talking and no touching. Turn around." He took her panties from her and hung them on the tip of the branch, a bright pink blossom on an otherwise bare tree.

Kat snapped her hand away and did as she was told, stamping her feet a little to take away the sting. She huffed, but didn't speak. She did, however, clamp her thighs together when she felt a growing wetness between them. Charles snickered and Kat felt herself flush red.

"I think my kitten likes to play." He ran his finger down her narrow landing strip of curls and laughed when she squeaked when his finger breached the barrier of her closed legs. "Yeah, she likes to play."

She relaxed her legs as he found her sweet spot and closed her eyes to enjoy the sensations. That was when he cracked her other cheek.

"To the boulder. Ready, set, go!"

"No!" she moaned. She was dazed enough that Charles had to turn her around and give her a bit of a push in the direction he pointed. The prickly grass turned to harsher growth and she found herself hopping on one foot and then the other as the stubble poked her feet. The daze was gone and the embarrassment of her bared behind bouncing with each hop slowed her further and she wasn't even close to the barely visible rock when Charles caught up with her. The stubble didn't seem to bother him.

She shrugged out of her tee and tossed it at his head, laughing when he had to pause to peel it off. Sprinting for the rock, her fists in the air in a silent cheer, Kat wasn't prepared to be swept off her feet and roughly tossed over his shoulder in a fireman's carry. She kicked her feet and tried to pound him on the back to protest the unfairness of it as he plopped her onto the wide boulder that arose a mere foot and a half from the ground. How in hell was she supposed to see that? To avoid another swat, she held her complaint and instead, put her hands on her hips and stuck out her tongue. Charles only laughed harder, damn him.

"You learn quickly, kitten, but you're ruining my fun."

Kat clamped her lips together to prevent a retort.

He positioned her up on the rock, facing him. This put her bottom half on display before him. She closed her eyes and her thighs.

"Open them," he ordered.

She wasn't sure if he meant her thighs or eyes, so she opened both just enough to claim she had obeyed. But her eyes went wide and her bottom clenched when he ran his finger along her slit and up her belly.

"Since you gave your shirt up freely, there's only one bit left. Take it off slowly so I can enjoy it."

It was on the tip of her tongue to say that at least one of them was enjoying this, but she kept the thought to herself and admitted, if only to herself, that she was enjoying this erotic game, too.

She inched her bra straps off her shoulders and watched his face, enjoying the hunger she saw there. In the darkness, his eyes glittered with it and she heard him release a ragged sigh, but all expression was gone by the time the bra was off. He simply stared.

She stood there, hands on her hips, eyes wide open and staring out over his head. She was cold now and she tried not to show it, but her teeth chattered a little. That seemed to bring Charles back from wherever his mind had wandered. He smiled.

"Cold?"

She almost said, "What the hell do you think? I don't have the body heat of a wolver." She'd noticed they all felt a little warm. Instead, she held her tongue and nodded. Her next giant shiver convinced him.

"Don't look down," he said.

She didn't need to. A soft golden glow illuminated the area around them. It was the same glow that filled the room when he healed Buddy. The warmth began at her feet and rose up her legs. When he reached the tops of her thighs, he moved to her arms and the same flush of warmth suffused them. He moved around her, never touching her, but wherever his hand hovered was warmed. Across her shoulders and down her back, the heat soothed her like a steaming shower at the end of a long day and as she often did in the shower, her head tilted back and she sighed with pleasure.

"Damn, kitten, you're beautiful," he breathed.

And then the light dissolved and her source of heat was gone. She almost cried out at the loss. Instead, she wiggled her rear end to show him he missed a spot.

"Always complaining." He smacked each cheek and on the cold flesh, it stung. "That's for trying to shorten your punishment."

Kat eeked and did a little dance with her feet, jiggling those stinging globes. It was as much for his pleasure as her relief and if he was distracted...

"Ready, set..."

This time, she was leaping from the rock before he got to "go". She ignored the stubbly growth jabbing at her feet. There was the bucket and suddenly, there was Charles picking it up by the bail before she reached it.

"Hmm, what should the penalty be if you've nothing left to forfeit."

Fully in the spirit of this extraordinary game, Kat slid her hand down the center of his chest and along the valley that separated the muscles defining his abdomen until she reached the button of his jeans. It was too dark to see his face from her position on her knees, but she took his sharp intake of breath as permission for her to continue. She freed his erection and took him into her mouth.

She played with him as he had played with her, teasing with her tongue and teeth and 'purring' once she had him fully in her mouth. She kept her hands behind her back as if tied. This was, after all, her forfeit and punishment.

Charles understood the gesture right away. "Finally," he sighed, "I've found a woman who likes to play."

She wondered vaguely about how many women he'd gone through to find her and had to remind herself that it was okay as long as she was the last in line. Still, the jealous thought gave her an idea for a bit of revenge.

She increased her efforts, teasing him with her teeth and working him with her tongue, sucking him deeply into her throat until his body tightened and his breath quickened and she knew he was reaching the height of his control.

Whereupon she pushed herself to her feet and took off for the barn, shouting, "Ready, set, go!" as she ran.

She was laughing and running full speed, her punishment over. She was sure she would win this leg of the race and the barn had to be warmer than the great outdoors. She had the door open before he caught her.

"You cheat," he said, laughing as he gave her a playful shove into the barn. He closed the door behind them. "You'll pay for that."

"I hope so," she laughed back. She threw her arms around his neck and pressed her body to him. She was shivering with a mixture of cold and excitement, but not for long.

Charles wrapped his arms around her and held her close, running his warm hands over her back and buttocks while he kissed her with all of the ardor she had come to expect from this strange and exciting man. Cold as she had become, she was strangely invigorated by the chase through the yard and anxious to satisfy the cravings her body had developed during her run.

The bulge pressing firmly to her belly through the rough fabric of Charles' jeans told her that in spite of his wet exposure to the cold, those cravings were shared. He'd enjoyed the chase and she found a certain pleasure and satisfaction in that, so when he gently pushed her away and took her hand to lead her into one of the stalls built along one wall of the barn, opposite the cars and trucks, she followed him willingly.

If the barn was warmer than the outdoors, the stall was warmer still, particularly after he closed both upper and lower halves of the door. The floor was covered in fresh straw and smelled sweet to her unaccustomed to nose. The walls were solidly built of fresh cut pine and sturdy hooks dotted the upper reaches holding various pieces of rope, leather, and metal which she assumed were used for horses. Faint light from the main part of the barn seeped over the tops of the walls giving an impression of the muted glow of dawn.

After looking about the stall, she turned to Charles who met her with a small white towel in his hands. Without a word, he began to rub her down with it. Starting with her arms and moving to her legs, he rubbed her briskly with the course cloth, heating her skin with rough friction.

"I want you warm and toasty. Raise your arms," he ordered as he began the vigorous application to her back.

Kat did as she was told, but not without question. Looking back over her shoulder she told him, "Charles, honey, I'm warm. You don't need to do this."

Her answer was another sharp smack on her ass, this one a little more painful than the last. "Ouch!"

"No talking during punishment and keep your arms up."

Chapter 16

Kat tried to step away, but an arm snaked around her waist and held her in place. "B-but I already served my punishment, the chase across the yard."

She was rewarded with another smack to the other cheek. This time she didn't lower her hands, but grabbed the fingers of one hand with the other and squeezed.

"Eavesdropping and lying. Two infractions, two punishments."

He was speaking to her back, but Kat heard the amusement in his voice.

"Charles," she pleaded.

Another crack on ass, this one hard enough to make her feet dance before he moved to her front and worked the rough cloth over her breasts which bobbled back and forth under his ministrations. He moved to the soft mound of her belly and the small pouch she could never be rid of no matter how much she exercised. It jiggled, too, and she was embarrassed until he kissed it and murmured.

"I love this part of you, so round and soft and feminine." He whispered it with his lips against her skin and in spite of what he was demanding of her, he made her feel sensual and sexy. Towel cast aside, his hand moved down between her legs.

"Open," he ordered and without thinking, Kat obeyed, again with both eyes and legs.

His finger probed more deeply this time than it had before

and Kat whimpered a little when with the moistened tip, he circled her clit. At the sound, he plunged his finger inside and slowly withdrew it. His eyes never left her face and what she saw in those glittering green orbs took her breath away.

She wasn't allowed to speak, so she inched her feet a little further apart as an answer to what she'd seen in those eyes.

Charles lifted the finger now coated with her juices for her to see and then he slowly drew it into his mouth and cleaned it with his tongue, sighing when he removed it as if he'd tasted ambrosia.

Kat was glad he walked behind her to retrieve something from the wall so she could close her eyes and sigh. She wasn't sure what this was, but she knew she liked it and would do whatever he required. No one had ever made her feel this way. She was his to command and yet she felt the power was all hers. She excited him. The waves of his magic crashed soundlessly against her and like an addictive drug, she wanted more.

She felt the heat of his chest at her back and then his hands were caressing her shoulders and following her arms up to her wrists where he wrapped them with something firm yet supple.

"Up on your toes, Katarina mine." Her body stretched until her toes barely touched the ground as he forced her hands upward where he hooked what she now realized was a leather thong about her wrists to a hook drilled into the support beam above them. Once her wrists were in place, she could put her heels back on firm ground, her body stretched, but not uncomfortable.

"Open," he said and she obeyed, but it wasn't enough and he tapped the inside of her ankles with his bare foot and she complied. With each tap of his foot, she spread herself further until she was spread so wide her weight hung from her wrists and her feet could only provide balance. Charles tied her ankles in place with the soft rope that dangled from opposite walls. He wrapped a silky cloth around her head, covering her eyes and blocking out what little light there was and then left her there, hanging in this vulnerable and precarious pose.

She didn't move. He didn't speak. The long silence gave her time to think about the position she'd allowed herself to be placed in and her mind wandered to places where she didn't want to go. In the position she was held in, she could only imagine one thing happening.

A little spanking she could handle. The sharp slaps to her ass stung, but they also excited her and caused her juices to flow. But this? Kat's mind shouted "No, no, no!" and yet she remained silent, her body tense and waiting and Charles let her wait.

He was watching her. She could feel his eyes wandering over her as his power sent those sensual flames of arousal pirouetting over her body. She thought, no, she knew she could feel the beating of his heart matching the beat of her own.

She'd trusted Charles from the beginning of this 'punishment' and he hadn't hurt her. He had, in fact, thrilled her with the adventure of it. She would trust him now. She forced her body to relax against the restraint at her wrists and settled more firmly on her feet.

"Ah, my Katarina, you are a treasure."

She sighed with bliss when his hands stroked lightly down her back, sending those electric tendrils of desire coursing through her. In such a short time, she'd come to crave them. Those wondrous hands stroked and caressed and tickled as they play along her arms and legs and danced over her stomach and back, never touching the places that craved their touch the most.

Finally, when she thought she could stand no more, those warm hands covered her breasts and continued to stroke and knead and heighten her tactile arousal. Her nipples were hard and tight, pebbled almost to pain and when he rolled them between his fingers and thumbs, she gasped with pleasure.

"Do you like this, kitten?" He asked as he gently rubbed the slight pain away.

Now that he'd given her permission to speak, she could only nod and gasp as he rolled her nipples again. She felt him nuzzle her hair and breathe deep of her scent and heard him whisper next to her ear.

"I want to hear my kitten purr."

His hands cupped the bottom of her breasts and he pulled her tightly against him. He kissed her neck and the sensitive place behind her ear. He caressed her shoulders with his lips and tongue, tiny darts of moist heat that made her quiver with need. He kissed his way down her spine to the base, all the while caressing and kneading the cheeks of her ass. He ran his finger along the crack that separated those cheeks, paused for a moment at the rosebud opening and she tightened against the possible invasion. His laugh was a deep rumble before he continued on.

She felt him sink to his knees in front of her where his tongue found a new playground and frolicked happily around her clit. She was so aroused from his previous attentions that it didn't take much to make her body dance to the tune his eager mouth played.

"Purr for me kitten," Charles ordered and Kat, the kitten, purred.

His mouth and tongue took her higher and higher until she felt ready to explode with the sensation and then he stopped and withdrew, stroking her thighs and buttocks until she calmed before turning his attentions once more to her cleft. He brought her to the edge, over and over, until she moaned with her need for release. She could feel the moisture dripping from her and each time he returned to her burning clit, she tried to angle her body and increase the pressure to give her the release she sought.

And every time she moved, she earned a smack on her ass from the hand that wasn't busy tormenting her along with an admonishment to stay still, an admonishment that was barely heard beneath the sound of her whimpers and moans.

"Tell me what you want, kitten. Tell me what you need from me."

Kat had trouble finding her voice, but she knew he wouldn't release her from this agony of need unless she told him what she wanted, needed.

"You," she breathed, "You. Oh god, please let me come, please."

"Did you just call me a god?" he chuckled.

He was asking this now? "I'll call you anything you want, you furry bastard, just let me come."

He let her come. He took her over the edge in a flash of light and sound that left her quivering with exhaustion. He wrapped his arms around her and held her through it and murmured of his pleasure in her ear.

His words were largely wasted. Kat was so caught up in the sensations coursing through her body that she couldn't hear or speak or see. She felt him unhook her wrists, felt him gently lowered her to the ground, felt him take her into his lap and felt his warm and comforting arms surround her. She whimpered and snuggled more tightly into his chest each time a tiny orgasmic aftershock exploded in her core.

Charles held her until sight and sound returned and as she dozed in his arms, she heard him murmuring above her.

"You are so beautiful, Katarina. You are all I ever wanted, a precious gift meant only for me."

Kat felt as if she could spend eternity right where she was, in Charles Goodman's arms. It didn't matter who he was or what he was. She knew this was where she belonged. With him.

Kat might have stayed there forever, but Charles had one

more thing on his agenda. When she had recovered enough to smile at him and draw circles in the hair of his chest with her fingers, he rolled her from his lap and into the straw.

"I want you all fours, Katarina. I need you on all fours. This isn't punishment and I promise you'll enjoy it. Please, do this for me."

It was the please that did it. She heard it in his voice and when she looked up at him, she saw it in his eyes. He needed this and what he needed she would give. She rolled to her hands and knees. Charles wasted no time in stripping off his jeans and entering her from behind. He groaned with pleasure as he seated himself firmly inside her and covered her body with his.

"One night when the moon is full, I'll chase you again, my Katarina. I'll chase you through the woods and fields and when I catch you, this is how I'll take you."

He began to move inside her, slowly at first, and Kat knew he was trying to be gentle with her after what he put her through, but she didn't want gentle. She wanted Charles. She wanted to fulfill his wants and secret needs as he had filled hers. Braced on her elbows and using her arms for leverage, she drove herself onto him, increasing her backward thrusts until he met her pace and pressure.

Once Charles understood that she wanted this as much as he did, he increased the force of his thrusts until he was pounding into her. The slap, slap of their bodies meeting in sensual pleasure echoed in the confines of the stall.

After what he'd put her through, she didn't think she could rise to the height of orgasm again, but she was wrong. He was pounding into her now as if he had a need to join the two of them into one. The magic surrounded them and she could feel the pressure building in him as it built in her. His body tensed in readiness for release and the hands that had been gripping her hips, curled around her body, one to her breast and one to her clit. One touch and she exploded and he followed on the wave of her orgasm into his own. She heard him shout her name, before she collapsed down into the straw.

Charles didn't withdraw from her, but again covered her body with his. He pressed his lips against the tender place where her neck joined her shoulder and kissed her there.

"Someday soon, Katarina Bennett, under the light of the full moon, I'll mark you here where my lips are now. I'll mark you here and you'll no longer be an Alpha's Mate, but the Alpha's Mate, my mate, Charles Goodman's Mate and being your Alpha, I promise to make you proud."

"You already do that, Charles Goodman," she mumbled drowsily through the blissful exhaustion that followed her orgasm. "You'll always make me proud. But Charles?"

"What is it, kitten?"

"Can you come down here beside me? I can't kiss you from this position and the straw is poking holes in my belly."

"You stay right there. I'll be right back."

"Bossy, bossy, always giving orders to the ones who will obey," Kat giggled sleepily, "You should start bossing the ones who don't."

"What did you say?" Charles asked quietly.

Kat was so tired she couldn't remember. "Whatever was in my head," she mumbled. "Are you coming to bed Charles? I'm cold without you."

"I'll be right there, kitten. I'll keep you warm."

"Charles?"

"Hmmm?"

"What's a...?" but she forgot what she was going to ask because Charles was back with a blanket to cover them and curling his body around hers, he was kissing her again.

Chapter 17

Kat awoke with a smile on her face, a solid chest under her head, a strong arm around her and itching almost everywhere on her body. The coarse straw beneath her scratched her hip and legs. The coarse blanket Charles pulled from the work truck to cover them scratched her other hip and shoulders. Her butt didn't itch or maybe it did, but in its frozen state, she couldn't feel it.

She'd learned a lot about her lover during the night, including the fact that the man lying flat on his back beside her was a blanket hog and there was only one cure for that. She pulled the blanket from him and straddled his knees, throwing the blanket over her back like a cape and laying herself down along his body. Now her back half might itch, but her front had a warm, firm mattress. She snuggled her head back into his shoulder and closed her eyes.

Until thirty seconds later when her mattress flipped her onto her back and covered her body with his. He left just enough space for his hand slid between them and work its way downward over her belly.

"Good morning, my beautiful kitten," Charles murmured in her ear.

"No." Kat followed the hand working its way down her body and stopped it in its tracks.

"Now, kitten, is that any way to greet your Alpha in the morning?"

"You're not my Alpha, Wolfman. You're my lover and the answer is still no." Kat stretched up to kiss him on the chin and soften her refusal. "Good morning."

"Your greeting is supposed to be..." Charles raised his voice to a falsetto. "Good morning my lord and master. Let me spread my legs for you so you can start your day with a smile."

Kat started to laugh. "You've been dreaming again or you're thinking of your other lover."

Charles looked offended. "I don't have another lover."

"Good answer! You get to keep your balls for another day."

"Geesh! You weren't this mean last night." He slid down her body until his mouth reached her breasts where he suckled first one and then the other. After several minutes of this he looked up at her and smiled. "You're purring."

The man just didn't give up. He'd let her sleep for a little while after she collapsed in the straw and then he'd taken her again, that time so sweetly, his gentleness made her cry. She'd pleasured him with her mouth the time after that and he'd returned the favor the time after that. The man had the stamina of a horse... or maybe a wolf?

She relented and stroked the hair from his forehead. "Of course I'm purring. The spirit is more than willing, but the flesh is beyond weak. It's plum wore out. I'll be walking funny for the rest of the day."

Charles rolled off of her onto his back. "Tell me about it," he muttered, staring down at his bobbing erection.

"I can fix that for you," Kat offered.

"You would too, wouldn't you?" He turned on his side to face her.

Kat closed her eyes and nodded her head, refusing to say aloud what she already knew. She loved him and she would be willing to help him in any way she could. It couldn't be possible in so short a time, but there it was. She loved him.

What she didn't understand and tried not to think too deeply about was why the whole wolver business didn't send her running for a point a thousand miles away. The whole idea of it should worry her a great deal more than love at first sight, but it didn't. Any normal person would have run screaming to the nearest psychiatrist, but then again, she wasn't normal. She'd never belonged to that world out there. Maybe, just maybe, she was where she was meant to be.

"Talk to me, kitten. I can see the thoughts swirling in your head. Tell me what you're thinking."

"I was thinking that I must be stark, raving mad, but I'm happy. I'm also thinking that you're not. Happy I mean." She, too, turned on her side to face him.

"I'm happy with you."

"I kind of got that," she laughed and then she sobered. "It's the rest of your life that worries me. You are not as at ease with them as you are with me. Why? You're their Alpha."

Charles closed his eyes and waited a full minute before he spoke. "I'm a fake. I'm not the Alpha it all."

He was waiting for her to say something, but Kat only smoothed his sleep tousled hair and smiled her encouragement.

"Do you want to know why I started this pack?" he asked and when she nodded, he continued. "It was revenge. Revenge, because my father gave my brother what should've been mine. I was the oldest. I was the one who was raised to be the Alpha. I was the one he lectured. I was the one he pushed and punished to make me into what he wanted me to be. But he failed and so did I. When he was sick and knew he was dying, he turned to Marshall, my youngest brother.

"I started this pack to show the two of them how wrong they were about me. I rejected everything my father stood for. My goal was to make enough money to finance my vengeance. I recruited other wolvers and convinced them to follow me. I didn't give a damn about them. The only damn I gave was the one I thought would show my father's pack how wrong he was in his choice of a successor."

Charles closed his eyes and steadied his breathing and Kat could see how hard this was for him. She continued to stroke his hair to comfort him and let him know she was listening.

"Don't get me wrong. Marshall fought for his place as the Alpha of the Rabbit Creek Pack and now that I'm older and wiser, I know he earned the right to serve. For a long time though, I hated him for it and if it wasn't for the lovely lady who became his mate, I might have destroyed him for it. That's the kind of man I became. Don't get mad, get even."

Charles leaned forward and kissed her. Soft and sweet, it was almost like saying goodbye. Kat could feel his sadness as if it was her own and her heart broke for him.

"And now?" she whispered against his lips, "What now?"

"Now I've met you and it may be too late. Now, when I see before me what it really means to be the Alpha, I also see it slipping from my grasp. The mantle hasn't fallen on my shoulders, Katarina, and without the mantle, I'm still a fraud."

"You are not a fake or a fraud, Charles Goodman. You're only a man or a wolver," Kat smiled and shrugged, "Who lost his way for a while. Where is this mantle? How can we find one? We can make this right."

"I have no money you know," he confessed. "That old truck out there is the only thing I own, that and the land. I owe more money on the cars than they're worth and the house is mortgaged to..."

"The hilt," Kat finished for him. "I know. I know. Why does everyone keep bringing up the money? I don't give a damn about the money. I never had any money. I don't know what it's like to have money. I do know what it's like to work hard to earn it and that's all I know about it, so can we drop the money business and talk about what's important? I want to know about this mantle."

"Who told you about the money?" he demanded. The hesitant, remorseful Charles was gone. The Alpha was back and he was pissed off.

"Jo did. She's worried about you, too, so get off your high horse and tell me about the damn mantle." Kat punched his chest to show him she meant business. The punch had no effect except to make him smile.

"You're cute when you're mad." He caught her small fist in his big hand when she tried to punch him again. "Okay, okay. The mantle isn't a piece of clothing that's kept hanging in your closet. It's a symbol, an expression used to describe the weight of the responsibility to the pack." Charles tapped his forehead with two fingers. "You can feel them and hear them. Literally. Their worries become your worries, their joys, your joys. You have to learn to control it or it will overwhelm you. Knowing each member of the pack so intimately is what gives the Alpha his real power to control his pack. It's a heavy burden to carry the mantle and in the wrong hands, it can be used to manipulate the pack into doing what's best for the Alpha instead of what's best for the pack."

"You can hear what people are thinking? Can they hear and feel you?"

Kat was thinking of the things they'd done during the night. She could feel the blush rising and was pretty sure it was turning her purple with embarrassment.

"Don't be ashamed of what we did last night," Charles said as if he could, in fact, read her mind. "We had fun. We gave each other pleasure. We made love. That's never something to be ashamed of." He tapped Kat's nose affectionately. "But no, if it will put your mind at rest, the mantle isn't like some kind of all-seeing eye. It's an emotional thing and I guess you'd call it a telepathic thing, though the speaking isn't done with words, although Marshall claims he can hear Elizabeth called his name."

Charles lifted her hand and turned her wrist until he could see her watch which was the only thing she still wore from the night before. "We better get back into the house and into our bed before the rest of them are up. We wouldn't want to be caught playing naked in the barn."

He arose in one fluid motion and pulled her up with him though she didn't have his animal grace. He grabbed his jeans up from the floor and slid them on.

"Uh, beastie boy? I think we have a problem." Kat rubbed her arms as stamped her feet all too aware of the chilly air now that Charles' body heat was gone. "My clothes are all outside and probably soaked with dew."

"I can fix that," Charles said, already shaking off bits of straw from the blanket.

He placed it over her shoulders and wrapped it tightly around her and then bent at the waist. One arm beneath her arms and one beneath her knees, he lifted her to his chest where she wrapped her arms around his neck.

It was a good solution and as it turned out, the only solution. As he carried her back to the house they found that every stitch of her clothing was gone. They were giggling and laughing like silly fools by the time they reached the back door. Charles kept trying to uncover her breasts as he trotted across the dew damp yard and Kat kept fighting him off.

She slapped his hand and shushed him one last time as she reached down and turned the knob. "If we get caught," she hissed, "I'll never..."

"I think we already are," he whispered and in a louder voice, "Good morning, Mrs. Martin. Up early I see."

"I like to get an early jump on the day," the housekeeper said conversationally as if it was perfectly normal for her half-naked employer to be passing through her kitchen with a fully naked woman in his arms. "Good morning, Kat. Your clothes are in the wash. I was just about to start breakfast. I'll have it ready by the time you're showered and back in bed if that's all right with you."

"Yes, thank you," Kat squeaked into Charles' chest where she'd buried her red face.

"That will be fine, Mrs. Martin," Charles told her sounding once again like the Lord of his Domain. "We'll be ready for it. It's been a, um, a strenuous night."

"Hmph," the housekeeper snorted, "Well, before you begin anything else that might be strenuous, be sure to check your bed. I think you might find an unwanted critter in it."

"Thank you, Mrs. Martin, we will."

They were at the foot of the stairs before their laughter sputtered forth, hissing and giggling like a couple of kids.

"Strenuous? Is that what you call it, a strenuous night?"

"Well what would you want me to say?" Charles screwed up his face and said in a dorky voice, "Gee thanks, Mrs. M. We were in the barn fucking our brains out all night and we're really, really hungry."

"Would you be quiet!" she giggled a whisper, "Keep it up and everyone will be awake. Bad enough Tilda saw me like this. I don't need half the house witnessing it."

Unfortunately, half the house did see her, obviously naked and wrapped in an old blanket with bits of straw sticking out of her hair. They all came running when Charles dropped Kat to her feet in the hallway when he opened the bedroom door and bellowed loud enough to rattle the windows.

"Get the fuck out of my bed!"

Fortunately, half of them weren't dressed much better or more completely than she. The next door down flew open and Ryker came charging out into the hall in a pair of olive drab boxers followed closely by Jo wearing Ryker's gray tee which was barely long enough to give modesty inches to spare.

Hyatt came barreling through the door to the back stairway like a caped Crusader with his flannel robe flying out behind him. Interestingly, or so Kat thought, his PJs looked like they might be silk. Once he saw the Alpha was unharmed, he turned his attentions to his sister who he tried to chase back into her bedroom with a flutter of his hands.

Tanner and Rhonda, who looked like two people who'd worn out the sheets, came running after Hyatt, Tanner looking ready for battle, Rhonda looking frightened. Rawley was there with his arm around the shoulders of the little freckled redhead. His face looked angry and hard and his free hand was clenched in a fist.

Two other young men, Kat couldn't remember their names, came bursting out of another door on the second floor. The lighter skinned of the two was completely naked and the other wore a shiny black thong that was so tiny it was obscene.

"What the fuck is going on out here?" Ryker growled, but Charles ignored him. He was too busy shouting into his room.

"Did you not hear me? Get the fuck out of my bed. Now!"

Stephanie came sauntering out of the room. "You needn't yell, Charles dear. I only came to keep you company after the hunt. We all know how you get after an evening in the wild. I must have fallen asleep."

She was wearing a black peignoir so sheer the dark silhouette of her perfect body was clearly defined. She stopped, just outside the door, to inspect Kat from head to toe.

"But I see you've expended your energies on the hired help."

Kat's fist clenched beneath her rough wool covering and she took a step toward the woman. "Bitch," she said clearly.

Stephanie's laugh was derisive. "As a matter of fact, I am, sometimes quite literally. I don't know who you think you are, but you're nothing to me."

"She's something to me," Charles snarled, "And that's all that counts."

"What is she, Charles? Tell us all. Please. Tell us all what she is to you." The woman's smirk turned her beautiful face ugly.

Charles put his arm around Kat and pulled her close. "Suffice it to say she's mine."

"But who is she, Charles? Where did she come from? What does she want? This isn't the time. Don't go all Alpha on us now. She isn't worth it. She may be a Mate, but that doesn't mean she isn't trash."

Charles took a step towards Stephanie, leaving Kat behind. He drew himself up as Kat had seen him do before when looming over Mrs. Martin. He suddenly appeared larger-than-life. Kat could hear the collective intake of breath and even the bold Stephanie stepped back and lowered her eyes.

Charles' voice was deadly calm. "You have one hour to pack your things and get out, Stephanie. You are no longer welcome here."

Stephanie looked up and her eyes flashed with surprise and anger. "You can't do that. I'm a member of the Council."

"Yes, I can. You may be a member of my Council, but I am the Alpha."

Charles seemed to grow even more in stature. His power seemed to swell the walls outward and when he turned that power upon Stephanie, she cringed.

"You breathe by my will and word. You have one hour to get out or I will throw you out and you'll be grateful that's all I do," Charles told her. Then he turned and addressed those standing in the hall after nodding to each, in turn. "Anyone else have anything to say? Good. Then thank you. Thank you all. I'm sorry you were disturbed. We'll meet tomorrow to go over my plans."

Alex, whose door had remained closed during the shouting, now opened it and took in the situation at a glance. Unlike the others, he was fully dressed.

Stephanie, finding no sympathy or support from anyone else, looked to him. "I've been banished, Alex. Would you come help me pack my things."

"Of course, Stephanie. Let's get your things together and I'll pull your car around."

He led her down the hallway to the stairs to her room.

Jo laughed and put her fists on her hips. "Bitch," she mocked, "Kitty Kat. Honey. Stephanie could tear you to shreds."

"I'd like to see her try," Kat challenged and said to the others. "I'm small, but I can take care of myself. I could have taken her." She shouted after the retreating Stephanie. "Even if she does outweigh me by thirty pounds."

"Ooo, low blow," Jo laughed. "Now tell her you're smarter than her, too."

"I probably am," Kat agreed and gathered her breath to shout again.

"Katarina! That's enough. It's over. Come to bed." Charles held the door and motioned with his hand. His power rippled over her and she felt the infuriating compulsion to obey. This was different from his commands during sex. Those she obeyed because she chose to.

She fought the compulsion and hesitated just long enough to let him know it and then she issued a "Hmph" Mrs. Martin would be proud of and ducked under his arm. As soon as the door was closed, she flung off her blanket and turned on Charles.

Hands on hips, she hissed at him. "Did you hear her? This isn't the time. Don't go all Alpha on us now," she mimicked viciously. "You can't do that," she continued. "Who in the hell does she think she is talking to you that way. You're the Big Bad. You can do anything you want. I could claw the bitch's eyes out."

Charles started to laugh. "I didn't know my kitten had claws."

"Well, now you know and it's not funny, Wolfman. She has no right to talk to you that way, the fancy-assed bitch, waltzing around in her sexy nightie, making herself at home in your bed." Kat was fuming and Charles laughing at her wasn't helping.

He was still laughing. "She has no right to talk to me that way and yet you call me Wolfman and Beasty Boy."

"That's different. Those are terms of... of affection. That bitch has no right to call you anything but Sir."

"I think you're jealous," he laughed.

"You're damn right I am."

Stephanie was everything she wasn't. She was those girls in high school who always made the cheerleading squad. She was those girls in college who never had to roll out of bed and run to class looking like death warmed over because they'd worked late the night before. She was those women who look down their noses at Kat when they picked their children up from school in their brand-new Volvo's wearing outfits that cost one of Kat's paychecks.

"She was in your bed! She was wearing that peignoir that would probably feel like silk in your hands. Her hands probably feel like silk, too. She's smart, she's rich, and she's beautiful, damn her. She's everything I ever wanted to be and couldn't. And now she wants you, too." Kat stamped her foot in an attempt to keep the water from filling her eyes.

Charles wasn't laughing now. He held out his arms to her, but Kat refused his invitation. She felt stupid and foolish for blurting out what she hadn't meant to say.

"Katarina. Come here."

The power and compulsion was still there and this time she reluctantly obeyed. Forehead resting on his chest she stood before him, ashamed of her confession.

Charles enveloped her in his arms. "Stephanie is all those things and yet, I would choose you. Do you think Stephanie would have played with me outdoors tonight? Do you think Stephanie would have made love on the floor of the barn? Do you think Stephanie would be angry on my behalf when the attack was against her? I like you, Katarina Bennett, and I think you may be the best thing that's happened to me in a long, long time."

Kat looked up at him, needing to see his eyes when he answered. "Do you really mean that?"

"Yes, I really mean that," he told her, but she'd already read the answer in his eyes and then those eyes took on the same sparkle they'd held just a little while ago. "You need to go get your shower, kitten, before I refuse to take no for an answer." His hands slid down her back to her rear where he gave her cheeks a light pat to send her on her way. "And kitten?" he laughed as he turned her around and gave her another playful swat on the rear, "Stephanie could never be as cute as you are naked and angry."

Chapter 18

"What's a mate?"

Kat was alone in the kitchen with Tilda making preparations for a late lunch. Buddy was out in the yard stacking wood from the fallen maple tree, the same tree that Charles had used for first base the night before. The others, all except Stephanie who'd managed to pack can be gone in one hour as directed, were in the dining room sitting around the long walnut table with Charles at its head.

He'd invited her to sit in on the meeting with his Council, but Kat had refused. Being his girlfriend wasn't the same as being a member of the pack or the Council and she wasn't the only one who thought so.

Earlier, on her way to the kitchen, she'd passed Charles' office door which was open a crack. She couldn't help overhearing him arguing with his Second, Alex. She'd paused just past the door to listen, knowing full well that this time, she was guilty as charged.

"I'm not saying you were wrong," Alex was explaining, "I'm only saying that perhaps you were a bit hasty in sending her away. Stephanie has an important role in our operation, Charles."

"And she can play that important role back in the city with the others."

"She's the one who came up with the idea of negotiating with the men who're using your land for their business. She should have been allowed to present her case."

"It's a dog fighting ring! And I can guaran-damn-tee whatever else they have going in there isn't legal either, so there is no case to present. I want them gone and Stephanie is off the Council. It's too damn big to begin with."

"I agree, but if you want to reduce the size, there are others we could probably do better without. Hyatt, for instance or Jo who does little but wisecrack her way through the meetings. Ryker is another we can do without. He's security. He knows his job, but has nothing to contribute to the running of the business."

"But he has a lot of ideas about the running of the pack and that's what we seem to forget, Alex. The Wolf's Head Pack should come before Wolf's Head Enterprises."

"They are one in the same."

"No. They're not and I'm coming to realize that more and more. We need to change. As a business, were flourishing. As a pack, we're falling apart," Charles said using the same words as Jo.

"Does this have something to do with Kat? I know you're enamored him with the girl, but..."

"Katarina has nothing to do with this. This has been coming for a long time."

"Forgive me, Alpha, but I beg to differ. I think she has everything to do with this and the pack has a right to know. I fully agree that Stephanie chose the wrong venue to voice her concerns, but that doesn't negate the fact that her concerns are real and shared. What do you know about this girl? Only that Eugene Begley found her at the instigation of your brother's Mate. A brother, I might add, with whom you've had a contentious relationship. Who knows..."

Charles had slammed his hand down on the desk and Kat was so startled she jumped. It was a good thing, too. She'd been so intent on listening, she'd failed pay attention to what was going on around her. Others were entering the hallway and she had just enough time to scurry into the kitchen before she was caught.

She didn't want to cause any further bad feelings between Charles and his Council, so instead of accepting his invitation, she'd helped Mrs. Martin straighten the rooms and make the beds and wipe down the bathrooms. She was, after all, an experienced hotel worker and she knew a lot more about that end of the business than what was going on in the dining room.

Now, she was helping the housekeeper prepare the massive lunch these wolvers required and since they were alone, Kat decided to use the opportunity to seek some answers to her questions.

Tilda didn't hesitate to answer. "A mate is a spouse. A mating is like a marriage."

"So it's nothing special?"

"Ah, well, I suppose it's special to the two doing the mating and if you want children it must be done. Unmated pairs can't breed. Why do you ask?" she asked cautiously.

"Is it forever?" Kat had read somewhere that wolves mate for life and she wondered if that was true for wolvers, too.

"For life, you mean? For most it is, I suppose, but what you're talking about is a true mating. That's when you meet the one you're meant to be with. That one lasts for a lifetime because the bonds are stronger."

Kat laid down the knife she was using to slice the tomatoes and frowned. Tilda's answer was closer to what she was looking for, but there was something else that Kat couldn't define. It was, she thought, another one of the codes she couldn't break.

"Sometimes, when I hear them talk about a mate, I get the impression it starts with a little 'm' but other times it seems to start with a capital. Like saying many wolvers are alphas, but only one in the pack is the Alpha. Lowercase, uppercase. You see what I mean? I'm asking because I think it has something to do with me."

Tilda turned off the three frying pans she had working on the stove and came to stand by Kat.

"What has the Alpha said about it?" she asked quietly.

"Nothing. I haven't asked him. But Jo hinted that she thought I might be special and Stephanie acted like I was threat. I'm neither one."

"And the Alpha said nothing?"

Kat blushed, knowing that the housekeeper already knew what she and Charles had been up to. "He hasn't said anything about a mate. He wouldn't would he? We haven't known each other that long," and then she blurted, "Mrs. Martin, I don't usually act that way around a man I just met. Usually? I've never acted with like that with any man. I haven't been with that many..."

"Hush, child. You couldn't help yourself. It's the way of the Alpha when he's searching for his Mate. Stronger women then you have fallen to it." Her consoling pat was awkward. She wasn't a woman who showed physical affection easily. "Are you sure he's not mentioned it?"

"No, but he did say... Kat hesitated. "He said he was convinced that I was the one," she said in a rush.

Tilda's comment wasn't what Kat expected. "Hmph. Fool man," she said, clearly irritated. She cocked her head in that way they all had when they were listening. "They're all arguing in there. We won't be overheard."

Kat almost laughed, remembering that she'd been 'punished' for eavesdropping when, with their hearing, these wolvers could listen to conversations that would be impossible for her to hear.

Tilda placed her hand over Kat's on the counter, a good indication what she had to say was important. "It isn't my place to tell you this, but them that should, haven't and that ain't right. Poor Emily didn't know neither and that's how she ended up locked in the bathroom. You're a bit ahead of her on that score. You, at least, know what we are and I must say I'm proud of the way you're taking to it."

"Emily. That's Charles' mother right? You said she wasn't a wolver, but not quite human either."

"That's right, child, just like you."

Kat pulled her hand away. "Oh no, I'm human. I know my mom and dad and everything. I never had any special gifts. I wasn't special in any way. I'm human, through and through."

"That's what Emily thought, too, and you're right for the most part, except for bein' special. You're an Alpha's Mate. You're a human woman born special and once you reach your womanhood, should you meet an Alpha and that's with a capital 'A'," she laughed, "He'd know you right away for what you are the minute he laid a hand on you. The instinct to mate is powerful in an Alpha and if he finds the one he wants, the magic is almost impossible to resist." She paused for a moment, waiting and watching for Kat's reaction. A minute passed, then two. "Are you going to say something or are you going to stand there with your mouth hanging open? You're meant to be an Alpha's Mate and our Alpha needs a Mate more than most."

"Why?" Kat's mind was reeling and it was the only word she could speak. That one word covered a lot of territory. Why was she born that way? Why hadn't she been told this before? Was this why she had always felt like she didn't belong? Why now? Why would these people consider her special when no one had before?

The housekeeper chose to answer the question that was most important to her. "Our Alpha needs his Mate to help him take this pack in the direction it's supposed to go. It ain't normal to have a pack of lone wolvers. That ain't the way the Good Lord intended. The men, they may go out to hunt and fight, but without their mates and families, they got nothing to hunt and fight for. They got nothing to protect. They can pair up with a likely woman, but they can't mate and if they can't mate, they can't breed. No young'uns, no families, no pack. It's the way it's always been and the way it always will be."

Kat was thinking about what Jo told her about traditions and there being more to them than she thought. "I don't see what all that has to do with me."

"It's got everything to do with you, girl. It don't matter how strong the Alpha is. If he don't find a Mate, the pack can't breed. You having your babies, allows them to have theirs."

"What exactly does that mean?" Kat asked worriedly. "Is the Alpha's Mate some kind of breeding machine having baby after baby just so other women in the pack can have theirs? Charles said he only has two brothers. Was he lying? Or was he trying to ease me into it. And how do these babies come out anyway, because I don't see myself raising a litter."

Tilda laughed at that. "Don't go borrowing trouble where there is none. It's the possibility is all, though with the first one there's usually a passel of others following right along. You'll have them one or two at a time, just the way your mother did. It ain't no different really, except for when they're grown they can go over the moon."

"I don't even know if I can have children." She'd made mistakes in the past and it was always a tense few weeks until the pregnancy test came out negative. She'd always thought she was lucky. What if she was barren?

"You'll have 'em," Tilda said with confidence. "Never heard tell of a Mate who couldn't."

"I don't know if I can do this. I think I need to sit down."

"You go sit and I'll make you a cup of tea." Tilda busied herself with the teapot and cups while Kat went to sit in a little room off the kitchen where a table had been placed for Tilda and her son.

"What if I'm the wrong woman for the job?" Kat muttered to herself. "What do I know about being the Alpha's Mate?"

Tilda answered as if Kat had called the question across the room instead of whispering to herself. "If you're the wrong woman, we'll all know soon enough, but I don't think you are. I see a lot of Emily in you. You're down to earth. You don't mind pitching in when it's needed and you're listening to what the Alpha's people have to say. You're on his side and it don't matter what side that is as long as it's his. You were ready to give that highfalutin Stephanie her comeuppance this morning because she insulted your man. If you ask me, and I know you ain't, you got the makings of a good Alpha's Mate."

Tilda brought in the tray, set it on the table and settled herself into the other wooden chair. She poured tea from the pot into two cups and handed one to Kat.

"Thank you." Kat took a sip of the steaming brew and sighed. Like everything else in the kitchen, Tilda knew how to brew a good pot of tea. "I'm keeping you from your work. They'll be hungry when they're finished."

"Then they'll be good and hungry by the time it's ready. If they complain too much, I'll serve them salad. That'll fix their wagons."

Kat laughed and her laughter was as refreshing as the tea. "Don't take their shit, huh?"

"Damn right I don't. I answer to the Alpha and no one else. You'd be wise to do that, too." Tilda sipped her tea, in no hurry to get back to fixing lunch. "So, what are you planning to do now that you know?"

"Nothing," Kat told her honestly, "Not until I've thought it through."

"At least you ain't a-howling and crying locking yourself in the bathroom."

"Nope. I'll fall apart later when I have more time. I'm not going to think about it right now. The children should be arriving soon and I need to get ready for their arrival."

Tilda nodded sharply to indicate she thought that was a wise decision.

Chapter 19

It may have been a wise decision, but it was one Kat couldn't keep. She thought about it while she helped Tilda finish the lunch preparations and all during lunch. She tried to concentrate on the conversations going on around the table, but her mind kept straying to the conversation in the kitchen.

Charles kept eyeing her with concern and touching her hand. She smiled weakly at his unasked question and closed her eyes to indicate she was tired and to let him know she was all right. Charles, however, wasn't buying it and after lunch, he detailed four of his Council members to the kitchen for clean-up and directed Mrs. Martin in no uncertain terms to put her feet up. He then grabbed Kat's hand.

"How would you like to go for a little stroll?" he asked cheerfully of Kat and practically dragged her through the front door. He set off at such a rapid pace Kat was almost running to keep up.

"It would be nice if you asked," she grumbled and tugged on her arm to release it from Charles' grip. His fingers wouldn't budge. Kat gave up and yelled at him instead. "This isn't strolling, it's power walking. Slow down!"

"I asked," he argued, keeping up the pace until they'd gone about fifty yards.

"It's only a question if you give the person a chance to answer," she said and tugged on his arm. "Slow down!"

She had to dig in her heels and skid a few feet before Charles got the message and even then she got the feeling he only slowed because he'd come as far as he wanted to anyway. He looked back at the house and readjusted their hands to a friendlier position as he slowed to a comfortable walk.

"What did Mrs. Martin say to upset you?"

Kat stopped walking, snatched her hand from his and smacked his shoulder with it. "You have a nerve, Wolfman. You spanked my ass for eavesdropping and here you are doing the same thing."

Charles' lips twitched. "Does this mean you want to spank my ass?" He sighed regretfully, "Because if you do, then I need to tell you that in this instance, what's good for the goose is not good for the gander. It ain't happening, kitten. Your bottom stays on the bottom. Which is all moot since I never spanked your ass for eavesdropping."

"You did so. I was there, remember." It may have made her feel hotter than hell, but it was still a spank.

Kat turned and stalked away, then realized she was marching every bit as fast as he'd been before. She slowed to a walk. It didn't really matter how fast or slow she walked. Charles would catch up if he wanted to.

"Then you should also remember that you got spanked for speaking out of turn, not eavesdropping. That was running the bases." Charles reached for her hand.

He was laughing at her and she'd be damned if she'd hold his hand. Se folded her arms across her chest. "You know what I mean," she huffed.

"I do, but I definitely think a refresher course is needed to jog your memory. You have a terrible memory, kitten, and I think we should jog it at least once a week, maybe twice. There's a great little clearing up here with an oak tree that would be perfect. I can see it now. A little rope, a few feathers and you won't believe what you can find on the internet..."

"Charles! Stop. You're making me angry."

"No I'm not. When you're angry, you get that little crease in your forehead. Right there." He touched the spot with his finger. "Okay, okay. Serious business," he said quickly when the crease appeared. "I still claim not guilty." He was now walking backward so he could speak to her face to face. "I didn't eavesdrop. It was the process of elimination. You were happy when I left you upstairs and you weren't when lunch started. Everyone except Buddy and Mrs. Martin were with me. Buddy isn't likely to say anything upsetting to you, Ergo..." He spread his hands and bowed.

Kat relented. "Mrs. Martin didn't upset me. She answered some of my questions. There were things I needed to know, things I should have been told," she said, giving him what Grams called her evil eye. "She told me about the wolver version of the birds and the bees. She told me about the Alpha's Mate."

Charles nodded. "So you and she had a chat."

Kat nodded. "She thinks I probably am one."

"Oh you are. You definitely are. I knew that the first time you kissed me. Scared the hell out of me." He wasn't laughing.

She wasn't either. "You kissed me. So when were you going to tell me?"

"If I recall correctly, I mentioned it last night."

They walked together, not speaking, not touching, up the narrow lane. She was so engrossed in trying to remember, she failed to notice when Charles stopped. When she finally realized she was walking alone, she spun around to find him standing in the middle of the lane with his hands on his hips.

"Why didn't you ask me?" he asked and there was something in his voice that told Kat this wasn't a curiosity question.

"Because at the time, I didn't know what I was asking. I was asking for clarification about some things I'd heard," she hedged.

"Is that it, or was it because you didn't trust me? The others don't. Mrs. Martin didn't trust me to heal her son. The Council doesn't trust me enough to follow my lead and support my decisions. Maybe you didn't trust me enough to ask about these things you heard."

"Trust you? I don't trust you?" She marched back toward him, her finger up and ready to poke him in the chest. "Damnit! I let you strip me naked while running around the damn backyard. I let you tie me to a beam in the barn. I don't do those kinds of things, Charles Goodman. I've never done anything like that in my entire life, but I did it for you and I trusted you wouldn't hurt me. So don't give me your 'You don't trust me' shit."

"Then why didn't you come to me?" he demanded.

"Because a girl doesn't go up to a guy she virtually just met, no matter how hot and heavy they've been making it, and ask about marriage... mating... whatever! And if she does, that guy is likely to take off for the hills." Kat threw up her hands and turned away.

"I said you were the one," he said as if that should be enough.

"Good God, Charles, guys always say stuff like that when they want to get in a girl's pants. You ought to know that being the charmer that you are."

"I never said it," he said defensively, "The women I've been with all knew it could never end in a mating. The only other unattached Mate I've met wasn't interested. She was in love with my brother."

"Did you love her?" Kat whispered, more to herself than to him, but in spite of her back being turned, he heard her.

"I was attracted to her. It's in the nature of the beast to be attracted to a Mate, but no, it felt like more of a game. In the end, we were friends. She's the one who made me see what Wolf's Head might be missing."

Kat turned back to see him smiling wryly. "What about me?"

she asked quietly, hating the catch in her voice, not wanting to hear the answer, but knowing it was important to them both. "Is what we share just the nature of the beast? Is this just a game? Because it's not a game for me, Charles. This is something that has changed my whole life."

Kat knew from the beginning that her reaction to all this wasn't natural, wasn't normal. These people could morph into wolves and yet she'd accepted that as easily as she would a change in their clothes. She'd had a harder time adjusting to Lucy Spellman returning to work as Luke Spellman after the school's summer break.

This was much more than an adjustment in perception and yet it didn't feel unusual. It felt right. For the first time since her mother died, Kat felt like she was where she was supposed to be. She felt like she'd met the man she was supposed to be with. She felt like she'd found her place and her place was beside Charles. And she was terrified to find out what it would feel like if all this was taken away.

"It's not a game, Katarina," he said solemnly. "What I feel for you is more than the nature of the beast. You are an Alpha's Mate, but am I the true Alpha? After this morning's meeting, I'm not sure. What if someone else is meant to be the Alpha of this pack? If it's not me, if I'm not the Alpha, then you and I can't be."

Over Charles' shoulder, Kat saw Ryker running with amazing grace and speed down the lane to meet them. He was waving one arm high over his head to attract their attention. There wasn't time to say what she wanted to, so she kept it short and to the point.

"You're a damn fool, Charles Goodman," she said as Ryker jogged to a halt beside them. "You are the Alpha of Wolf's Head pack. If the others don't see that, then they're damn fools, too. I'm new to this Alpha's Mate business and even I know the difference. Now, do I have to kiss him to prove it?"

She pointed her thumb at Ryker who stepped back with his hands, palms outward, in front of his chest to ward her off. His usual stone cold face cracked enough to show his surprise. He looked to his Alpha.

"What the hell?" he asked as if someone here had lost their mind.

"She wants to see if kissing you is different from kissing me," Charles explained.

Ryker took another step back. "Sorry, ma'am, but didn't you just say you were an Alpha's Mate?"

"I did," Kat agreed.

"Then if there's any kissing to be done, you should be directing your attentions that way." He pointed to Charles. "Like you said, he's the Alpha."

"See? One down and..." Kat paused. "Just how many are in this pack?"

"Only fifty three."

"Then forty-eight to go. You've got Jo and Hyatt and Mrs. Martin and Buddy. They're definitely in your corner." She meant it as a joke. In her mind, Charles was the Alpha and that was that.

"He's got more than that, ma'am." Ryker seemed to understand what she was talking about only he wasn't smiling.

"How many?" Charles asked, as serious as Ryker.

"Twenty-five if it comes down to it. More if you knock some heads."

"Heads? Whose heads?" Kat was walking between the two and had a crick in her neck from looking up.

"You and I need to talk, Ryker."

"I've been waiting for you to ask."

"I was afraid you might be one of them."

Ryker chuckled and it sounded odd coming from that granite mask. "I could take you in the fight, but I'm not smart enough to run the pack. I'd probably kill half of them. Easier that way."

"He doesn't really mean that, does he?" Kat asked Charles worriedly. The man looked like he could do it without batting an eye.

Charles smiled at her and winked.

The look that Ryker gave her said he'd do it in a heartbeat. Then he ignored her and spoke to Charles. "We make a good showing tonight and you'll probably convince a few more." he said to Charles. "Oh, and Marcus called to say they finally found the cubs. He'll be bringing them in tomorrow. Wanted to know if we had any cages."

Chapter 20

"It's our land. We have every right to drive them off."

"We'd be better off to charge them rent, a percentage of the take. Alex had a good point. They'll only move their business elsewhere."

"It's dog fighting!"

"It's money!"

"You wouldn't say that if it was your pup instead of Buddy."

"We don't have any pups and we have the brains not to get caught. Buddy should never have been allowed to run."

"We've got pups now. I overheard Ryker on the phone."

"Yeah, and who's bright idea was that. I didn't sign on to be a foster parent."

There were a half dozen voices all shouting over the top of one another from the room where the television blared. Ryker moved toward the door, but Charles stopped him with a signal from his hand. Alex was coming down the hallway shaking his head.

"They're only blowing off steam. I'll settle them down."

"No." Charles moved the hand he held up to Ryker and showed it to Alex. "I've let you do enough of my dirty work. It's time I did it myself."

"It's my job. I'm your Second."

"And now it's my job. I'm your Alpha."

"Charles, I don't think this is a good time to…"

"Go all Alpha on you?" Charles finished the sentence for him.

"I've heard those words before, Alex, and I disagree. I can't think of a better time."

He slid the doors to the TV room back and the crowd roared. The roar was from a televised football game, but Kat thought it was appropriate. Ryker followed on his Alpha's heels and once inside, he slid the doors closed behind him and stood in front of them, blocking the exit and the view.

There was some harsh talk, a bit of swearing, but Kat couldn't hear what was said and then she felt that wall expanding power again. There was a crash. The TV went silent. There was another crash, followed by a groan. Kat didn't know why they thought Charles shouldn't go all Alpha. She found it pretty impressive. She bent in half to see if she could see past Ryker's big body and wondered if she could ask him to move.

There were more thuds. Kat knew what those sounds were. She'd worked in enough low life bars to recognize the sounds of body blows. She bobbed and weaved herself, trying to get a better view. There were two of them getting a pounding, maybe three.

"Don't just stand there, Ryker. Back him up," she muttered. "Ooo, good one, Big Bad!"

Alex sniffed at the nickname. "This is your fault," he accused.

"Yeah, yeah, sure. Like I told him to go in there and start a brawl." Kat stood and made a display of wiping imaginary dust off her hands. "It's all over but the mopping up."

"This isn't any way to run a business." Alex scowl was centered on Kat.

"Probably not, but this isn't about Wolf's Head Enterprises. This is about pack." Kat stared at the handsome man for a moment. "What do you have against me?"

"Nothing, Ms. Bennett, nothing at all. I'm sure you're a fine young woman and an excellent teacher."

Alex didn't look her in the eye, hadn't looked her in the eye since he arrived, not even when he'd shaken her hand to say hello. He spoke to the air over her right shoulder, just like he did when they first met, just like he did at meals or when they passed in the halls. She'd seen this behavior when she was a kid living in the old neighborhood. There were some people with whom you never made eye contact.

She remembered reading that animals were often the same way. Direct eye contact could be interpreted as a challenge for dominance. How much of the animal was in these wolvers? Surely Alex couldn't see her as a threat?

"Why are you afraid of me, Alex?" she asked quietly and sure enough, he looked surprised at her question, but he didn't look at her.

"Afraid? No, Ms. Bennett, I'm not afraid of you. If I'm afraid, it's for you, not of you. You've been placed in an unfortunate position here and I'm afraid you'll find nothing but heartache in the end."

Alex did look at her then and what flashed through his eyes wasn't fear, but a challenge. It startled her.

"Your presence will precipitate a battle that need not be fought," he said, answering her unspoken question. "And in the end, it will destroy this pack. Charles will be forced to make choices he is not equipped to make."

"If you have so little confidence in his abilities as your Alpha, then why do you stay? Why do you serve as his Second?" she asked.

"As you said yourself, Ms. Bennett, it's about the pack. This pack is mine. I was there at its inception and I will see it preserved."

"What is it you want to preserve, Alex? How will it be destroyed? I only want to see Charles happy and I think I can do that for him. None of what's going on has anything to do with me. This all started long before I arrived."

"And except for your arrival, this all, as you put it, would have resolved itself. It can still resolve itself and I am determined to make that happen. It would be best for all concerned, Katarina, if you left now. Then all you would suffer is a broken heart and our Alpha would remain intact."

"Your Alpha will remain intact whether I stay or go. I'll go when my contract is up or when the Alpha tells me to and not a moment before." She heard the doors behind her slide open. "And just for the record, Alex, the name's Kat, K–A–T. I may not run with the big dogs, but I still have claws."

Alex nodded as if to an opponent, which Kat supposed she was, and turned to the opening doors.

Kat silently cursed herself. While engaged in her mini-battle with Alex, she'd missed her opportunity to eavesdrop on what was said behind the closed doors. She noted happily, however, that Charles was looking none the worse for wear and except for a slight bruise on his right cheek, he'd come through the brawl unscathed.

Two of the young men following him with their heads lowered were not so fortunate. They were both bruised and battered and they would both be in the market for new shirts. A third emerged with his head held high and a proud grin on his face, though he looked little better than his peers. This was Tanner and he gave Kat a wink when he caught her eye.

Three more, all untouched, followed and Kat thought maybe she should start a list of names to keep track of yeses, noes and maybes. She really had to learn some names. She couldn't keep thinking of them in terms like Naked and Speedo.

"Charles, we really need to discuss this," Alex said and his disapproval was clear.

"Damn right we do," Charles snarled. "My office."

Kat did a mental happy dance and smiled her approval at Charles. He said something to Ryker that Kat didn't catch and then he kissed her cheek and gave her arm a quick squeeze. Power still rippled the air around him and she got the impression his show of affection was more a statement to the others than for her.

"Jo! Hyatt! My office. Now!" Charles shouted and he pointed to Tanner. "Go find Rawley. Check the barn. He said he was going to work on the truck. I want you two in on this, too."

"Sure thing, Alpha!" Tanner looked like he'd won the lottery.

*****

They were in the Alpha's Office for most of the afternoon and while Kat was tempted to spend the time with her ear to the door, she knew Charles would tell her what she needed to know later when they were alone. Besides, there were too many people milling about for her not to get caught.

She did, however, make note of those who lingered in the hall, writing their description when she couldn't remember the name and adding a frowny or smiley face depending on their reactions as they slowly passed by the office door. Damn them! Their hearing was so much better than hers.

In between snooping on the snoopers, she readied her classroom for her student's arrival. She finally had names, ages and sexes and once she wrote them down, her fuzzy memory began to clear and what she'd been told by Eugene Begley started to return. Knowing what she did now, she wondered if Mr. Begley's powers of persuasion weren't some kind of Wolver hoo-doo, akin to Charles' power, but in no way as potent.

There was no doubt she would have her hands full with her five students, none of whom were proficient for their ages in reading or math. There were three boys ages fifteen, ten and nine and two girls, the older being thirteen and the younger, a tender four year old. They had all suffered the most horrible neglect, most likely from birth if one could judge by their names.

The oldest boy, River, was named for the place of his birth

on the bank of an unknown river, the girls, Forest and Meadow, followed suit. The other boys were named for the pickup trucks in which they were born, Ranger and Dakota. At least the names weren't awful and Kat shuddered to think what names they might have been forced to carry if they'd been born in an alley or the back room of a bar.

No one knew their exact dates of birth or last names, only that they'd been found on land belonging to the Wolf's Head Pack after a band of rogues had been run off by Charles' brother Marshall. By pack law, they were Wolf's Head's responsibility and therefore Charles' as Alpha.

He'd funded the renovation of a small, former school building about two miles from the house where the children could live and learn, but Kat was convinced they would be better served with some semblance of family life here in Hell Hall.

Around the dinner table that evening, she was gratified to learn that most of the women agreed with her. The first to speak up was one of Stephanie's cohorts.

"They need to learn what a real pack looks like," Rhonda told the men. "How else will they form the bonds they'll need in the future. They've grown up rogue. That's no way to live."

"If Marcus isn't joking about cages," Becky added, "They must be pretty wild. They need a strong hand and some tough male guidance and they'll get more of that here than isolated with Kat. No offense," she added, smiling at Kat.

"I don't think he was joking," Ryker muttered.

Kat chose to ignore the Security Chief's remark. "None taken," she smiled back at Becky, "But if living rogue is what they know, I think they're going to need loving kindness first. They need to see that life isn't all harsh and cold."

"I think Kat's right," redheaded Becky added with a wink at Rawley. "I think it will be good for us all to have a few kids around and I'm sure they'll be glad to be here rather than where they were. It must have been awful to be left alone like that. Good food, warm beds and a gentle touch will bring them around faster than cages."

"A wolver cub needs to know they'll get their head cracked if they don't fly right," Jo said bluntly.

Kat thought the woman would be on her side and was surprised when she wasn't.

"If you ask me, these kids would be better off being locked down for a time, brought back to health and trained physically before you inflict them on the rest of us."

"Then it's a good thing no one asked you," her brother interrupted. "Fortunately, our Kat has a heart, unlike you who misplaced yours when you were twelve."

"I haven't misplaced it. I just don't let it rule my head or in your case..." Jo paused and grinned when Charles cleared his throat "...all right, message understood, we're at the table." She turned back to Kat. "You're thinking in terms of children. These are cubs. They'll be dirty and sticky and snarly."

"In other words, like human kids who've been neglected and allowed to run wild," Kat laughed and turned to Charles. "Well?"

He raised his hands to fend her off. "Don't look at me. This is your area of expertise. You were hired to do the job and I expect, one way or another, you'll get it done. It might be best, however, to reserve judgment until after we've met the little critters. Don't go..."

"Borrowing trouble where there is none," Buddy finished for him. The yardman was clearing the table of empty plates and loading them onto a tray for his mother.

"I don't think your Alpha needs the advice of a..." Alex began.

"Hired hand? Maybe, maybe not, but I can always use the advice of a trusted friend and Buddy has been my friend since I was in diapers." Charles nodded and winked at the man who beamed in return.

Kat silently cheered and saw Jo suck in her cheeks to stifle a laugh. Score one for Buddy and oh, too bad, none for Alex.

"Best friend," Buddy agreed, "Not BFFs, though. That's for girls." He piled a few more plates on the tray. "You going hunting tonight?" he asked hopefully.

"We are, Buddy, but it's not the kind of hunting where I can take you. I do have a job for you. I need a man I can trust."

"I can do it," Buddy said solemnly. "You can always trust me."

"I know I can and that's why I'm going to give you another chance to go over the moon."

It was Ryker who interrupted him this time. "Alpha, are you sure?"

"Absolutely. Leave the dishes there a minute, Buddy. I want you here, looking at me." Charles stood and waited for the man to come to him. "I need someone to patrol the grounds to protect Kat and your Mama and the other women. I need you to watch and listen and smell. If you see or hear or smell anyone who doesn't belong, you get Kat or your Mama. Don't wait until you see who it is. You hear me? You come straight to the house."

"I can do that," Buddy said after each sentence, "I can do that."

"Alpha?" Mrs. Martin stood in the doorway, looking terrified.

Kat couldn't blame her after what had happened the last time, but Charles was aware of that, too.

"Trust your Alpha," was all Kat said.

Tilda stared at her for a moment and then went to Buddy's full tray. "I'll just clear this away," she said.

Charles ignored the exchange, but Kat felt his power raise up just a notch. "This is the most important thing I've ever asked you to do, Buddy. I ask it because you are my best friend and because I am your Alpha. You have to ignore the call of the wild and obey me, your Alpha. It's a rule. The most important rule.

You must always obey your Alpha."

"I can do it, Alpha. I can do it."

And Kat was confident that Buddy would.

Chapter 21

The men were going on a hunt and their prey were the men who operated the dog fights that were taking place in an abandoned building on Wolf's Head land.

"Is it going to be dangerous?" Kat asked when they were alone in their room after dinner. "Isn't there another way? A safer way?" These were the questions she would have asked earlier, but she refused to publicly cast doubt on the Alpha's decision.

"You sound like Alex," Charles complained. "Of course there's another way, but charging them rent is not an option and it's likely they're already paying off the authorities to look the other way. I know these people, Katarina, maybe not as individuals, but I know their kind. My father had to deal with them. My brother, Marshall, has had to deal with them. A show of force is what they understand. Anything less is seen as a weakness. They'll think they've won."

"Will they have guns? You can't go up against guns, Charles."

He laughed at that. "Just because I live in a highly secured high-rise in a low crime area of the city, doesn't mean I'm unaware of the evils that lurk in the woods. I grew up here, remember? You don't run an outfit like that with that much money floating around and not be armed. So are we. We'll run as wolves, but we'll fight as men. They won't know we're there until we're on top of them. We'll run them off, take the place apart, and take care of the animals."

"What will you do with them?" Realistically, Kat knew that some of those dogs would be beyond saving, but it was hard to envision a mass slaughter. They didn't deserve that.

"I called my brother. He knows someone who knows someone who'll quietly move in when we've done our job. The Rabbit Creek pack has members working all over this mountain."

"Someday Wolf's Head will, too. You'll see to it." He'd thought of everything as she should have known he would.

"You are so good for me, kitten." He drew her in and kissed her forehead. "Your belief in me makes me believe I can do anything."

"Don't let it go to your head. I believe in Santa Claus and the Easter Bunny, too," she laughed, lifting her chin so he could transfer his kiss to her lips. "Go get 'em, Big Bad. Go show those little pigs who's boss Alpha around here."

"Wait up for me?"

"Like I could sleep while you guys are out there playing with firearms. Are you sure they all know what end the bullet comes out of?"

Wolf on wolf, she was sure of their competence. She'd heard some of the stories about their forays into the wild. But guns? When these guys said shoot from the hip, they were talking business tactics and their OK Corral was a board room.

"Don't be fooled by the Brooks Brothers suits and Italian loafers. Most of these guys grew up like I did. Don't forget, most packs live close to the wild. Riker's trained them well. They know how to work as a fighting unit inside the boardroom and out. There's nothing to worry about. They'll be fine."

*****

Kat watched them go. She was alone on the patio when the men went over the moon. This time there was very little horseplay and they were all dressed in dark jeans and black cotton T-shirts. She'd wondered how they would transport the guns, but the problem was easily solved with leather satchels whose straps could be looped over the neck once the change to wolf was made.

She watched as they changed, no less fascinated than she'd been the night before and wondered where Jo was and why she wasn't watching, too. The other women had opted to stay indoors. The forecast promised more rain and a light mist was already beginning to fall.

When the bright light faded and the beasts departed, Kat stayed where she was. A lone white wolf came out of the mist running toward her at full tilt. He skid to a stop just inches from her feet and barked at her insistently. She wanted to laugh, but didn't.

"Alright, Buddy, I get the message. I'm going in, but I want you to stop by the kitchen windows every time you make a pass. I'll be watching out for you just like you're watching out for me. Okay?"

The animal snorted and nodded his head. He understood.

"Don't forget. The Alpha is counting on you and so am I."

Charles didn't believe there was any danger, but he wanted Buddy to feel like he was part of the pack. If Buddy believed he had an important role to play, he would be less likely to follow the call of the wild. It was a matter of trust and they all had to trust that their Alpha was right.

For the next few hours, Kat waited and watched. For a while, Tilda waited with her. Just as Charles predicted, Buddy kept his promise and circled the grounds as he had been shown and stopped by the windows with each pass.

"He'll be fine," Tilda said as if Kat was the one who doubted it. "I expect they'll be out until the wee hours. They can afford to sleep late. I can't. House this big, I can't afford to let the work get ahead of me."

"You need to talk to the Alpha, Tilda," Kat told her. "With all these people, this job is too much for one person."

"It won't be forever. They'll all be heading back to the city soon." Tilda yawned and rolled her shoulders. "With just you and the cubs, I'll get my rest."

Kat snorted a laugh. "Sure, because taking care of eight people is no big deal, right?"

Inside, she wasn't laughing. What Tilda said made perfect sense. The others would be leaving soon. They had jobs to go to, work to do. She said an absentminded good night to Tilda, her thoughts on the future.

They'd been playing house here at Hell Hall and she had allowed the fantasy of it all to hide the truth. This wasn't a fairytale, in spite of the fantastical beings she'd discovered. Charles would be leaving for the city soon and leaving her behind. How long would he be gone? How often would he visit and when he did, how long would he stay? How long before he forgot to come visit her at all?

"Stop it!" Kat said the words aloud and looked at the old schoolhouse clock that hung on the kitchen wall. Ten minutes! She leaned over the sink to get a wider view of the yard. There was no sign of Buddy. Had he passed by while she was busy holding her private pity party? Or had he missed his check-in?

She grabbed a jacket from the row of hooks by the back door and ran out onto the patio, calling the white wolf's name. "Buddy! Buddy, where are you?"

She ran to the edge of the field, the perimeter of the area around the house where Buddy was to patrol. He couldn't have gone that far in such a short time. Buddy travelled in a clockwise pattern, stopping at the spot where his circuit began and trotting to the house to prance by the kitchen windows before returning to the point of origin to begin the trek again.

"Buddy! Buddy!" If Buddy had felt the call and answered it, he could be anywhere and might take hours to find. Or, God forbid, they might not find him at all. There were miles and miles of forest on this mountain. Buddy could run forever and never be found.

Calm down, she told herself. It was only a few minutes. Even if he was running wild, he couldn't have gone that far. She thought about going back to the house to get Tilda and the others, but decided to follow Buddy's route instead. If she could find him, maybe she could lure him back to his assigned task and no one need be the wiser. If they were caught, Buddy would never be allowed to run again.

Slowly, her eyes adjusted to the dark. Following Buddy's route counterclockwise, Kat trotted along, scanning to either side and hoped to run into him as he completed his rounds.

It was full dark, darker still because of the cloud cover and misty rain. The silence set her teeth on edge. Like those gothic novels she read as a girl, the dark and the silence brought a portent of evil.

"Don't go down those dark stairs alone with only a candle to light your way!" Those words could easily be translated into something more apt. "Don't go wandering along the edge of the dark woods without any light at all." Nothing good ever came of either one of those scenarios.

Where the lane curved around the barn, a flash of white caught Kat's attention, so quick and faint, she thought it must be her imagination. Then it happened again.

Buddy was running back and forth in a frenzy as if he was caught behind some kind of invisible fence within the trees. He ran back a few feet and then forward to a line imperceptible to Kat, but very real to him. He suddenly changed his direction and ran along the unseen fence for a couple of yards and then turned back.

Kat watched, mesmerized by the white wolf's strange behavior. She thought at first he might be tied, but there was no telltale jerk of his head when he reached the end of his tether. She stood, stock still, in the shelter of the trees and watched and finally saw what held the wolf. It wasn't a fence or tether, but two dark shadows, quietly working in tandem to drive him back.

She saw the flash of vicious looking fangs as one snapped at his panicked face. The other lunged at his side. The wolves weren't attacking. They were confining him, preventing him from moving forward to... to what?

These wolves weren't part of Charles' pack. He would never send someone to test Buddy's strength of will and certainly not to torment him this way. These wolvers, and she was sure that's what they were, had a mission and suddenly she knew what it was. They were there to prevent Buddy from alerting the house to their presence. No, not their presence, someone else's. Someone who was heading for the house.

The other women were back at the house alone, asleep and vulnerable. If someone wanted to harm them, they would have no warning and no defense. She should go back to the house and alert them, but she didn't know where the intruder was. He would be a wolver, too, and as man or beast, he'd be faster and stronger than her.

Buddy, on the other hand, was fast and strong, too. If she could distract one, he might be able to outrun the other.

She reached around with her foot until she found a branch that was long enough and felt sturdy. There was no time to strip it down to create a pole and it would make too much noise. Hefting the branch, she ran toward the wolves shouting.

"Run! Call the Alpha, Buddy. Run!" She took a deep breath, charged the nearest wolf and screamed.

The scream was high and loud and it echoed through the night and drew the attention momentarily away from Buddy.

"Run! Call Charles! Buddy, run! Ooooph." The branch made contact with the wolf. It yelped, snarled and snapped at the branch, breaking off the ends with his teeth and lunging body. A fork in the branch was the only thing that saved Kat from the lunge that followed.

"Char-r-r-les!"

The name turned into another scream, this one unplanned, but just as loud and piercing. Kat swung the branch in an arch, her only protection against the wolf. This was as far as her plan went. It was up to Buddy now.

A frightened howl tore through the night. That was Buddy. She was sure of it. Her heart soared at the sound and then sank in misery when the howl became a scream of pain and then abruptly cut off. Sorrow filled her, but she didn't let herself cry. She hadn't sent Buddy for help. She'd sent him to his death.

The wolf snarled and grabbed the branch that she'd begun to lower in her defeat. His jaws slowly crunched down on one thick length of the fork and the wood splintered under the crushing force. It was a threat, a warning of what he could do. The animal's eyes never left Kat's face.

Across the yard, two upright shadows ran toward them. The wolf's ears flickered at the sound of their boots clumping across the ground. His eyes, however, never strayed from Kat's face and she knew he recognized the runners.

Kat also saw what the wolf and men did not. Two long dark shadows slinked along in their wake. She shoved the branch at the wolf with renewed effort.

"Bastard! Bastard! Bastard!" she screamed to keep attention on her and not on the shadows.

"Shut her up!" one of the runners hissed. They slowed to a trot.

"At least we got somethin' out of this," the other one laughed and Kat recognized the voice. "And I owe this one, big time." It was one of the men who'd trapped Buddy.

Both men's heads turned in the direction of an approaching

wolf running at full speed from the field behind the barn. It yipped and snarled and barked as it ran. Kat thought it was the second wolf, but the one guarding her snarled and turned to face the newcomer as if he was the enemy.

Kat took advantage of his neglect to attack with what was left of her branch. She stabbed at the wolf's side, but the wolf's body spun with her thrust and her failed blow only served to draw his attention back to her. His snarling jaws grabbed the useless branch and wrenched it from her grasp.

The next few moments were a blur of flesh and fur. One of the men drew a gun from his waist. Kat screamed. The two slinking shapes sprang into the forms of leaping wolves. The running wolf leapt with no decrease in speed, driving the enemy wolf into Kat who was rolled to her back in a torrent of snarling fur.

Pain lanced through her head as they rolled over her, driving the breath from her lungs and when she was finally free of their crushing weight, she curled herself into a ball, her mouth opened in another scream that had no air to fuel it.

The screams tearing through the night weren't hers. Something wet and sticky spattered her face and she clamped her mouth shut, covered her ears with her hands and closed her eyes in an attempt to shut out the mayhem surrounding her.

Chapter 22

Her eyes were still closed, but her hands were no longer covering her ears. Her knees were no longer curled into her chest. She was flat on her back and the ground beneath her was no longer hard and damp. She was, however, still wet and cold and when she finally managed to open her eyes, it was to find a mouth full of white teeth grinning into them. It was a full ten seconds before she realized the battle was over and done and the teeth were no longer sharp and pointed, but even and flat. The teeth were surrounded by pale lips in a paler face with sparkling eyes.

"Buddy?" Kat whispered.

He was alive and whole and happy.

"There. What did I say? She's fine. Had a bit of a bump is all."

Mrs. Martin was standing over them, wrapped in an old flannel robe. It took Kat a moment to figure out that her eyes were fine and the housekeeper's misshapen head was the result of curlers.

"Were you scared, Kitty Kat? Mama said you was scared, but you didn't look scared to me. You looked like one of them lion tamers at the circus, 'cept he weren't no lion and you got no chair." Buddy laughed and then frowned. "But then you curled into a ball and wouldn't wake up and Charlie had to carry you home."

"Charles? Where is he?" She sat up on the sofa, swung her legs to the floor and grabbed Buddy's hand until the wave of dizziness passed.

"The Alpha says you're to stay right where you are. He'll be back," Tilda said firmly. She wrapped a fleece throw around Kat's shoulders. "He's busy with Jo. The fool girl got herself tore up some, but he's taking care of it. She'll be fine and he'll be back down to take care of you."

"Jo? What happened to Jo? Did they get in the house? Is everyone else okay?" Oh, God, what had she missed?

"Everyone's fine," Tilda assured her. "Or they will be. The Alpha took her over the moon and set her to watch same as Buddy, but he kept that to himself. She wasn't to do naught but sound the alarm if someone should come snooping around."

"You sent me runnin' to Charlie," Buddy took over. "I was scared, but I was runnin'. Trouble was, that mean old wolf was runnin', too. He almost got me, but Jo, she come flyin' out of nowhere and wham!" Buddy clapped his hands together so suddenly, Kat jumped and a whoosh of pain expanded in her head. "Knocked him clean over. I kept runnin' and I called, just like you told me to do. I howled my heart out."

"I heard you, Buddy. I heard you. You were wonderful."

"Charlie, I mean the Alpha, he heard me, too. He was in my head and I knew he was a-coming." Buddy patted the side of his white head. "In here. I knew it plain as day." Buddy was silent for a moment and then he spoke to the floor. "Charlie told me what to do, but I didn't do it. He told me to call and then lay low, hide until he came, but I didn't. That mean old wolf had Jo and he was hurting her bad. He had his teeth in her just a-shakin' and a-tearin' at her."

Buddy raised his head and his finger and Kat knew there was another rule coming.

"Boy wolvers are bigger and stronger than girls and you ain't never supposed to hurt a girl. He made her cry, Mama," he said as if that would explain everything.

And it did. Tilda stroked her son's head. "You did good, son. I'm right proud of you."

"Finish it, Buddy! What did you do?" Kat wanted to hear the rest.

"It made me mad, so I ran back and I whupped him. I whupped him good." Honest to a fault, he added, "Jo helped. We whupped him together and he ain't gonna hurt no one no more."

"Oh Buddy, you're a hero." Kat gave him a quick kiss on the cheek and his pale pink face turned red.

"No ma'am, that was Jo," he said, "She was bleeding bad and I wanted to hide, but she made me follow her and we snuck up on those two men. They were going to hurt you, Miss Kitty Kat. We jumped on them and then Charlie came running in and then Tanner and Rawley and it was a big ole mess and Jo was just lying there all bloody and you wouldn't wake up and Mama came running and then I was really scared, but Mama said the Alpha would make it all right." Buddy grinned. "And he did."

"Well, you're my hero, Buddy, and so is Jo." She looked around. "Where are the others? How long have I been here?"

"Some's upstairs, some's across the way waiting on the Alpha, and some's cleaning up in the kitchen and the bathrooms. They came back as he was carrying you here. That man's going to be wore out with all the fighting and coming and going and now the healing. You've only been out but a few minutes." Tilda glanced over her shoulder at the murmuring from beyond the door. "I need to get back to the kitchen. They're not likely to sleep and after a night like tonight, they'll want to be fed."

"I can help," Kat volunteered and this time rose with only a wince. If she held her head straight and steady, it hardly hurt at all.

Tilda hesitated. "I don't know, the Alpha, he's..."

"Busy and tired and has more to worry about than me helping you make sandwiches. God," Kat started to shake her head and thought better of it, "I can't believe I did that, Tilda. I have never, ever fainted in my entire life."

"It happens," Tilda said, smiling cryptically and then immediately reverted to her role as housekeeper. "There's ham, roast beef, chicken salad and half a dozen cheeses. We ought to be able to put something together out of that. We'll lay it out on the kitchen counter and while they're busy chowing down, I'll get that front hall mopped up." Mrs. Martin shook her finger at no one in particular. "There's got to be some changes around here, I'll tell you that. Half of them came in shaking their wet coats and padding about with their muddy paws as if nobody ever taught them no manners." She was still grumbling to herself as she headed down the hall. "Hmph. Acting no better than untrained dogs. From now on, they want fed, they'll do they're changing before they come into the house and they'll use the back door."

"Mama tends to get grumpy if you don't wipe your feet," Buddy explained helpfully. He put his finger in the air in the gesture Kat now realized he learned from his mother. "Just because you was born a beast don't mean you can't act like a civilized human being."

"She's got a point," Kat laughed and then winced and rubbed the back of her head where the pain was centered. "We'd better go help before we're in the doghouse, too."

They were halfway down the hall before Buddy laughed. "Doghouse! That was a good one, Kitty Kat."

*****

Kat carried a tray loaded with sandwiches and beer upstairs. The others were congregated in the kitchen arguing about the night's events. Charles, Ryker and Hyatt were still with Jo. Kat tapped softly on the door with the toe of her shoe and eased past Hyatt when he opened and held the door. Ryker, strong, stone cold Ryker, lay on the bed, his long muscular body molded to Jo's tucked beneath the covers. One arm cradled her head and the other was wrapped protectively around her.

Charles sat, slumped in the chair by the window, his head held in his hands. He looked up at her entrance and then back down.

Kat had seen what the healing magic cost him in energy and each time he shifted it cost him more. The man must be exhausted.

She placed her tray on the nightstand and nodded to Ryker, who hadn't moved but watched her with narrowed and focused eyes. Jo's face was pale and she didn't open her eyes.

"How is she?" Kat asked Ryker in a whisper.

"She'll live," Jo said through barely moving lips. "Can you all just go away now?"

"Sure, honey. Sorry," Kat apologized.

Ryker started to rise.

"Not you," Jo mumbled, "You get your warm ass right back where it was."

"That wasn't my ass," Ryker deadpanned, settling back down.

"I know and if these people would leave I have other places that need to be warmed by the part that's not your ass." Jo opened one eye. "Go away," she said to the others.

Hyatt looked worriedly from his sister to Kat. "I don't think..."

"That's right, Hyatt. You don't think. Otherwise you'd be thinking I'm about to throw your ass out of here," Ryker growled. "Now go and take him with you." He pointed his chin at Charles.

It was obvious that Jo was fine and didn't need anyone but Ryker. It was kind of sweet and Kat looked to Charles to share a smile.

He didn't look up. His head was still bowed and now she

noticed the tremor in his hands as they gripped the sides of his head.

"Charles?" Kat went to her knees in front of him. This was more than exhaustion. "The others are in the kitchen, Hyatt. I'll take care of the Alpha."

Thankfully, Hyatt didn't argue.

She laid her hand on Charles' knee and he finally looked up. His eyes, always so bright and glittering with fire, were dull, a green so dark they were almost black. They were filled with a painful knowledge she hadn't seen in them before.

"Do you need...?" Ryker started to rise.

"No! We're fine." She didn't mean to snap, but she didn't apologize. Whatever was wrong, she knew Charles didn't want it shared.

"He's tired is all."

She maneuvered her shoulder under his arm and he rose with her. His weight almost buckled her knees, but somehow she managed to get him out of one bedroom and into the next. She eased him onto the bed where he resumed his position of hands gripping head.

"Oh God," he moaned, "Make it stop. Make it stop. They're all in my head."

"Who's in your head?" She'd no sooner asked than the answer dawned and she understood.

There was no question now as to who was the rightful Alpha of the Wolf's Head Pack. The mantle had fallen on Charles' shoulders and it had fallen hard.

As gently as possible she undressed him and forced him to lie down under the covers. Then she undressed and climbed in beside him and held him and rocked him and stroked his hair and offered what comfort she could, her own headache ignored and forgotten.

She heard the others pass their door on their way to their

rooms and finally, with the house silent and asleep, Charles slept, too.

Kat tried to sleep as well, but her dreams were haunted by the dark green eyes so filled with pain and it was as if she could feel it, too. Was it only his pain, the pain of the adjustment to the terrible weight he now carried? Or was it the pain of his pack, unsettled and unhappy with his leadership?

Chapter 23

Kat awoke to the faint light of daybreak, the lump on her head a mere sore spot, her headache gone and Charles sleeping peacefully beside her. She stretched a bit, carefully so as not to awaken Charles and snuggled back under the covers. They'd had a long night and there was no reason not to catch a few hours more sleep. Then she remembered. The children were coming today!

There was so much to do. Bedrooms would need to be rearranged. She wanted the children settled and quickly, no shifting of bedrooms from here to there as the adults moved out. This was to be their home and she wanted them to see they were planned for and wanted. These children would need more than a teacher. They needed someone to love them as well.

They would no doubt feel lost and alone and frightened just as she'd felt when her father left her with a grandmother she barely knew. Grams' hugs and kisses had meant a lot to that nine year old girl. Poor as she was, she'd made sure Kat had a bed with a new and pretty pink coverlet to welcome her into her new home and that small gesture had made Kat feel wanted and welcome.

She carefully rolled to her side to slip from the bed, but Charles rolled with her and captured her waist, hauling her back, nuzzling her neck and hair.

"Go back to sleep," she whispered. "It's early and you need your rest. You've had a rough time of it. I'll send Buddy up with some breakfast later. You'll be starving after last night." She started to pull away and Charles tightened his grip. "Come on, Big Bad, I don't have time. The children will be here soon and they'll need me," she said quietly and tried again to pull away.

"I need you," he grumbled, pulling her closer. The hand at her waist began to roam. "Last night I thought I couldn't survive it, the crushing weight of it. That's what happens to an alpha who's not strong enough to carry it, you know, and I wasn't meant to carry it. My father knew that."

Kat relaxed back onto the bed and stared at the ceiling. They suffered from the same thing, she and Charles. She'd spent her whole life wondering why she wasn't good enough for her father's love. Why couldn't he stop drinking for Kat as he had for her mother? She remembered their quiet conversations. It was part of the code she hadn't been able to break as a child.

"You can do this, John. One day at a time," her mother would whisper when her father was in one of his sad and miserable moods. "Do this for me. One day at a time. I believe in you, darling."

John Bennett would cling to his wife like a drowning man. "I'd be lost without you, sweetheart," he'd say to her. "You are the Master of my fate, the Captain of my soul. You keep my sails to the wind. You light my way. You keep me from floundering in the shoals."

Her father always was one for flowery speech. Kat didn't understand what the words meant until she was much older and once she did, she worked hard had to create the life she thought her parents had, believing that someday, maybe, her father would come home.

Charles had spent his life afraid of not living up to his father's expectations. He was incapable of being the Alpha his father wanted him to be.

Who were these men who continued to rule their lives; one

from the bottom of a bottle, one from the bottom of a grave? She was tired of it and it was time to put an end to it.

"Your father was a goddamned ass. Welcome to the club," she whispered fiercely.

Charles chuckled softly at her ferocity. "He wasn't, you know. He was a great Alpha. My brother Marshall..."

"Is nothing like him either," she snapped though her voice never rose above a whisper. She rolled in his arms until they were nose to nose and placed her hand on his cheek. "Your father stuck to the old ways. He couldn't change and his pack suffered for it. He's probably rolling over in his grave at what Marshall has done to his precious domain. You told me that yourself. Marshall wanted to keep the old and found ways to take it in a new direction. You want new and modern, but need to blend in the old ways necessary for your pack's survival. Two different roads leading to the same destination; what's best for the pack, your pack, not your father's. Wes Goodman wanted to create a mini-me. Well tough shit, he didn't get one. What Wolf's Head got is something a whole helluva lot better. They got you, Charles Goodman, and you're going to be the best damn Alpha the Wolver world has ever seen." Kat punched his shoulder for emphasis.

"Hey! Shhh, don't cry." Charles ran his thumb over her cheek.

"I'm not crying," she protested even as he kissed the tears from the corners of her eyes.

"Good," he said between kisses, "Because I'd like to finish what I started to say about last night." He rolled her over him and into the middle of the bed where he straddled her hips to keep her in place and rested his weight on his elbows to either side of her head. He toyed with her short, unruly curls while he spoke.

"I was being crushed under the weight of it all and then you touched me. You held me and I felt your touch run through me. Not like this," he said, chuckling as one of his hands left her curls to roam over her breasts and down the center of her body to her mound, leaving behind its trail of magic. The chuckle turned into a laugh when, without thinking, Kat inched her body up until his hand was firmly between her legs.

"This is good," he told her as his fingers danced and played in a new nest of curls, "But what I felt last night through your touch was different. For the first time since I was a pup, I felt like I wasn't alone. I didn't have to pretend to be someone I wasn't or to guess what a real Alpha would do. I felt your belief in me. It was your touch that gave me the strength to bear the mantle. I am the Alpha of Wolf's Head Pack."

"I never doubted it, but" Kat whispered against his lips as she moved against his fingers down below, "For now, can you just be my Big Bad Wolf?"

Charles cocked his head to the side for a moment, listening, frowned in concentration and then brought his attention back to her and smiled.

"With pleasure," he said right before his lips covered hers with a kiss that was filled with the Alpha's magic.

*****

As it turned out, there wasn't that much to do to get ready for the children's arrival. Mrs. Martin, housekeeper extraordinaire, had everything under control and Kat was beginning to suspect there was something magical about her, too. She never seemed to hurry, but never seemed to fall behind. She was grateful for any help she received but didn't seem to need it. When Kat entered the kitchen, the woman was ironing pillow cases, something Kat found extraordinary in itself. Did anyone still iron pillowcases?

"Good morning. Everyone else still in bed?" Kat asked as she poured a cup of coffee, ready with her pad and pencil to make her list of things to do.

"Hmph. Them that's still here," Tilda grumbled. "Mr. High and Mighty took half of them off last night back to the city."

"Alex?" A plate of cinnamon rolls sat on the counter, still warm from the oven. Kat debated for half a second before taking one. Nature walks would be good for the children and for the calories she was sure were settling about her hips.

"None other." Tilda neatly folded the finished case and snapped another straight before placing it on the board. "Said they had a business to run and playtime was over as if what happened last night was a game." If the pillowcase had been alive, she would have killed it the way she was slamming the iron along the board.

"What did happen last night?" Kat never did get the whole of it.

"I thought the Alpha would have told you." Tilda looked at her suspiciously.

"We were... ah... both pretty tired."

"Hmph." Tilda finished the case and set it with the others. "Likely wasn't something he cared to talk about."

"Why?"

"They got their butts whupped, that's why. Guess you already know there was wolvers out there. With humans. I never saw the like, never heard of it before. They knew the pack was coming, waited until the Alpha brought them home so they could act as men and that's when they attacked, both man and wolver. The pack wasn't ready and Ryker tried to hold them together while the Alpha flashed them back, but they panicked and they were lucky no one got killed." She slammed another case onto the board. "And all Mr. Alex Prissy Pants said was what do you expect? You can't put a group of civilized men up against rogues."

Kat suddenly remembered the line of wolves walking along

the edge of the trees on her first night here. Charles had said she was mistaken because he'd known none of his pack had arrived. He hadn't known about the others.

Rogues, Kat knew, were single, mostly male wolvers who had left their packs for various reasons, either by choice or because they had been shunned and called Outcast for some serious offense against the pack. Like many of the outcasts from human society, they formed a criminal element in the wolver world.

While they might band together in smaller groups, they could not form a true pack. They had no Alpha. They could not mate and so their small band couldn't grow except by the addition of more rogues.

Kat wondered, but didn't ask, if anyone had noticed the similarities between a band of rogues and the original Wolf's Head pack.

"Does the Alpha know?"

"I suppose he does." Tilda looked at her meaningfully. "Now."

"You know?" Kat asked.

The slow blink of her eyes and slight nod of her head said she did. "They all know."

Of course. They would. They could feel their Alpha just as he could feel them. They'd all known all along that he wasn't a true Alpha. No wonder he didn't hold their respect. Kat thought again about their resemblance to the rogues. Some of them might not be too happy to learn that the mantle had fallen on Charles' shoulders. Alex, perhaps, most of all.

"Well," Kat said and placed both hands on the table, "they know he's their Alpha now."

"That they do." This time Tilda's nod was decisive. "Rawley and Tanner are upstairs with Buddy moving beds from one room to the other. I've put the three boys in one room and the girls in another. Seeing as how they've been living, I figured they'd want to be close, but there's no call to pack them all in one room. By the time they're finished, I'll have the sheets ready to make up the beds."

"Rawley and Tanner didn't go back to the city?"

"Nope. Them and some of the others refused to go."

"So the lines are drawn then." Kat wondered how many had stayed.

"Maybe, maybe not. Some of them might not understand who's giving the orders now. Seems to me that Alex feller has been given a mite more power than he ought to have. For some, the Alpha's going to have to lay down the law."

Kat thought of yesterday's scuffle. "I'd say he's ready to do that."

"I'd say it's past time he did."

"Past time he did what?" Charles asked coming into the kitchen followed by Ryker and a yawning Jo.

"Lay down the law as the Alpha should," Mrs. Martin stated bluntly and without trying to hide the fact that she was talking about him.

Instead of taking offense, Charles laughed as he poured a mug of coffee and passed it to Ryker who passed it to Jo. "I think you should have been born a male, Mrs. Martin. You would have made one helluva Alpha."

Tilda's firm nod showed her agreement. She unplugged her iron and set it aside and moved the ironing board out of the way. "I've got pork chops and biscuits in the oven. All I've got to do is scramble your eggs."

"Good, because I'm famished." Jo slid onto a stool and rested her head in the hand propped up by the elbow on the island. She still looked tired, but was no longer pale.

"Then why don't you cook the eggs," Ryker suggested.

"Careful, Ryker, you'd be taking your life in your hands,"

Hyatt said from the door. Of them all, he looked the most rested. He was wearing a red plaid flannel shirt and a pair of jeans that both looked like they'd been taken from their packages that morning. "My sister has never cooked a decent meal in her life. It was Mother's one failing as a teacher of domesticity and it broke her heart."

"I can cook," Jo defended herself and laughed. "If it comes in a package with the microwave directions on the back. With a good variety of restaurants, who needs to cook?"

"Have you seen anything that even looks close to an eating establishment around these parts?" her brother asked.

"No, but there will be some. I've seen the plans." Jo stuck her tongue out at Hyatt. "In the meantime, we have the marvelous Mrs. Martin, who's a better cook then dear old Mom ever hoped to be."

The marvelous Mrs. Martin rolled her eyes at the flattery.

Chapter 24

Charles went to his office immediately after breakfast and from the dull roar emanating through the door, it was clear to everyone what he thought of half his Council being sent back to the city without his blessings. He then left with Hyatt to meet with the wolver architect whose design they were using for the new community.

Ryker took the remainder of the men and put them 'through their paces'.

"They are taking them back out tonight," Jo told her as they were making the beds in the children's rooms. She was great with the fitted bottom sheets, but had to be shown how to square the corners of the top ones. "You know, you can actually pay someone to do this for you."

"Take them back out where?" Kat asked as she folded the top of the sheet over the blanket. They looked like they'd been ironed, too.

"To the same place they went last night."

"How? Half the men are gone." If, as Tilda claimed, they were beaten the night before, what could they do with only half the manpower?

"Ryker says he can do more with a few good men, than with an army of halfwits. He says that after getting their asses chewed last night they'll be paying more attention to what he has to say today. Besides, tonight they'll have their Alpha to hold them together."

"Was it really that bad?" Kat straightened the last coverlet, a pretty yellow with a ruffled edge, one of a pair that Mrs. Martin produced from the huge linen closet on the third floor. They were bright and cheery and perfect for the girls.

"According to Ryker, it was a near disaster. They were lucky someone didn't get killed." Jo lowered her voice to a whisper. "We've got a traitor. Someone tipped them off. Charles says this time no one is to know until it's time to go."

"Do they know who it is?"

"No, but they have their suspicions. They knew about those guys months ago when we first started bringing things down here and getting this place ready. Alex, Stephanie, and a few others met with them and Alex paid them off. They never said anything about rogues. There are a lot of illegal businesses down here in these mountains. The Rabbit Creek pack over on the other side has had trouble before, but this side of the mountain is our land now and Alex said there was a more civilized way to take care of the problem."

"Looks like his way didn't work."

Jo lifted her eyebrows and shrugged. "Looks that way doesn't it?" She stood back and admired their handiwork. "Now that we're done with your work, come on downstairs take a look at mine. I'll show you what Wolf's Head Bluff is going to look like in a few years."

Jo led Kat to a small room next to the one Charles used as an office. It had been set up like a makeshift conference room with two long white folding tables pushed together to make one large one and folding chairs all around. From the closet in the corner, Jo withdrew a large tube of rolled paper and several heavier office items to weigh down the corners after the paper was unrolled. Once the paper was spread she stepped back and opened her arms.

"This is Wolf's Head Bluff, a modern community for the

modern wolver."

"Holy shit!"

"Yeah," Jo nodded with a satisfied smile. "This is my baby. We needed an architectural team to pull it all together into a detailed plan, but the basic concept is mine. It can't be done overnight. The whole thing will take years to complete, but what the hell. We'll be around a long time."

It was, as Jo said, a community. Not just a sub-division, but a whole village, with a square surrounded by small businesses and winding lanes dotted with mixed housing that included a small development of condominiums, and both smaller and larger single family homes. Except for the condos, each dwelling came with a good portion of land with plenty of green space in between.

It wasn't, as Jo said, an architectural plan, but an artist's rendition of what that plan could look like. It was an amazing piece of work that covered thousands of acres of land. Kat was speechless for long minutes as she traced her finger along the roads and read the small print under each tiny drawing. Some of the homes already existed.

After giving Kat some time to absorb it all, Jo started pointing out special features.

"There's Hell Hall right there and the school and the clinic. A lot of packs have to make do with a vet for their medical needs. We're not exactly built like our human cousins and visiting a doctor can be risky. Charles is hoping his brother, Mike, might come back to run the clinic. He's a doctor, you know. More and more of our people are getting higher educations and we should be making a place for them within the packs instead of forcing them to work in the human world."

"How many of you are there?" Kat had been thinking in terms of a half dozen packs of fifty to a few hundred members.

"Compared to the human population? Not many, but we're

in the thousands and growing. There are packs all over the world. Some we don't even know about. Look at Rawley. His ancestors sure as hell didn't hail from the Scottish Highlands," she laughed. "We come in all shapes and colors and sizes. You ever hear about the rediscovery of red wolves in Mexico?" Jo raised her eyebrows. "I don't know for sure, but it makes me wonder..."

"How have you been able to keep the secret?" This was amazing, mind boggling.

"In the past, we settled in isolated areas, but the world's a smaller place now and the wilderness is disappearing. Times are changing faster than we have. We have to adapt. We were almost wiped out of this country and not so very long ago. If you kill us in wolf form, that's the way we stay. We have to make sure it doesn't happen again. And someday when our numbers are high enough..."

"You'll have to come out of the woods."

Jo laughed. "I like that. If you'd said out of the closet, I was going to have to rip you up. We're not ashamed of who we are, but we know what can happen. We've seen it before, silver bullets and all."

"Is that true? The legends?"

"Nah. Any old bullet will do." Jo cocked her head. "Your cute little puppies have arrived. Got your rolled up newspaper ready?"

*****

A half hour later, Kat wasn't sure if a rolled up newspaper would do the job. The phrase 'raised by wolves' came to mind, but wolves would have done it better.

First contact was at the dark blue panel truck used to transport the children and Kat was offended on their behalf. Damnit! These were children, not cargo. She was horrified until she saw the condition of the driver, Marcus, who leapt from the driver's seat with surprising agility for a man shaped roughly like a barrel of muscle.

Marcus looked a little beat up and torn. He also looked like he was using the last of his restraint not to kill someone. Ryker, who'd come running with the rest of the men when the van pulled up, sealed his lips, pulled on his earlobe and turned his back, but his shaking shoulders gave his mirth away.

"Next time, you pick the little bastards up," Marcus growled, "See who's laughing then." He used a key to open the side door. "Had to break off the lock heads and handles on the inside, so they couldn't escape. Again. They busted the windows out of the passenger van we had them in."

He slid the door open, reached inside and snatched his arm back. "Goddamnit! The little bastard bit me! Can I get some help over here?"

Ryker and another man moved forward and removed a child of no more than eight or nine who growled and fought like his life depended on it. A third man rushed forward to grab the boy and held him, the boy's arms pinned to his sides with feet kicking the air. Another boy, a little older, followed. This one seemed a little more cooperative or perhaps a little smarter. He calmly allowed his captor to walk him away from the van and then bit the man's hand and took off running.

It would have been comical if he hadn't drawn blood. The boy was fast and almost made the trees before he was caught. This one's vocabulary seemed to be limited to four letter words which he used freely as he was dragged back to the others.

While the boy was chased down, two girls emerged from the van. Not willing to take the chance that she wouldn't run off, too, Tanner grabbed the elder of the two by her upper arm, not cruelly, but firmly. The girl went ramrod straight and wouldn't move.

"Stop it!" Kat ran to the girl who was frozen in terror. She slapped at Tanner's arm. "You're frightening her, you big ox. Come on, sweetie," she said to the girl. "They're big and ugly, but they won't hurt you. I wouldn't let them. Come on, Forest. You'll be safe with me. My name is Miss Kat and I'll be your teacher." She put her arm around the girl's shoulders to lead her to the house.

Forest blinked twice and her eyes focused on Kat. She gave a quick nod and began to move with her. After a few steps and frightened as the girl was, she stopped and turned and reached her hand out toward the van.

"Meadow," she whispered.

"They'll bring her. She'll be all right."

"Damn right she will." Jo, who'd been watching the debacle from a front window, came striding through the door. "Damn fools. More jackass than wolver. You," she pointed at Tanner, "Go tell Charles to get his a-a-... his Alphaness out here. Knock some sense into these idiots."

She marched to the van where Ryker held the fort and stuck her head inside. Words were exchanged and if Kat hadn't already heard a mouthful from the runaway, Ranger, who now seemed quite content with his inactivity, she might have covered poor Forest's ears.

As it was, the girl stared at the open van door as if she expected blood and screams to come pouring out of it.

All that emerged was Jo with the tiny girl called Meadow in tow. The child's thumb was stuck in her mouth like a cork and she looked up at Jo with big blue eyes.

When they came abreast of Kat and Forest, Kat stooped to child eye level to say hello and was greeted by a snarl of blond hair on the back of Meadow's head.

"It's all right, Meadow. No one here is going to hurt you," Kat said to the snarl. "Why don't you come to the kitchen with Forest and me? I'll bet Mrs. Martin has some cookies and milk just waiting for a tea party."

Jo rolled her eyes and mouthed, "Tea party?" She looked down at the child who held her two fingers in an iron grip. "Don't mind her, kid. She means well, but doesn't know sh... shazam about some things. Cookies and milk sound pretty good, though, but not until you wash those hands. What is that? No, wait, don't tell me. I'd rather not know until after I've washed mine."

Two things happened simultaneously as Jo was speaking. Charles and the architect pulled up just as a tall, bone-thin teenaged boy with his hands tied behind his back broke from the van. The boy ran around to the back of the van and into the front of the blue Tahoe. Fortunately, Charles was rolling to a stop and most of the force came from the boy himself. He hit the grill, bounced off and stumbled into the rear doors of the van before he hit the ground.

Charles and Ryker reached the boy at the same time.

"What the hell's going on here?" Charles roared. "Why's this kid tied? Ryker?" and before Ryker could answer, "Marcus!"

Marcus came running, holding the ice pack Mrs. Martin had given him moments before.

Ryker patted the kid down to make sure everything was working.

"Get him out of those things," Charles ordered. "We don't tie up kids. Why Marcus?"

"This is why." Marcus pulled the ice pack away from his face. "And this." He pulled his shirt collar away from his neck. "You want to see the rest? Or would you like to hear about chasing them all over the fucking mountain for four days."

He snarled at the boy and stamped his foot as if about to attack. Hands now free, the boy reacted with an attack of his own. He swung with a full roundhouse punch aimed at Marcus' head. Ryker captured him much as the younger boy had been held, wrapping his arms around the boy's chest in a bear hug although River was much too tall to lift off the ground. He did, however, try to stomp on Ryker's booted foot.

Ryker tightened his grip. "Seems like you're aching to know what it feels like to be crushed by a car. I can help with that."

"Ryker!" Kat screamed the name. What was wrong with these wolvers? She looked to Charles for support and found none.

"River, right? The Chief can make it happen, River," Charles said to the teen.

The place suddenly erupted as the two younger boys exploded into kicks and punches and screams that triggered a new outburst from River.

"Get your goddamned hands off them," he shouted. "Fuckin' bastards! It was my fault. Leave 'em alone."

"Charles!" Kat wrapped her arms around Forest and pulled her into her chest, hiding her from all that was happening around them.

Little Meadow watched it all with the same wide eyes, her thumb plug in place.

"Enough!" Charles roared. "Enough, Damnit!" His power expanded and rolled over them all in a compression of air and all noise and movement stopped. Everything stopped.

"You two." He pointed to the younger boys who were now cowering with their heads lowered. The sandy haired one had fallen to his knees. "You use those feet for anything but walking or those fists for anything but stuffing your faces and you're going to feel mine. Are we clear?"

The dark haired one gave him a look that could kill, but gave him a sharp nod of his head. The sandy haired was shaking so badly, it was hard to tell if he nodded or not.

Charles turned back to River, still locked in Ryker's embrace. "You're right. I hold you responsible." He raised his voice. "So if the rest of you want him to suffer for your screw-ups, go right ahead. No fur off my tail."

Kat couldn't believe what she was hearing. These were children. Wild, yes, but children nonetheless. He was threatening them with bodily harm. She and Charles were going to have to talk about this when they had some time alone.

"All of you go into the kitchen and get yourself something to eat. Now!" he shouted when no one moved. He turned his back on them all and went back to the Tahoe in which the architect had wisely remained.

Jo looked down at her tiny charge and saw the dark shadow on the ground at her feet. "Well, shit," she muttered.

"Nope. I'm pretty sure that's pee," Ryker snickered as he marched by with River in tow.

Poor Meadow had wet herself. It was the only sign of the little girl's fear.

Chapter 25

"Get out of my kitchen. Git now, git!" Mrs. Martin shooed them with her apron like a flock of unruly chickens that had pecked their way through her kitchen door. "The day I can't handle a litter of pups is the day I hang up my apron."

Most of the adults backed away, but Marcus stood his ground. "They'll run," he warned. He folded his arms, prepared to stay. "I've already chased them all over the fucking mountain. I'm not chasing them again."

"You watch your tongue or the only one running is going to be you," she threatened. "Grown man making a little girl wet herself. You ought to be ashamed, you..."

"The Alpha did it! Not me," Marcus complained, sounding very much like a kid himself.

"He wouldn't have had to if you'd done your job proper. Miz Jo, why don't you take your friend into my sitting room and get those wet bottoms off. You can wrap her in that coverlet until this feller here brings her something dry to wear."

As she led Forest to one of the stools that lined one side of the island, Kat wondered if Charles could do anything wrong in the housekeepers eyes.

"Don't be afraid," she whispered to the young teen who hadn't raised her head since the outdoor altercation and moved like an automaton. "No one here will hurt you."

The two younger boys didn't need to be told. On seeing the plate piled high with cookies, they scrambled up onto stools. The sandy haired one reached for the plate.

"Don't you dare," Mrs. Martin warned. "In this house you'll eat off your own plate and none other and not until your face and hands are washed."

The boy looked at River and withdrew his hand only after the teenaged leader gave a slight shake of his head.

Mrs. Martin already had a wet towel in her hand. The dark haired boy drew back as she approached, but she was not to be put off. She raised her index finger. "You don't wash, you don't eat. That's the rule. You may have to eat a peck a dirt before you die, but you don't have to eat it all in one sitting." She looked the boy in the eye. "So what's it going to be?"

After a moment's deliberation and another glance at the plate of cookies, the boy held out his hands. Mrs. Martin attacked them with a vengeance and moved on to his face, giving it the same treatment.

"What's your name, boy?" she asked when she finished.

"Ranger."

"Well, Ranger, you're a pretty handsome fella when you're cleaned up. Miz Kat, will you put a couple of cookies on one of them little plates and pass it over to Ranger here?" She turned the towel around to the clean half and went to work on Dakota. "Let's see what's under all that dirt and muck" she said as she scrubbed away. "Well lookie here, Miz Kat, we got us another fine one."

Kat had the plate ready for Dakota. "He is a handsome one, isn't he?" she said. Dakota had the cookies stuffed in his face before the plate touched the counter.

The housekeeper ignored the boys' manners and rinsed the towel. She handed it to Forest who used it and returned it without raising her head. Mrs. Martin said nothing, but stroked the girl's head and continued to do so even when the girl stiffened.

"You and me got some baking to do," she said to the girl. "These boys are going to need cookies and cakes and good homemade bread. Miz Kat's got enough to do in the schoolroom and that one," she motioned to Jo who was washing Meadow's face at the sink, "Ain't worth squat in the kitchen. You think you can help me out?"

"I don't know how," Forest whispered.

"Nobody knows how 'till somebody shows 'em. We'll do just fine, you and me. You'll see," she told the girl and turned her attention to River. "You look like you could do with a might more than cookies. Never saw a feller so skinny and still be standing. You wash up and I'll fill you a plate," she told him.

River didn't move and Marcus took a step forward.

"It's all right, River," Kat intervened. She didn't want another contest of wills, not now when the others were just settling down. "We'll worry about cleaning up later. Let's get you fed."

"Everything all right in here?" Charles stood in the doorway.

"Everything's fine, Charles," Kat said quickly. She busied herself passing out more cookies and pouring milk. "Just fine. Mrs. Martin was just going to make River a sandwich. She thinks he needs fattening up. I'm sure you have other things to do. You can take Marcus with you." She smiled.

"That's who I'm here for. Tanner can keep watch." He smiled back.

"But..."

"Tanner can keep watch."

She was distracted by the sound of water running behind her. River was washing his hands. She looked back at Charles and gave him what she thought was a significant look. "Can we talk?"

"Later, Katarina. I have other, more important, things to take care of now. I'll talk to you later tonight. Late tonight," he said firmly. "If I have the time."

She could tell by the way he said it that she wasn't to question it. She also knew how it sounded to the others. She was being put in her place.

*****

Lunch was a near disaster, a feeding frenzy of monumental proportions. The children acted as if they'd never had a decent meal before. While they abided by Mrs. Martin's rule of eating from their own plates, once those plates were full, they dove in, cramming their mouths with chunks of meat and cheese and deviled eggs. They ignored the forks and spoons and shoveled it into their mouths with their hands, Dakota going so far as to lick the mashed potato directly from the plate and, like Oliver Twist, they held out their plates for more.

Kat was repulsed by the display, but held her tongue only because it was their first day and they had been through enough. Tilda was having a hard time holding hers, too, and Kat was sure she restrained herself solely because Kat had touched her hand and shaken her head in a gentle 'no' before the woman could interfere. They had time to teach them table manners. There were other things they needed to learn first.

Like using the bathroom.

After their cookies and milk, the first order of business had been baths. Since the younger boys smelled the worst, Kat decided they should go first. She chose Ranger because he seemed the most tractable and Rawley volunteered for the job.

The kitchen exploded when Rawley tried to take him out. This time, even Forest attacked without hesitation. Rawley was not going to separate one from the others. With Becky's help, Kat and Mrs. Martin managed to pull everyone apart and Rawley volunteered to take the two boys together.

"Are you sure?" Kat asked. She didn't think he was a willing volunteer to begin with. Becky certainly wasn't.

Rawley grinned. "Two half pints? I think I can handle it."

River, who'd watched the whole thing from his place leaning against the sink because he'd refused to sit with the others, whistled and gave a sharp nod.

"Go," was all he said and the boys went.

"You could have prevented that," Kat said to him, "You could have told them to go as soon as it was suggested. Why didn't you?"

River's answer was a curled lip.

"We're your family now, River," Kat told him gently. She could feel Forest watching from beneath the bangs that were much too long. "You have people you can rely on, people you can trust. The Alpha..."

"Fuck off."

Tilda glared at the boy. "You mind your tongue when you talk to Miz Kat. She's here to help you."

"Shut up, old woman. Save it for the young ones who don't know any better."

"River!"

"What?" he asked with the same curl of the lip.

Charles walked in with a tray of dirty dishes followed by Jo with an armload of empty platters.

Charles took in the food strewn floor and counter, Forest with her head bent and her hand frozen on the last bit of cheese on her plate, Meadow staring with her thumb stuck in her mouth and River, sullen and confrontational.

"What happened?"

"Lunch," Kat told him, a little too brightly. "I'm adding table manners to my lesson plans. Rawley took Dakota and Ranger upstairs for a bath."

"Tanner! Get in here! You're back on duty."

"Charles. We're fine."

"No, we're not," River mumbled under his breath.

"No, we're not," Charles said aloud. "I don't have time to

chase all over creation after these kids. My brother made that mistake and his Mate went into early labor for her trouble."

"I didn't touch her," River snarled.

"You didn't have to. She was so worried when you took off, she insisted on joining the search. She was afraid for the little ones. I'm not as kindhearted as my brother. I won't give you the chance to harm what's mine."

"Elizabeth? Is she all right? Is the baby all right?"

"Babies. Twins and they and their mother are doing fine, no thanks to him."

"Thank you God," Kat said for the sake of Elizabeth, the babies and for River. That was a burden no child should have to carry and there was no use explaining it wasn't his fault since Charles had already declared it to be. "He wasn't the only one that ran, Charles. The other children did, too." Kat knew River was the leader, but they were forgetting that he was a child, too.

"He was the one in charge. He takes the responsibility."

There was no point in arguing here in front of the other children. It would only make things worse. River's fists were clenched and he was ready to fight. Forest's body was quivering in fear and little Meadow had her thumb in her mouth.

Becky's burst of giggles interrupted the moment when Rawley brought Dakota and Ranger back, leading them not so gently by the scruffs of their necks. The boys were clean and shiny, their hair towel dried and sticking out every which way. In spite of the big man's grip on their necks, they were grinning. Rawley was soaked to the skin from head to foot.

"They never saw a shower before. They liked it," was all he said in explanation. He looked at River. "You're next."

"I've seen a shower before," River snarled.

"Glad to hear it. I wasn't much looking forward to soaping you down. While you shower, I'll clean up the mess those two made." It was said with a smile, but it was clear Rawley wasn't asking. He was telling.

River slammed his fist into the cabinetry behind him and Kat waited for Charles to explode. He didn't.

"Looks like you've got this handled," he said to Rawley and then to the women, "Can you handle the others for a few minutes while I speak to Kat?"

Chapter 26

"You can't want that, Charles."

"It's not a matter of want. What I want has nothing to do with what is. Those cubs are wild and I don't know if they can be tamed."

They were walking along the lane, holding hands, but Kat now realized this wasn't an afternoon stroll for lovers who would find little alone time over the coming days. Charles wanted them to be out of range for sensitive wolver ears.

"They're children, Charles, children."

"They're not. They're wolvers. We don't call them cubs or pups as terms of affection. We're mixed breeds, Katarina, and the wolf can be as strong as the human in us. It takes mental strength and discipline to control that and that control has to be learned early, so that when the change comes, they won't succumb to the Call. That's why the packs don't want someone like Buddy. They're afraid of him answering the Call of the Wild. Wild wolvers, Kat, have to be eliminated."

"No!" She looked at him in horror, not believing her ears.

"Yes," he said forcefully. "It's our dirty little secret. Every time we go over the moon, the temptation is there not to come back. Running free as a wolf is exciting, exhilarating. The speed, the feel of your body, every sight and smell is intoxicating. There are no rules, no boundaries. Some, a very few, choose to answer that Call. They'll take a trip to Yellowstone or the northern wilds of Canada and they won't come back. Sad, but accepted." Charles looked at her sadly.

"Some don't plan it. They're just not strong enough to withstand it and those are the ones who pose a threat to the safety of the pack, because they will likely draw the attention of humans."

"These are children. They can be taught." She refused to believe otherwise.

"There are instances of human children being raised wild and no matter how well they're treated, how diligently they're trained, there are certain things they never learn or understand. They're probably the closest to what their caveman ancestors were like. They run on instinct and cunning and their communication skills are basic. They don't ever fit into society. They can't.

"Now flip the coin. Think about what a wolver child raised wild will be. Like humans, it's very rare. Unlike humans, there's nothing written, only stories passed down. Feral wolvers are a nightmare come true. They are the stuff of human legend."

Kat let go of his hand and turned away, so upset by what he was hinting that for a moment she couldn't speak. Charles let her go and said nothing more.

"So what are you saying?" she finally asked. "Do you just take them out behind the barn and shoot them. Eliminate the problem?"

"No. I'm not saying that. I'm saying you need to be aware of the problem. River is the most functional, but he's been raised rogue and he's almost ready to go over the moon. He may never fit in for other reasons."

"He's a boy, a fifteen year old boy!" she cried, unable to understand how Charles could pass judgment on so young a child.

"No," Charles said firmly, "That's a human misconception. He's a man or on the verge of becoming one and you need to see him for what he is, not what you want him to be."

"And the others. Are you so ready to write them off, too?"

"I'm not writing anyone off," he said, losing patience. "I'm trying to say that I just don't know. There's something wrong with the girl, Forest. I can feel it, but I don't know what it is. The two boys are almost feral. The little one, as far as anyone can tell, has no speech. I've talked to my brother and he has the same doubts. They're one step away from animals, Katarina, and I don't know if they can be brought back."

"Well I know," she said. "You'll see. They'll come around."

It was their first, but not their last argument over the children.

*****

Eleven wolvers were on the hunt. An unhappy Rawley and Tanner were left behind to guard the house along with Buddy who was once again allowed to go over the moon and patrol the grounds. He'd proven himself capable as Charles had known he would.

They left a little after ten o'clock and would not return before midnight. Busy settling the children into their beds, Kat did not watch them go. Still angry, she didn't want to watch them go although she'd lifted her lips dutifully when Charles came to say goodbye.

Kat and Charles had barely spoken to each other for the rest of the afternoon and evening and Kat felt their emotional distance more deeply now that there was bodily distance as well. She felt him moving away from her, putting miles between them, and it made her miserable.

Now, she realized her mistake. He wasn't going out for a jog. He was going out to fight. He could be injured or worse.

"Don't let the sun go down on your anger," Grams used to tell her. "Not with those you love. Anger festers and grows in the dark and that makes it harder to be rid of in the morning."

Kat had not only let the sun set, she'd rebuffed his overtures for peace and she was ashamed.

She'd taken what Charles said as a personal attack on her abilities and each time one of the children acted out during the afternoon and evening, she was sure he saw it as her inability to cope.

Now, having had time to sit and think, she realized that wasn't true. The children didn't defy her personally. When they cooperated it was because they were doing what they wanted to do anyway and not because they'd been asked or told to do it. Otherwise, they defied or ignored everyone and did as they pleased, although Tilda Martin seemed to have more influence than anyone else.

"What are you smiling about," Jo asked.

After a near brawl over bedtime, the four younger children were finally tucked in and River was ensconced in a chair in the boy's room from which he refused to budge. Jo had poured two glasses of wine and led Kat out to the patio where she pulled an outdoor heater close a table and offered Kat a seat. Until Jo spoke, they'd sat in silence enjoying the peace.

"Tilda," Kat told her. She didn't want to discuss her other problem just yet. "I was thinking about what you said about women being alphas. Charles says she would have been the Alpha if she'd been a man. She has a way with the kids. They listen to her."

"At least they listen to someone," Jo laughed.

Her resolution not to discuss the problem faded as quickly as it was made. "What if they won't listen to us? What if they won't conform? What if the feral side is too ingrained?" she whispered. She told Jo what Charles had said. "What do you think?"

"Shit. Poor Charles is what I think."

It wasn't what Kat expected. "Poor Charles! More like poor

children."

"Yeah, well, it depends on how you look at it, doesn't it?" Jo said after a sip of wine. She looked out over the yard and fields to the woods beyond. There was a look of longing on her face. "If the cubs are too feral to readjust, they'd be happier living in the wild, don't you think? It's better than going rogue if you ask me. They'd belong to nature. They'd have a place in the grand scheme of things, you know? A rogue has no place at all. They can't get along in the human world and they don't fit into a pack. If they're Outcasts and have their families with them, they can form a familial pack, but it's temporary and lonely."

It was a different way of looking at it, but Kat couldn't get past the thought that these were children. "But why poor Charles?"

"Because the decision will be his and his alone. It's the Alpha who offers a young adult a place within the pack. The safety and wellbeing of the pack comes first and if he thinks they'll be a threat, he'll refuse them entry and then it will be up to him to decide their fate. I've never seen it happen, but I've been told an Alpha can make the beast permanent and after a while you forget what it was like to walk upright. I wouldn't want that decision on my plate."

"I hadn't realized," Kat said thoughtfully.

"Yeah, being the Alpha is a lot more than being ubermale. Sometimes, when the Alpha of a pack is really provoked, they'll say something like, 'You breathe by my will alone.' or "You live by my will alone." That's not an empty threat. They may appoint councilors or have those they can ask for advice, but that's a courtesy. They don't have to. By Pack Law, the Alpha is the ultimate judge, jury and executioner."

Jo shook herself as if trying to shake off her thoughts. "I wouldn't worry about it yet. He's not going to send a kid off to the wild. There are some that would, but not Charles. He's not that cruel. So," she smiled her reassurance. "There's plenty of time before he has to make that kind of decision."

"He says River is almost ready to go over the moon," Kat whispered understanding now why Charles was so worried.

"Shit."

"My thought exactly. I don't know what to make of him. He comes across as a belligerent asshole who doesn't give a shit about anything, but there's something about that that doesn't sit right."

Kat poured herself a little more wine and offered the bottle to Jo. She should be tucked up in bed since she suspected the children would be up early, but she knew she wouldn't sleep. She was too worried about the children's fate and Charles. Oh god, how she wished him to come home.

"Tilda thinks he's so thin because he's starving, but that doesn't make sense. The others aren't plump, but they don't look unfed. Except for Forest. She's way too thin and she eats like a bird, but she eats."

In the kitchen, Kat had noticed River repeatedly wiping the saliva from the corner of his mouth. She thought it might be a sign of his nervousness since he seemed to show no others. Tilda's observation made her think of it differently.

"Have you noticed how he doesn't eat until the others have been fed?" she asked Jo. "It didn't matter how much food was out there. I thought his refusal was just being obnoxious. What if he's starving because he lets them eat their fill first?"

"Rawley said River has scars. Bad ones. He didn't look too closely because he didn't want to aggravate River who, Rawley says, enjoyed the shower though he wasn't about to admit it. Rawley also said there weren't any outward signs of physical abuse on the younger boys." Jo shrugged. "I didn't see any on Meadow and believe me, after the number of times she wet herself today, I am intimately acquainted with that child's body."

"Oh jeez, Jo. I'm sorry I left that to you. There was just so much else going on."

"Hey, no problem, though you might think about a box of those diaper thingys. You know, the ones that look like underpants? There's a one gallon bladder in a half pint kid. She does know how to use the toilet, just not very well."

"It's fear and I'm pretty sure it's only of Charles. Forest is afraid of all the men. She hangs her head when any of them are in the room. She shrinks down and lets her hair fall over face like if she can't see them, they can't see her I don't know if it's shyness or fear."

There was so much to teach them, so much they needed to know. The three Rs were no longer a priority, though she'd present them as if they were. Social skills had to take precedence. The children's lives depended on it.

After talking with Jo, Kat better understood Charles' responsibility and concern about the possibilities, but that didn't mean she found the alternatives acceptable. In spite of the altered circumstances of her living here and being with Charles, she'd been hired to do a job and she would see that it was done. She had people who were willing to help and she wasn't too proud to ask.

"How long will you be here?" she asked her friend and she smiled as it dawned on her that this was another first. She had friends. In all her life, she'd had few acquaintances and never a friend unless she counted Grams.

Even Brandon had not been a friend. They talked about his studies, his days in the hospital training, his interests, his needs. They didn't share. She honestly hoped that it was different between him and his new wife. In spite of what happened between them, she wished him happiness in his new life. If it hadn't been for Brandon's betrayal, she'd have never ended up here where she was a part of something magical, where it felt good to say she had friends.

"... moving part of the operation down here. Eventually he'd like to bring most of it here and leave a satellite office in the city. Like most of us, I can do my job from anywhere and with any luck, the real estate business is going to be booming around here. Maybe I'll leave Wolf's Head Enterprises."

"What?" In the midst of her reverie, Kat only half listened to the answer to her own question. "I'm sorry. My mind wandered off track for a moment."

Jo laughed. "It's not like you don't have a few things on your mind. I said I've been thinking about leaving Wolf's Head Enterprises and going off on my own."

"No! You can't! Not when I just found you."

"Sorry kid, but I've got my eyes on someone else and I don't think Charles is into threesomes."

Kat sputtered a laugh. "He better not be. I wasn't listening because I was thinking about how nice it is to have a friend. You. I've never had one before."

Jo looked at Kat curiously. "Damn, Kat, no family, no friends. How in the hell did you survive? I couldn't stand being alone, though I have to warn you, being in a pack means everybody's business is everybody's business. It can be annoying sometimes."

"I can live with that."

Kat could live with a lot of things, but not with losing these children or Charles.

She froze at the muted sound of gunfire in the distance and looked for reassurance from Jo. She found none.

Chapter 27

They waited for what seemed like hours. Rawley and Tanner altered the course of their patrols, Rawley as wolf, Tanner as human. Buddy continued on as scheduled, a blatant guard that could be timed and watched by prying eyes.

An explosion ripped the dark fabric of the sky overheard, a fire ball soaring upward and ballooning out in red and yellow. It was several miles away and yet the windows of Hell Hall rattled with the waves of air and sound that rolled over the trees and across the fields.

Tilda came running, her hair dotted once more with the pink spongy bumps of her rollers. Becky, who'd gone to bed earlier and Rhonda, who'd apparently chosen Tanner over her friend Stephanie and stayed behind, came running downstairs.

"What's happening?"

"Don't know," Jo didn't take her eyes from the sky above the trees. "But I hope it's their problem and not ours."

"Rawley only said they were going out for a run."

"I guess they got sidetracked."

"Maybe it has nothing to do with them," Kat added, but no one thought that for a minute.

"Jeez, and to think I told Stephanie this place was dull as dust," Rhonda giggled and then frowned. "Do you think they're all right?"

"Yes, I think they are," Kat told her. There was a lightness in her head, a smile in her mind that wasn't hers. "Yes, they're definitely all right."

They all stood transfixed by the glow that slowly faded to a soft orange light in the sky and then the world came alive again when Kat shouted, "The kids!"

She raced through the house and up the stairs, first to the girl's room and opened the door. The beds were empty, the covers gone.

"Shit, shit, shit." Kat stamped her foot. Charles wanted the hallway watched and she had refused. She ran to the next door and threw it open.

River sat in the chair by the window with his hands lightly gripping the wooden claws at the end of the arms and his feet flat on the floor. He hadn't moved an inch from the time she'd put the boys to bed. He was watching the glow in the sky just as they had been. He turned slowly at her entrance as if he'd expected it.

The boys' beds were empty, too, and Kat opened her mouth to ask what the hell was going on when movement on the floor caught her eye. The four younger children were curled in a tangle of blankets sound asleep on the floor.

"They'll have to learn, you know, sometime, but not tonight," she whispered. She smiled to show she wasn't angry and shrugged. "I was afraid they'd be frightened by the explosion. I shouldn't have been. They're with you."

River's facial expression never changed, but his eyes changed slightly, giving away his surprise.

"You should get some sleep, too, honey. You've had a long day." Kat didn't wait for the response she knew wouldn't come. Softly, she closed the door on River and his sleeping charges.

Tanner was on the phone when she walked back into the kitchen.

"Ah, yes, this is Charles Goodman, over at..." He gave the address and a thumbs-up to Kat. "My guests and I were enjoying the night air and heard the explosion. I wouldn't be bothering you, but with the sirens and all, the ladies were a little frightened. Seems like there's a fire and well, you know how women are. They insisted I call to make sure we weren't in any danger. Yes, yes. Thank you very much, sir, and I surely do appreciate your taking the time. Yes, sir, I will. Bye, now."

He hung up the phone and grinned. "That's called establishing an alibi. The Alpha is on his way home."

Kat smiled and nodded her thanks, but she already knew. She could feel Charles coming closer and closer. The pressure in her chest eased at the same slow pace it had grown as he moved away. Charles' magic had planted the seeds of a connection between them and the vine was growing longer and stronger every day.

*****

This homecoming was better than the last. They came across the fields, men alternating with wolves, walking abreast with their heads high and shoulders back. They stopped at the edge of the nearest field and because there were so few of them, the Alpha's bright light flashing each of them home was clear and distinct.

Beginning with their Alpha at the center, the golden glow surrounded each in turn, starting as a shimmering ball covering the wolf. It elongated as the man within straightened in a swirl of strange shapes and reached his full height. There was a final burst of brightness and man stood where once was wolf.

It was a marvelous display and Charles bowed to the round of applause.

Kat ran to him and threw her arms around his neck and kissed him while he whirled her in a broad circle and kissed her back.

"Show off," she laughed when the twirling stopped and the kiss broke. "I gather it went well."

Charles put her down and started walking toward the house with his arm around her shoulders. "Better than well. They had some kind of drug lab running in an old trailer on the property. The place stank to high heaven. Now it smells like ash. That was Hyatt's doing."

"Gas and a match. It was nothing." Hyatt, who was walking with his sister and Ryker, didn't look like it was nothing. He looked proud as a peacock.

A squeal of fright behind them had Kat's head snapping around, but the squeal had already turned into giggles as Rhonda took off for the woods with Tanner hot on her trail.

Ryker raised his fingers to his lips to whistle, but Charles stopped him.

"Let them have their fun." He bent down and gave Kat another quick kiss. "I'll save ours for the bedroom," he whispered and then a little more loudly, "How are the cubs. I see the house is still standing."

"They're fine," she answered and glanced up to the boy's window, sure they were being watched. "They're sleeping all curled together on the floor. I don't think they like beds."

Charles frown wasn't what she expected. Kat thought the children's sleeping arrangement was rather endearing all tangled together like that. They reminded her of a litter... Oh. She frowned.

"They'll learn, Charles. You'll see. River wasn't with them. He was in a chair by the window. He's keeping watch over them, Charles, protecting them. They didn't try to run away," she said, thinking that, in itself, was an improvement. "They know they're safe here."

"Or they're waiting until our guard is down and their strength is up."

Kat stopped abruptly, forcing Charles to stop with her. She put her hands on her hips. "Look, I know it's your job to look at the dark side of this. I understand that now where I didn't before. The safety and well-being of the pack comes first. I get that. I really do." She looked over her shoulder to make sure the others were well ahead and out of hearing range.

"You can't let yourself get too close to them," she continued, holding his cheek in her hand and stroking him lightly with her thumb. "I understand that, too. It would be too painful when... if..." She forced herself to say the words. "If you have to send them into the wild. But Charles, you have to give them a chance. They've had years of living like animals. That won't come undone overnight. You have to show them you have faith in them. You're the Alpha and they'll believe it if it comes from you."

Charles gripped her shoulders and looked deeply into her eyes. "You understand it's not a decision I want to make."

"I know it's not," she told him, "And if it comes to that, I won't pretend to like it, but I won't stop loving you because of it. I trust you. You're my Alpha."

Charles' somber face split into a grin. "So you love me, huh?"

"Yeah, I think I do," she said as she took his hand and they started back to the house.

"I knew you would. Who could resist this handsome face, this muscular physique, this..."

"...swollen ego, that furry tail, those muddy paws." Kat shook her head, laughing. "Come on, Beasty Boy, let's get you something to eat and go to bed."

"Not in the mood for another run?" he asked with a leering arch to his eyebrows.

"No," she said firmly, thinking of the boy upstairs watching from the window, "You said bed and I'm holding you to it."

"All righty then. Bed it is." He stopped her before they entered the house. "I love you, too, you know."

"I knew you would. Who could resist..." But she couldn't

think of anything to say.

"The most beautiful woman and understanding soul I've ever met." He said and she knew it wasn't one of his silly pickup lines.

"Oh, you're good, Wolfman. Very good," she smiled.

*****

Several days later, the television news was still reporting on the meth lab explosion and the subsequent discovery of a dog fighting ring. Talking heads described the perils of meth addiction and animal rights activists protested the cruelty and immorality of gambling on dogs killing each other for sport. Everyone wanted in on the act.

The violence was attributed to two rival gangs. Two men were killed along with several large dogs that lost their lives in the fire. The county Sheriff made a statement about the drug trade infiltrating the countryside and assuring the populace that they were doing everything in their power to combat the problem and urging the citizenry to report any suspicious behavior.

"Yeah right," one of the younger men sneered. "Like there wasn't a deputy's cruiser parked out front the first time we stopped by. The only ones running these bastards to ground is us."

"We didn't get them all," Ryker reminded them, "And I still want to know why in hell they're working with humans."

Kat watched River out of the corner of her eye. He was watching and listening from just beyond the doorway to the TV room. He shook his head in disgust and turned back to the schoolroom, reminding Kat of where she should be.

Dakota, the bloodthirsty nine year old, was straddling a sofa cushion on the floor of the schoolroom. "Kill 'em dead," he shouted in his odd froglike voice and stabbed the pillow with a ruler. "Take that and that and that!"

"Dakota, stop that," Kat admonished. "There'll be no pillow killing in the classroom. Put it away and let's get started." She pulled the pocket doors closed behind her.

"But that's how you do it if you don't have claws and teeth," he argued. "You slash and stab until they're dead, dead, dead..."

"Dakota!"

"...and their blood and guts are all over the floor and then you have a party. We killed them dead!" he shouted one last time.

"Dakota! No!" Kat took a deep breath and after a short tug of war, removed the ruler from his hand. "We must never rejoice in another man's death be he human or wolver."

Dakota looked at her as if she had two heads. "Huh?"

The words were too big for him. "I'm saying it's not good to be happy about someone getting killed. Killing isn't good."

"They're happy." Dakota pointed at the door.

"They're happy the bad people are gone. That's not the same. They would be just as happy if no one died."

"They deserved to die." River spoke so quietly it almost passed unnoticed.

"Maybe they did," she said quietly, "But that doesn't mean we should enjoy it. Now let's get out our reading books and get some work done."

It was difficult to explain it properly to the children when she wasn't sure how she felt about it either. The more she saw of these wolvers, the more she recognized their primal instincts running close to the surface. Some of them took pleasure in the kill and even those who didn't saw nothing wrong with those who did.

In business, they were ruthless, though Charles swore they were above board in everything they did. They had to avoid scrutiny by the various government agencies that kept track of businesses like theirs. In play, they were aggressive and as Jo so crudely put it, constantly measuring their dicks against the next guy.

A psychologist would label them Type A personalities, but it was more than that. They were territorial and their first thought when threatened was to eliminate the threat. The preservation of the pack was their sole moral compass and the wiser heads of the pack hierarchy kept many of them from following their baser instincts.

That too, she was beginning to believe had more to do with pack preservation than a sense of right and wrong. They couldn't afford to attract the outside scrutiny of the human world. She wondered what would happen if the Wolvers did someday come out of the woods. Under the wrong leadership, they could make organized crime bosses look like pansies.

*****

After what felt like a six minute reading lesson and two hundred and twenty-six minutes of "Please sit down. Let's put that away. No, no, we don't eat crayons. Be careful, that sharp!" Kat was ready for a break.

"How about we go outside for a walk? We could all use some fresh air and you can run some of that energy off. What do you think?" she asked River who had ignored the lessons and the children, and spent all his time staring out the window to the trees beyond.

He looked at her and turned back to the window where he spent most of his time staring through the glass. He could hold the same position for hours at a time and his stillness was uncanny, particularly when his stare was directed at Kat. She could feel his eyes boring into her back and it made her stumble and stutter when she presented lessons. She wondered if he took satisfaction in that.

There was no way to tell. He didn't look away when she turned to confront his stare, but his face showed nothing.

Questions he was forced to answer were preceded by a snarl and the only time he smiled, if a smirk could be called one, was when Kat begged him to intervene and help her maintain some minimum of discipline.

Still, there was something about him that touched her. He had an innate ability to lead and the children were quick to follow. He never raised his voice or his hand and yet she was sure they would follow him anywhere. There was a danger to this, she knew. Sooner or later, they would have to transfer their loyalty to Charles and the pack, but for now, she needed the boy.

When she explained that they would no longer sleep on the floor, but in a bed like all good wolvers do, a riot ensued. It was River who settled them down and offered a compromise although it came in the form of an order.

"Dakota, Ranger, you two sleep in that bed there. You don't have to use the pillows. Forest, Meadow, pick a bed in the other room. Meadow, no whining. Forest will hold you if you're scared and the bathroom doors will be open. I'll be right here. Say good night to Miz Kat."

He made the boys brush their teeth and the girls brush their hair, but refused to help out at the table. His face was already filling out with Mrs. Martin's cooking, but he still refused to eat until the younger ones were fed and he eschewed the use of utensils of any sort.

He was a strange mixture of cooperation and defiance, pushing the children to learn some skills and ignore others. He rarely smiled, but the children held no fear of him except for Forest who trembled when any male came too close.

As for Kat, she wanted to rest her hand on his shoulder and stroke his hair away from his brow. She wanted to tell him how proud she was of him for taking on these kids. She wanted to tell him it was all right, now. There were other people here to do the job, but she said nothing. Any overtures of kindness were met by hostile glares and a curled upper lip.

Outdoors, River became a different person. He laughed when Buddy played Bear in the Woods with the younger boys and he whirled Meadow high in the air until she giggled with delight. He brought the shy Forest wildflowers. And he ran. River ran like the breeze that skimmed over the new grass, so light and playful. He ran like the gusts caught in the trees, leaping, dodging, laughing. He ran for miles, always staying within sight of the other children, always ready to run back if one of them called his name. Outdoors, he was free of the burdens that weighed so heavily on his young shoulders.

Kat decided that outdoor activities should become part of their daily schedule. The others needed time to play. River needed a time and place to be free.

Chapter 28

Charles, however, had little time for play or freedom and was more and more confined to his office. Alex was still in the city with a contingent of others whose missions were to transfer the various operations to the Hell Hall location. This should have been a tedious, but facile procedure, since most of their work was stored in a main server with off-site back-up. It was simply a matter of moving hardware. Or it should have been.

During the move, it was discovered that certain client files had been misplaced while others had been deleted altogether leaving some financial statements altered and suspect.

Charles was left with the daunting tasks of trying to rebuild computer files from existing hard copy, while informing clients of their investment status. All this was made more difficult because their Chief Financial Officer, namely Alex, had left everything in the hands of Stephanie who was at this moment basking in the sun in South America and refusing all forms of attempted communication.

"It's not like something like this hasn't happened before," her friend Rhonda explained to anyone who would listen. It was Rhonda who told them she was at the Copacabana Palace in Rio. "The place always falls apart when she leaves town. Everyone calls her a bitch, but no one gives her the credit she deserves."

"Why would they when she's already said it first," Jo countered. "She earns a damn good paycheck for what she does and you can't say Charles doesn't recognize her for it. She gets away with murder and all because she's good at what she does. I've even said she's the best damn negotiator we've got and I'd probably say it more often if she didn't always beat me to it."

The children were in bed and the women were spread over Kat's bedroom, gossiping and painting their nails. Charles, Ryker, and Tanner were out roaming the property as wolves.

In addition to all his other problems, Charles was having trouble at the job sites where work on the new roads had begun. Some heavy equipment had been damaged and several vacant houses that were due to be refurbished had been vandalized. The men were convinced it was the work of those who were absent from the raid a few nights before.

"I don't like Stephanie," Kat confessed only because her feelings were made known the night Charles found Stephanie in their bed. "But regardless of my personal feelings, I think ditching the pack to go clubbing in Rio is a shitty thing to do. She knew she was needed to reassure clients and help with the move. Charles was planning to leave her in charge of the city offices. She could have had the best of both worlds."

"You don't understand," Rhonda argued, "She couldn't stay. She had to get away for a while. She was heartbroken, humiliated."

Kat understood humiliated, but heartbroken?

"Rhonda, you are such a romantic," Jo laughed, "Or is that what she told you? Honey, you have to have a heart before it can be broken." She stroked a last layer of polish onto her nails. "Note to self. Hair and nail salon, top priority in new development. If Stephanie's 'heartbroken', it's because her little plan for world domination has been foiled by our little schoolteacher here."

"World domination? Like Wolvers Unite!" Kat giggled. "I doubt even Stephanie could pull that one off. Wouldn't she need some badass Alpha to act as titular head?"

"Not the whole world, just ours and she thought she had an Alpha in her pocket. You screwed that up royally." Jo waved her hands to dry the nails and eyed the unopened bottle of wine. "How many smeared fingernails does it take to open a wine bottle."

"Give it here. Mine are dry." Kat reached for the cork screw with one hand and the bottle with the other. "So," she asked as casually as she could, "Were Charles and Stephanie... ah... an item?"

"An item?" Rhonda giggled, "They were hot and heavy."

"A year ago," Jo snorted, "And it was a lot hotter and heavier on her part. She had visions of being the power being the throne."

"She did not," Rhonda argued, but without much heat. "She loves him. She thought she had a chance to work it out with Charles when she came here."

"Right. She was just seeking consolation for her broken heart when she spent the rest of that night in bed with Alex." Jo snorted in derision. "Or was she setting herself up with the one guy who might be persuaded to take over the pack. Food for thought, I'd say."

"But she's not an Alpha's Mate." Kat was thoroughly confused.

"There was never supposed to be an Alpha's Mate. We didn't want one. Remember? I admit one of the things that attracted me to this pack was being recognized as an alpha. I wanted to hear someone say it out loud. Charles gives us that recognition, but Stephanie wants more than alpha status. She wants the whole shooting match and she knows the only way she'll ever get it is to rule side by side with a weaker Alpha. That's the only way she can be top wolf."

"She only wants what's best for the pack," Rhonda said loyally. "She calls me almost every day and always asks how things are going. She wants to know everything that's going on and she wants to be a part of it. She just doesn't know where she stands with Charles." She looked pleadingly at Kat. "She thinks you've turned him against her."

"Me? I don't give a damn what she does as long as she doesn't do it in Charles' bed." Kat had a history before Charles just as he had one before her. It was pointless to get upset over things that were over and done as long as they remained over and done.

*****

Kat was learning about surviving in the woods and while some of what she learned made her cringe, like when Ranger laughingly showed her how to find and eat grubs, other things she found fascinating. Forest shyly introduced her to fiddleheads, the small, curled fronds of a newly emerging ostrich fern. Dakota thought her wits were clearly dim when she couldn't tell the difference between a good mushroom and a bad one. He found it hilarious that her choices could kill them all.

River patiently showed her how to set a snare and while her soft heart broke for the rabbits they caught, she did enjoy the stew Mrs. Martin concocted from their harvest. The housekeeper had no sympathy for the greedy creatures.

"Just wait until you wake up one morning to find half your garden gone, then you can tell me all about the lovely little bunnies."

The children showed her where a variety of birds nested in the trees and a fox den built into the earth. They showed her how to follow the deer and the shallow caves that would make good places to sleep.

Buddy always came with them and Forest usually stayed home, preferring the company of Mrs. Martin in the kitchen.

She was slowly coming out of her shell and she blushed with pride at the least little compliment to her awakening skills. Tilda swore the girl chattered when no one else was around though said little about her previous life. What little she did say led Tilda to form some strong opinions about the girl's behavior.

"That child has seen things no child should see. She worries about the women in the house, but you and the Alpha most of all," she told Kat one morning in the kitchen. "You watch her. Every time one of you gives a man a bit of sass, she cringes. She hangs that head of hers down every time a man walks by, but she's watching and waiting.

"Yesterday, Ryker called me from the kitchen and he sounded put out, but it wasn't at me. He was giving some of the younger ones a good telling about leaving their plates and glasses about. He said I wasn't to be picking up after them. They were big and ugly enough to do it themselves. When I got back to the kitchen, that girl was curled up in the corner, froze stiff with fear. She clung to me and cried. She didn't say so, but I suspect she thought I was in for a beating."

Kat nodded in agreement. "I've noticed it, too, even with River. If he asks her to do something, she scurries to do it. Tilda, you don't suppose he's..."

"Not for a minute. I've seen him cuff those two boys, not hard mind, but enough to get their attention. Never seen him raise a hand or his voice for that matter to either of the girls. He'd never hurt a one of them. I think he'd die for 'em. And I've never seen him watching Forest like a boy does a girl, like a man does a woman. No ma'am. Those cubs's got nothing to worry about from River."

"You like him, don't you?" Kat had notice how the thickest chop always found its way to River's plate along with the largest slice of pie. They'd had pecan pie three times this week and she wondered if it was his favorite. Tilda showed her love with food.

"I do," Tilda answered without hesitation. "Life's been hard on him, too, and he don't trust a one of us as far as he could toss us. Can't say we've given him a reason to, but you watch him with those kids. He loves 'em, though he probably wouldn't own to it and I expect that's because he's been raised to see it as a weakness. I know what some of these wolvers are watching for, but I'm telling you here and now that boy's not wild. The softness has been wore out of his body, but it still abides in his heart."

"I think so, too," Kat said thoughtfully, "And I think I understand his anger. When my mother died, I was so angry with her for leaving me even though I knew it wasn't her choice. I blamed her for my father's drinking and I was angry with him for leaving, too, but I didn't know it then. All I knew was I was so, so angry. It was years before I realized where the anger came from. For River, it has to be so much worse. I was lucky I had Grams. When I think about it, I don't know how she put up with me."

"She just kept on loving you, same as you'll do for these cubs."

*****

She told Charles about it later that night when the house was quiet and they were walking up the lane in the dark. Between his business and the children and a houseful of people, it was hard to find time to just be together and talk.

"They need you, you know. They need to see you're not the man they think you are. They need to know you, not the Alpha."

"And how am I supposed to do that? The big one snarls and clenches his fists every time I walk by. The little one pees. The girl freezes like a deer caught in the headlights and the boys duck and run for cover. They've been here long enough to know I'm not going to eat them alive."

"You could start by learning their names. You, boy!" she snapped her fingers and mimicked Charles' deep voice, "Is not how you begin a friendly conversation."

Kat was learning that her lover was not a patient man. He wanted everything done yesterday. There were dozens of workmen about the place, most hired from his brother's pack across the mountain, and Kat was amazed at how quickly the abandoned houses were being whipped into shape. The roads were still mostly mud, but new loads of gravel were delivered every day. The school had been transformed into temporary offices awaiting the construction of the new headquarters for Wolf's Head Enterprises.

He'd already sent out emissaries to other pack Alphas, seeking out members of their ranks who might be looking for a change. He wanted only those who could leave with their current Alpha's blessing and first approached those whose packs had become too large and unwieldy for their territories.

They were at the end of the lane when he spun her around and kissed her, laughing at her mimicry. "I have never said 'You, boy!' in my life. I am not Ebenezer Scrooge."

"Of course not! You're spending way too much money to be Scrooge. And where's it all coming from, might I ask? You went to great pains to tell me you were broke."

Charles slid his hands into the back pockets of her jeans and pressed her up against him. "There's broke and then there's broke with excellent credit. I've made and piddled away fortunes before. This time I won't piddle it away. Don't worry, I won't let you down."

"You couldn't let me down. I'd live in a tent with you," Kat giggled, "As long as there was another one for the children."

"Ah, back to the cubs. We need to find something to take your mind off them," he said with a laugh and moved his pelvis against hers. He kissed her again and then looked up to the sky. "Damnit. Can we get a week without rain?" Fat drops were beginning to fall. "I was hoping we'd have a chance to play. A good chase would do us both good."

Kat pushed him away and took off at a run. "Then chase me back to the house," she called over her shoulder. It was a race she couldn't win, but Charles always made losing so much fun.

He caught her twice before they reached the house, allowing her escape after a brief and playful struggle each time. Her shirt was unbuttoned and her bra undone by the time they reached the front door.

The television was on, but the doors were closed and Kat was laughing when he caught her on the stairs, flipped her over and worked her zipper down while holding her hands to the step above her head.

"Charles! They'll hear us," she sputtered, trying to wiggle her way free. She lost one of her shoes on the step below.

"Good. Then they'll know not to open the doors." He latched onto her breast and sucked hard while working her jeans down over her hips.

"Oh!" Her sneakered foot managed to get a grip on the step and she pushed upward and away which only served Charles purposes as her jeans slid down as she pushed up. He peeled them from her legs.

"No!" she squealed as he freed her naked foot and she pushed up again, kicking out her sneakered foot to free it of the jeans that were now hampering her escape.

Charles was rising, preparing to lunge over the top of her, and her sneaker caught him between the legs.

"Oomph!"

She pushed herself up another few steps, not knowing whether to laugh or be concerned. She didn't think she hit him that hard, but Charles' face said otherwise.

"Now you'll pay," he growled. He grabbed the trailing denim and pulled.

Sneaker and pant leg came off with a jerk, throwing him off balance. Kat scrambled up the steps squealing, "No, no, no. I'm sorry. I'm sorry."

"You're gonna be."

She half ran, half crawled to the bedroom door, burst through and stumbled to the other side of the bed, trying not to laugh as Charles barged in, slamming the door in his wake.

"You're in for it now," he growled as he circled the bed, stripping his shirt off over his head.

Kat scooted across the top, taking half the covers with her. Charles was right behind her. Tossing the covers at him, she dodged his grasping hand. She managed to reach the foot of the bed before he untangled himself. A lamp spilled to the floor.

Kat tried to wiggle beneath the high bed, but Charles grabbed her ankle and pulled her out. His laugh was maniacal, an evil genius laugh from the worst of horror movies and Kat started to giggle. The giggle turned into an 'oomph' of her own when Charles tossed her onto the bed where he made short work of removing her sagging bra and shirt. He climbed up her body and straddled her waist.

"Now you're going to pay, little kitten, but first let's get rid of your claws." he picked up her shirt and tore it in half.

"No!" she shouted. Her wardrobe was meager. She couldn't afford to lose a shirt.

"I'll buy you another," he whispered in her ear. He used her torn shirt to tie her hands to the headboard.

"Oh, no!"

"Oh, yes!"

Breathless and panting, she squirmed against her bonds. The air was filled with his magic and as he slid down her body she thrust her hips upwards in invitation.

"Oh ho, now you want it." He began with her breasts, kissing and sucking and tugging with his teeth until she was arching up to meet his mouth. "You're enjoying this too much," he growled and moved farther down to attack her belly with teeth and tongue, moving to the sensitive spot on her side where she was most ticklish.

"Please, please," she begged, "Not there." She was screeching with laughter before he finished his assault and then he moved downward between her legs.

He slipped his arms beneath her thighs and spread her wide. Holding her hips motionless, his tongue began to work her already excited clit.

"Oh god," she moaned. The man had a magic tongue. She tried to thrust her hips upward to seek an explosive end to the torture, but he wouldn't let her move. She grabbed the shirt tied to her wrists and begged him for release. "Please. Please!"

She thought it was the banging of the headboard until Charles paused and swore. "Damn it to hell," he shouted. "I'm busy."

The banging on the bedroom door came again. Charles threw the sheet over Kat's nakedness, but left her tied and went to the door and threw it open. And slammed it just as quickly.

He came back to the bed and yanked on his jeans.

"Who is it?" Kat whispered, still aching but cooling fast.

"Visitors." He was back at the door. "What?"

"You were making a lot of noise."

It was Jo and she was laughing. Charles body blocked her view, but not that of the tall man behind her. Ryker gave Kat a wink.

"And?" Charles didn't sound happy.

"Well," Jo sputtered, "Since you're awake, we thought you'd want to know that our little girl can talk. She woke me up, but it was Ryker she wanted. She said, "Miz Kat's hurt. Help."

"Shit."

"That's what I said," Ryker deadpanned.

"We told her you were okay, but I think Meadow needs to see for herself." Jo was enjoying every minute of this.

"Hang on." Charles closed the door and came to the bed. "You're going to say this is sweet. I beg to differ." He tossed her the robe that hung on the bathroom door.

Kat was tying the robe as he opened the door. "See?" he said, "She's fine."

A puddle formed at Meadow's feet.

Kat pushed him aside and knelt in the doorway. "Oh, honey, it's all right. We were playing a game," she explained, ignoring Jo's snort. "I'm sorry we woke you."

Kat fetched a clean nightgown without waking Forest and clean and dry, brought Meadow back to their room.

"Meadow's going to sleep with us, tonight," she said sweetly.

"Sure, sure," Charles said with a smile that was patently false. "It's a big bed. There's plenty of room to sleep." He threw back the covers and Kat was relieved to see he was wearing boxers. "God knows we're not going to use it for anything else," he muttered.

Kat giggled as she climbed over Meadow to the center of the bed. There was no way the child would sleep next to Charles. She leaned over Charles and kissed him on the lips.

"Be a good boy," she whispered, "And I promise I'll make it up to you."

He kissed her back "You bet your sweet a... I'm sure you will, dear."

"I love you," Kat said as she turned her back on him and settled her arm over the sleepy child beside her.

It wasn't until morning that she thought to wonder why Meadow had woken Ryker and Jo and not her protector, River.

Chapter 29

The day began the way every day for the last three weeks had begun; with a feeding frenzy in the kitchen. Eggs and toast and bacon and ham were shoveled into mouths with hands and fingers and in Dakota's case, a face in the plate.

Charles had banned them from the dining room until they learned some manners and Kat whole heartedly agreed. The kitchen floor could be mopped. The dining room carpet could not. Until they developed some manners, the children were relegated to the kitchen.

Kat worked with them every day, three times a day, and either they couldn't or wouldn't learn. She had to remind herself a hundred times a day that they were raised like animals and they couldn't be expected to change overnight.

"Ranger," she said patiently. "Remember what I showed you. Hold your fork this way."

Ranger laughed and nodded. He laughed and nodded at everything. He picked up his fork and allowed her to mold his fingers around it. Holding the fork in his hand, he proceeded to stuff the food into his mouth with the other hand.

Dakota seemed to think his spoon was a catapult to be used to bombard the girls with bits of his food which afforded him the opportunity to steal larger amounts of food from their plates.

Forest, at least, ate daintily with her fingers, but she ate hardly anything at all. The others all ate as if half-starved but were only slightly underweight, however Forest was now thin to the point of emaciation and Kat suspected an eating disorder. Could wolvers suffer from anorexia? No one knew for sure, having never run across it before. Charles promised to call his brother, Mike, a doctor who served a large pack out west and hopefully they would learn how best to handle the problem.

River sat back in his chair, angry and defiant. Kat knew he could handle a fork and spoon. She'd watched him in fascination as he twirled a butter knife in his hand, weaving it in and out of his fingers so rapidly, the blade was almost a blur. He refused out of pure belligerence. The younger boys looked up to him and took their behavioral cues from him.

Meadow was the most cooperative. Though she hadn't spoken again, her eyes took in everything that was happening around her. She tried to mimic what Kat showed her and struggled through each meal with a concentration Kat found endearing. Kat praised her lavishly for her efforts and was rewarded with the occasional smile. Sadly, the child froze every time another was reprimanded, no matter how mildly, and Kat had to wonder if the little girl's cooperation was a result of her wish to please or her fear of punishment.

Punishment was another thing Kat and Charles argued over. He thought she was too lenient. She thought he was too harsh.

"They're just children, Charles. They don't understand. No one's ever taught them the first thing about civilized behavior."

"They're wolver children. They're as much beast as human and the beast has been allowed to run wild. They need to be tamed, Katarina, and mollycoddling them with kisses and hugs isn't going to do the job. You'll notice they settle down when I come in the room."

"That's because they're afraid of you! You walk in acting like the Big Bad, and scare the bejesus out of them."

"Well someone sure as hell has to or this house is going to come tumbling to the ground. They've broken four windows, shattered a patio table with the rock they dug out of the yard which, by the way, they found while digging a pit to line with sharp sticks. And who the hell gave them the matches so they could light the woodpile on fire? Dammit! We could have lost the whole barn. They need to be punished, Katarina, and if you can't do it then the Big Bad is going to do it for you."

It was the main reason why she'd said nothing to Charles or anyone else about River's nighttime excursions. The question had nagged at her after the night Meadow woke Jo and Ryker. Why hadn't she gone to River? The answer was because River wasn't there. He left sometime after the children were asleep and she had no idea how he got out or where he went, but he always returned before they awakened.

Kat chose to believe that he needed to run. He needed to feel free to escape if he wanted to and coming back each night meant he wanted to stay. Charles would only confront the boy and make matters worse. River was already over tired and edgy.

Kat took a deep breath and went on with the disaster that was breakfast.

The classroom wasn't much better. With only five children, it should be easy to give each one individual attention, but every time she sat down to work with one or two, the others would be into something they shouldn't. River refused to do anything even though it was evident he couldn't read. Forest stopped working and stared into her lap, if you weren't right beside her, encouraging her. She was the only one who could read and write, but her skills were minimal. The others had no education to speak of. A lesson in counting had turned into a disaster when Ranger and Dakota decided to pelt each other with the blocks Buddy had cut for her as a teaching aid. Meadow, who was building a tower with her own set of blocks, joined in the vicious fun.

When she'd asked for River's help, he curled his lip,

shrugged and did nothing.

After two weeks, she'd finally managed to impose some kind of order and discovered one way to get them to sit and listen. They liked stories. When she pulled out a book and read to them or told them stories from memory, they sat quietly and listened to her speak. Even River, who pretended not to, listened.

Perhaps she could use stories to open the door to other forms of learning. Today, she had one for Meadow, who was afraid of everyone, but particularly of Charles.

Once upon a time," she began when the children were all seated and waiting, "There was a ferocious looking wolver who lived far away across the sea in a land called Scotland." Kat growled the word 'ferocious' and snarled a little over 'wolver' and that was enough to make little Meadow shiver. Not wanting a wet lap, Kat shifted gears.

"Ranger? Would you bring us that globe, please? I'd like you to show Meadow where Scotland is." She steered the boy's finger in the right direction. "Yes, that's it. See, sweetie? Scotland is a far away land. Here we are, way over here." Leaving Ranger to point to Scotland and placing her own finger over their home. "Nothing can hurt you from way across the ocean." After a little geography lesson and listening to the other's questions, Meadow was ready to move on. Settling her arm more firmly about the girl's waist, Kat continued.

"Now, everyone knew how mean and cruel those wolvers in the woods could be, so when her mother insisted she bring a basket of food to her ailing grandmother, Little Red Riding Hood, whose real name was Meadow, was very worried and a little afraid, but she was also very brave."

Meadow's head snapped up to question Kat with those big blue eyes.

"Oh, my! Will you look at that? The girl in the story has your name. She must be a very special girl, don't you think?" Kat kissed the real Meadow's forehead and earned another smile.

"You made that up," Dakota accused.

"Oh no," Forest defended, "I think I read somewhere that was her name."

The girl's defense of her warmed Kat and she smiled her thanks. Forest beamed.

"That's a lie." Dakota wasn't going to let it go.

"How would you know? You can't read?" Ranger piped.

Kat could see where this was going so she quickly resumed her story. "Meadow knew her grandmother needed help and she was determined to bring her that basket, no matter what. So she donned... that's a fancy word for put on and I'll be checking to see who uses the word tomorrow. Meadow donned her bright red cloak with its winter warm hood and carrying her basket over her arm, she set out for Grandmother's house."

"Is that Grandmother's house like your house or like our house? Does it have lots of rooms or just one?" Ranger asked. He liked details.

"It's a good, sturdy house," Kat told him, thinking of the hovel in which they'd been found. "Made of stone, but not so big and fancy as *our* house. Our house would be much too big for one Grandmother to live in." They needed to understand that this was their home. She described the three room cottage of her imagination and Ranger questioned her until he was satisfied. She then went on with Red Riding Hood's walk through the woods.

"She's going to get eaten," Dakota said in his froggy croak, "Or at least get beat up. It's what they always do."

Kat wasn't sure if he was concerned or excited by the thought.

"They do worse than that," Forest whispered.

The words and the way they were said broke Kat's heart. Forest was at the age where boys and men should be a fascinating subject of speculation. She should be wondering about first kisses and first dates or if a boy's smile meant he liked her a little bit more than a friend. Instead, she hunched her shoulders to hide her blossoming body and wore her hair dirty and ragged to hide her face.

That face became bright and animated in the classroom or when she was with Mrs. Martin in the kitchen. It was a beautiful face that went slack and vacant in the presence of any adult male. Forest even became shy around Buddy and River who, to Kat's knowledge, had never been offensive to her. This girl had seen too much sexual abuse and yes, perhaps rape, to instantly change her opinion of men and no matter how gentle, Buddy was a man and a giant one at that and River was a big, rough, boy.

"Why don't we listen to the story? You may be surprised at how it ends."

Kat heard a rustling outside the door and glanced up to see Charles' blond head and green eyes pop out and back to hide behind the jamb. She heard a snicker that wasn't his coming from the same direction and assumed she had an audience. River heard it, too, and she felt him stiffen at her back where he always seemed to be, always watching, always waiting.

She drew the story out as long as she could, switching to a schoolroom lesson when Meadow became too upset at the scary parts. Kat felt bad about adding those parts, but being scared was part of the story and necessary to the lesson.

"We all know that poor Meadow grew up in the city and had no wood ways at all. I'm pretty sure she would poison us with her choice of mushrooms and it was a good thing there was a path to follow or the poor Miss Red Riding Hood would fall over her own feet." There was some giggling at this reference to herself and even the dour faced River's mouth curled upward a bit instead of his usual downward frown.

"But that was the problem, wasn't it? There were too many

paths turning this way and that and before you know it, Meadow, our Little Red Riding Hood, found herself turned around and completely lost."

"Are you sure this girl's name isn't Miz Kat?" croaked Dakota.

"Oh no, Miz Kitty Kat wouldn't be alone in the woods," Buddy said from the doorway. He crossed his ankles and sat with a thump on the floor. "I'd be with her so she wouldn't get lost. She might fall down some, though."

"Oh, no, it's definitely not Miz Kat," Kat laughed and the silent child on her lap looked up into her eyes and smiled. After a hug, Kat continued. "Meadow was lost and alone and very, very frightened. It was getting dark and the woods called to her with strange sounds that she'd never heard in the day. The path branched off in three different directions and she no long knew which path to choose. She'd chosen so many wrong ones before. Poor Meadow didn't know what to do and she started to cry."

The real Meadow looked like she was about to cry, too. Buddy crawled over and placed his hand on her knee. "Don't you worry, Meadow. If nobody comes to save you, I will."

Meadow relaxed somewhat, but her thumb went to her mouth and her tiny finger curled around her nose. With her arm around the child and Buddy's hand on her knee, Kat went on. She tried to sound growly and fierce.

"Why are you crying? a terrible voice demanded. A mean looking giant stood in the middle of the path. His blond hair was all messy and his face was all grizzled because he hadn't shaved in days," Kat said as a hint to the man behind the door.

"Stop your crying and tell me what's wrong. Meadow knew who this man was. He was a wolver and she'd heard the stories about how terrible he was. At first, Meadow was afraid to speak, but the big wolver pestered and pestered and finally, Little Red Riding Hood told him."

"Now that you've told me what the problem is, I can fix it, the scary man told her and quick as a flash he turned into a wolf. Climb on my back and I'll carry you to Grandmother's house. And that's exactly what he did."

"And then he ate her." Dakota really was a little savage.

"He did not!" Kat wasn't about to have her story ruined now. "There were bad wolvers in those woods, but he wasn't one of them. He took her straight to Grandmother's house and when Grandmother was fed and cared for, that wolver took Red Riding Hood home and after that, every time Red Riding Hood needed help, he was there. He was the Alpha of a very good pack and guess what?"

Meadow looked up with her questioning big eyes.

"When Little Red Riding Hood grew up, she mated that wolver. Yes she did, because she was an Alpha's Mate. And that big wolver whose name was Charles, brought Meadow to America along with his pack and they lived happily ever after. The End."

Everyone seemed satisfied with her story, including Dakota, which surprised Kat because it included no murder and mayhem. Ranger stared out the window, daydreaming she hoped of being the wolver who rescued damsels in distress. Forest had a faint smile on her face. She was old enough to know it was only a fairytale, but hopeful at the end that it just might be true.

Buddy sat up and offered his hand to a smiling Meadow to help her slide from Kat's dry lap and Kat stood and stretched, satisfied with a story well told until she turned and found River with his eyes blazing with anger.

"Why do you tell them that bullshit when you know it isn't true?" he snarled. "That's not the way it is."

"It was a story, River. I wanted to…"

"Keep your fucking stories to yourself. They need to hear the truth. The Alpha and his Mate lived happily ever after." He spit the words. "You think you know so much. They think they know it all." He hissed, referring to the others in the house. "A band of rogues can't have an Alpha. Where in hell do they think we came from? We had an Alpha. Ask Forest. She's his daughter and she watched him kill her mother, his perfect Mate. He would have killed us, too, but we ran. Tell her, Forest."

Forest's eyes were watching the floor. Her lips trembled. Meadow was staring at him with big frightened eyes. The other two boys just stared.

All her work here today was for nothing. She'd try again. It was all she could do. But worse than ruining her story, she knew Charles was listening at the door. She had to handle this and quickly or they'd be arguing about the boy again.

"Now is not the time, River. We'll talk about this later and you can tell me..." She placed her hand on his arm.

Kat didn't think he meant it, not even as it happened. He threw up his arm to cast her hand off and when he did, his arm flashed out and pushed her hard enough to make her stumble back against the chair which crashed to the floor.

"Get off me, bitch!" River shouted.

Chapter 30

"River!" Charles roared the name so loudly Kat was convinced the windows rattled.

Dakota hit the floor and belly crawled under the table. Forest froze and the pencil she'd been holding in her hand snapped in two. Her eyes were still glued to the floor. Ranger inched his way behind the overstuffed chair and ducked. Little Meadow's thumb plugged her mouth and a puddle formed on the floor.

Charles stood in the doorway, pointed his finger at the offending teenager, then slowly swung his arm to point toward his office door. He was the ghost of Christmas Future pointing to Scrooge's gravestone. "My office. Now."

"Honey, it's all right. He didn't mean it. We were just..." Kat tried to explain.

Charles ignored her, cut her off, in fact. "You, too," he said to her and then to the frozen girl at the table, "Forest, help your sister get cleaned up."

River curled his lip as he slunk by his guardian and Kat winced when she saw Charles' hand twitch. She tried again.

"Charles, it was an argument. He's just a boy."

She saw his jaw tightened and he continued to point down the hall. "Now," was all he said.

Kat followed River to Charles' office. This wasn't something that should be taken care of in front of the children anyway.

Charles shut the door behind him. It wasn't quite a slam, but he did it with more force than was necessary. He pointed to the chair in front of his desk and looked at Kat.

"Sit." He rounded the desk and took his place behind it.

Kat sat and immediately leaned forward toward the furious River who was standing in front of her. She had to stop this before it escalated.

"You can't keep going off like that, sweetheart," she said gently. "You have to talk it out and not in front of the other children." She reached for his arm to comfort him, but he slapped her hand away.

Charles raised his hand, his power rolling off him in waves. Kat could only imagine what it cost him to keep his tone quiet and even. "You need to listen to her, son."

"I'm not your damn son," River snarled at Charles and turned to Kat. "And I'm sure as hell not your sweetheart. I don't have to tell you shit. So you can both fuck off." River turned his back on Charles and walked away.

Charles was around the desk and across the room faster than Kat could rise from her chair. River managed to get his hand on the doorknob and began the twist of his wrist to open it, but the latch never clicked.

There was a sudden blur of bodies, a roar of anger, another curse or two and an animal-like growl and then a crash as River was thrown up against the door. Back to it, toes barely touching the floor, River dangled from Charles' hand which was large enough to circle the front half of the boy's throat. Charles' thumb and fingers touched the door.

Charles brought his face so close to River's, Kat thought they were about to touch noses, but the Alpha stopped a couple of inches away. And this was The Alpha, the Lord of his Domain. The air hummed with his power.

"I am your Alpha," Charles snarled. "You eat at my table. You sleep under my roof. You exist by my will alone. You will be my omega until I tell you otherwise. If I call you Dirt, you will answer with respect. Do you hear me?"

River stared at Charles, his eyes wide and frightened.

"Do you?" he shouted when the boy didn't answer.

With his neck pinned to the door, the teenager couldn't speak, couldn't nod. Kat held out her hand to Charles, ready to point this out.

Charles must have sensed her movement. His head snapped around and he glared at her. "Don't," he said sharply. Just that one word. Don't.

Kat was a poker player. She knew when to hold 'em and when to fold 'em. She folded her hands together and sat back. It wasn't obedience so much as a show of trust that he knew how best to handle the boy. Her way wasn't working.

Charles turned back to River. "Katarina is mine. Mine. She will be The Mate. More importantly, she will be *my* Mate. You will treat her with the respect she deserves or you will answer to me, just as any other full adult would answer to me. Are we clear?"

This time, he didn't have to ask twice. River blinked and his chin moved a fraction of an inch in an attempted nod.

"Thirdly, you feel the need to swear at me, you go right ahead, but you do it in private. Out at the barn, in my office, I don't care. You need to express yourself? I'm the Big Bad. I can take it. But..." Charles' hand closed a little tighter over the boy's throat. "No one talks that way to my woman or any other woman in my pack. Not if they want to keep their tongue. Blink if you'd like to keep yours."

River blinked and Charles eased him to the floor.

Kat had expected a snarl or a surly look after the dressing down but instead, River straightened his shoulders and looked Charles in the eye.

"I am your Alpha," Charles repeated. "As a member of my

pack, you will obey me in all things, but this one first and foremost. You will not raise a hand to any woman in anger. Harm any woman inside my pack or out and I will deliver the penalty myself and that penalty is death. If punishment is to be meted out to a woman of my pack, then it will be done by my hand or under my orders and it will be rare, if ever. Are you with me, son?"

River nodded and Charles nodded back in some masculine wolver exchange and then Charles stood aside and the boy came and stood in front of Kat.

"I'm sorry, Miz Kat. It won't happen again."

"I know it won't, River. You're a man of your word," Kat said solemnly and was grateful the words came so smoothly. Inside, she was shaking.

He was a man. Before her misty eyes, River changed from the boy she thought he was into the young man Charles expected him to be.

And then he smiled. This man, created by the magic of the Alpha just moments before, smiled where the boy never could. Kat went up on tiptoe to kiss his cheek. Charles cleared his throat behind her.

"Oh stop it." She waved her hand at Charles. "Our boy's become a man. I'm proud of him and I can kiss him if I want. Look at him, Charles. When he smiles, he's almost as handsome as you," she teased and winked to share the joke with River and his grin broadened.

"Next time shake his hand. Save your kisses for little boys. And me."

Charles couldn't have said anything better to raise River to the ranks of men.

"You'd better get going while the going's good," she told River in a conspiratorial whisper and motioned to the door that was now free to open. "Go tell the others your news. They'll believe it if it comes from you. We'll see you at supper."

"Dining room," Charles added which earned them both another grin.

Charles held the door open and when it closed behind the young man, Kat was on her feet and throwing herself into Charles' arms. She slid her fingers over shoulders that had never seemed so broad, up that glorious neck and into that noble head and crown of golden hair. Drawing his lips down to hers, she kissed him. Hard. And he kissed her back.

"If this is what it gets me," Charles laughed when the need to breathe finally broke them apart, "Poor River will be apologizing every day for the next twenty years."

"It wasn't the apology, though that was really sweet. It was you. When you go all Alpha like that, work your magic like that, you are so hot. What was that all about, anyway? What did you do to make him change like that?" She poked his chest with her finger. "And don't tell me nothing."

Charles' hands cupped the cheeks of her ass and pulled her so close she had to lay her head all the way back to look up. He brought his nose down to hers.

"I told him he was an adult and that I would treat him like an adult. I issued an invitation to join the pack. He accepted."

She understood it now, River's elation, but, "You said he'd be your omega. That's the last in line, the bottom of the barrel."

"It is, because that's where he belongs. That's where every young wolver begins. It's up to him to rise above it and he will. I know he will. He's had a hard life and he's stood up to it well. He's strong and he's looked out for those kids. Ryker will find a way to channel that anger. River's ready to be taken over the moon."

"That's why you argued with me, told me to stop treating him like a child. He's not a child. Probably never was."

"Never had the chance to be and we can't give him those

years back." Charles kissed her nose and gave her ass cheeks a quick squeeze. "What we can give him is the support of the pack to complete his journey into manhood. That's what I was offering him."

"You also said I'll be your mate. Were you asking me to marry you?" She tried to ask it lightly, as if his answer didn't matter, but it did. Oh, how it did.

"No," he said and locked his arms around her to hold her close when she would have pulled away. "It was a statement, not a question. I said you'll be my mate. The way we are now, you sharing my bed, is setting a bad example for the children. We need to make this right."

"So you're only marrying me for the sake of the children," she huffed.

"That and so you don't run off with some fifteen-year-old omega. I have a reputation to maintain you know."

"Well that's the suckiest proposal I've ever had," she complained and she meant it, too.

"You had the flowers, ring, and bended knee last time and look what it got you."

She pushed away from his chest and turned to walk away. "Yeah, a lame-ass pack of wolvers and a Big Bad who doesn't know his dick from his elbow when it comes to romancing a girl."

"I think the little kitten needs a reminder of what this Big Bad can do with his dick," he growled.

Kat felt the ripple of his sexual power, squealed and ran for the door, found it locked, and laughing, circled around the chair and ran behind the desk with Charles hot on her heels. She dodged one way and then the other until Charles lost patience with the game and vaulted over the top of the desk, scattering papers and pens everywhere. He captured her lips with his mouth as he captured her body with one arm. The other arm swept the remainder of the desktop contents onto the floor.

"Big Bad and his dick are about to fuck your brains out," he whispered in her ear.

Kat struggled against him, but not too hard. "Hey! What about using bad language to your woman?"

"That wasn't bad language. It was a statement of intent."

Kat squealed again as he bent her over the desk and proceeded to show her exactly what he meant.

****

Later, when she'd pulled herself back together and straightened her clothes, Kat went back to the classroom and found them working quietly at their books. Dakota looked as if he was finally making an effort and Ranger was trying to hide his grin.

For the first time, Forest was scribbling away in her journal, something Kat had encouraged her to do, but never required. She glanced up a little worriedly at Kat, blushed and quickly lowered her eyes and Kat understood. She was covered with the Alpha's scent and not even River's word could convince her that Kat wasn't hurt. Time and example would be the only cure for that.

She put her hand on Forest's shoulder and bent to whisper in her ear. "He asked me to be his mate. I'm the happiest woman on earth." She smiled at the girl's wide eyed shock. "He's never hurt me. He never will. Ask River what he said about women in his pack."

Meadow was sharing the sofa with both River and Buddy, happily sitting between the two, listening to Buddy read. River followed Buddy's finger with an intensity she'd never seen from him before. He, too, was making an effort to learn.

This classroom which only minutes before had evidenced her failure, now proved her success. As a teacher, this little band of children - and two young adults, she reminded herself-

fulfilled her in more ways than any full classroom ever had. These children needed her and needed the pack and they were growing to love her even though they didn't know what love was. She was teaching them more than reading and writing.

She was teaching them to live without fear and she wasn't teaching them alone. She had the Alpha and his pack. She knew there was still a lot of work to be done. Dakota was still a blood thirsty little devil and Rangers laughter covered a mountain of fear. Forest was still wary of men and Meadow had yet to talk normally. This idyllic scene wouldn't last forever, but right at this moment, she felt there was hope. Whatever River had told them seemed to work.

She looked over to where he sat and found him watching her. She smiled and mouthed the words "Thank you" and her heart skipped a beat when his lips moved, too.

"You're welcome."

The moment of peaceful and studious diligence passed, not because of the students, but because Charles, their Alpha, strode through the door.

"Little Red Riding Hood," he said. He pointed at Meadow and crooked his finger. "Come here."

Her eyes went wide and Charles laughed and that made her eyes grow wider.

"And don't worry about piddling on the floor. We all know you're empty. Come here. Your Alpha awaits."

He held out his hand and it was River who slid her to the floor.

"Go on. Meadow, and remember that you're brave."

Taking very tiny steps, she made her way across the room and placed her hand in the giant's paw. In one swift motion, he tossed her up and over his shoulder and onto his back. Her arms circled his neck in a choking hold. Seating her more firmly, he grasped her legs and jogged a little in place.

"Someday soon I'll let you ride my wolf, but for now we'll do it this way."

He began with a gentle trot around the room, but soon was at a full gallop. Down the hall they flew, Meadow's laughter trailing behind them. It was the first happy sound she had made. Kat wanted to cry for the joy of it, but they didn't give her a chance. The boys were clamoring for a turn on the wolf and while they were both too big for that type of play, Charles galloped away with them without complaint.

They whooped and hollered and when it was Meadow's turn again, they were chased from the kitchen by a laughing Mrs. Martin. Jo, who'd been hiding in the office with Ryker and Hyatt, held the front door open for wolf and rider to escape. The men followed along with the boys and soon the yard became a battlefield of riders and horses with a squealing little girl cheering them on.

Kat and Jo closed the door on their fun and headed to the kitchen to join Mrs. Martin who was filling a plate with cookies and had glasses already set out for the milk. Kat put the kettle on for tea.

"This is the way it's supposed to be," Mrs. Martin said approvingly.

But Kat wasn't listening. The battle had moved to the back of the house and as she watched the Alpha laughing the loudest, she couldn't have loved him more.

Chapter 31

Like all the decisions he'd made since becoming the true Alpha, once Charles decided they would be mated, plans were immediately underway.

"I wonder what he would have done if I'd said no," Kat mused.

The ever practical Tilda looked up and mumbled through a mouthful of pins, "Ya didn't. That's that."

"He probably would have run you down and taken you the old way. That's what I would have done." Jo, who'd organized everything, but had no domestic skills at all, held out an old metal lozenge box filled with straight pins for a refill.

Kat stood in the center of the breakfast table while Tilda deftly turned up the hem of her mating gown. It wasn't the gown she would have chosen to be married in, but it was lovely in its own simplistic way.

The gown was white silk, gathered under the bust in an empire style with long sleeves gathered at the elbow and wrist and a long fall of lace that fell over her hands. The neckline was a deep scoop that showed off the tops of her breasts just enough to be enticing without flaunting her well endowed chest. The gatherings at waist and arm were dotted with tiny pink rosebuds and according to Tilda, it was exactly like the gown Emily had worn when she was mated to Charles' father. And she should know since she'd made that one, too.

"What do you mean the old way? I thought this was the old

way," Kat said, referring to the gown. While very pretty, it was designed for freedom of movement as were her shoes which were nothing more than satiny ballet slippers.

Part of the mating ritual involved something called the Chase. She would run through the woods while Charles chased her as a Wolf. According to Jo, the longer she could evade him, the more fun everyone would have and then, in the privacy of a spot he had chosen for the occasion, they would mate.

"It's only symbolic of the old ways. In the good old days the Mate wasn't always willing." Jo laughed. "Hell, I bet they were never willing. They were captured and running was their one hope of escape. Of course, running also triggers the instinct to chase, so... Haven't you noticed that this dress resembles nightgown?"

Kat's eyes widened in horror as she looked down at her dress. It did look like an old fashioned nightgown. Holy shit. "You mean they were... forced?"

"Yup, and with the whole pack there to watch." Jo laughed again when Kat paled and swallowed visibly.

"Nobody's going to be watching us, though, right?"

"Sure. Didn't anyone tell you you'd be spending your wedding night under the watchful eyes of a hundred and fifty guests?"

"No!" Tradition was all well and good but there were some things she simply would not do.

Tilda spit her pins into her hand. "Stop your nonsense, now," she admonished the laughing Jo, but she was laughing, too. "There'll be no such goings-on. All of that was hundreds of years ago. Nobody does that today. Some of the men will follow you on the Chase, but once you're caught they'll leave you in peace to do what needs to be done."

"Okay then." Kat nodded her head, relieved, and then bit her lip worriedly. "Will it hurt?"

Jo cackled at that. "It's a little too late to play the blushing virgin now, isn't it? As I recall, you even have some experience being roped and tied."

"Jo!" Kat cried and then whispered, "Not that. The other."

Charles had explained it to her, showed her how it would be done, but the thought of it frightened her little. During the ritual, while they were physically mating, he would bite her, bite her hard enough to draw blood and at that moment, she would become part of the pack.

The thought of becoming a true member of this wondrous society she had discovered thrilled her. It was a fairytale come true. The idea of running through the wild in wolf form, side-by-side with Charles, excited her. The biting? Not so much. She wasn't into pain. A little paddling on the ass didn't count.

Jo shrugged. "Don't know. Never knew a Mate well enough to ask. The Alpha from Rabbit Creek will be there with his Mate, Elizabeth. I guess you could ask her."

"Sure," Kat sighed, "Hi, Elizabeth. Nice to meet you. You don't know me from Adam. So how was your wedding night? Did your most intimate moment hurt?" She looked down and gave the grinning Jo the evil eye. "Sure," she repeated, "I can do that."

Tilda inserted the last pin and patted Kat's bare foot. "You'll do fine. With what you two get up to, a little nibble on the neck shouldn't be a far stretch."

"How do you know what we get up to?" Kat eyed the woman suspiciously.

"If you don't want folks to know, then you shouldn't be doing it in the backyard for all and sundry to see. You forget, darkness isn't the same for us as it is for you. We can see just fine." Tilda gathered her scissors and loose pins and placed the pins in the metal box before taking it from Jo and closing it with a snap.

"Oh. My. God. Is nothing sacred in this house?" Kat's blush

had gone from red to purple.

"It's sacred. It just ain't secret."

"What? What did I miss?"

Jo looked from one woman to the other, but neither woman was telling.

*****

The week leading up to the mating was a relatively peaceful one. Since the incident with River and the resulting wolf rides, the children had settled down in the classroom. Mrs. Martin laid down the law in the kitchen, when yet another glass when flying off the table to shatter on the floor.

"That's it." She slammed the dishtowel onto the counter as if she hoped it might make a resounding crash, too. She marched to the table and began clearing half empty plates, going so far as to snatch the biscuit out of Ranger's hand. "I'm done. You can eat pig slop out back of the barn and be grateful we don't keep pigs." She put her fists on her hips and stared the boys down. "I ain't cooking one more meal for you. No cookies, no cakes, no pies," she said glaring at Dakota who liked his sweets. "No fried chicken and mashed potatoes with gravy." That was for Ranger, who couldn't get enough of the crisp and savory treat.

She didn't ignore the girls, either. "No chocolate chip pancakes for you, young lady, until you hold that fork like a fork instead of a shovel. And you." She shook her head sadly as she pointed at Forest. "I'm so-o-o disappointed in you, Miss Forest. You've helped me in this kitchen. You know how much work goes into laying out a meal in this house and it don't bother you atall when it's thrown on the floor? I thought you'd have more respect for yourself and your hard work.

"So here it is, you ungrateful pups. You can whittle down to nothing right here on my kitchen floor and I'll weep when you're gone, but I ain't feeding you one more thing. And don't go looking at Miz Kat for sympathy, because she ain't got no say here. This is my kitchen and who I feed is *my* say."

Kat shrugged to let them know there was nothing she could do. In addition to missing half their breakfast, she'd give them the morning without their snack and talk to them before lunch about how to go about changing Mrs. Martin's mind. They should be hungry enough by then to come to their own conclusions.

"It's not all about manners," River said from the door. He ate with the adults now but always took time to stop by the kitchen. "It's about Miz Kat and Mr. Charles, too. They got their big mating party coming up and there'll be lots of folks there looking us over. I won't have you shaming the Alpha or his Mate with your bad manners. It's time you started acting like children instead of beasts. You listen to Miz Kat and do what she's already showed you and no more fussing at the table or I'll be the one feeding you scraps out behind the barn. You hear?"

Kat pressed her lips together to keep from laughing out loud. River, the main instigator of this uncivilized behavior, had executed a complete about face and was now insisting the heathens attend church.

The children, however, missed the irony as well as their breakfast and snacks. They were ready to apologize and promised better behavior well before lunch. Not realizing the self-incriminating aspect of their performance, they were true to their word and by supper were using their utensils like old pros, evidence that they knew how all along or at least from the time they were first shown.

They weren't the only source of surprise. Alex returned from the city with the rest of the pack to join in the festivities. Charles swore he could feel no animosity from any of them and Kat was happy for him, but she questioned their sincerity.

"Are you sure they're with you, Charles?" She knew that some were fence sitters, but surely there were some who resented the changes taking place. A week or two wouldn't cure their dissatisfaction.

"I'm not a mind reader, Katarina, but as they say in the hills where I was raised, my mama didn't raise no fool. I don't trust any of them, but I have no reason to judge them either. Alex did what he thought best and since I never insisted he run decisions by me in the past, I can't really fault him, can I? I can only tell you what I feel. They're well fed, happy and satisfied."

"Satisfied with what?" she wanted to ask, but didn't.

Charles was more relaxed than he'd been since Alex left and she didn't want to cast doubt where there should be none. She didn't like Alex, didn't trust him or his loyalty to Charles, but she also knew her personal prejudices could color her opinions.

Her initial reaction to Jo was a case in point. What she thought the woman was and what she turned out to be were two very different things. Jo had become a dear friend and it was to Jo she voiced her concerns.

"Now that the mantle has fallen squarely on his shoulders, could you hide your feelings from The Alpha?"

"Why would I want to?" Jo seemed genuinely perplexed.

"I don't know," Kat hedged, "I'm trying to figure out how it works, I guess. Okay. Suppose you were planning a big surprise birthday party for him. Would he know?"

"Why? Are you planning one? He's coming up on forty, you know." Jo looked ready to take up her PDA and start the planning.

Forty? Really? She was marrying this guy and had no clue how old he was. Was something wrong with this picture? No! Kat shook her head to clear it of the distraction. "I don't care how old he is and I'm not planning anything. It's just an example. Could you hide it or would he know?"

"He'd know I was happy and excited, but he wouldn't know why. Not unless I kept an image of balloons and a Happy Birthday sign in my head and even then, he'd have to look for it."

Jo frowned and squinted her eyes suspiciously. "Are you hiding something?"

"No! But what if other people are, Jo. Who stands for Charles and who doesn't?"

"Hell, how would I know? That's the Alpha's business, not mine. I don't want to see it happen, but if he's challenged, there's nothing I can do to stop it."

"Who can?"

"No one. Once a challenge has been made in earnest, that's it. There's going to be a fight. That's Pack Law. But just because someone pisses and moans about some decision the Alpha's made, doesn't mean they're going to stage a coup. Anyone who issues a challenge puts their life on the line. It's a fight to the death, Kat. You don't just wake up one morning and say 'I think I'll challenge the Alpha today.' And if you win? You sure as hell better have the majority on your side or you'll be the one facing a challenge tomorrow. A simple challenge can grow into a tremendous mess, Kat. That's why there's so few of them."

"Who in the pack is strong enough to beat him, other than Ryker?"

"It doesn't matter," Jo didn't raise her voice, but she was shouting in exasperation just the same. "That's not the way it happens. At least it wouldn't if I was running the show. I'd find the biggest, dumbest wolver I could. That's who I'd put against the Alpha. My guy would get beat and I'd put up another and another until the Alpha can barely stand." She nodded her head in satisfaction. "Now I challenge him. I attack when he's at his weakest. I told you before. It's not just physical strength. It's cunning, too. I'm weaker physically. I'd have to find my strength in other ways."

"You're not helping, Jo."

"I know and I'm sorry about that, but you've got to understand, Kat. We're wolvers. We're not human. The survival of the pack is first and foremost and we follow its Alpha. The Alpha, not the man. In a good pack, they're one and the same and a pack that loves their Alpha is a happy and fortunate pack. We don't have to love the Alpha or respect him, but we are compelled to follow him for the sake of the pack. Without the pack, there's chaos."

"So when Charles and Ryker were counting up those for and against, they weren't talking about one team against the other." This was more serious than Kat first thought.

"No. They were looking at how many challenges there would be before the Alpha wins."

"Or before he dies," she whispered to herself.

Jo punched Kat's shoulder with her fist. "Buck up there, lady. You're going to be the Mate. Charles doesn't need your worry. He needs your faith. Tradition says that a true Mate has more power over the Alpha than any other member of the pack. Her belief in him gives him strength. That's a tradition I'm going to believe in. You need to believe in it, too."

Chapter 32

Kat tried to follow Jo's advice. She tried to keep her mind filled with happy thoughts, but when she had a moment alone, the darkness of worry would creep in and fill her with such pain she had all she could do not to buckle under the weight of it.

She loved him. Oh, God, how she loved him and the thought of losing what she'd so recently found tore at her heart and brought tears to her eyes. She wanted to tell Charles how she felt. She wanted to share this almost overwhelming emotion with him, but Jo was right. Charles didn't need her worry or her fear, so she smiled and went through the motions of the last few days before her mating as cheerfully as she could.

It wasn't always hard. There was excitement everywhere. Buddy had mown the new grass to a velvet smoothness and the men were erecting huge tents to shelter the guests. As Jo predicted, there would be close to a hundred and fifty wolvers most of whom Kat didn't know. In addition to Charles' small band, his brother Marshall would be there with his Mate and a contingent of Rabbit Creek's finest and a few other Alphas and guests from nearby packs.

She worried about where they'd put them all if it rained, but no one else seemed concerned. Everyone swore the day would dawn sunny and warm and stay that way throughout. Kat could only trust that their animal sixth-sense was more accurate than the weather reports.

There was no point in holding school. There was too much

going on inside and out for the children to concentrate.

Forest could always be found in the kitchen at Tilda's side practicing her newly learned skills. At the housekeeper's insistence, she pulled her hair back in a ponytail now and held herself more erect. She was still overly timid and perhaps always would be, but she no longer quaked with fear when the men walked by and she sometimes smiled shyly when they flattered and fussed over her baking.

Meadow, no longer afraid of her Alpha, followed Charles around like a puppy, and twice they'd found her asleep tucked up in the kneehole under his desk where she quietly played while he worked.

The younger boys were bundles of energy that seemed capable of being in six places at once. Kat finally gave up trying to keep track of them, satisfied that they were safe under the eyes of so many wolvers and they always managed to show up to be fed. Tilda assured her that this was as it should be.

In one fell swoop, Kat had a mate and a family. It wasn't the house in the suburbs with the white picket fence and they certainly weren't the two children she'd envisioned, but she was happier with her makeshift brood and her soon-to-be mate than she'd ever have been with Brandon.

River still worried her. His change from boy to man hadn't wavered and the solemn Ryker had taken the young wolver under his wing.

"They're two of a kind," Jo declared with some pride.

Kat thought so, too, and she was confident the older wolver would be a good role model for River. Ryker was strong and solid and no-nonsense, but underneath the hard surface there was a compassion in the man that he tried to keep hidden. River would be fine if he followed in Ryker's footsteps.

He still, however, escaped each night and Kat wondered how long she should keep his secret. River and Charles were on firm if not companionable footing with each other and she hesitated to bring up anything that might upset that delicate balance. There was so much else going on that needed Charles' attention.

"A penny for your thoughts," the man who was constantly in them said from behind her as he slipped his hands about her waist.

"I was thinking of you," she told him, leaning back into the firmness of his chest, "And the children and Tilda and Buddy and Hell Hall." Kat tilted her head back to look up at him with her eyes filled with tears. "I'm happy."

"I'll take your word for it," Charles chuckled and kissed her nose, "Though it beats me how women can be happy and cry at the same time."

She ran her knuckle under her eyes. "I've wondered that, myself. Are you happy, Charles? With all this? With me?"

Charles paused for a moment before he spoke. "If you'd asked me a year ago if I wanted a Mate and a family and a falling down estate, I would have laughed in your face. I wanted fast cars and a sleek, modern apartment in a high-rise. Now, I wonder how I could have been such a fool."

He released her and led her over to the schoolroom sofa that was already spotted with unknown splotches made by children's sticky fingers and made her sit. He got down on one knee and took her hand in his.

"All this makes me happy. Even the cubs make me happy, but none of it would matter without you. You're the heart of my house, kitten, the center of my soul. Your love and trust are honors I don't deserve. I want to be the man you see in me. I want to make you proud. You make me whole. You make me complete. You make me laugh. So, Miss Katarina Bennett, I'm formally asking for your hand on bended knee. Will you please be my Mate and love me as I love you."

With his free hand, he held out a small black velvet box,

opened to show her the gold and diamond band within.

"We wolvers don't do engagement rings or wedding bands. Jewelry tends to get lost in the change, but I thought you might like this."

Kat was crying openly now, snuffling like a baby. "Well it took you long enough." She tried to laugh, but she couldn't. She held out her hand for him to slip the ring on her finger. "I accept your proposal, Charles Goodman, and I will love you with all my heart for as long as we both shall live and then some." She leaned forward for a kiss.

"How touching! And to think I'm the only witness to this momentous occasion."

Stephanie stood in the doorway, smiling benevolently. "Let me be the first to congratulate the happy couple."

Charles rose, still holding Kat's hand. "I thought you were out of town."

"Ah yes, and shame on me, Alpha. I shouldn't have left you with so much going on. You needed me here, but I needed time to readjust my thinking and my plans. That's done now, so here I am, rested and ready. I wouldn't have missed this for the world. Our Alpha has found himself a Mate." She walked toward them and held out her hand to Kat. "You'll be just what we need."

*****

"I smiled and said thank you, oh so politely, but it wasn't easy," Kat said later to Jo as they stood out on the patio watching Stephanie make the rounds among the men. "I feel sorry for her in a way. I know what it's like to have all your plans ruined."

"That's why you'll make a good Mate. You try to love everyone. There's no snarkiness in you. That'll be my job." Jo offered her a glass of wine. "So are you ready for this? They'll start showing up tomorrow morning. It's an all day affair."

"When do I get dressed for the mating?"

"You may as well do it first thing, by afternoon at the latest.

You only get to wear it once. It won't be worth much by the next morning."

"No saving it for my daughter?"

"Not unless she's into muddy and torn," her friend laughed.

"It's a planting moon," Tilda said beside them, "A good fertile moon to begin a family under." She winked at Jo. "You and that wolver of yours should be looking at that, too."

"Now tell me I'm not getting any younger, Mom." Jo rolled her eyes.

"Well, you ain't and neither is your man." Tilda was not to be deterred. She had her Alpha and her Mate and she was set on creating a flourishing pack single handedly. She'd been dropping hints all day about the single wolver women who were bound to be attending the mating.

"Okay, okay!" Jo threw up her hands. "Next month during the Honey Moon. The big guy's got a thing for honey," she confided.

"I'm not going there. I don't want to know," Kat laughed. "But I'm happy to hear it."

"You and my real Mom," Jo said, glancing at Tilda. "She cried. I'm now under orders to give her a granddaughter. Shit! We haven't even talked about kids."

Tilda was lost in thought. "I thought I was missing a jar. I reckoned it was them boys. Not missing any bread or biscuits, though."

The younger women burst into laughter. Tilda looked from one to the other and turned an odd shade of red. "He didn't need any bread, did he? That rascal had his own honey bun!"

Jo's laughter stopped abruptly and she stared past Kat's shoulder. "What's up with him? I haven't seen that look in days."

Kat turned and saw River at the corner of the house, staring out onto the patio. His lip was curled and he looked like he didn't know whether to curse or spit. She followed his eyes, but there were too many clustered around Charles to pick out the victim of his animosity.

Charles stood by Alex and a fawning Stephanie, who'd been so affable and apologetic since she arrived that Kat felt something akin to a hairball in her throat. Next to them, Tanner and Rawley passed their time with two other men who'd returned with Alex. One of them had received the physical talking to from Charles in the TV room.

Right behind them, Becky was chatting with Rhonda while keeping one eye on Rawley and Kat wondered if Rawley had a favorite moon like Ryker. If not, Becky was more than ready to supply him with hers.

There were more men and a few women, but none of them looked particularly guilty or suspicious. Ryker, with a sixth sense for trouble, looked over the heads of the others, caught River's scowl and moved toward the teenage, but when he got close enough to speak, River turned his back and walked away.

It pained Kat to see him this way. She thought he would be happy and excited. Tomorrow would be a big day for him, too. Tomorrow, Charles would take him over the moon for the first time and he would be welcomed into the pack as a full-fledged member.

She'd thought River might want his own day, separate from hers and Charles, but Charles explained that it was not an event, more an acceptance after repeating a few words of loyalty. The important part for the young wolver was running with the pack. Still, Kat expected to see River more excited than angry.

There was nothing to be done about it now. After the mating, when the company was gone and things had settled, Kat would make the time to talk with River.

Chapter 33

As promised, the day dawned bright and cloudless and also as promised, guests began to arrive soon after breakfast. Tilda had been cooking for three days, but there was no way the vast amount she'd prepared would feed this crowd all day and into the night. She didn't seem concerned and Kat soon found out why. The two large festival tents Charles supplied were only the beginning.

Men brought out chairs and tables from trucks and cars and women brought out baskets filled with baked goods and platters of fried chicken and ham and pork roasts and beef. Gigantic coolers of lemonade and kegs of beer appeared along with huge tubs of ice packed with bottles and cans.

Canopies went up to offer shelter and shade when day became warm and fully enclosed tents appeared across the field on the edge of the trees answering the question of where all these people would sleep.

Older children ran everywhere, hugged or scolded depending on the need, by anyone who was near. And babies! Kat had never seen so many babies!

Marshall, Charles' brother and the Alpha of the Rabbit Creek pack, arrived early with his Mate, Elizabeth, and two small, but chubby babies in tow.

"It's my fault," Elizabeth explained about the babies after introductions were made. "The pack was without a Mate for a long time before I came along. They're making up for lost time!"

and then she frowned, "They explained the part about the babies, right?"

One of the babies started to cry, joined by her brother. "I knew this would happen," Elizabeth laughed, handing the squalling infant to Kat. "Do you have a place where I can feed them in peace?"

An hour later, the schoolroom was transformed into a nursery as the nursing Elizabeth took charge of organizing the place where mothers could relax away from the chaos outdoors. Older women kept watch over the sleeping babes so younger ones could join in the gossip and fun.

"It's one of the things I love most about the pack," Elizabeth said later when the babies were fed and asleep. "The teamwork. They help one another. *We* help one another. That's not true of every pack, but with a good Alpha to lead them, that's the way it will be and Charles will be a good Alpha. Now that he's pulled his head from his ass," she laughed.

Kat bristled at that. "Charles is a good Alpha and he'll make a success of this pack. You be careful what you say about my mate."

Elizabeth wasn't offended. She laughed again. "You love him, don't you? Not just the Mate hoo-doo." She waved her fingers like a magician. "You really love him. Not every Mate does, you know. Sometimes it's just the hoo-doo. I had a hard time with that."

Kat realized she'd just passed a test. "I didn't," she said honestly. "I'm a believer in fairytales and this one is mine. I'm looking forward to my happily ever after and I'm terrified someone will wake me up and it will disappear."

"You don't know how happy I am to hear that, because once the deed is done, there's no turning back. You're stuck with each other 'till death do you part." She smiled and took Kat's hand. "Charles has changed since you came along. It's in his face and in his voice. There's more confidence than bravado. That's a good thing. And now," Elizabeth said, looking up at the women standing in the doorway, "I think your entourage is waiting."

*****

It was almost time. Kat stood in front of the mirror for one last look before her mating. The dress, so lovingly created by Tilda, who'd become so much more than a housekeeper, flowed over her body like a waterfall of silk and clung to all the right places. It was a lovely dress and its simplicity suited her as no expensive boutique gown ever could.

Jo had done her makeup, scolding her when she protested that it was too much. As usual, Jo was right. The face staring back at her was someone from a magazine with smoky dark eyes, flawless skin and full, rosy lips. For once in her life, she was one of those women she envied. She was beautiful.

The afternoon had flown by with eating and drinking, games and music. Kat was introduced to hundreds of people whose names she couldn't possibly remember. It was like having the reception before the wedding only Kat was too on edge to eat and too afraid the alcohol would go to her head to drink. She hadn't seen Charles long enough to have a conversation and she was pretty sure there was a conspiracy among the guests to keep them apart. The sun was setting and people were beginning to gather under the largest tent. It was time.

Walking to the door, she glanced through the window and happened to see Forest standing apart from the crowd, head hanging and her hands twisting together at her waist. Kat thought she knew what might be wrong and decided there was still enough time to before the ceremony to gather the younger members of her brood and use Mrs. Martin's sitting room to have a little talk.

"Have you ever been to a mating party before?" she asked when she finally got them all rounded up.

"No, but I like it. There's lots of food and kids and nobody's made us wash our faces all day," Dakota declared.

Ranger nodded his enthusiastic agreement. "Lots of kids, too."

"What about you, Forest?"

The girl nodded slightly while keeping her eyes on the floor.

It was what Kat was afraid of. She took a deep breath and began, "I've never been to one either, but I wanted to tell you what I think will happen because I don't want you to be scared. The Alpha will say a few words and then I'll take off running into the woods. You might hear some laughter and you might hear some squeals and you might hear some screams. They'll be the same kind of screams Meadow makes when Buddy pretends he's a bear. It's all in fun. Then the Alpha and I will spend some alone time together and we'll be home smiling and happy in the morning. "She looked from one to the other. "Any questions?"

The younger children eyed the door, wanting to make their escape. They, at least, were sure that Miz Kat would come to no harm and Kat let them go.

"Wash those hands and faces first and leave the dirt in the sink, not the towel," she called after them and then she turned to Forest, who hadn't moved an inch. "You know what's going to happen, after the Chase I mean."

The girl nodded and then looked up with such agony in her eyes that Kat was brought to tears.

"No," she said, "It's not what you think," and then she amended, "It's not what you've seen."

Forest's eyes told her it was true.

"Wolvers are beasts and men," Kat said gently. "The wolvers you knew chose the beast. They were cruel and heartless and they didn't love their mates. That's wrong, Forest, so very, very wrong. Our Alpha enjoys his beast in other ways, but not when he makes love. That's what will happen between us, sweetheart, we'll make love. It's still sex, but a different kind. He loves me and I love him and we'll share the joy of that love together. Charles won't hurt me, not ever and he'd kill any man who tried."

"You'll have babies," Forest whispered.

"I guess I will." Kat smiled, thinking she understood what worried the child. Fear of another abandonment was something she was familiar with. "And when I do, I'll love that baby as much as I do you and the others. That's the wonderful thing about having a heart." She tapped Forest's chest with her fingers. "There always room for one more to love."

But Forest didn't smile back. "What happens when you don't give him a son?" she asked in a whisper.

Oh God, Oh God. Kat had hoped Forest would one day talk about what River had blurted in the schoolroom that day. Now was not the ideal time, but she couldn't pat the girl on the head and send her on her way. This chance might never come again.

There was a knock on the door. "They're ready and waiting," Jo called.

"Then they'll have to wait some more. Forest and I are having a chat. The Alpha will understand. You can make something up for the guests."

Kat got down on her knees in front of the girl and looked up into her sad and frightened face. "Is that what happened to your mother? She didn't have a boy?"

Forest shook her head. "She had them, but they died and he beat her. Every time one died, he beat her. He hit her other times, too. Lots of times. Sometimes he hit her because of me, but the worst times were when her babies died." Once started, the girl couldn't stop and she poured out all the horror she'd kept bottled inside. Her shoulders heaved and she gasped for air, choking on her tears.

Kat gathered the child in her arms. "How horrible. For your mother, for you. How horrible. I'm so, so sorry."

Forest melted into her and Kat sat back, her legs curled beneath her and the girl on her lap. Forest was almost as tall as she was, but that didn't matter now. This was a child who needed her mother's lap and that comfort had been viciously taken from her. Kat's lap was a poor substitute, but all she had to offer.

Forest clung to her, soaking the front of her gown with tears. "She wanted to leave. She tried, but she was the Mate and she couldn't. She had to go back. She had to."

"I know, honey, I know," Kat whispered, when in fact, she hadn't known until now.

"Once the deed is done, there's no turning back." That's what Elizabeth had said only a few hours before. The magic and the bonding that would occur tonight was more than words, the magic more than great sex. There was no divorce court for an Alpha and his Mate.

"That's why we left."

"What?" Hadn't Forest just said they couldn't leave?

"That's why we ran away. He killed my mother and then said I was old enough. I would have to do," Forest sobbed.

Kat gagged on the thought of a monster using this poor child. She tried to turn it into a clearing of her throat unsure of whether expressing her revulsion would be a good idea or bad. Good won out.

"That monster. That beast," she cried with a venom she never knew she possessed. "He should be put down like a rabid dog."

"He s-said an Alpha's daughter could be a Mate, too. Is that true? Will I have to be a Mate?"

"You don't have to be anything you don't want to be, my precious, darling girl. I don't know if it's true or not and it doesn't matter right now. We can ask Mrs. Martin, later. You're young and shouldn't be worried about such things. You have to understand that no one and I mean no one will ever make you do what you don't want. Charles and the wolvers of this pack would die before they let that happen. You understand that what that animal wanted from you is wrong because you were his daughter and a child and because you're someone of value. You have choices. Your mother had choices and he took that away. For that alone, the monster should be shot."

Kat picked up the edge of her gown and wiped the girl's tears, looked around for a box of tissues for her nose and seeing none, offered Forest the hem of her dress's lining. "Blow," she said and at Forest's horrified look added. "It's going to be muddy and shredded from my run through the woods. Who'll notice a little snot? We'll blame it on your brothers."

Forest smiled a little. "They're not really my brothers, you know."

"I know, I know, and I'm not your mother and Charles isn't your father and Meadow isn't our daughter either, but we may as well start thinking in terms of brothers and sisters and daughters and sons, because like it or not, we're a family now and our family is part of this pack. We're not alone anymore, Forest. We have each other and we have the pack."

There was another knock on the door and Kat helped Forest to rise. "We're in trouble now," she laughed and wiped away the last of her tears. "They'll think the Mate's run off." She stopped before she opened the door. "Are you all right? Because if you aren't, I can do this Mate thing any old time. They can party on without us."

"I'll be okay," Forest told her and Kat knew it would be true someday if not right now. People didn't heal from those kinds of wounds overnight.

"I know you will. Come on then. We've got a mating to attend."

Chapter 34

The crowd parted to form an aisle for Kat to make her way to her beloved mate. Her nose was red, her eyes were swollen from crying and her dress was soaked with tears and the drippings from Forest's nose. She'd stopped at the kitchen sink long enough to wash away the now smeared makeup that Jo had so carefully applied and laid her battered crown of rosebuds aside. She was coming to him naked, so to speak, with none of the sleek trappings of the women he was used to.

So be it. This was what she was, the real Katarina Bennett. She wasn't glamorous and never would be, but after her time with Forest, she knew she could offer Charles and his pack something more. She had arms to comfort those in need, laughter to share their joy, and tears to share their sorrow. If Charles was to be the head of this pack, she would be the heart.

There were murmurings in the crowd as she passed, some no doubt thinking she'd had an attack of cold feet. In truth, her heart was more determined than ever to see this through and make it work and when she saw Charles hold out his hand and the look of loving relief on his face, her last doubt fled.

She took his hand and with the physical contact, the rightness of all this flooded through her. It was beyond the sexual heat of his magic. This feeling burned in the core of her heart. Kat kissed his cheek and the crowd murmured their approval and relief.

Charles kissed her hand and held it high above their heads in a display of togetherness. "You see?" He said loudly. "I told you she hadn't run away. She couldn't," He straightened his shoulders, tugged on his shirt cuffs and shook his golden hair into place, a proud and preening peacock. "I had Ryker hide her car and keys."

Kat rolled her eyes at his nonsense, but their guests loved it.

"Family emergency. Forest needed me," she whispered softly for only Charles to hear, "Sorry."

"Don't be," Charles whispered back, "It comes with the territory. I think it's in your job description." He turned to the guests.

"Before we begin the mating and the Chase, I'd like to welcome the newest member of Wolf's Head Pack. River, step forward and be recognized."

Kat held her breath, afraid that the River the crowd would see would be the sullen and angry River of the night before. She needn't have worried. The young man who stepped forward was solemn and humble and a little afraid. And no wonder, Kat thought. He was dressed in a loin cloth; a strip of cotton banding around his hips with a square white flap fore and aft to cover his nakedness.

"Is it your wish to join Wolf's Head Pack?" Charles asked, loud enough for all to hear.

"It is," River answered quietly, his voice shivering with emotion.

"Will you swear to uphold Pack Law no matter the cost?"

"I will." River's voice gained strength and he nodded his head as he spoke.

"Will you swear to place the needs of the pack above your own and follow your Alpha in whatever he may ask of you even unto death?"

"I will." River's answer was loud and clear.

"Who stands for this man?" Charles called to the crowd.

"I do," Ryker shouted immediately. "I stand for this man."

"I do." Tanner's voice came with Ryker's last word.

"I do," shouted another and another, each voice coming faster than the one before until the tent rang with the voices of the Wolf's Head Pack.

Whatever River expected, it wasn't this. His eyes went wide in his surprise. He squared his shoulders and stood tall.

When the voices subsided, Charles spoke again. "Who do you stand for?"

"I stand for my Alpha and the Wolf's Head Pack."

"I stand for those who stand for me," Charles shouted and his power rolled over the crowd. "We stand for those who stand with us. *We* are the Wolf's Head Pack."

A roar went up from the members of the pack and Charles raised his arms and spread them wide. Light surrounded the supplicant, so bright Kat could barely see the twisting and reforming of limbs. Where once stood a young man, a new made wolf emerged, long and rangy just like the man. A child's voice called out in awe and was quickly hushed.

Charles placed his hand on River's dark head. "Henceforth you will be able to run under each full moon and at your Alpha's behest. Welcome, River, member of Wolf's Head Pack."

This time, the whole crowd roared their welcome.

Clearly bewildered, River looked around at the crowd.

"Come stand beside me, son, until you get a feel for it," Ryker ordered and River obeyed.

Unused to walking on four legs, he stumbled through his first few steps. There was another quick flash of light and Ryker now stood as a massive gray wolf beside the new member.

"That, was amazing," Kat breathed.

"It will be more amazing when it happens to you," Charles laughed and then sobered. "You still want to do it, right?"

"As long as I don't have to do it in a loin cloth in front of a crowd," she laughed.

"In front of a crowd? No, but I was counting on a little less than a loin cloth." Charles wiggled his eyebrows suggestively.

The crowd had hushed and were waiting. "This is it," he said and took her hand in his.

"This is Katarina Bennett, the woman I have chosen to be my Mate. She came to us by accident..."

"No accident if Eugene Begley sent her!" someone shouted and the crowd laughed.

"Maybe unannounced is a better word," Charles laughed and the crowd laughed with him. "But she took to us like a duck to water or a wolf to his pack. The first time she saw me go over the moon, another woman might have cowered and cried. Not my Katarina. She stood beside me and fought."

"She saved my life. She saved my life," Buddy told everyone around him until Tilda told him to hush.

"She did indeed and mine, too," Charles went on. "She has a kind heart," and here he gave a nod to his brother's Mate, Elizabeth, "Something I've been reminded is important in a Mate. She's intelligent and wise and loyal and beautiful. Most beautiful when she sacrifices her dress to comfort one of my own."

He smiled down at her and murmurs of approval rippled through the crowd. Kat kissed the air to blow him a kiss. He'd made her excuses to the crowd without betraying Forest.

"But most of all, I love the woman. She makes me who I am and who I will be and I'll spend the rest of my life telling her so." Charles took both of her hands in his. "Katarina Bennett, I take you as my mate and as the Mate of the Wolf's Head Pack. I take you into my bed so the pack will flourish and into my heart so that I may flourish as their Alpha."

One more, he turned to the crowd. "I give you Katarina Bennett, The Alpha's Mate of Wolf's Head Pack."

A cheer went up and Kat blushed. "Can I say something?" she

asked.

"They always do," someone called from the crowd.

"Make it quick. The moon is rising," yelled someone else, but it was all in fun and Kat wasn't offended.

"I haven't had a family of my own for a very long time now," She told the guests and the pack to which she would belong, "I have one now, because you took me in. This is all very normal for you, but for me, it's a fairytale come true. Bless you all for being here to welcome me and bless this man for loving me the way I've come to love him. I know I have a role to fill as the Alpha's Mate and I'll try my best to do it right and Tilda Martin will be there to tell me if I don't." Kat smiled at the crowd's chuckle. "But I want it made clear that I would follow Charles Goodman anywhere, not because he's a wolver, not because he's the Alpha of Wolf's Head Pack and not because he's the Prince of my fairytale, but because he's the man I love more than anything on earth." Her eyes found Forest on the edge of the crowd, watching silently. "I freely choose to take Charles Goodman as my mate."

Charles took her in his arms and kissed her as the crowd cheered. "Are you ready?" he asked. "I'll give you two minutes, no more."

"Catch me if you can, Wolfman!" Kat pushed him away and ran.

She lifted her skirts and sprinted for the trees and felt more than saw the power rising behind her as the men went over the moon under the influence of the shining orb rising high above the treetops. She'd be caught. That was a given, but she'd give them the best Chase she could.

The surrounding trees were fully dressed in their spring finery, but the light from the moon was bright and gave her just enough light to see by. She'd planned her route and knew her path. It was one she walked frequently with the children. Two minutes was not a long time when the creatures who were after you could run like the wind, so she kept up her pace as long as she could.

Kat heard them enter the woods and would have laughed at all the noise they made, knowing they did it on purpose, but her breath was coming fast an her heart was beating faster. The excitement of the Chase was getting to her, too. She took a narrower path to the right.

She screeched when a deer suddenly appeared in front of her, leaping high over a patch of underbrush, startled from its nighttime bed. She paused to catch her breath and found it strange that the animal had come from the left when the noise of the wolves behind her came distinctly from the rear and to the right. But deer were notoriously stupid and were known to run into cars rather than away so the thought was no more than a passing one. The deer was safe from the hunting wolves. She was not. She laughed and ran on.

Her goal was a small pool of water fed by a rushing stream that flowed over an outcropping of rock into a short fall of water. Buddy had taken them there several times and Dakota and Ranger thought it great fun to climb the rocks and crawl behind the sheet of cascading water to hide in the shallow cave worn into the stone at the back. It would make a wonderful place hide and catch her breath.

The wolves behind her were closer now and she picked up her pace. She was almost there. She could hear the rushing water up ahead and the closeness of her goal gave her speed.

She found the steam and followed the narrow path along its edge until she came to the falls. The rocks were slippery with moss, but not a dangerous climb. She looked down at her gown, the hem already muddied from her run, shrugged and removed her shoes for the climb, a lesson she'd learned from the boys.

In less than a minute, she was crouched behind the falls and peering out at the pool of water below. This was a secret the boys had kept to themselves. You could not be seen behind the falls, but the world was visible to you. She started to laugh, but it caught in her throat, choking her to silence.

A wolf stood by the pool and it was certainly not Charles. It stood in a patch of moonlight and she could clearly see its unkempt and dingy brown coat. Unlike the smooth, shining coats she'd seen on the wolvers of Wolf's Head, this one was rough and uneven with what she realized were scars. This was not a guest from the mating. She was sure of it.

This was a rogue and by the way it stood and stared into the trees beyond the pool, she knew she'd seen it before. This was the wolf that Forest spoke of when she recounted her mother's life and death. This was the wolf she'd seen leading the others along the edge of the trees the first night she spent at Hell Hall.

Charles had doubted her vision because he believed the rogues had been run off just as now he believed they'd been run off again.

Kat held her body as still as the stone surrounding her, afraid that even an intake of breath would attract the monster's attention. She prayed the rushing water would be enough to disrupt her scent.

The wolf raised its head, testing the air. It stared at the waterfall for one long moment and then its tongue came out to slather across its jaws.

Chapter 35

"Charles!" Kat cried in her mind, "Oh God, Charles, come quickly. Charles!" The game was over. The Chase was done. She wanted Charles here beside her with his arms around her, telling her she was safe from the menace of this rogue wolf. "Charles," she cried again in her mind, "Charles!"

Like a warm ray of sunshine on a cold winter's day, Charles voice was suddenly flowing through her mind. It was different, hard and raspy, but it was Charles. She knew it in her heart of hearts.

"Kaa-taa-rinaaa," it called and she heard his worry and concern in her name.

She closed her eyes and silently called again, "Charles!"

A howl sounded, clearly close by, followed by another and another and a few sharp barks.

The rogue raised its snout and snarled, showing off its yellowed teeth. Its head snapped toward the sound of the oncoming wolvers and it turned in the opposite direction to trot off into the cover of trees.

Kat wanted to run, to bolt from her hiding place and race toward the sound of the approaching wolvers, but she held herself still until the great golden wolf was in sight.

"Charles, oh Charles."

Kat scrambled from her hiding place, icy water splashing over her gown and hair in her haste to get to the safety of her wolver lord. She threw herself at him, circling his silken ruff with her arms, sighing with relief now that the danger had passed.

"He was here. He was here," she said over and over. "The monster, the rogue. The one I saw by the trees. He's here, Charles. He's here."

Charles, the wolf, chuffed and barked what was clearly an order and half the assembled wolves silently moved off into the trees. The others stayed close by, fanning out in a circle, watching and waiting. No longer noisy and playful, they were on the alert and ready for attack.

Kat stood and moved away from her wolf and watched as Charles changed back to a man. Her man and as she had his wolf, she threw her arms around his neck and clung to him for dear life.

"I saw him, Charles, I saw him and don't you dare tell me I didn't. He was standing right there." She pointed to the spot. "And I think he was looking for me all along." She told him about the deer. "I don't think he knew, at first, where I was hiding, but he found me. Just before you howled a warning, he found me."

Charles held her close and rubbed her back. "Hush now, you're safe. The others will keep looking. I'll take you home."

"But Charles, our mating! We can't go home."

"We can and we will. There'll be no mating in these woods tonight. There's nothing that says we can't mate in our bed where I can keep you safe and warm." He patted her rear end and kissed her nose. "I promise I'll make it a night to remember."

Kat stepped back from his embrace. "No."

She said it so vehemently that several of the wolvers snapped their heads around to stare. Now that Charles was here, she was no longer afraid. Conscious of the wolver's scrutiny, she stepped closer to Charles to whisper her plea.

"This is the only night we get, Charles. It only happens once. You want to bring back tradition to the pack? Well this is where it should begin. With us, Alpha and Mate. I want this, Charles, and

I want it done right. I know you have the place all ready and waiting and that's where I want to be, in the place that you've prepared for me.

"I'll be safe as long as you're with me. I've happily gone along with everything you've planned because I want to be a part of you and your pack, but this I want for me. I want to be mated in the wild and before the dawn calls us home, I want to run free by your side as a wolf."

"Are you always going to be this stubborn?" Charles asked.

"Only about the really important things," she said and smiled because she knew she had made her point.

"So be it," he said resignedly. "It's not a good idea to start your mated life with an unhappy woman. Just give me a minute with my men and I'll carry you off to the place I've prepared. It's right up there, a little way beyond the falls."

"You knew I'd come this way?"

"Who do you think showed Buddy this place and who suggested he take you and the children here time and time again?"

"You're a sneaky and conniving man, Charles Goodman," she laughed. "A sneaky and conniving man."

"I know," he said proudly, "Though we prefer to call it clever and cunning."

*****

They weren't completely alone and no matter how much she begged, Charles would not let her have her way in that.

"You deserve my full attention, kitten, and I can't give you that and guard you, too."

"He's gone, Charles. Your men would have found him if he was still here and he wouldn't dare come back with all these wolvers around." Kat was talking to his neck, her arms wrapped tightly around it as he carried her up the slope.

Eight wolvers flanked them, four on each side. When they

reached the mating place, they would spread out in a wide circle to protect the couple within. Charles promised Kat the wolvers would be far enough away that they wouldn't interfere with her privacy.

"But I'll know they're there," she grumbled.

Charles laughed at her complaints. "They're there every night; on the other side of the wall, across the hall, above our ceiling. They know what we do, kitten. You purr loud enough."

"And with that image in my head, I may never purr again," she giggled.

"You'll purr and loudly. I'll see to it. Now close your eyes." he said.

She could feel his head nod and rise as he gave silent orders to his men and she heard the quiet rustle of their feet as they moved away and into their guard's positions. When she could hear nothing more than the sound of her own breathing, Charles stopped and set her on her feet.

"Now you can look."

"Oh Charles, it's beautiful," she said when she opened her eyes.

The grassy clearing wasn't what she expected at all. It wasn't large, no more than ten or twelve feet across. All but one of the tree branches had been cleared away so a circle of moonlight defined their woodland room. From the remaining branch, a canopy of sheer, white netting cascaded from its circular frame to settle around a bed of downy white duvets sprinkled with rose petals. White pillows with crocheted lace edges were piled high at one end and next to their bed, a silver tray held a shiny silver bucket with champagne, two flutes, and a crystal bowl of strawberries.

"You're not the outdoorsman I thought you were," she laughed softly. "I had something completely different in my mind."

"I know," he said, unbuttoning the buttons at the back of her dress. They were tiny, but his fingers were nimble. "Smelly sleeping bags and a campfire or worse yet, a bed of moss."

"Jo told you!" Kat turned to him laughing.

"She's a loyal member of my pack and she wanted this night to be perfect for both of us." He slipped the gown from her shoulders kissing each as it was bared.

The gown pooled at her feet and she left it there along with her thoughts and worries for the wolvers standing guard in the darkness. The magic surrounded them and sent a thrill of pleasure through her at each place his flesh touched hers. Charles was as naked as the day he was born and she ran her hands over his chest glorying in the feel of the curly blond hair beneath her fingers.

She wondered briefly if she would ever get tired of the feel of him and decided she would not. When she was old and gray, she would still take pleasure in laying her head against his shoulder and running her fingers through the hair of his chest and along the line of his stomach. He would be old and gray then, too, but she would love him then as much as she did now.

A tear fell from her eyes to his skin and he held her away to look at her face. "Second thoughts?"

"No! Not ever. I meant what I said and don't you ever question it again. I love you, Charles Goodman. I always will."

"Happy tears then. You never struck me as the weepy type." His fingers traced the lace along the edges of her demi-cup bra.

"I never was until I met you." Kat closed her eyes to savor the feel of his hands at her breasts and sighed with pleasure as he freed the clasp and his mouth found her hardened nipple.

"You're purring," he chuckle against her.

"Softly," she whispered, "So only you can hear."

He brought his lips to hers and they kissed lovingly, deeply, with a quiet passion that was different from their kisses before as if both were aware that this coming together was more important than the others. This night would seal their fates together for the rest of their lives.

Charles kissed her as if they had the rest of their lives and when his lips left her, she whimpered a plea for their return.

"Patience, kitten, patience."

He'd left her mouth but his kisses didn't stop. He left a searing line of pleasure with them over her breasts and stomach. He removed her shoes and cast them to the side and then bared each leg of its stocking. When the stockings were gone, he kissed her through the tiny triangle of silk that covered her most intimate part.

"Beautiful, so beautiful," Charles whispered as he kissed the silk of her panties again. "As soft and as silky as the woman beneath."

Kat let her head fall back and said a silent prayer of thanks to Jo who'd ordered the expensive underwear, insisting her old nylon things wouldn't do.

"I like them," Charles chuckled deep in his chest, "But I love what they're hiding more." He hooked his thumbs in the barely there sides and slid them over her hips and down her legs and cast them aside along with the gown still pooled at her feet.

"This is how I love you best," he said as he rose, "Soft and naked in my arms. Come, kitten, you must be cold." He led her to the bed and pulled back the cover to tuck her beneath.

Kat knew the spring night air was chilled, but she felt nothing but warmth at his touch and his words. The champagne and the strawberries sat forgotten as they tasted the sweetness of each other.

She pleasured him with her mouth and hands as he pleasured her, their passion rising and peaking together, but without release. His fingers danced over her clit until her need was almost painful and then he turned her and gently raised her hips as he knelt between her legs behind her.

She cried out when he entered her, not caring who heard. He filled her with his passion, driving into her with a force she relished and absorbed. Closed eyes opened wide when she felt him in her mind, his pleasure and fervency melding with hers. Higher and higher they rose together until an almost unbearable desire for completion overtook them both.

He covered her then, his chest against her back, still driving deeply into her and then his mouth was at the soft place where her neck met her shoulder, the place where he'd found she was most sensitive. He kissed her, licked the spot once and then bit down, his teeth instantly breaking through the tender skin.

Kat's cry was not one of pain, but of ecstasy as her body orgasmed in an explosion of sensation and light that rocked her to her core. Charles' body shuddered against her and he cried out her name as he reached his release with her.

She couldn't breathe. She couldn't think. She could only feel his love bursting inside of her. He was her Alpha. She was his Mate. She collapsed onto their bed of pillows and down.

Charles rolled to the side and gathered her to him. "Are you all right?" he asked and when she didn't answer, he asked again. "Are you all right? Did I hurt you?"

Kat started to laugh. "If I say yes, you'll think you hurt me. If I say no, you'll think I'm not all right." Her body began to shake. "No," she said suddenly, "No, I'm not all right. I can feel them Charles. I can feel them all in my head. I can feel them all in my heart."

Charles pulled the covers up around them and held her close to his chest. "It's the pack. You're their Mate. Lie quiet for a minute until you get used to it."

They laid there, quiet in each other's arms, bathed in the moonlight and the afterglow of their lovemaking. She could still feel the pack, but it was no longer shocking nor painful now that she knew what it was.

"Is this what you felt when the mantle fell?"

"No," he told her quietly, "You share only a small corner of the mantle. The burden of it is mine to carry."

"Oh Charles, I'm sorry. I didn't understand."

"That's part of the burden of carrying the mantle. No one but another Alpha would understand. It's a fortunate Alpha who chooses a Mate whose heart is willing to carry even a small part of it."

No one had asked her if she was willing to carry this and yet now that the feelings were becoming more settled in her mind, she knew that she was. This was no burden, but an honor; to be trusted with the emotions of her pack.

"It's love," she said as sure of it as she was her own name. "The Mates who love their Alpha share that love with the pack. It's the ones who are taken against their will that can't share the mantle. Their love is stripped from them. They've nothing to share."

Chapter 36

The champagne bottle was empty as was the bowl of strawberries. Kat dozed, safe in her lover's arms and reluctantly roused at Charles' gently prodding hand. It was still dark and her woodland bed was cozy.

"Leave me alone, beasty boy. I'm having a lovely dream and you're ruining it." She snuggled in closer to the warmth of his body beside her.

"Too tired to go for a run?" Charles said quietly next to her ear.

She loved that voice, his sexy voice, so deep and rumbly.

"I don't run," she mumbled, "You know that, beasty boy. I read someplace that it's bad for the knees and ankles. That's my excuse and I'm sticking to it. I'm a city girl. We only run for the bus."

She opened one eye and smiled coyly. "Unless, of course, some Big Bad Wolver comes along and wants to play. Then we'll run and run until he catches us."

"I'm going for a run," Charles said, tossing his covers off and rolling to his feet.

Kat stretched lazily, reaching her hands high over her head which allowed the covers to slide down and over her breasts.

"Come back to bed, Big Bad" she coaxed.

"My wolf wants to run. I thought my Mate would want to run with me."

Kat was suddenly wide awake. "Holy shit. How could I

forget? What time is it? How long do we have?" She crawled to the edge of the bed and onto the ground. On hands and knees, she looked up at her mate. "How do I do this?"

"You don't. I do," he laughed, "And you don't have to start on your hands and knees although I must admit, the position is enticing. It reminds me of..."

Kat sat back on her heels. "I figured if I'm going to end up on all fours anyway, there was no reason to get up."

"Your right," he said, "I like that position even better. You're just the right height to..."

"Get your mind out of the gutter, beasty boy. I thought we were going to run." She pushed herself to her feet and then looked around. "Are they still out there?" she whispered.

"They are."

"Can you make them go away?" She stepped closer to Charles, feeling exposed in a way she hadn't felt before. "When we change, I mean."

"They can, but they won't. They know their duty." He pushed a stray curl from her cheek.

"Will they run with us?"

"Yes," he said firmly and raised his finger in warning. "And there'll be no changing my mind. They'll keep their distance ad let us be, but they will run with us and they'll keep watch."

"So they'll see me when I stumble over my four paws and fall on my snout, when I step on my tail and then chase it."

"You won't fall on your snout or chase your tail. If it itches, I'll scratch it for you." He took her hand. "Are you ready? Of course you are," he answered himself and they were suddenly engulfed in light and magic.

Kat was so stunned, she didn't have time to think about what was happening to her body, as her form shrank and expanded into something new. Bone remolded as muscle reformed. The momentary ache in her face was replaced with a sharp tingling sensation over her entire body. A sharp poke in her rear end startled her and then it was done.

Charles' wolf was grinning at her. She could feel his laughter even though he made no sound. Her nose twitched, attracted by the scent of the bed. Hmmm. Sex smells. Good smells. Charles smells. Better smells.

Charles started to walk away and she followed him, cautiously at first, because four legs moved differently than two. She looked behind her at her tail and frowned. It dragged. She tightened her muscles. It rose and she smiled.

She heard Charles laugh again and order her to follow. He wasn't speaking in words, but his meaning was clear. They walked a ways and then he began to trot. Kat had to trot to keep up. Then he ran. Energy burst through her limbs and suddenly she was flying over the ground.

Sound was everywhere. Birds called in the trees. Squirrels skittered along branches, something rustled through the leaves at her feet and she jumped, skid, stumbled and ran on. Charles stopped abruptly. Kat stopped, too. Deer. Where? Ah, there. Kat's stomach tightened at the sight of the doe grazing peacefully fifty yards off. She was hungry. Hunt? No! She wasn't ready for that.

Charles ran on and Kat was aware of the others running with them. Pack. Pack was good. They reached a clearing. Charles chuffed and an image formed in her head. She understood. Two wolves home. Report. She saw an image in her mind of a grassy area in front of them. Three wolves left. Three wolves right. Female follow.

Her human mind was still active, but subdued. It marveled that she could see so well in the dark. Her wolf was unimpressed. The sights, smells, and feel of the night were more important. The Alpha was more important. The placement of the wolves surrounding them was more important.

Charles faced her and placed his face next to hers, eye to eye.

He laughed and bumped her snout with his. She bumped his back and suddenly they were bumping and pawing, mouths open, teeth flashing. He hit her hips and knocked her off balance. She regained her footing and lunged. He bowled her over and straddled her body. She kicked with her feet, rolled and took off. He chased. She evaded. She laughed. This was fun. This was play.

Occasionally, Charles glanced at the sky, checking the time, she eventually realized. Her wolf had no sense of time passing. There were things a wolver had to learn.

They played and ran until Charles said stop. It was time to go home. Home? This could be home. Run, play, hunt, eat, sleep, mate. Good. Her human mind gave an emphatic No! Home, children, food, mate. Game over. Time to go home.

She was trotting toward the Alpha when the warning flashed through her. No! Run! and then Down! Kat was confused. She hesitated. A sharp CRACK! Gun. A cry of pain, a yelp. Charles ran past her. RUN! HOME! His directions were clear, but where was home? A picture of Hell Hall blossomed in her mind and suddenly she knew where home was. Kat ran.

Two of the wolves ran with her and she was grateful not to be alone, but where was Charles? Her human mind told her to call out to him. Her wolf instinct told her not to. She was not his concern. As they ran through the trees, ignoring the path, she kept Hell Hall in her mind and let her feet fly. They knew the way home.

As they reached the edge of the woods, one of the wolvers, nudged her gently, side to side and chuffed. Stop. Her instinct said run. Don't stop until you are home. Safe. The wolf nudged her again, more forcefully and she stumbled. Stop! Kat stopped.

The wolvers to either side of her flashed and came home. Kat looked around, expecting to see Charles and then her human mind remembered that this was the full moon. The men could come home without his aid. She could not.

"Stay here until we signal it's safe," one said. He was naked, but neither her wolf or her human cared. Both wanted her mate, her Alpha.

Kat sat on her haunches to show them she understood.

The two men were halfway across the field before Ryker came trotting out to meet them. As if given some unseen signal, other men came from the house and tents and travel trailers along the far side of the field. Ryker waved her in.

She hesitated, suddenly conscious of her wolf body among all these humans. A tall, rangy, dark wolf suddenly separated from the men and trotted her way. River!

He trotted up to her and tossed his head in the direction of the house. Come. Home.

She yipped and if she'd been human, she would have covered her mouth. Where did that come from? She felt River laugh. He understood. He was new to this wolf business, too. Together, they trotted toward the house.

Now what? Kat was quickly learning the disadvantages of being a wolf. She understood everything they were saying, but no one was saying what she wanted to hear and she either wasn't skilled enough or it was impossible for her to communicate. What was happening? Where was Charles?

Bless her dear, curler covered head, Tilda brought her a bowl of water. Need overcame self-consciousness and she lapped at it thirstily, finally moving aside for River to drink his fill.

"You should come inside," Tilda told her.

Kat could only sit back on her haunches and stare dumbly at the woods to voice her refusal. River sat beside her.

All the other men had apparently come home. Why hadn't River? She tried to form a picture of his human self in her mind with a question mark. The picture reformed into his wolf. No!

River snarled. Kat snarled back. River snarled again. Kat

chuffed in exasperation and gave up. Teenaged wolves were as obnoxious as human ones. And then she thought maybe first timers couldn't come home on their own. Maybe they needed the Alpha or another male to show them the way. River wouldn't be the type to ask.

She, on the other hand, was stuck here as a wolf until the Alpha brought her home. If he didn't make it back until after sunrise, she would be a wolf until darkness fell again. Shit!

She blew out air through her lips to show her irritation, laid down facing the trees and lowered her head to her outstretched front legs. River mimicked her position and together they waited.

And waited. And waited. Her wolf had no sense of time, only fast and slow, and her human had no watch. Her wolf waited a long, long time. Her human understood it might be only minutes, but she was a wolf and minutes had no meaning. Shit!

When Charles finally came walking through the trees as a man, Kat was on her feet and running. She heard people yell at her to stop. She dodged the hands that would hold her back. Her mate, her Alpha was home and she felt an overpowering need to be near him, to see him up close, to feel his touch.

She was vaguely aware that he carried another human in his arms, but that was not nearly as important as her need to be near him. She circled him, felt her head begin to shake back and forth in happiness and her body followed, right down to the tip of her tail.

Charles didn't laugh or show any signs of greeting. It was like a slap and it was enough for her human side to take notice. Tanner lay unconscious in Charles' arm. His side was bloody and the smell was irritating to her nose. Charles was bloody, too, but she knew it was Tanner's blood and not his own. She could smell that, too, but she could also feel his weakness. She whined and nudged Tanner's hand. His breathing was shallow and his heart beat slow.

"He's lost a lot of blood," Charles said, "I repaired the damage, but..." His knee folded under him.

"Give him to me." Ryker held out his arms.

"I've got him." Charles pushed himself up and trudged a few more steps.

"Don't be a damned fool," Ryker snapped. He all but shoved Charles back and took Tanner's body by force. "Godammit, you've done what you could. There's others who need you."

Charles nodded reluctantly and followed Ryker, the other guards, all in human form following closely behind.

Kat walked quietly by Charles' side, tense and chastened, with her tail now hanging between her legs. She understood. First law; pack comes first. Second law; she'd let her wolf rule her human, something that must not be done.

Charles' hand reached down and scratched her head. It was like a blessing, her Alpha's forgiveness. She stayed where she was, content at his side, lesson learned.

Chapter 37

"We were too damn close to the road," Charles said, "I should have known better."

"How you figure?" Ryker asked angrily. "You had guards against wolvers. Who the hell would expect some fucking asshole with a rifle at four in the morning? It's not a fucking highway. It's an unpaved back road. We own the land on either side. No one lives there. He was probably banging his girlfriend, saw you guys and decided to take a potshot at a couple of dogs to show off."

Kat remove yet another plate from the table beside Charles. He'd been eating almost constantly since he awakened from his nap, a nap where he had slept like the dead for almost four hours. Healing Tanner and bringing River and her home had sapped a great deal of his strength and his magic.

"Bullshit. I saw that truck, Ryker. The guy was alone and the plate was covered in mud. He fucking knew what he was firing at. Someone firing at dogs doesn't run back to his truck and take off. They don't expect to be chased. That shot was meant for me or Kat. Tanner was in the trees out of sight."

The plate wobbled in Kat's hand. She used her other hand to grasp it tight.

"Can I get you another hamburger?" she asked weakly when Charles glanced up.

Charles nodded. "Please. Bring two. You need some, too."

She would have laughed if they weren't talking about

murder. He always fed her something from his plate. It was a bit silly to Kat, but Charles seemed to enjoy it so she never protested until today. He'd been feeding her nonstop since he'd awakened and come downstairs and he'd insisted she stay nearby while he talked with his men. Now she understood why.

The conversation went on. "Who knew you were there?"

"Who was there when the boys reported back?"

Kat took the plate over to the grill where Buddy was serving as chef in a white cook's hat and apron. Hamburgers and hot dogs were his specialty and also the only thing Tilda let him cook.

"Two more burgers, please."

"Two more coming up." Buddy plopped two more burgers on the grill and moved a half dozen hotdogs to the side away from the flame. He regarded Kat for a moment and then asked, "You all right, Miz Kat? You're not still crying, are you? Cuz Mama says what's done is done. No sense crying over it. You learned your lesson. Now that's enough."

Everyone, it seemed, knew she'd been reprimanded. Buddy, having seen her ears down and her tail between her legs, thought she'd cried, but it wasn't until she was human again that the humiliation set in.

"I'm fine, Buddy." She smiled to show him she meant it. "Jo says it happens to everybody."

Actually, Jo had laughed first. "Looks like the new pup got her nose whacked." It was only after she saw how miserable Kat was that she'd added. "It happens to all of us, you know. It's easy to let the wolf take charge, especially for the women. We don't get as much practice."

It helped a little, but not enough. It was no way for a Mate to act and it had to have embarrassed Charles. Kat had wanted to apologize, but when he brought her up to their room and brought her home, he was so exhausted, he fell back on their bed immediately asleep.

More humiliating yet, it was she who had to make the rounds of the departing guests and thank them for coming. Alex, as Second, came with her which made it that much worse. He politely refused all offers of help, saying the pack could stand on its own, but she could tell he was unhappy, angry even.

It was he who was speaking now to the group gathered around Charles.

"Alpha, I think we need to rethink this move. There's been damage done to the worksites, costs are escalating. We have leases to honor back in the city. If we're going to shift our client base to strictly wolvers, we've got to start making face to face contacts..."

"We're staying."

"I'm saying delay it, not abandon it. Recruit more wolvers, ones who can fill the needs here better than we can..."

"Godammit, Alex, are you deaf! We're staying. You want more members? Talk to John Morgan, Blue Ridge Pack. Marshall says he's got a couple of young men who mated Rabbit Creek girls who are missing their Mamas. Marshall can't take them. He's got a hard enough time finding work for the ones he's got. Call Burt Hennessey, Lowland Pack. He says he's outgrowing his territory. Same with Zeb Trehune. He's talking about a possible split and that's a nightmare."

"Sending us his malcontents will be a nightmare for us, too," Alex argued.

"Give men jobs, homes for their families, maybe they'll be contented instead," Rawley added. "My brother..."

"Who gives a shit about your damned brother? You have no idea..."

"Know more than you do..."

"If you had to..."

Buddy froze, hamburger half way to the bun as Charles

straighten and seemed to expand. The magic rippled the air.

"Oh, oh," he whispered.

"Alex, shut the fuck up. I've spoken. You don't like it, resign as Second. I'll find someone else to do the job."

"No," Alex said sharply and Kat could see how much effort his refusal took. "This is my pack. I serve it well."

When he said no more, Charles nodded at Rawley. "I give a shit," he said. It was another slap at Alex and everybody knew it. "What about your brother."

Kat gave Buddy a relieved smile. "Let's get those hamburgers served."

This time, she held her ground and refused Charles' offer of food and his insistence that she stay.

"I have children to care for, work to do. Everyone's working but me. It's not right."

"It's your mating day," he said and held her hand tightly. "You shouldn't have to work."

"It's yours, too," she said, pulling against him, "And I don't see you sitting back to relax. Come on, Big Bad, let me go."

"Yeah, Big Bad, let her go," Ryker said, and the others laughed.

Charles tugged her hard enough to pull her over the arm of his chair. "You'll pay for that," he said before he kissed her.

"I hope so," she laughed. "Now let me go."

*****

After helping Tilda finish straightening the downstairs rooms and fending off Jo's questions about her mating night with Charles, Kat headed for Tanner's room.

The injured wolver had been asleep since they brought him home. Everyone agreed that this was best, but Kat was worried about Rhonda. She'd been sitting by her lover's side since they'd brought him in.

Becky reported that the young woman had refused to eat or

drink, so Kat fixed a tray with tempting tidbits leftover from the mating feast and a glass of the sweet ice tea Ronda was so fond of. Rhonda wasn't a favorite of Kat's. She seemed too artificial and Jo was wary of the woman because she was a friend of Stephanie's.

"I automatically deduct twenty points off my friendship scale if they like Stephanie and another fifteen if they kiss her ass. Rhonda's not the brightest bulb in the chandelier, so I gave her ten points back," was how Jo explained it. "How anyone that stupid can be that good at her job defies explanation."

Kat wasn't sure exactly what Rhonda did, but she knew the woman was devoted to Tanner and Tanner seemed pretty fond of her, too. She knocked on the door and entered quietly to find Rhonda lifting her head from the bed where it had been resting on Tanner's pale hand. Her eyes were red and swollen.

"I brought you a tray. Tanner probably knows you haven't eaten and knowing won't make him feel better."

"Do you think so?"

"I do. He likes to see you eat. He's just like Charles that way, always feeding you."

Rhonda giggled a little. "That's a sign of love, silly. Everybody knows that."

"I didn't," Kat laughed softly. "I think you guys should get together and write a book, the Mate's Handbook, Everything an Alpha's Mate Needs to Know. There are so many little things going on that I don't understand."

"It goes back to the early days when wolvers hunted for their mates. It's like saying I want to take care of you. I guess it's kind of stupid, but it's tradition." She smiled and stroked Tanners hand and then took one of the little salami cornucopias filled with cream cheese and took a bite, chewed and swallowed. "I love these things."

"Good. I brought you sweet tea, too." Kat handed her the

glass.

"You remembered?"

How could she not? Every time someone asked if Rhonda wanted something to drink she'd ask, "Got any sweet tea?" Never iced tea or tea, always sweet tea. Kat just smiled.

"I know what you mean about not understanding," Rhonda told her after taking another tidbit from the plate. "Our pack was big and we had our own schools. I didn't have much to do with humans until I went to college. It was like living in a foreign country, England or someplace. We spoke the same language, but I didn't understand half of what they said."

"Like they were speaking in code and you didn't have the key."

"Exactly!" Rhonda was delighted that Kat understood. "And they knew it. I didn't dress right, either. I started copying what the popular girls said and did and then I felt better."

And you're still doing it, but Kat didn't say it aloud. Instead she asked, "Why did you join Wolf's Head?"

Rhonda sounded like she'd be more comfortable in the familiar surroundings of her own pack.

"Because of Tanner," Rhonda said simply. "We're from the same pack. He's four years older than me, but I've loved him since the first time he came to supper with my brother. I was six."

"Six?" Rhonda was using the only chair in the room, so Kat sat on the corner of the bed. "How about Tanner?"

"Oh no," Rhonda giggled. "It took him way longer. We just got together last year." She sighed and then frowned as she looked down at Tanner. "You don't think he can hear us, do you? You won't tell anyone, will you? I know it sounds stupid..."

"I won't tell and I don't think it's stupid. I think it's the sweetest thing I ever heard and someday you should tell him. I bet he'd think it was sweet, too."

Tanner groaned and both women stopped talking and watched until he groaned again. He half opened his eyes.

"Tanner?" Rhonda brought her face close to his and when he smiled, she kissed him. "Oh, honey, I've been so worried."

"You always taste like sweet tea, baby," Tanner mumbled, not fully awake, "Got any left? I'm thirsty. Hungry, too."

"Soup," Kat said, smiling. "You feed him kisses and sweet tea. I'll get the soup."

*****

In spite of her promise, Kat told Charles about it that night when they were snuggled together in bed. This was swiftly becoming her favorite part of her day. Charles would lie back on his pillows with his arm around her and she would curl up beside him with her head on his shoulder and her hand on his chest and they would talk of the simple things that made up their lives. It was their version of 'How was your day, dear?' and it worked both ways.

Charles would tell her about the progress of the renovations and construction, how the business was doing, who irked him and who made him laugh.

Kat would tell him about the children, what they learned in the schoolroom and out, what they said that made her think and what they said that made her laugh. When she told him about Forest, he held her while she cried.

It was mostly because of that that she told him about Rhonda and Tanner. She wanted to end her day with a smile.

"I'm a little ashamed. Rhonda's not what I thought she was," Kat confessed. "Jo says she's good at her job, so she's smart, but I don't think she really knows it. She's really very sweet, but I don't believe she thinks that's enough for other people to like her. In some ways, she's a lot like me, feeling like the people around me are talking in code. I feel that way when you talk about business with the others. The terms are foreign to me. And wolver terms and culture?" she laughed. "The only time I ever heard about being over the moon, someone was talking about falling in love."

She was ready for Charles to laugh and tease her and was therefore surprised when he didn't.

"That's one of the things I love most about you, my Katarina. You're open to seeing the best in people and you don't mind sharing your weaknesses with them. They see that and they feel it and they trust you. It's a wonderful quality to have for an Alpha's Mate."

"Except when I'm a wolf who acts like an ass," she whispered. His having to reprimand her still stung.

"All it showed them was that you were just like them. They appreciate that, too."

Kat snuggled closer and closed her eyes. It was good to have someone to share your secrets with.

Chapter 38

There was one secret, however, Kat failed to share with Charles and the longer she waited, the harder she found it to tell.

River was still running off at night and returning in the wee hours of the morning.

Two weeks had passed since their mating, two weeks of confinement to the house and yard, two weeks of antsy children who needed a run in the woods, two weeks of snarling wolvers who were overtired from working all day and patrolling all night and still the harassment continued.

"Ryker's going to be bald the way he's pulling his hair out over this," Jo told Kat one afternoon while she took a break by the pool. Ranger deliberately splashed water up onto her bare feet. "Get out of here you little beast, before I ask Mrs. Martin to cook you for supper." She grinned maliciously. "I like little boys, especially when they're served with carrots and onions."

"Mrs. Martin wouldn't listen," Ranger shouted back, "She likes me."

"Don't be too sure. She wasn't real happy when she found that snake in your bed the other day," Jo laughed. They'd all come running when the housekeeper screamed.

"That wasn't my fault! He got out of my pocket and got lost." Ranger had a habit of pocketing anything that jumped or wiggled.

"You'd probably taste like old shoe leather anyway." Jo banished him with a wave of her hand.

"Come play with us, Auntie Jo."

"I, unlike some people I know, have to work for a living. I'm taking a break and then it's back to the grindstone," she told him and turned to Kat with a wrinkled nose and curled lip. "Auntie Jo?"

Kat laughed. "And Uncle Ryker. They decided that if they were going to be brothers and sisters, they needed aunts and uncles."

"Poor Uncle Ryker. I think he'd like to spend more time with the kids. I think he'd like one of his own." She frowned.

"You don't?" Kat found that hard to believe. Jo tormented the children mercilessly, called them names and was sometimes as crude as they were. They loved her for it and regularly asked her to join in their fun. In spite of her loud protests to the contrary, Jo loved them, too.

"I don't know. I like them best when I know I can hand them off to someone else and babies are so, so tiny. I wouldn't know what to do with one. I'm not very maternal."

Kat thought otherwise, but it wasn't her decision to make, so she kept her mouth shut. "So what's this about Ryker going bald?"

"Pack security is Ryker's baby and he feels like a failure as a father. He knows the men are tired. Hell, he even lets some of us women ride shotgun on patrol." She laughed without amusement. "He's willing to let us risk our nails dialing our cell phones for help. Like the damned things work up here." She shrugged. "He makes new schedules. He changes the routes and the times, but it doesn't matter. The vandals show up where we aren't. He can't track them, either. There's too much water, too many streams and ponds. They lose the scent. The damage they do isn't major, but it's annoying and time consuming to repair and as Alex so frequently points out, it's costly. He's going nuts over it."

Kat nodded. "So is Stephanie. All she does is complain about the 'drain on our resources,'" she mimicked in a snooty voice and then relented. "I shouldn't mock. She has a right to be concerned and she's gone out of her way to be nice to me. In a sticky sweet kind of way."

Stephanie felt pleased. It was the only way Kat could describe it. Since her mating, Kat felt more attuned to the feelings of others and she understood what Stephanie felt but not why. Why should she feel so pleased when she was still off the Council and nothing with the pack was going as she'd planned?

She'd moved her things into Alex's room and Kat had regaled Charles with her visions of Stephanie poured into black leather complete with whips and chains and Alex splayed on a cross taking his punishment.

"Damn. I guess this means I'll have to return those packages that were delivered in plain brown wrappers," he'd said.

"Not until I check out what's in them," she'd giggled.

"Just don't trust her," Jo was telling her now.

Kat most certainly didn't.

*****

She was reminded of her conversation with Jo three days later when River once again disappeared.

Charles had gone to the city and had a late dinner planned with clients. He'd done this before and, as in the past, he promised to drive home that night even though Kat had urged him to stay in the city. The fool man didn't understand that she worried more about him driving back in the middle of the night than she did spending the night alone.

Kat couldn't sleep. She never did until Charles was safely home.

"Of course," Jo laughed when Kat told her, "Makes perfect sense, because everyone knows that ghosting around the house in the middle of the night is the mystical answer to keeping drunks off the road."

The words were said in jest, but when two o'clock came and went, they haunted Kat.

Drunks? She hadn't thought of drunks. She'd been thinking more along the lines of falling asleep at the wheel. Oh, God, never mind drunks on the road. What if he never made it out of the parking lot?"

Kat knew she was borrowing trouble, but she couldn't help it. Restless, she began what Jo called ghosting around the house, wandering listlessly from room to room without purpose or direction.

When she found herself at the far end of the second floor hallway where the children slept, she quietly opened the door to the girl's room. They were fine, sleeping peacefully; Forest curled up in a tight fetal ball and Meadow sprawled across the bed amidst the pile of stuffed animal her Auntie Jo had purchased.

The boy's room held no surprises either. Ranger and Dakota were sound asleep and River was gone. Kat was already overtired and anxious and River's absence put the proverbial icing on her distressed cake. She became angry, so angry that she failed to notice Dakota and Ranger were now sleeping in separate beds.

River had crossed the line. She would no longer keep his secret or turn a blind eye to his wanderings. She plopped into the overstuffed chair in which he usually slept, crossed her arms over her chest and settled in to wait. She would wait there until he returned and confront him and tell him in no uncertain terms that he was to stop his midnight meanderings.

It was all perfectly planned except the culprit never came home.

*****

Kat awoke with a start to find an upside down face staring into hers.

"It's okay. She's awake," Dakota croaked as he stepped back and righted his head.

"What time is it?" Kat asked groggily. She rubbed her hands over her face and combed through her curls with her fingers.

"I dunno," Ranger shrugged, "Whatever time it is we get up."

"Shi...sha...shoot! Charles!" What did he think when he found an empty bed? "Where's River?" she asked impatiently.

"I dunno." This time it was Dakota. "He gets up before us sometimes."

"I'll just bet he does." She'd also bet he came home, found her asleep in the room and made himself scarce. "You boys be good and get dressed. Then go to the kitchen for breakfast. I'll be down shortly."

Kat ran to the Master bedroom. The bed was as she'd left it, neatly made with three throw pillows arranged at the head. Kat turned and flew down the stairs to the kitchen, stumbling over her untied robe as she went.

Half the people in the house were already there, filling their breakfast plates to carry to the dining room.

"Has anyone heard from Charles?" she asked and heard the panic in her voice.

"Isn't he home?" someone asked and Kat was saved from saying something she would regret when the phone rang.

She pushed Hyatt, in the process of answering it, aside.

"Hello?" It had to be the police or the hospital. It had to be something bad.

"Hey kitten. I was expecting Mrs. Martin to answer."

It was Charles, sounding disgustingly chipper and obviously unharmed. The tension she'd been carrying exploded.

"Don't you kitten me you idiotic, fool of a furry asshole," Kat shouted into the phone and then looked around shame-faced at the kitchen full of people staring back at her. "I didn't mean that," she told them.

Jo snorted a laugh. "Oh, we've called him that lots of times, but the part about getting our throats ripped out keeps us from saying it aloud. Hyatt's called him much worse."

"I have not!"

Jo waved him off. "Keep going, girl. Whip his furry ass."

"I know you didn't, kitten," Charles was saying on the other end.

"The apology was for them, not for you. For you, I meant every word. Where the hell are you? I've been worried sick." And not just about you, she thought, but didn't say.

"I'm still in the city. We finished up so late last night I decided to spend the night. I didn't want to wake you."

"Oh yes, because it's so much better to wake up in an empty bed." She wasn't going to tell him that she'd never gone to bed. "You didn't answer your cell," she accused.

"I forgot it. It's on the charger in my office."

"I had you splattered on the road somewhere by some drunk driver, shot in some parking lot for your snakeskin boots, flattened by an eighteen wheeler while you bent to change a tire. That was a terrible, terrible thing to do to me, beasty boy, and I've been half out of my mind."

"Guess you love me, huh?" Charles chuckled.

"Yes, but I'm thinking of changing my mind. When are you coming home?" She was pouting. She knew it. She didn't care.

"Before midnight," he told her and before she could say a word, he continued, "That's the best I can do, kitten. There are some contacts that need finalization and the client wants to meet for another working dinner. I shouldn't be too late. As a matter of fact, I promise I won't be too late. If I'm not home by midnight, you'll have reason to worry."

"No. If you're not home by midnight, you'll have reason to

worry." She wasn't ready to let go of the anger.

"Kitten?"

"What?" she asked impatiently.

"If I died, you'd feel it in your heart, a gut wrenching pain," he told her gently.

"Oh." Most of the anger drained out of her. "I didn't know."

"I love you, Katarina."

"I love you, too, but you still should have called. You could have been stuck in a ditch or semi-flattened by that truck."

"You're right."

"Damn right."

"All right, damn right," he laughed, "Now that that's settled, will you find Hyatt for me."

"He's right here." She handed the phone to Hyatt.

"What a way to start the day, huh?" Jo crowed, "Hearing the boss get beat up by a hootchie cootchie dancer."

The others laughed and Kat looked down. Her robe was wide open and framing the bright pink nightie that barely covered what it needed to. She dragged the robe shut and belted it as she stomped out of the kitchen waving her hand over her head.

"You can all go to hell for all I care, every damn one of you. Wolvers, bah!"

The crowd behind her laughed harder.

*****

Her worry over Charles alleviated, Kat turned her concern to River. She questioned the children repeatedly until she was sure they were telling the truth. They didn't know where he was. They didn't know where he went. But she was also sure they knew something, because they all acquired the same closed look they had when they arrived.

Kat called it their us-against-them look and it said, "Keep your mouth shut. Don't cooperate. Protect each other at all costs." They were a mini-pack unto themselves and River was their leader. Kat wondered if they would ever be able to transfer that loyalty to the larger Wolf's Head Pack or if River would always be first in their minds and hearts.

She was still half convinced that he'd come home during the night and found her sleeping in his chair, knew he'd been found out and was either making himself scarce or had run off again to avoid questions and consequences. If that was the case, Kat was confident he would return sooner or later. He was as attached to the children as they were to him.

Sooner passed and later arrived and there was still no sign of River. By the time the school day was over, Kat's concern had turned to full-fledged worry. She was still, however, reluctant to voice her fears to anyone else. They would feel obligated to tell Charles and she didn't want to see the wounds between them reopened over something so simple as teenaged stupidity.

She began to ask, surreptitiously, if anyone had seen him. No one had, but everyone assumed he was with someone else, even Mrs. Martin who always had her finger on the pulse of the house.

"He's been working with the road crew and taking his meals with them."

She even told Kat where the crew could be found, but River wasn't with them.

Jo didn't bat an eye. "I haven't seen him all day, but then again, I haven't seen Ryker either. You want to find River, find Ryker. They've become joined at the hip."

Ryker was alone. "Haven't seen him. Check with Mrs. Martin. She was talking about fencing in her vegetable garden to keep the rabbits out. Buddy can't do that alone."

Buddy was the only one that showed some concern. "He was supposed to help me, but I guess he forgot. I ain't mad at him, though. He's got a lot on his mind."

"Has he said something?"

"Nah, he don't talk much, but that's okay because he says I can do the talking for the both of us. It's how he looks, Miz Kitty Kat. That's how I can tell. He looks off into them trees and his face gets all hard and ugly like Mama's does when she's had it up to here." Buddy slashed his fingers across his throat. "I don't ask no questions when Mama's had it up to here." He gestured again. "And I figured I'd be wise not to ask River no questions neither."

It said a great deal about the teenager's recent behavior that no one found her questions suspicious. Those first few weeks, they'd watched him like hawks, sure that he would bolt. Now, he'd become so much a part of the fabric of their lives, the thought of him running away never crossed their minds. He was a member of the pack.

When suppertime came and there was still no sign of River, Kat knew she had no choice. She told the others everything.

"He'll be back," Hyatt said with a confidence Kat no longer felt. "I used to take off now and then when I was his age."

"But you always told Dad where you were going and when you'd be back," Jo argued.

"The poor boy could be lost or hurt," Stephanie offered which was something Kat feared, but hadn't voiced and she was touched by the woman's concern until Stephanie added, "I thought you were in charge of the children."

There was that pleased feeling again and this time, Kat thought she knew why. Stephanie was pleased that Kat might be blamed. The damned woman couldn't put aside her own interests for a minute.

"This is just what we need on top of everything else," Alex grumbled.

The discussion went on for several minutes until Ryker spoke. "He's not lost. He's too wood wise and I don't think he's run off unless Kat's right and he knows he's been caught and is too stubborn or afraid to come home and face the music. In which case, I'd take the odds that he's hunkered down someplace close. My biggest fear is that he's been injured or..." He shrugged, unable to say the word.

It was a small consolation that no one had heard any gunshots during the night.

Chapter 39

Kat felt useless and totally responsible. Whatever had befallen River was her fault. She should have told Charles immediately, the very first night she discovered River's nighttime excursions. Charles and the others would have known how to handle it best. At the very least, she should have talked to River, questioned him and made him promise to stop. What made her think she could handle these children, these wolver children, on her own? She'd only just learned that these beings existed. What made her assume that she knew how they thought?

She was alone. The others were gone and the house echoed with their absence. They were all out searching, the women in cars and trucks, the men on foot and that was made more difficult because of Charles' absence. They could cover more territory more safely as wolves, but that was impossible with their Alpha so far away.

Even breaking the speed limit and driving recklessly fast, it would still be two hours before he arrived and Kat feared what she would see in those beautiful green eyes. This was her fault.

They'd called him and Ryker reported what had happened clearly and concisely with no judgment in his voice. Right now, everyone's main concern was River, but once he was found, however he was found, the judgment would come and it was what she deserved. This was, after all, her fault.

She'd sent the children to their rooms, with directions for

Forest to see that they all went to their beds. It was still early, barely dark out, and their silent acquiescence was testament to their own fears and concerns.

"We'll find him," Kat told them as she kissed each goodnight. "Everything will turn out all right," she said and they looked at her as if they knew it was a lie. In their world very little turned out right.

Tilda was in her room where she claimed to be napping and she'd advised Kat to do the same. "You'll be no good to anyone if you're dead on your feet. You've been up for almost two days. You'll hear the phone if it rings, though I reckon they'll send someone back if there's news." Cell phones were spotty at best in the hills.

So Kat was alone with her thoughts and her guilt. She stared out the window of the schoolroom, willing the tall thin body of a teenaged boy to walk across the field with his head hung down, remorseful and repentant. She didn't care where he'd been or what he had done. Kat just wanted him home. Home with the pack where he belonged.

The reflection of four children in the glass had her turning around. They stood in a line and there was no mistaking the guilt on their faces.

"Tell her Forest. You're the oldest. Tell her," Ranger urged, obviously not wanting to be the bearer of the news.

That alone told Kat it was serious. Ranger was usually eager to tell everyone's news.

"You know where he is." Kat made it a statement.

"No ma'am. We didn't lie," Forest said carefully, "But we know what he's looking for and Meadow knows how he gets out. She followed him once."

Dakota started to explain in a rush. "We wanted to tell, but River said..."

"That's not important now," Kat interrupted, "What's

important is you tell me what you know. What was he looking for?"

"The hide."

"The hide?"

Ranger nodded his head. "Them."

Kat looked to Forest for the translation though she thought she knew.

"Them. Where we came from. They've done it before, pretended to be a man and his wolfdogs. It looks like they're trained, see? They move in on a human pack's business and pretend to help. The wolfdogs are used as..." Forest looked to the others for the word she couldn't find.

"They kill people," Dakota said in a matter of fact way that was frightening.

"And listen real good to find out who to rob," Ranger added.

The others nodded their agreement. The wolvers disguised as highly trained dogs were used for enforcement and spying. Men would talk freely in front of a dog.

"Then when things go sour or there's money enough, they take it and move on," Forest finished.

"And none of the humans can complain because what they were doing was illegal in the first place," Kat concluded.

"They don't leave any humans to do any complaining. You don't want anybody recognizing you the next time you come round." Dakota looked at the others and shrugged as if to say, "Somebody has to say it."

"How does he get out?" Kat asked Meadow. She kept her voice smooth and soothing even though her heart was thundering in her chest. "Can you show me?"

Meadow looked to the others and when they nodded their encouragement, she took Kat's hand and led her to the cellar door.

Kat had never been down in the cellar and had taken Tilda's

word that it was as cold and dank as an old stone foundation could be and was only fit for spiders and other crawly creatures who spent their lives in the dark.

Cautiously, with her hand on the child's shoulder, she followed Meadow down the rickety stairs and the warning she had called as a girl came to mind.

"Don't go down those dark, drafty cellar stairs in the middle of the night with only a candle to light your way, you idiot!"

Kat stopped and turned back. "Ranger. Go get a flashlight from the kitchen drawer. Make sure it's one that works." The boys and Meadow loved to run around in the dark chasing each other with the beams. They went through batteries faster than ice cream.

She didn't wait until the faint light from the open door disappeared. She hit the flashlight's button as soon as it was securely in her hand.

The cellar was much smaller than she thought it would be and judging by the fallen shelves was probably once used for winter storage. Something scurried over her foot and she jumped.

Behind her she heard Dakota stomp and croak happily, "Gotcha."

Kat didn't ask what he'd got. Meadow led her across the room, sure of her direction and pointed to and old pie safe that had been pulled out from the wall. The opening in the wall was crude, made by removing the irregular shaped stones of the foundation. Hinges were affixed to the wall, but the door was long gone. Kat shined the light inside.

It was not a secret room, but a passage cut from the earth and shored up with rotting timbers and stone. Someone had built this to smuggle goods or whiskey or the human cargo of slaves long, long ago. From where she stood, Kat could see it slope deeper into the earth. The flashlight's beam could not reach its end.

"You children go back now," she ordered and pointed to the pale light hovering over the stairs. "Forest, I want you to wake Mrs. Martin and tell her where I've gone. She'll alert the grownups." They all nodded, but didn't move. "Go on. I'm only going to the end of the tunnel. If River was hurt, he might have made his way back here and the sooner I find him, the sooner he can get help. You've done a wonderful job, but now it's time for you to go back upstairs."

They reluctantly left her and she waited until they were on the stairs before she ducked into the entrance and began to walk.

The passage was narrow. Kat doubted two men could walk abreast. It was not straight forward as she had first thought. It zigzagged through the earth. The floor was hard packed earth and the walls, once neatly framed with wood and stone, were crumbled in spots with tree roots reaching their gnarled fingers through the opening to reclaim what was rightfully theirs. Chunks of stone littered the path along with the skeletons of long dead rats and mice. Kat winced as one of them crunched beneath her feet.

She alternated between shining her light ahead and lowering it to the ground at her feet and twice, she shined it behind her when she thought she heard a noise. But there was nothing and she thought perhaps all the rats and mice weren't dead. The thought gave her no comfort.

She passed a spot where the wall had completely collapsed, evidence of her greatest fear; somewhere along its length the tunnel had collapsed on River.

Long minutes passed as Kat moved as quickly as she could. The floor began to slant upward and there was still no sign of the end or of a collapse. How far had she come from the house? She rounded yet another corner and she could see a ladder propped against the end wall. She had reached the end.

Kat ran, eager to be out of this long hole in the ground. Before the thought had fully formed that this was a small room and not a tunnel, hands grabbed her and she screamed. She fought. She kicked.

More screaming followed, not her own, and one of the men shouted and cursed and flailed his arm back ward. There was a thud and Kat stopped struggling.

"No! Stop! Stop! We won't fight! We'll do whatever you want. Don't hurt him. Oh God, don't hurt them."

She ran to Dakota who'd been thrown against the wall. He was dazed, but conscious. His nose was bleeding. Ranger still struggled against the beefy arm that held him. Meadow stood immobile by the ladder, her thumb in her mouth.

"Stop it. All of you. Ranger, stop!" She looked at the man holding the boy. "Let him go. He won't run."

"Fuck off bitch." He shoved Ranger toward the ladder. "You run, we kill your little sister here and then the bitch."

Kat helped Dakota to his feet. She thought about pushing him toward the passageway and telling him to run, but she was afraid their captor would make good on his threat. She steered him toward the ladder.

"Just do as you're told and you won't be hurt," she told them as calmly as she could.

"Yeah, that's right. Listen to the bitch and you won't be hurt," the first man said.

The second one laughed. He didn't believe it either.

As she lifted Meadow up onto the first rung that was higher than the others, she glanced back and caught the tiniest of movement at the mouth of the room.

Kat let her foot slip off the rung and fell back into the man behind her, drawing his attention to her instead of to the girl plastered against the wall.

"Watch what you're doing, bitch." He gave her a shove up the ladder.

"Damn kids," Kat muttered loud enough for Forest to hear. "I told them to go to Mrs. Martin."

"Yeah, well it saved me and Top some time not having to go get you. We didn't want the old lady anyway."

Kat didn't want to think about what they might have done to Tilda and she prayed that Forest understood her message and this time did as she was told.

The outside of the passage was no more than a hole in the ground. With the wooden cover over it and dead leaves scattered about, it could easily be mistaken for an abandoned well. She'd hoped there would be a building nearby, but once her eyes adjusted to the darkness, she realized they were in the middle of nowhere.

Top pushed Dakota forward and laughed when the boy snarled. "You got your father in you, cub. He was a mean bastard, too."

"My father's going to come get you and you're gonna be sorry."

"Hate to break it to you kid, but your father's dead."

Dakota stopped and looked back at Kat and Top dragged him along. The boy was referring to Charles and Kat hoped he was right. She gave a slight shake of her head to tell him his father wasn't dead.

Once she realized their destination wasn't nearby, Kat began to think. She was so frightened it was difficult at first, but then reason prevailed. They were wanted alive or these two would have finished the job back at the tunnel and once she accepted that they were temporarily safe, her mind started to work.

If Forest went back, it would be reasonable to assume the men would start their search at the tunnel. They would follow the trail from there. Kat knew they would use both scent and sight so she snapped every twig she could and trampled every tall plant she could find without making it obvious and when little Meadow tripped and fell, Kat dragged the poor child a few feet before righting her, hoping to leave her scent behind.

When they came to a stream and were forced to walk in the icy water, she remembered what Jo had said. She purposely set Meadow up on the bank to walk. It was a good minute or two before it was noticed and she was forced to pull her back in.

"It's too deep and cold for a little girl," Kat complained and hoped that they allowed her to continue.

"Tough shit. She walks in the water or you carry her."

Kat carried her, but managed to stumble and fall to the side, catching herself on the bank.

The boys seemed to understand her intent. Dakota suddenly howled and jumped for the bank.

"Something bit me!" he screamed and rolled in the weeds in pretended agony.

He got a cuff to the back of his head for his efforts which gave him an excuse to howl again loud enough to be heard if there was anyone near enough to hear. The boy flashed Kat a grin as he rubbed the back of his head and Top yelled.

"Will you shut that kid up!"

Ranger, more timid than Dakota, fell more often, too. He wasted no time rolling on the ground, but Kat saw him wipe his hands through the weeds each time before he stood.

Meadow began to cry loudly as if she, too, understood.

Kat shushed her quickly.

After what seemed like hours, they reached their destination, another hole in the ground.

Chapter 40

"What is this place?" Kat asked of the giant oil drum they were forced to climb down into. It was an underground bunker of some sort and she had a feeling that this was not the whole of it. Top had disappeared through a door to the side, leaving it open and she could hear nothing from the room beyond. She was surprised when the man called Kirby answered.

"This place? Beats the hell out of me. One of them old survival types lived here. Didn't do him much good. He didn't survive." The man grinned and in the light from the overhead fixture, Kirby's need for intensive dental work became apparent. Added to that, he had an ugly scar that ran across his eye and over his nose that made his appearance both sad and frightening.

Kat gathered the children to her. "What do you want from us?"

"Not a goddamned thing. I would have been done with you the minute we found you, made it easy on ya, you know?" At his malicious laugh, Kat was afraid she did. "But I'm not the boss, you know?"

Top came back in and jerked his head toward the door. "They said bring 'em up."

Kat hurried the children along, picking up Meadow when she didn't move quickly enough. She didn't want these animals to touch any of them again. They passed through two rooms; one used for storage and one a bedroom. The bed had no sheets, no cases on the pillows and there were blankets and sleeping bags spread everywhere. They had to walk on them as they passed through. Dakota's foot caught in a tangle of blankets and he fell to the floor. Top grabbed him by the scruff of the neck and threw him forward.

"Leave him alone!" Ranger ran back to his brother.

Top took a step toward the two boys with his hand raised.

"Back off and get them up front," Kirby ordered and shoved them forward.

They passed through another bedroom, neater and less occupied than the last and from there into a kitchen that reeked of grease and spoiled food. Ranger pushed through the next door and then scrambled back. He grabbed Dakota's shirt and pulled him back to the safety of Kat, a safety she couldn't provide. They squeezed through the door as a single unit.

"How sweet. Mother Goose and her goslings." She stood beside an ugly giant of a man. "Leon, allow me to introduce you to Katarina Bennett, the key to our success. Or do you go by Goodman now? Not that it matters. By tomorrow you'll go by nothing at all."

Kat had seen the woman as spoiled and somewhat greedy, but to stoop this low, to deal with the lowest, most disgusting form of criminal? No, she hadn't seen that.

"My God, Stephanie, what have you done?"

"What should have been done months ago." Stephanie propped her fists on her hips. In her designer clothes and two thousand dollar boots, the woman looked perfectly at home standing in the midst of filth. Kat's nose itched with the smell of the place, but Stephanie didn't seem bothered by the smell of unwashed bodies and inadequate plumbing.

"Where's the girl?" Leon asked.

"There's the girl," Top said, "This is it, boss. You said the woman and the kids and that's what we got."

"The girl, Goddamnit!" Leon glared at Stephanie. "You said

she was there."

"She was, darling, she still is, but you don't need her now. You can have her later when our work here is done." Stephanie stroked his arm. "When we're in charge, you can have anything you want. You'll have nothing to do but keep the pack in line, spend money and play with your little friends. You've got five out of six. There's no need to be greedy."

"The deal was I get the girl. She's mine." His hair was long and coarse, a dirty looking brown and his curled lip exposed long and yellowed teeth.

Kat knew who this was and she swallowed the bile that rose in her throat. The boys knew, too. This was the wolver they had run from.

"Stephanie, you don't know what he is. You don't know what he's..."

"I know a hell of a lot more than you do," Stephanie snapped, whirling toward Kat with her manicured finger pointed dangerously close to Kat's eye. "I know that the cash cow that was our pack is running dry and dying a slow, painful death. I know I can revive it if people get out of my way. Leon here is going to make that happen and the first step to making that happen is to get rid of you. Poor Charles will be consumed with grief. It will weaken him and then Leon will finish it." She laughed shrilly. "It appears that my Alpha is bigger than yours." She ran her fingers up his arm seductively. "It's time for you to take the first step, Alpha."

"Not until I get the girl."

Stephanie tossed back her mane of perfect hair and huffed. "Oh for heaven's sake, you'll get the goddamned girl. Now kill her!"

Leon moved faster than Kat thought possible for a man of his bulk. Stephanie was grabbed about the neck and flung up against the wall before she could squeak in surprise. Her tongue was caught between her teeth and her eyes bulged.

"Don't try to order me around like I'm one of your prettyboy lackeys," He roared into her face, "*I* say what's done and *I* say who does it. This bitch is a Mate and if I don't get mine back, I'll take this one instead." He tossed Stephanie to the ground and slammed out the door.

Kat had backed the children as far away from the brute as she could. She was more frightened now than she was before. The threat against her was nothing compared to the idea that Forest could be returned to this monster and there was nothing she could do.

Stephanie picked herself up from the floor and wiped the spittle from her face, not in the least subdued. She brushed at the sleeves and lapels of her jacket. "A Mate, a Mate. They all want a Mate. How does it feel to finally be popular?" she sneered.

"Is that why you're doing this? Charles chose me over you? You can't be an Alpha's Mate, Stephanie. That's not my fault That's not their fault." Kat nodded toward the children.

"You think this is about you?" the other woman asked, looking at Kat the way she had the first time they met. "You couldn't be more wrong. You're nothing more than a baby making machine to them. Who cares?" She flicked her wrist. "This is about the pack, the way it's supposed to be, the way Charles said it would be. *I* should have stood at his side. *I* should have run the business and I would have, given time. Alex is a poor Second, though he'd make a perfect Alpha. Your arrival just confirmed my belief that a change in leadership was necessary."

"You could still have that, Stephanie," Kat lied, thinking sympathy might help her cause. "You bring us back and Charles will be so grateful he'll give you everything you want."

"Oh, I'll get what I want and Charles will get what he deserves. Charles will come to your rescue, dear Kat." She smiled and placed her hands together by her cheek as if in payer. "Oh

Charles, Charles," she called in a sing-song voice, "Come quickly. I've found our Mate. Please, Charles, hurry before it's too late." She smiled, flipped her hands open and shrugged. Her face sobered. "Then I'll introduce him to Leon and it will be too late for Charles, too."

"The pack will never accept that monster as their Alpha."

"I don't expect them to. That's part of the plan."

The woman was insane. "What about River?" Kat demanded.

Stephanie motioned to the men standing guard in the corner. "You," she said, pointing to Top, "Go back and get the girl and don't screw it up this time. You," the finger moved to Kirby, "Bring in the boy. Let the Kitty see what's been done to her cub," she told him.

River, beaten almost beyond recognition, was dragged from yet another room off to the side and dumped unceremoniously onto the floor. The boys were there before Kat, pushing past Kirby and falling on their knees beside their hero and calling his name.

"I need something to wash his face with," Kat told Kirby as she knelt on the floor to the other side. "My God, what is wrong with you people?"

Once again, Kirby surprised her by disappearing for a minute, taking Ranger with him for insurance, and returning with a wet rag and a bottle of water that he tossed to her feet. She checked River's body over as well as she could, found nothing that looked fatal though the bruising on his side looked swollen and angry.

"Why, why would you do something like this?" she asked angrily of Kirby. He wasn't much bigger than River, but he scars on his Face and fists testified to his abilities.

"I didn't, boss did. I only held him."

River groaned and tried to sit up. "I'm sorry," he rasped through split lips. "The Alpha's going to kill me."

"No, he won't." Kat helped him to his feet and then to the only chair in the room. "He'll be grateful you're alive just like I am."

"I wanted to find them for the Alpha," River said through swollen and bloody lips. I wanted to show him I was worth of the pack." Beneath his mask of blood and contusions, his face was pale.

"I know, sweetheart I know." She was afraid he was going into shock.

Kirby left them after a time and Kat thought of making an attempt to escape, but when she made her way to the back entrance, she found a snarling wolf lying in wait and she'd no doubt there was one at the front.

They waited and waited. Meadow had fallen asleep and the two boys were exhausted. River dozed fitfully in the chair. Kat curled on the floor next to him resting her head on his knee.

She closed her eyes and called to her mate "Charles, please, I need you." She'd called to him repeatedly since the moment they were captured. Surely he was home by now and close enough to hear her cry. "Charles! Charles! We need you!" and the tears she'd held back from the beginning of their ordeal threatened to break through her dam of restraint. "Charles!"

She was so desperate to hear from him that at first she thought it was her imagination. His voice was so clear she turned to see if he was in the room.

"I'm coming, Katarina. I'm coming."

"River," she whispered, shaking the knee on which she'd been resting, "They're coming. They're coming!"

River roused and started to rise just as the door opened. Stephanie entered and raised a gun.

"Showtime!" she said and pointed the gun at Kat.

Time slowed, but not enough.

River shouted, "No!" and lunged.

Stephanie fired once.

Kat raised her hand, fingers splayed as if her palm could stop the bullet.

Meadow screamed.

Ranger and Dakota charged toward Stephanie.

Kat found her voice and time sped up.

"Stop!"

She grabbed the boys as they flew past and almost swung them off their feet in her haste to remove them from the line of fire. She pushed them back toward the corner with the screaming Meadow.

"See to your sister," she ordered and then looked straight at Stephanie. "You stupid, stupid woman. Whatever you want, this isn't the way to get it."

She turned her back on the stunned woman and knelt beside River, who had crumpled to the floor and was bleeding badly.

"I wasn't planning to shoot," Stephanie pouted.

"Then you shouldn't have been waving a gun," Kat snapped. She rolled River to his side. His eyes were closed and his breathing was shallow.

"He shouldn't have gotten in the way," Stephanie argued, "It wasn't part of the plan."

"And heaven forbid anyone from getting in the way of your plans." Kat didn't try to hide her disgust.

Stephanie waved the gun toward the door and the rising commotion outside. "You need to come with me. Or would you rather your precious children watch you die, too."

"You do what you need to do, Stephanie, but if you need me, you'll wait until I'm done here." Kat took the chance that the woman really hadn't planned to shoot or kill, only threaten. She motioned to Dakota, who was watching the scene intently while his brother comforted Meadow. "Bring that pillow over here."

Kat watched him carefully as he brought the pillow to her,

ready to intervene should he try to extract his own revenge. She took it from him and placed it under River's head and then grabbed Dakota's hand when he would have turned away. "Take off your shirt." She folded it into a thick pad and placed it over the wound. "Hold it here, press it tight and don't do anything foolish. Your brothers and sister need you," she told him and hoped her message got through. It was the best she could do.

She pressed a kiss to the young man's forehead and whispered, "Hang on, River. Help is here. Hang on."

Kat nodded to Dakota, he was in charge, and winked her reassurance to Ranger and Meadow now reduced to whimpering in the corner. She then walked calmly past Stephanie's gun and out into the night.

Chapter 41

The yard, a large roughly circular patch of hard dirt surrounded by various pieces of rusted equipment, was filled with wolvers, both man and beast. Kat's eyes sought Charles and found him in the open center of a ring of spectators as if this was a sporting event.

The cleared patch of earth was filled with wolvers and the animosity between the members of the pack and the rogues was clearly evident. Snarls, snapping jaws and shouted oaths abounded. Ryker and Alex wove their way through the throng to settle and sometimes threaten the members of their pack when their goading grew out of hand.

"Katarina," Charles called to her with a question in is voice.

"I'm fine." Kat wasn't sure if that was true or not, but she had to believe that River's wounding was not intentional and from the looks of things, Charles had more desperate worries.

"But your boy's not. River's dying in there." Stephanie stuck the barrel of the gun into Kat's neck. "Ryker, she'll be dead before I hit the ground."

Ryker who'd been wending his way across the yard toward them, now moved away, far enough to be perceived as no threat.

"She's not lying, Alpha," Rawley called from the door. "Cubs are okay, but River's bad."

"I challenge for the Pack," a voice boomed.

Stephanie sighed and muttered, "I swear it's like living with the Beverly Hillbillies." Louder, she called to the man a few feet away, "Call him off, Leon. Don't waste a man. Let the Alpha attend to his boy. Please," she added belatedly and then she smiled and winked as if sharing a secret. "You won't be sorry."

Icy fingers crawled up Kat's spine at the shrewd look that passed over his face while he assessed Stephanie's request. "Withdraw, Bear. Let the man through."

"Thank you," Kat whispered, all too aware there was an ulterior motive behind Stephanie's request that had nothing to do with saving River.

When Bear withdrew, Kat understood what was going on. Stephanie had known Charles for a long time. She knew what kind of man he was and the choices he would make. This was part of the plan Jo had spoken of before; use up the Alpha's magic, wear him out with challenges and let the final victory go to the chosen replacement.

Beating River had been part of the woman's plan as had Kat's death. Shooting the boy hadn't been intentional but it was a practical replacement for Leon's refusal to kill the Mate. Hadn't Stephanie all but said that Leon as Alpha wasn't part of her plan?

"No," Stephanie laughed unkindly, "Thank you or thank River for giving me just what I wanted without sacrificing another pawn." The gun pressed more firmly into the soft flesh of Kat's neck.

Charles walked past the few wolvers who weren't his own. He glanced at Kat, no more than that. Just a glance and yet she could feel his confidence and hear him in her head telling her it would be all right.

"I know it will," she sent out to him and felt the link between them close behind her words.

She felt his power, though, as it rolled out from the bunker's door and the light that followed sent a ripple of comment through Leon's wolvers.

"What the fuck is that?"

"He's a healer, stupid."

"Ain't no such thing."

"Must have a lot of the mojo."

There were murmurs among the Wolf's Head, too.

"He should have left it 'till after the fight."

"The challenge should have come first."

"He knows how much magic he loses every time he heals. He won't have enough left." This last was said by Tanner whose own life was owed to Charles' magic.

Kat wanted to scream, "He's your Alpha! Have faith!" but their words were said and there was no calling them back.

Long minutes passed and the light never wavered. River's wounds must have been severe. Wonder grew into impatience as the crowd became restless. Finally the light faded and the power receded. Charles emerged. His shoulders were slumped and he stumbled as he walked through the surrounding wolvers to the center of the makeshift ring.

Ryker shook his head as if their cause was lost.

"Damn, that healing shit has taken a lot out of him," he said to no one in particular and his words hurt her more than the others. From Ryker she'd expected loyalty.

Kat tried to open her link to Charles to tell him that she, at least, still believed, but the connection was closed and she understood. He'd need all his magic for the fight to come.

"Poor Charles looks exhausted. How tragic," Stephanie said, though she sounded gleeful and not like it was a tragedy at all. "Save the boy and lose the pack. That's Charles' leadership for you."

"He hasn't lost yet," Kat said through gritted teeth.

"Aw, how sweet. Faithful to our Alpha to the bitter end."

"Not your Alpha. Mine"

"I challenge for Alpha," Leon shouted to the crowd and strode to the center of the circle.

"He'll be no one's Alpha when this is over," Stephanie said triumphantly "And it's all over but the final blow."

Kat felt the woman's body tense with anticipation and felt her own antipathy rise. She had never hated anyone as much as she did this woman right at that moment in time.

The two men squared off, facing each other about twenty feet apart. They raised their arms and the whole yard was filled with light as all men were sent over the moon to their wolves. They snarled and snapped and Kat surveyed them all, separating foe from friend, though friend was a term she was now hesitant to use.

There couldn't be more than a dozen of the rogues, but every one of them, no matter their size, looked like they fought for a living and fought hard. If it came to a battle, there would be bloodshed.

Charles and Leon raised their arms again and in another burst of light their wolf forms appeared. Charles rose on unsteady legs. His tail was up and curled over his back a sign of his dominance but his head hung a little lower than normal, not quite so proud.

His opponent stood tall, broader of chest and heavier in body. He was massive compared to the sleekness of Charles. Leon knew it too. He almost pranced as he walked.

The two wolvers snarled and shook their heads, mouths open to display their teeth, one's white and sharp, the other's yellowed and deadly. Warily they took each other's measure, the golden and the brown. If the outcome was based on beauty Charles' wolf would win hands down, but in this clash of tooth and claw and strength, Leon looked the better formed.

They circled, snarled again and then with a roar leapt at each other. The course of their surge took them higher than a man's head and had they collided chest to chest as the rogue wolf intended, sheer weight and size would have brought Charles down.

But as their fur touched, Charles' body turned, seemingly unable to keep up his momentum and make the height of the great brown wolf. Seeking to right his ungainly fall Charles scrambled with his legs and raked the larger wolf's underbelly with the claws of his flailing hind legs. Somehow his body completed its midair roll and Charles landed on his feet. His legs collapsed like springs and he remained upright, though clearly shaken.

Without Charles' body to absorb the impact and slow him down, Leon sailed past his intended target and landed heavily. He tumbled, righted himself, and skid to a stop. Blood dripped from his underside.

Both sides roared their support, short howls of approval and yips of canine applause, but Leon's angry snarl soared out over the rest. He whirled to face Charles who stood panting with his head hanging down. Leon gave him no time to recoup his strength or power. He leapt, covering half the ground between them, snarled triumphantly and charged across the remaining yards. He meant to broadside Charles to drive him to the ground. Without his feet beneath him, Charles would lose his maneuverability and thus his ability to avoid Leon's razor sharp teeth.

The broadside only partially worked. Fangs grazed Charles' back. He was hit, but once again shifted his position and his hip took the blow rather than his more vulnerable ribs. It spun him counter clockwise which brought his jaws in direct contact with Leon's flank. In an immediate response, Charles tore a chunk of flesh from the back of Leon's leg.

Leon howled, whirled back, his body twisting into impossible angles and snapped at air. Charles was no longer there.

He'd spun away and stood head down and panting, awaiting

Leon's next move. Kat began to suspect that all was not what it seemed. She held her breath.

Twice more the two wolves clashed and each time the brown wolf was out maneuvered and was left with another bleeding laceration. Charles had not completely escaped the punishing blows of the rogue and one hind leg was bleeding badly.

The wounded Leon was limping now, but his anger fueled his strength and he charged again. There was a surge of power in the air that raised the hair on the back of Kat's neck. Charles head snapped up, his green eyes glowed in the reflection of the surrounding lights and his body seemed to expand.

He leapt to meet Leon's charge and the fight was on. The two joined with a clash of tooth and claw. They tumbled together, a twining of gold and brown. They rolled, snarling and snapping, across the open area scattering the wolves who formed the ring around them. Blood joined the swirl of gold and brown, spattering across the dirt along with the saliva of never closing jaws.

The two broke apart, came together and broke apart again. Both wolver's muzzles were smeared with blood. They circled, but now it was Leon whose step faltered. His breathing was labored. One eye was filled with blood.

Kat held her breath and forced herself to watch. She was the Mate and owed it to her Alpha. She wanted to look away, to refuse to witness the slaughter that was about to occur. She no longer feared for Charles' survival only the scars this might leave on his soul. He was the Alpha, but not a killer and she knew in her heart he would avoid this if he could and his next few moments proved it.

Leon lunged one last time. Charles dove beneath the brown body and rose with a powerful thrust that sent his opponent sailing behind him to land on his back. With lightning speed,

Charles turned and pinned the massive wolf's neck to the ground in a lethal hold.

The surrounding wolves hushed as they waited for the jaws to close over the bloodied throat and end the challenge, but the jaws didn't close. His point of victory made, Charles pulled his head back and stared at the brown wolf. Leon turned his head to the side with a submissive whine, admitting his defeat.

"Coward," Stephanie whispered behind her and Kat knew the comment was for Charles and not for the defeated wolf.

Charles turned and walked away. It was Kat's scream and the roar of the surrounding wolves that made him turn as Leon rolled to his feet and sprang for Charles' back sinking his fangs into the golden ruff that surrounded Charles' neck.

This time there was no mercy. Charles leapt with wolf on his back, twisted in midair and landed on his back with Leon crushed beneath him. Jarred free of the larger wolf's grasp he plunged his muzzle into Leon's throat. His jaws clamped shut. The rogue wolf thrashed once and lay still.

The yard erupted as, having no regard for Pack Law, Leon's wolvers attacked. Kat saw Ryker charge at the giant called Bear. Hyatt and Rawley leapt from the porch in tandem and cornered a wolf that was trying to slink of into the woods. For a few minutes pandemonium reigned. The rogues were fierce, but outnumbered and the battle was short lived though as Kat had predicted, bloody. Her heart swelled with pride for her Wolf's Head Pack.

The battle however, wasn't over. There was one more wolver to be dealt with.

Charles ignored the chaos around him and stalked toward Stephanie who had not released her hold on his Mate.

"Challenge him, Alex! Challenge him now!" she screamed at the grey wolf watching from a few feet away. "You should be the Alpha. You want it! You know you do! Fight for it! Challenge him!"

Alex lowered his head, flattened his ears and tensed the muscles of his impressive wolf's body. He snarled, showing a row of razor sharp teeth, not at Charles but at Stephanie and braced his body to attack.

Stephanie's game was over.

Charles flashed to human and Kat cried out at the wounds that were revealed by his human flesh. A deep gash ran across his abdomen and blood ran down over his shoulder from the wound in his neck. His jeans were torn at the thigh and a dark stain spread over the denim.

Stephanie released her arm from Kat's throat and Kat thinking the drama was finally over, took a step forward.

"Oh Charles," she breathed and felt Stephanie's arm rise beside her.

Charles shouted and raised his hand.

Kat grabbed for the gun now pointed at Charles.

Light flashed as Alex leapt, knocking Kat away as he bore down on Stephanie, now transformed to her wolf. Her gun lay useless at Kat's feet.

The sleek black she-wolf screamed and scrambled from beneath Alex's gray one and tore off for the trees. With a nod from Charles, the gray took off after her.

Charles wavered. His knee buckled as he took another step toward Kat, but she was there to catch him and he righted himself and looked around at his pack.

"I stand for those who stand for me," he shouted to them all and he raised his hands above his head to bring them home.

A scream echoed through the trees and Charles paused and waited with his arms raised and his Mate supporting his unsteady frame.

Alex, his muzzle showing flecks of blood, trotted to his Alpha and bowed low, his allegiance proven and clear.

The yard was suddenly engulfed in light as Charles brought his Wolf's Head Pack home.

"We stand with those who stand with us," his wolvers shouted.

"I stand for my Alpha and the Wolf's Head Pack," Alex, ever formal, declared.

Charles nodded his acknowledgement. "I never doubted it, Second."

"If you had lost..." Alex continued but Charles cut him off. Some things were best left unspoken.

"I know. It's why I chose you as Second. You stand for the good of the pack."

Chapter 42

"Ow! How's a man supposed to eat when you're stabbing him with that thing."

"From now on, it's Big Baby instead of Big Bad. I've never seen such a whiner. This isn't easy for me either, you know." Kat clipped off another knot of white thread and pulled the remaining stitch out of his thigh. It wasn't true. It was much harder putting them in than taking them out.

Meadow giggled from her perch on an end table where she sat cross-legged with a plateful of rare steak on her lap. She stabbed another chunk with her fork and offered it to Charles.

"Open, Papa, eat."

"Use sentences Meadow. You're a big girl." Since the battle, Meadow had begun to speak, mostly to Charles, and Kat insisted she learn to do it properly.

"Big Bad, Big Girl, Big Meanie," Charles laughed, pointing to each in turn.

Meadow giggled and Kat tried to frown, but she only made her face look funny and Meadow giggled all the more.

"You're spoiling her, Charles," she said as she removed the last stitch and patted his thigh.

There would be a scar on his neck and stomach as well as his leg, in spite of her best efforts to sew a fine seam. The healer could not heal himself, but when it was suggested they call his brother to do the job, Charles refused. He said he wanted a reminder of what he could have lost. Kat needed no reminder. It was all around her. Every day.

"We spoil each other and now that these damned stitches are out I can spoil you, too." He wiggled his eyebrows suggestively.

"I'm looking forward to it."

And she was. In the days since the battle they had little time to themselves and what intimate time they had, needed to be carefully choreographed. If Charles split more stitches while they were in bed, they'd never hear the end of it. It was little enough, but Kat was grateful for every moment of it.

River needed care and not just for his wounds though they were serious enough. The bruising and swelling over his abdomen and side were the result of his damaged liver and spleen.

Charles had taken care of the worst of it and stopped the bleeding from the gunshot wound, but knowing what he had to face, he had reluctantly agreed with Rawley and left the rest to nature. As it was, the necessary healing had depleted his magic, though his total exhaustion had been a ruse to fool an overconfident Leon, something Charles' wolvers recognized and played along with.

River still felt responsible for endangering them all, even though he'd been assured by everyone that the plot would have come about eventually. Stephanie would have seen to that. She'd already attempted the kidnapping once before when Rhonda had inadvertently told her the women and children were alone at the house. He seemed to come around a bit when Ryker pointed out that if it hadn't been River, who could take it like a man, it might have been Kat or one of the cubs who wouldn't have survived that kind of beating.

The Alpha needed caution. He tried to do too much too soon and split his amateur stitching twice. Kat pled and Mrs. Martin scolded and Ryker finally threatened to tie him down if he didn't take up a post on the sofa and stay there.

Forest was the hero of the hour. She'd run back to the house alone in the darkness of the tunnel and awakened Mrs. Martin. Together they'd gone out and found some of the others.

It was Rhonda, the one they all thought was not so bright, who placed Stephanie at the center of the trouble. Stephanie had bragged a little too much, though Rhonda never suspected it was anything more than talk until Kat and the cubs were taken.

Jo, along with Hyatt and Tanner, followed the tunnel and the trail left by Kat and the boys. The two men made short work of the guard at the back of the bunker and Jo led the cubs home.

"The hardest part about it was keeping Dakota and Ranger quiet. They wanted to go back and join in the fight." Jo laughed when she told Kat about it later. "Those wolvers hurt River and made their sister cry. Those two boys were hell bent on revenge. It would have served the bastards right if I'd sent the little demons back. I hope they're around to give my kid a little bit of the beastie someday."

"Your kid? Someday?" Kat asked with a laugh of her own. "I thought pups were a sticky fingered pain in the ass."

"Oh, they are and they still start out too tiny, but Ryker and I talked and, well, if I don't like them, Ryker says I can just turn them over to you and Mrs. Martin."

Jo's mating to Ryker was only a week away and Tanner and Rhonda would be mated the following month and Kat had a feeling there would be more to come. Their pack would be growing, not only through the recruitment of families, but through families born of the newly mated pairs.

The indomitable Mrs. Martin was in her element with her scolding and cosseting and feeding of the revolving residents of Hell Hall. Buddy now ran with the pack and Kat loved him as the brother she never had. She was his Kitty Kat.

Alex would never see her as his Kitty Kat nor would she see

him as her bosom buddy, but they had learned to respect each other's position and Kat would forever be grateful to him for doing what must be done and relieving Charles of the burden of doing it. She couldn't love Alex, but she would never again question his loyalty to the Wolf's Head Pack.

*****

Kat ran her fingers over the puckered marks at the back of Charles' neck. Four small scars made by the rogue's fangs, four tiny punctures that could have taken him away from her forever.

She'd waited for him, naked and kneeling on the carpet in the center of their room, hoping for a night of play now that he was fully healed. Charles happily agreed with her plan.

Now, he captured the hand and pulled it away, carrying it to his lips where he kissed her palm. "Don't," he said gently, "Don't think about what might have been, kitten. Think about what is and what will be."

Kat smiled and when he released her fingers she brought them to his chest where she began unsnapping his western style shirt. As each button popped from its mooring, she separated the fabric and kissed the spot beneath.

"Easy for you to say," she whispered, her lips against the blond curls that tickled her nose. "You didn't see that night from my perspective." She moved to the next button. "You knew you had reserves of magic. I didn't."

Charles ran his fingers through her curls. "I told everything would be all right." His breath hitched when her lips found the reddened line that backslashed across his ribs and abdomen.

She pulled the shirt up and out from the waistband of his jeans to finish her unbuttoning. "That's what the hero always says right before he thinks he's going to die."

The buckle came next. It was a big buckle, oval in shape, with a wolf standing tall and howling at the sky embossed in the silver. It fell heavily to the side as she released the catch. The button and fly were undone and spread to continue her kisses along the scar's full length to where it ended just above his hip.

"But I never had any intentions of dying."

"The hero never does."

She slid the jeans and silk boxers beneath down over his hips and his erection sprang free. It bobbed in front of her nose and she went to captured it between her lips, but instead... she burst into tears.

"Well damn," Charles laughed hoarsely, "I've never had that reaction before. I always thought it was pretty good looking... as penises go."

Kat knew he was trying to make her laugh and she tried but it came out a sputter that turned into a sob. She sat back on her heels and covered her face with her hands, unable to stop the pent up fear and terror she'd held in her heart from pouring forth.

"Hey now, hey." Charles kicked the jeans from his legs and cursed when the bunched denim caught on his foot. He freed it and kicked the offending jeans to the side and then he was on his knees in front of her. "What is it, kitten, what's wrong?" His hand was shaking as he ran it through her curls. "Tell me."

She tried. Each time she opened her mouth to speak, fresh sobs erupted.

"Delayed reaction?"

She nodded her head and wailed. Not once since River disappeared had she cried, not when they were taken and she feared for the children's safety, not when she worried about Forest's possible return to the thing she feared most. When River was shot she'd felt as if her heart was ripped from her chest and when Charles faced off with that brutal rogue, with her new found happiness crumbling beneath her feet, she'd faced it passively with false courage. Even with a gun to her throat, she'd given no sign of the panic she felt. Her hands never shook with her terror as she stitched Charles' deep wounds.

But it was there, hiding inside, and this simple act of playfully undressing her mate brought it home. In that one night, her fairytale turned into a nightmare. She'd come so close to losing it all.

Charles let her cry while she blubbered and mumbled and hiccupped her way through it. When she was finished and there were no tears left, he wiped her eyes with his shirt and made her blow her nose. He lifted her to her feet and she slid up his body until her head rested on his chest. She wrapped her arms around him and clung to him, her liferaft in the storm.

He let her rest there for a moment until her breathing slowed and then gently moved her away with his hands beneath her arms. He kissed her eyes, her nose, her cheeks and the corners of her mouth.

"I'm a mess" she mumbled and would have turned away, but his hand held her head firmly in place.

"Yes, but you're a beautiful mess and you're my mess and I'll be forever grateful for the day I found you swimming naked in my pool."

Kat tilted her head and brought her mouth to his in open invitation, an invitation he accepted as his tongue plunged within. She whimpered, still not quite past her teariness. Charles' arms tightened around her and pulled her close to press her breasts to his chest.

His erection felt warm against her belly. She needed him, needed that warmth inside her, reassuring her that they were both alive and their future was bright. The Alpha's magic coursed through her, warmer and richer than before because she now knew how precious it was, how easily it could be extinguished.

Kat pulled away and led Charles to their bed, the bed where they would laugh and play and snuggle and talk and someday create children together and share the richness of their lives until they were old and gray.

This was her fairytale and he was her Wolf King, the Master of his Domain and the Captain of her heart. He was her Happily Ever After. He was her Alpha and she was his Mate.

#####

About the Author

Jacqueline, known as Jackie to her friends, lives in rural southern Ohio with one lovable husband, one spoiled dog and one disinterested cat. She believes coffee is a food group and always has a pot brewing. When not writing, she can usually be found with her nose in someone else's book or working in her garden. She also spends a great deal of time chasing deer and rabbits who apparently also like gardening.

Jackie loves hearing from her readers and is always willing to chat. She can be reached through her website at http://jacquelinerhoades.com or at mailto:jackie3049@gmail.com

Excerpt from Guardian's Grace

Book 1 of the Guardians of the Race

This was a mistake. Grace knew it when her best friend Alice cornered her at the elevators after work and she knew it when Alice dragged her, protesting, into the little apartment that shared a landing with her own to dress her up in what Alice called 'a sexy little number' and Grace called one step up from a street walker. Why, oh, why had she said yes?

But, of course, she knew why. It was guilt. She'd avoided Alice all week because she hadn't told her friend about getting laid off. Alice, with her rose colored glasses, would see this misfortune as an opportunity to try something new, to embark on an adventure, to meet new people. The woman never saw a problem that couldn't be fixed and Grace needed a little more time to get used to the idea of being unemployed before hearing about how wonderful it all might be.

So here she was, at a retirement party for a guy she barely recognized, sitting at a group of tables surrounded by twenty people she didn't know, wearing a little black sheath that covered a great deal less than decency should allow and a pair of thin strapped stilettos that almost guaranteed foot pain in the morning. A crystal pendant disappeared into her cleavage and sparkling teardrops hung from her ears.

The buzzing in her brain was a continuous thrum and it wasn't from the lights or the music or the three glasses of wine she'd sipped her way through. It was the people. There were just too many people with their emotions rolling off them in waves, heightened by the music and alcohol.

Grace looked around at the crowd, smiling, talking, drinking and dancing. Happiness, anxiety, lust, fear, and even a smattering of violence blazed through her head and she winced as her heart seemed to take up the throbbing beat of the music. The place was a cacophony of sensations and she didn't know how much longer she could hold out. She couldn't handle this many people on her best day and today definitely wasn't her best.

Today had been her last day to take the elevator to the basement storage facility where she'd spent the last six years scanning box after box of paper files onto her computer. It didn't pay much, but she didn't need much and the peace she enjoyed made up for the lack of dollars. No one ever came down to her little cloister and that was what made the job so perfect. No people meant no psychic vibrations and none of the violent headaches that accompanied them. Unfortunately, she'd been too efficient and worked herself out of a job.

"Come on. Dance with me. You've been sitting there all night." Alice, wearing a flirty red dress with glittery trim at the hem and deeply scooped neckline, shimmied in front of Grace. Her smile was wide and her eyes sparkled. She held out her hands. "How are you going to attract attention if you don't display the goods?"

"I'm not a piece of meat, Alice."

Her friend laughed. "Oh, honey, in that dress you're a prime rib."

When Alice leaned over to whisper, Grace could only imagine the view the swirling skirt offered from behind.

"In that dress, you're as sexy as sin." The bubbly blonde's face became serious. "You really don't have a clue, do you?" Then she shook her head and laughed again. "Never mind, come dance with your best friend."

And Alice was her best friend. If truth be told, Alice was her only friend and had been since seventh grade when yet another foster placement dropped Grace into yet another school, her eighth or ninth. She was no longer sure. Thirteen year old Alice immediately took her in and unlike most of her classmates, never saw Grace as weird, only different. The friendship continued right through high school as did the foster placement.

She and Alice lost touch for a few years after high school when Alice remained at home to attend Junior College and Grace was cast out on her own when her foster child funding was cut off at the age of eighteen. Then six years ago, when Grace moved into her current cheap, fourth floor walk-up, there was Alice, ready to say hello to the new neighbor and reminding Grace that there were, after all, good things in every life and Alice was the best thing in hers.

At twenty-seven, her life was a confined and lonely one. She didn't like it, didn't want it, but it was the only way she could survive. She often thought that without Alice's friendship, she might have succumbed to desperation and depression.

Grace smiled as she joined Alice on the dance floor and laughed outright as Alice lifted her arms and began swirling her hips to the heavy beat of the music. She raised her own arms and began a much slower mime of her friend. It was then that she saw them.

Across the room, standing against the wall, arms crossed over massive chests, were two of the most beautiful men she had ever seen, twins, each the exact replica of the other. Soft light surrounded them as if they stood in a spotlight on a stage. Only their eyes moved, searching the room. She smiled in appreciation.

"Whoa, girl, I didn't know you could move like that," Alice's admiring voice broke through.

Grace's heart skipped a beat as realization dawned. The buzzing in her head was gone, leaving only the music. The tension that had been her body's constant companion was replaced by a peaceful swaying rhythm. This was heaven. She kept her eyes on the twins and let her body fall under the seductive spell of the moment.

"Alice," she said softly, after another song began. "Eye candy at one o'clock." She gestured with her eyes.

Dov elbowed his twin lightly in the ribs. "That girl over there is staring at us."

"Woman."

"What?"

"Woman. You can't call a female over eighteen a girl. It's sexist. Chauvinistic. Politically incorrect."

"Whatever," Dov replied, shrugging off the criticism. "She's staring at us."

"She can't be. We're in white light. Humans can't stare at what they can't see."

"I'm telling you, she's staring at us. Look," Dov directed with a slight poke of his chin. "Right there. Goddess body, skimpy black dress, dark hair with the blonde streak. She's dancing with the sexy boobs in the red dress."

"Idiot. You've got to stop saying stuff like that. You can't refer to a woman as sexy boobs in a red dress." Col looked disgusted.

"Blonde. I meant blonde. Sexy blonde in the red dress. Okay? And she's still looking. She's pointing us out to her friend."

"Shit. You're right." Col motioned with his head. "Let's take it outside."

"Eye candy?" Alice squealed. "Did you say eye candy? I can't believe you said eye candy!"

Grace huffed in exasperation. "You say it all the time. Now quit making fun of me and look behind you, over by the wall. And don't be your usual obvious self."

Alice made a casual turn and kept on dancing. "Ooo, you mean red shirt, dark hair, and dreamy eyes?" She completed her turn and faced Grace.

"What guy in the red shirt? I'm talking twins! How could you miss them? White tees, light blue jeans, at least six feet of hunky body. Each."

"Twins! Where?" Alice shrieked and spun around.

It was too late for subtlety. Grace pointed. "Right there in the light."

But they weren't there. And neither was the light they were standing under. Her eyes darted around the room. They had to be here. Somewhere. They were way too big to get lost in the crowd.

"They were there, Alice. I swear. They were right there." Grace pointed across the room.

"So they left. No big deal, honey. We'll catch them another time. Now that you're getting in the swing of things, we can go out anytime you want." Alice winked. "You really let yourself go for a minute there, girl. You were something to see." Her eyes lit on someone over Grace's shoulder. "We'll catch those twins another day, but right now I think I'll go introduce myself to the cutie in the red shirt. Don't leave without me, now."

She watched as Alice danced her way across the floor toward her intended conquest. Grace tried to keep the smile on her face, but knew it was becoming a grimace as the buzzing of emotions around her returned. She glanced at her watch. The few minutes of reprieve had been wonderful and it gave her hope. If it could happen once, it could happen again, right? But for now, the buzzing was back with a vengeance.

She returned to her table, took a sip of wine and tried to take an interest in the dancers on the floor. She scanned the room again hoping to catch another glimpse of the gorgeous twins, to no avail. The buzzing in her head grew stronger and the migraine that always accompanied the sensory overload was building along the side of her head. It was too much and she knew it was time to go home. She wasn't going to ruin Alice's night out, just make her apologies and find her own way home.

She once again scanned the floor, this time for Alice and Mr. Red Shirt and quickly spotted them heading for a hallway at the back of the club.

She blinked her eyes, shook her head and blinked again. She couldn't be seeing what she was seeing. Mr. Red Shirt wasn't the cutie Alice claimed. Grace's heart stopped and she choked on the bile that rose up in her throat. Red shirt's face had elongated, his chin jutting forward with snarling lips curled back exposing jagged, feral teeth. His brow bulged over blackened eyes and it appeared he had no nose at all. Grace shook her head again, trying to dislodge the nightmare image. This couldn't be real.

Her rational mind told her that this was a hallucination. Someone must have drugged her wine. It all made sense. That's why her brain buzz had temporarily disappeared. That's why she saw the beautiful twins who weren't there. That's why she was now seeing this monster while Alice walked calmly at his side, laughing and talking as if she didn't have a care in the world.

Grace grabbed her purse and followed the couple across the floor. If she was hallucinating, whether from drugs or simply because she had finally gone over the edge into insanity, she needed to get to a hospital and she couldn't trust herself to get there alone. She needed Alice. Alice was all she had.

She reached the empty hallway in time to see a rear exit door close. Something was very wrong. Hallucinations or not, Grace knew that Alice would never follow a complete stranger into a back alley alone. Alice was fun and flirty. She wasn't stupid.

Grace sprinted for the door.

Excerpt from Guardian's Faith

A Guardians' of the Race Novel
Coming in 2013

Having only recently crawled from the dark cavern of her madness, Faith Parsons seriously considered crawling back in. At least it was quiet there. For a while, her mind had cut off most sight and sound, most thought for that matter, and Faith found she sometimes missed the absolute silence. The silence within her mind wasn't deafening as some writers claimed. She thought of it more as restful, serene, and healing.

There was a lot of healing going on in this House of Guardians lately and while she didn't mind using her powers as a Daughter of Man to help repair the injuries they inflicted upon each other, she wished they could batter and bash each other a little more quietly. When they weren't screaming at each other in mock battle rage, they were laughing and joking and thundering around the house, egged on by the twins, Dov and Col, who weren't yet Guardian's but were full-fledged trainees and certainly old enough to begin acting like sensible adults.

Following the recent trouble at Moonlight Sanctuary, the Paenitentia enclave several miles outside the city, and the popularity of Nardo's video games, there had been an upsurge in young Paenitentia men signing up for long-unfilled positions within the Guardians of the Race. This House had become a clearing house for these recruits where they were put through a rigorous initial training meant to weed out those who didn't have the right stuff. Those that passed would be sent on to other Houses to complete their instruction.

Faith wasn't sure how Canaan, the Liege Lord of this House, had earned this dubious honor, but there it was. There were eight new recruits living here now along with the seven people who called this House their home. Add to that number her sister Hope and Hope's Guardian mate, Nico, who lived across the alleyway and the old, but harmless vampire, Otto, and his mate Manon, and you had quite a crowd around the dinner table and none of them were quiet.

The place was like a damn bus station with people running in and out, in and out and like those in the bus station, most of them, most of them were strangers. Faith hated strangers. They frightened her and she'd had enough fright in her twenty eight years to last a lifetime, thank you very much. It was her problem, she knew, and no one else's fault, but there it was; strangers coming in waves of two or three or four. She would no sooner get used to one batch than another would be flowing through the door, coming upon her unawares, bumping her with the door while she was doing laundry and they came in, laughing or shouting to each other, from the garage. It was a good thing she had no voice or she would have spent half her time screeching from startlement.

And that was another thing, she thought as she stripped the sheets from one of the guest rooms' beds, guests. At least that's what everyone else called them. Faith thought of them as cattle buyers coming in from out of town to get an up-close look at the House's current stock of muscle bound bulls. Every week or two, someone new arrived.

None of the other women seemed to mind. Grace, Lord Canaan's Lady and pregnant with their first child, fussed over them all like a mother hen, clucking over the recruits' injuries and stuffing the visitors with the goodies that constantly flowed from her oven in the huge kitchen at the back of the house. Hope spent her days taking care of the business end of Nardo's games. She closed her office door and didn't come out until it was time to set the table for supper. JJ, Faith's best friend and the only known genetic mix of Paenitentia and Daughter of Man (other than the child Grace carried) was Nardo's mate. She worked beside the men in the gym, training recruits. For Faith, it was the only thing she enjoyed about the comings and goings of the House; the look of shock and awe on the faces of the new recruits when JJ set them on their all too macho asses.

She smoothed out the wrinkles of the fresh sheets and pulled up the blanket, making sure it was perfectly even on either side of the bed before pulling the downy comforter into place. She dusted the dresser and night stands, straightened the pillow on the overstuffed chair and resolved to vacuum later when she did the hall. This was all she was good for; hotel maid for a House of Guardians.

Faith felt her job as healer was superfluous. Yes, the golden glow from her fingertips aided the healing process, but the Paenitentia were remarkably fast healers to begin with. Unless a bone was broken, or a wound was particularly deep, her services weren't really necessary. As a matter of fact, things outside the House had been so quiet lately none of the Daughter's talents were necessary.

Like Faith, all the women were Daughters of Man, an ancient collective of women whom some called blessed and others called witches. No one knew how many Daughters still existed in the world. History had not been kind to their numbers and many succumbed to insanity or death if their powers weren't fully realized. Faith tried not to think about that too deeply. There was a time, not too long ago, that she would have preferred death to the life she was forced to lead.

"Why the pensive face, poppet? Have the Terrible Two been leading their band of miscreants on another rampage?"

Broadbent, also known as the Professor and the Guardian Faith felt most comfortable with came down to stand beside her, his long beaklike nose preceding his head around the corner to look into the parlor and then down the hall to see why she hesitated at the foot of the stairs. There was no one there.

"What is it, then?"

Faith sighed, smiled and signed. *"Nothing unusual. Too many people. Too much noise. Wondering what I'm doing here. What purpose do I serve?"*

Her body had healed and so had her mind, but her voice was gone. Sometime between her rescue and her return from her emotional exile, her voice had disappeared. Working with JJ, her best friend among the women, she developed a sign language, part American Sign and part her own, that allowed her to communicate with the members of the House. Even the recruits caught on quickly.

"You're our healer."

"Cuts, bruises and broken noses. They heal themselves."

"You help Grace with the cooking and cleaning and I know she finds it a great comfort that you'll be here when her time comes." He lifted his hand to touch her shoulder and winced inside when he saw her flinch. "I beg your pardon," he said as he drew back.

"No." Faith caught his hand and brought it to her opposite shoulder so that his arm was around her. *"My fault. I don't mean to do it and I know I hurt you every time I do. I'm sorry."*

"Hush now, poppet. I feel privileged that you allow me the honor of touching you at all. I know how hard it must be and I admire your bravery." He led her into the parlor and when he had her seated on the antique settee, he closed the door to give them privacy to talk. He settled his long body next to her tiny one, angling his long legs so that their knees were almost touching. Almost.

"I'm not brave," she signed. *"Hope and Grace have stood up against Demons. JJ hunts them while I…"*

"Survived. Lived. And I am so very glad you did. Every day, I admire your courage in facing your fears and overcoming them. You are gentle and kind, a true lady."

Faith shook her head. *"You don't know me, what I've done, who I was before."*

Her life had become a series of Before and After. Before her mother died and After, when she saw what a cruel man her father was; Before she ran away to avoid her sister's fate and After, when she ran wild in the city; Before she was captured by a demon and forced to be his plaything and now, another After. The other Afters had held hope and plans for the future. Faith saw no future now.

"My dearest Faith." Broadbent reached for her hand, but waited until she nodded before taking it in his. "Who you were doesn't matter. Who you are does."

Who am I? She asked herself and answered. A scarred husk of a woman who has nothing to offer. She had her healing touch but what good did it do here where no one needed it and she was too terrified to leave this House of Guardians to offer it to those who did.

The other Daughters, Hope and Grace and JJ, had left lonely, unhappy lives to come here and discover new ones with purpose and men who loved them. There was none of that here for her and yet, she was afraid to leave. The city terrified her and where else did she have to go.

"Faith."

Broadbent's voice called her back from her maudlin reverie.

"There's something I wish to speak with you about, something over which I have thought long and hard." He slid to his knee in front of her. "Faith Parsons, it is my consummate desire to have you as my mate. I promise you I will care for you and shelter you and protect you from all you fear with every breath in my body, every beat of my heart. I will be loyal and faithful and I will share with you all that I have. You will never be in want."

Faith's eyes widened in shock and Broadbent misunderstood.

"I understand, dearest, that consummating such a union would be too much to ask, but I am willing to wait until you find it in your heart to trust me with such a precious gift. You needn't share my bed unless you choose to. My parents have spent their mated lives in separate bedrooms as do most others of their social set. It wouldn't feel unusual to me. Please, my dear sweet Faith, consider my proposal. I offer it with the most honorable of intentions."

How she wished she could say yes and be what he wanted her to be. If she'd met Broadbent when she first came to the city, she would have laughed at his gangly body and funny clothes. She would have made fun of his flowery speech. Faith was glad she hadn't met him then. If she had, she never would have gotten to know this gentle and generous man. She never would have heard the stories of his bravery and loyalty from his fellow Guardians.

Sometimes, on her worst days of mental withdrawal, it had been Broadbent's voice, kind and always cheerful, that brought her back from the depths. He read Jane Austin to her and it was just what she needed; gentle stories of another time, where civility ruled. Jane Austin would have liked Broadbent for his courtesy and honesty. She also would have frowned at the offer of a marriage without love.

Broadbent loved her, but not in the way a man should love the woman he asked to be his mate. And she loved him. How could she not love this dear and noble man? But she couldn't be the mate he deserved. She couldn't love him in that way and she wouldn't torture him with waiting for her to change. That part of her was dead. She ran her fingers along his cheek down to his chin and then she signed.

"You flatter me beyond measure," she told him and hoped he heard Miss Austin in her words, *"To think a man so honorable and good should make such an offer to one such as I is a compliment beyond any I have had before or likely will hear again. But I would be remiss to accept such an offer from a man who does not love me."*

Broadbent started to protest, but she stopped the movement of his lips with her finger.

"Nor I him." She smiled to soften the blow. *"We love each other as brother and sister should, but that is not the kind of love to bring to your mating bed. You know it's true. Not once in your proposal did you offer me your love. You couldn't, you dear, sweet man, you couldn't lie about something so important."*

"Strong matings have been built on less."

"But you deserve more."

"Is this where you ask if we can still be friends?" Broadbent asked as he moved back to the settee and settled in with a sigh.

"Can we?"

Broadbent smiled sadly. "I don't have so many I can afford to turn one away. I did mean it, though. We could make a go of it. We wouldn't have what the others have, but we would have each other. It's awkward being the lone wolf."

"You're not alone. Dov and Col aren't mated either."

"Ah, you wound me. First you turn down my offer and now you lump me in with the irritating idiots."

At that moment, one of the irritating idiots was banging on the parlor door. "Hey Faith! You in there? Gracie wants to know what happened to the sweet potatoes." He jiggled the locked doorknob.

Faith sighed and signed quickly.

"They're already in the oven," Broadbent called her message. "She hid them behind the roast so you and your band of heathens wouldn't eat them before dinner."

"Broadbent? Hey Col! Broadbent's tryin' to put the moves on Faith in the parlor. He finally found one that couldn't scream. Don't worry Faith," he called through the door. "We'll have you out before he figures out what to do with it. Canaan can snap this lock open just looking at it." There was the sound of a scuffle. "Ow! Jeez JJ, I was only having a little fun. Let go my ear!"

Broadbent stood and offered Faith his hand.

"*I'm truly sorry if I've hurt you*," she told him and couldn't stop the tears. "*And I meant what I said. I'll carry this in my heart, always. You'll find someone, someday. I know you will.*" Faith smiled through her tears. "*And then you'll happily bless the day that I said no.*"

Excerpt from Changing Times

A Hidden Mountain Romance
Contemporary
Coming in 2013

Cob Thornton eased his way through the town he hadn't seen in twenty years. There were a few more vacant storefronts, a few more boarded over windows. His mother had written of Doc Hanson's passing. Murray's store was gone, too, but he smiled when he saw the lights on in the corner diner. Someone must have taken it over. Much to his childhood dismay, the Brinsons had closed it when he was eight. How he'd loved sitting at the counter with Rollie, ordering coffee and pie as if he was one of the men. Mrs. Brinson always left plenty of room for sugar and milk in his cup, but that hadn't mattered back then.

He was tempted to stop, grab a cup of coffee and see how the place had changed and it must have. Everything changed. He only hoped his home hadn't changed too much.

His uncle sure as hell hadn't changed. They'd argued twenty years ago when Cob enlisted and hadn't spoken since. His mother had written though, and he'd called her once a month until the letters stopped and his calls went unanswered. The bastard hadn't even bothered to tell him his mother had passed.

Well, the old man would have to get used to having him back. Half that house and half that land was his mother's and now it was Cob's and he had plans, big plans. He'd scraped and saved and invested his money for twenty years. He'd dreamed of coming home to the mountain for twenty years, too, though that wasn't the plan when he left. Now he was back and no one was going to stand in his way.

Cob passed the Post Office, also new, and noted the mailbox marked 'Tolliver' seated on a post of rusty tire rims welded together. He wondered which Tolliver it was. When he was a kid, every other person you met was either a Tolliver or related to one.

It wasn't Dan's. Cars were too damn fast for Dan. His mailbox would sport a wagon wheel or a horse head.

Instead of narrowing, the road widened and was paved. This was new also. Rollie had given John Preston right of way through his land, but would never allow a public road. Things changed.

The lane to the house hadn't changed. It was as overgrown and rutted as it was when he left. The yard, however, was completely different; no cans, no bottles and holy shit! Were those baskets of flowers hanging from the porch?

He parked the truck and retrieved his duffle and his mother's lessons kicked in. Front doors were for guests. Cob headed around to the back. As he rounded the rear corner of the house, debating whether he owed his uncle the courtesy of a knock, he was brought up short by a sight he never thought he'd see, a woman other than his mother hanging clothes in his uncle's backyard. It couldn't be.

He paused to watch and think. Her back was to him and her long, brown curls bounced along her back as she pegged a towel to the clothesline running between two posts. She was tall and slim as far as he could see. Her legs, extending from a pair of modest shorts were long and as finely shaped as any he had seen. Her shirt was sleeveless and showed a pair of muscular arms, but it was one of those wide, smocky things so he couldn't get a good idea of her waist.

Her line was sagging and she bent to pick up a wooden prop at her feet and Cob got a good look at a rounded behind, a little wider than perfect, but eye-catching just the same. She picked up a man's shirt from her basket and that's when everything clicked.

The clean front yard, the flowers, a woman hanging laundry in the mowed back yard. He looked beyond her and saw a vegetable garden, something Rollie would never keep, but Cob's mother always did.

Things change. Some other family was living in his house and that could only mean one thing. His uncle was dead.

Cob was surprised at how hard that hit him. How many times had he wished his uncle to burn in hell? He never once thought the old bastard would actually do it. His mother was always frail, but Rollie was like Big Rock; granite hard, immovable and eternal. He was looking forward to having a knock-down-drag-out with the old man. Cob was no kid anymore. He had plans and ideas and the money to make them happen. He'd rehearsed the scene so many times in his mind and now it would never happen. His shoulders sagged.

"Oh God, not Rollie." Rollie was at the bottom of all his dreams. Rollie taught him everything he needed to know and some of those things had saved his life a time or two. Rollie was his only living kin and the best damn distiller of illegal corn whiskey in the mountains.

Cob dropped the duffle and leaned against the house.

Lorelei heard a dull thud and a quiet groan and dropped the wet overalls back into the basket. She looked up at wooden screen door that led to the kitchen.

"Rollie? Rollie honey? You okay?" If the old man fell again because he refused to use the damn walker, she'd kill him herself. It was hard enough to pick him up last time and it niggled at the back of her mind that the old fart did it on purpose, just so he could cop a feel while she helped him up. He never fell when she was at work or if he did, he picked himself up. "Rollie?"

"Godammit woman, can't a man have a minute's peace?

What do you want?"

Breathing a sigh of relief she called back, "Nothing. Sorry." She bent to pick up the denim pants from the basket.

"He's alive?"

Lorelei eeked and spun. She held the overalls out in front of her like a shield. "Who the hell are you?"

"Cob Thornton and this is my house, so who the hell are you?"

"This is not your house, buddy." She took a step back and toward the stairs. "Rollie?" she called as loud as she could. "We got company! Now!"

"You live here? With him?"

"What if I do? It's his place." She dropped the pants and took another quick step toward the porch and safety. She hated showing this guy her fear, but she'd been in this place before; alone and at the mercy of a strange man and she wasn't pregnant then. "Rollie!"

Cob stopped, mouth open. The woman was pregnant, belly swollen and about to pop. Rollie had a woman? A young and beautiful woman. A pregnant woman. Shit! What'd the old man do, win the lottery?

He raised his hands in a gesture of peace, not wanting to frighten her any more than she obviously was. He heard the door open. "I won't..." hurt you, he started to say.

"Damn right. You won't do squat. Stay right there, Mister."

Rollie, looking older and a lot smaller than Cob remembered, stood on the back porch holding a shotgun that wavered vaguely in Cob's direction.

The woman, now behind his uncle, reached for the gun. "I got it, honey."

"The hell you do. It's my legs don't work. I can shoot just fine." He rested the barrel on the rail.

Hands still in the air, Cob said quietly, "Rollie, it's me, Cob, your nephew," he added, in case the old man had lost his mind as well as the use of his legs. He stared at the woman's middle. Obviously other parts worked just fine.

"The hell you say. Cob's dead. Been dead these last fourteen years."

"Then how the hell am I standing here now?" Cob thought for a minute before he came up with something the old man would understand. "Did they ever send you a check?"

"Don't deal in checks. It's cash money or nothing. Anybody who knows me knows that."

Cob's head dropped to his chest. He gave it a quick shake and picked it up again. "You are as thick as the soles on a banker's shoes, Rollie Roper." It was what his mother said over and over when he was a boy.

Rollie took his finger off the trigger. "Step on over here so's I can get a good look at ya."

Rollie handed the shotgun to Lorelei and leaned over the rail to get a better look. The boy had been tall and skinny when he left. This feller wasn't as tall as Dewey Tolliver, but he was twice as broad.

"What was your Mama's name?"

"Oh, for God's sake." Cob started to lower his hands and then noticed how the woman held the weapon. She looked a damn sight more competent that Rollie.

"My mother's name was Abigail. My father was Elijah. I was born in this house, or so I was told, in the same damn bed as you were, though I hope to God it wasn't the same damn mattress. We came to live with you when I wasn't much more than a baby. You had an old hound you called Boner that my mother hated though I didn't understand at the time it was the name she hated, not the dog. He lived under that porch you're standing on and you told me he would eat me alive if I dared leave the house without you or my mother. I believed it, you old bastard."

Rollie slapped the rail. "I'll be damned. I thought you was dead. Got notice from the gov'ment."

"That I was wounded, not dead. Didn't you listen to what they said?" He started to drop his hands again, stopped, looked at the woman and completed the move when she nodded and lowered the weapon, though she didn't put the safety on when she cradled it across her arm.

"Didn't talk to 'em. Saw the car and the uniforms and knew why they were here. They don't send a car lessen you're dead. You best come in since you ain't." He turned, tottered, and was rescued from falling by the woman.

"Good to see you, too," Cob muttered as he went to retrieve his duffle.

When he entered the kitchen, Rollie was sitting at the table and the woman was leaning over him, rubbing his back and cooing something into his ear. There was an aluminum walker next to the table. Rollie didn't look good. Maybe she thought she and the baby would inherit this house when the old man died. She wasn't wearing a ring. Still...

He heard Rollie blow his nose. The woman leaned further in and kissed the top of his uncle's head. "Thanks for being there, honey. You're my hero. I'm going out back to finish hanging my wash." She glared at Cob, but spoke to Rollie. "You call if you need me."

Cob moved out of the way as she passed. For a woman 'great with child', she moved gracefully without the waddling gait he'd noticed in other women in her state.

She stopped just past him and turned her head. "Don't upset him again," she warned.

Upset Rollie? His uncle wasn't the one held at gunpoint, was he?

The screen door slammed behind her and he turned his attention to Rollie.

"Who the hell is she?"

Printed in Great Britain
by Amazon.co.uk, Ltd.,
Marston Gate.